MISTY R. PHILLIPS

Heart of Gaia

Calamity Crew Book One

To my husband, for being my support, my inspiration, and the reason I've gone mad.

Contents

Content Warning — iii

1 The Siren's Call — 1
2 Home — 10
3 Old Friend — 19
4 A Breath of Fresh Air — 30
5 Holy Lands — 36
6 The Thief — 44
7 Razin — 57
8 Storytime — 58
9 Gold is Good — 65
10 The Mark — 76
11 Stuck in the Past — 82
12 The Songbird — 88
13 Romo — 95
14 Decisions — 105
15 Deadly Duo — 115
16 Angels — 127
17 Scars — 137
18 Party time — 148
19 Set Sail — 160
20 Basic Training — 173
21 No News is Good News — 184
22 The Valkyrie — 196
23 Into Gaia — 209
24 General Markham — 218
25 Dana and David — 226

26 Halftime   234
27 Sasfierm   244
28 The Mountain   253
29 Connections   266
30 Descendants   277
31 The Escape   293
32 City of Olympia   306
33 Adventures in Olympia   319
34 Hermes' Piper   328
35 The Priestess   340
36 The Healers   357
37 The Siren's Song   367
38 Just a Fantasy   382
39 One with the Earth   389
40 Clockwork Soldiers   401
41 Mother Gaia   412
Epilogue   421
Like it, Love it, Hate it   424
About the Author   425

Content Warning

This book is intended for adult readers and covers many dark and mature issues.

For an extensive list of content warnings, visit www.mistyrphillips.ca

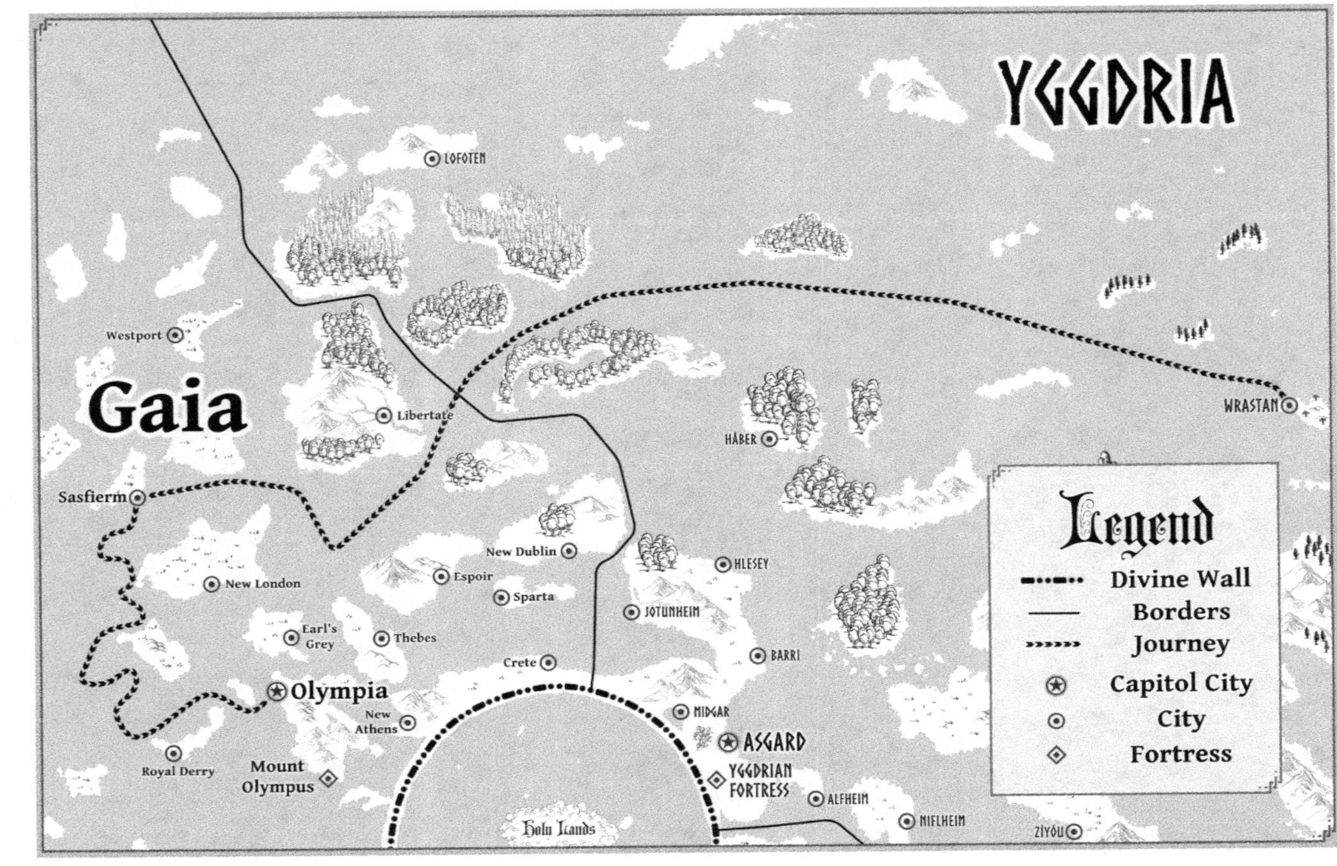

YGGDRIA
Gaia
LOFOTEN
Westport
Libertate
HÅBER
WRASTAN
Sasfierm
New London
New Dublin
Espoir
Sparta
HLESEY
JOTUNHEIM
Earl's Grey
Thebes
BARRI
Crete
Olympia
MIDGAR
New Athens
ASGARD
YGGDRIAN FORTRESS
Royal Derry
Mount Olympus
ALFHEIM
NIFLHEIM
ZIYOU
Holn Lands
Legend
Divine Wall
Borders
Journey
Capitol City
City
Fortress

1

The Siren's Call

"Come all you bold seamen, wherever you're bound. And always let Nelson's proud memory go round." It was an old song, made long before the Calamity destroyed their world. A song that many sailors sang hoping for a better future. It wasn't a song normally heard on a pirate ship.

The song didn't seem odd to the drowsy man, dressed in far too many stripes, sitting in the gently swaying crow's nest as a blackened flag flapped lazily above his head. He just smiled and hummed along as that wonderful voice filled his ears.

"And pray that the wars and the tumult may cease. For the greatest of gifts—" a gentle hand rested on his shoulder, as the woman's sensuous voice sang in his ear, "—is a sweet, lasting peace."

A dull smile spread across his face as he turned his heavy eyes beside him. There, glowing in the moonlight, sat a strikingly gorgeous woman—her soft olive skin beckoning him to reach out and touch her. She smiled at him from beneath waves of perfect auburn hair, where only one eye could be seen, sparkling with excitement. Bewitched by her beauty, he reached out to caress her face, those luscious lips pulling him in close as she continued her song.

Bang! Crash! "Blast ye damn, dirty cheat," bellowed from the deck below, followed by incoherent shouting and cursing as a scuffle broke out between shipmates.

The striped man snapped from his stupor, seeing the woman before him clearly. While still beautiful, she seemed far less perfect and far more dishevelled. She wore a simple black and red outfit littered with patches, her hair haphazardly tied up with a shimmering silver pin.

"Y-yer The Siren!" he stammered, taking a few clumsy steps away.

"That I am," she breathed in a melodic voice. "And what do you plan to do about it? Tie me up? Tell me I'm a bad girl?" She undid a few buttons on her shirt, showing off a little more skin. "Or perhaps you'd just like to run me through? Right here?" She tapped above her left breast, thumping a bird in flight tattoo. "Many have tried—many have failed."

He considered her for a moment, making no effort to hide where he was staring. As his blood rushed from his brain, he shook himself from her enchantment. He knew all too well what happened to men like him at her hands.

The pirate scurried over the edge, screeching, "She's here! The Siren be here!"

The warning echoed throughout every corner of the ship. His shipmates sprang to action—the deck swarmed with almost a hundred buccaneers readying themselves for battle. Not a single man on that ship took the warning with a light heart. Lorelei the Siren was a pirate's worst nightmare.

The lookout scrambled to the edge. As his feet prepared to leap, his body yanked backwards. There was no fighting against that strength. An all so familiar pressure of cold steel pressed against his neck.

"Too bad," she sighed in his ear, her sweet, soft scent filling his senses. "I do prefer having some fun first."

His heart raced and a cold sweat beaded on his brow. As he was about to whimper for mercy...

Slice.

The blade cut deep and slow. Blood sprayed over the crow's nest. Lorelei's face twisted in a wicked grin.

Swarming below, anxious buccaneers gathered, demanding their lookout to reveal the position of The Siren. What they received in response, however, was a bloody body plummeting at alarming speed.

Crash.

Blood, guts and gods knew what else covered the unsuspecting brutes. Mixed cries of rage, fear and anguish filled the air as the men identified their lost comrade.

"Yikes, that would've hurt if he was still alive," Lorelei called out with a giggle, drawing all the snarling faces to look up at her smug grin.

The crowd yelled and growled, crying out for her head. They scrambled to get their hands on the woman. They didn't need to bother.

Lorelei had no plans of hiding out. With a joyful whistle, she swung down into the crowd, landing with ship-rocking force upon the deck.

She smiled at the swarm of apprehensive men surrounding her. It was a smile of excitement and eagerness. "Aw boys, you don't really want to fight little ol' me, do you?"

"Is that really 'er?" asked one man, dressed in rags. "I thought she'd be bigger."

That smile twisted into a sneer, just enough to bare her lovely white teeth. "I'm tall for a girl!"

The smelly bastards laughed. Apparently, they were starting to get their courage back. Something about surrounding one woman made them feel tough.

One even had the gall to suggest, "Let's kill her quick and give 'er head to Konstantin."

"Or we could tie her up and have some fun," cackled a gaunt man.

With that on their minds, all faces turned to her with eager, wicked grins as they crept steadily toward her.

Unlike most women they had encountered in her position, she let out a cackling laugh, and sang a bouncing tune.

"What will we do with a drunken pirate? What will we do with a drunken pirate? What will we do with a drunken pirate?"

With furrowed brows, the men exchange glances. She raised her hand, pausing her song with a suspenseful long note that echoed across the silent ship. Her face twisted into a vicious sneer that made the men around her

take an involuntary step back. With quiet intensity, she breathed,
"We kill them."

Her fist closed. Death whistled in. Spears and arrows pierced unsuspecting pirate flesh. Screams of pain and terror rang through the air, and Lorelei bathed in it, laughing that melodic laugh. Those who survived the initial attack slipped and slid their way across blood and entrails to reach the mocking woman. Once again, death greeted them. Multiple shadowed figures closed in, slicing their prey away with ease.

Now dead or scattered, fighting off reinforcements, only a handful of shaking adversaries kept their attention on the legendary Siren. Lorelei's gaze pierced through every one of them, taunting them with that smirk, eagerly awaiting one of them to make a move.

A hulking man readied his axe, charging in for the kill. Such a tiny foe must have seemed a simple kill. Still, the Siren remained still. Not a muscle moved until the mammoth took a wide swing.

No one saw what happened.

One moment he was in a lethal charge, the next, his body was in two pieces, rolling into unsuspecting spectators. The axe remained in the woman's hand, her stance low and solid, her blood-soaked grin sending shivers through their spines.

"Ooo, this could be fun," she chirped, giving the axe a swing. "Who's next?"

As the bloody battle raged above, one petite woman weaved gracefully below deck, avoiding any of the angry pirates rampaging upwards. She wasn't particularly sneaky but, as usual, they were far more concerned about the deadly Siren than her blonde little friend, Astrid.

Astrid was a decent fighter, but not nearly as talented as Lorelei, and certainly not enough to go into battle without some sort of armour. So, atop her customary flowing dress, she wore a form-fitted leather breastplate. The tools of her trade hung from her belt, and a small staff was strapped to her back. As was her usual, her feet were completely bare. She just couldn't stand shoes, even during battle. She needed that connection with the world around her. Shoes made everything so lifeless.

A scream penetrated the air, and Astrid felt the woman's panic in her bones. She raced through the hull, coming to a halt before a dank, dark cell holding a handful of prisoners. The rusted bars and rotting wood were quite an odd sight for the ships they usually hunted. But no time to dwell on that. Not while there were people to rescue.

A crooked-nosed pirate stood by the cell, looking over the prisoners like they were his last meal. "What do you think, sweetheart? Want to show me a good time before the Siren shows up?"

A terrified brunette cried and pleaded as the man took her by the hair. The rest of the slaves cowered in the corner, not wanting to take her place, while the man's crewmate stood at the door, begging his buddy to get moving—that they needed to be on deck. His words went flat. A strike to the neck sent his paralyzed body falling to the floor with a dull thud.

The abuser turned his attention to the little blonde girl in the doorway.

She gasped at his comrade, and giggled, "Now, how did that happen?" She smiled sweetly and innocently at the snarling man in the cage, rocking on her bare feet.

With a guttural growl, he threw the poor, terrified woman down to the dungy, dirty floor. In a single motion, he drew his sword and charged with a cry of rage. He took a swing. Astrid gracefully dove under. He caught her tiny wrist with his meaty hand, a sick grin on his face.

She jabbed into his shoulder with her free hand, weakening his grip. Before he realized it, her wrist was free. One more strike to his neck, and another just below the opposite ear, and his body fell uselessly to the floor.

He tried with all his might to rise, but the only thing he could do was slur a confused, drool-filled, "What?"

Astrid hopped lightly over the useless, big-nosed man with a sprightly giggle. "Don't worry, it will wear off in a little while. Just be glad I'm not

Lorelei."

The man's previous prey still lay cowering, sobbing on the damp floor. Astrid kneeled beside her, laying a soft, comforting hand on her shoulder. "Are you hurt?"

The brunette looked up at her and took a shuddering breath. Astrid's kind emerald eyes visibly brought calm to the woman. With a half-hearted smile, she shook her head and weakly rose to her feet, gently nursing one hand.

Astrid voiced a tiny gasp. "No, you're hurt. Let me see."

"It's nothing," she whispered hoarsely. Still, Astrid held out her hand, and the woman let her look at her crooked finger.

"It's not nothing," said Astrid, reaching into her pouch. In the blink of an eye, she had the broken finger cleaned and bandaged.

As the woman admired the efficient work, Astrid turned to the rest of the prisoners. They still sat cowering in the dank, mildew encrusted cell staring at her in confusion. She gave a quick head count. There were eight, just like the report said.

She gave them her sweetest smile, then dipped into a curtsey. "Well, come on now, you are cordially invited to join The Siren and her crew on the Oasis."

Up above, the battle raged on, with the nasty marauders clearly at a severe disadvantage to the trained and Blessed crew of the Siren. Perfect for a prisoner escape. Astrid peeked her head onto deck, and finding their coast was clear, motioned for the handful of prisoners to follow. They hurried toward the edge. Freedom was in their sights.

Not for long.

A woman blocked their path. A woman who seemed very keen on the classic pirate look. She raised a rapier to Astrid's throat.

"You're a woman!" Astrid exclaimed, rather obviously.

"That's right," she cackled, "And don't you go thinking I'll take it easy on you because of it."

A couple of slaves attempted to take off the other way but found a dull, square-jawed man blocking their retreat.

"Oh, no, no! Perish the thought. It's just such a delightful change of pace. Usually, these battles are all men. Good for you for breaking the mold," Astrid praised, a small smile upon her face.

The woman burned bright with embarrassment. "Uh… well, thank—"

Woosh, thunk.

An axe stuck in the woman's chest. She stood there for a stunned moment, axe embedded strong, then fell dead to the ground.

The prisoners cried out in surprise and horror.

The dense man blocking their retreat gagged. "E-Ella?"

His sadness did not last long.

A red and black blur jumped on his back, twisting his head with a loud crack. Down went the big guy.

Once again, the prisoners cried out in horror at the gruesome scene as Lorelei stood over the dead bodies, humming a merry tune.

Astrid crossed her arms and glared. "Was that really necessary?"

"Well, I suppose you could have handled them, but I saw the opportunity and took it. Can't risk losing one of the main reasons we're here, right?" She slapped one of the nervous escapees on the behind, leaving a nice red handprint on his pants.

"But… she was a woman! We could have—"

"What? Let her live? Take it easy on her? Just because she was a woman?" Lorelei wiped her hands off on her pants, rolling her eyes at Astrid. "That's pretty sexist."

Astrid just continued to glare, lip pursed, unable to come up with an argument.

With a spine-chilling grin, Lorelei continued, "Anyway, women pirates are the worst. Only someone truly psychotic lives among those that treat their sex like utter crap. I should know, I was one."

"Yes! Exactly. And you—"

A battle cry rang out, cutting Astrid short, and turning Lorelei's attention to the action, a scowl replacing her grin.

"No time for discussion. Get the escapees to the ship."

With a dejected sigh, Astrid replied, "Right." Off they went.

Lorelei stood relaxed and ready. She drew her straight sword, engraved with her teacher's symbol of two entwined dragons around the blade, and took a deep breath. She thought, A strong mind breeds a strong body.

The horde closed in.

"A cut to the jugular, a stab through the heart, a knee to the balls and don't forget your part," she sang, slicing, stabbing and kneeing the pirates accordingly—leaving a wake of dead bodies behind her.

As a squealing, broken-balled man fell to the ground, Lorelei kicked him onto his back, mounted him, and brought her sword to rest on his throat. Fear and confusion filled the man's eyes as she stroked his cheek with her free hand.

"I need you to listen carefully," she purred, "because if I don't like what I hear, you join your friends."

He nodded carefully as he strained his pinned arms to root around in his pocket. Lorelei didn't care. It was normal for them to squirm away.

She bore those golden eyes into the man's skull, a fiery determination about her. "I want you to tell me where Konstantin is docked. What part of the ocean is he in?"

A smile flicked on and off the man's face as he continued to squirm beneath her. "Ye know I can't do that."

"You will if you want to live."

The sweat poured off of him as he mumbled, "Living… were never an option on this ship."

Lorelei pressed the sword deeper into his throat, about to question him further, until she heard the worst sound possible.

Click.

She leapt off of the man, not bothering to look at what she knew was in his hand. "Abandon ship!" she screamed at the top of her lungs, sprinting to the rail.

First came a deafening silence, then the ear-shattering boom. An overwhelming pressure flung her from that damned ship.

2

Home

Lorelei's eyes snapped open. She stabbed that violet-eyed bastard right between the eyes. Konstantin's photo flapped mockingly at the disturbance, and Lorelei just scowled. His picture was the only one on her board that didn't have an "X" through it.

Konstantin Razin. His crimes should have been a one-way ticket to Purgatory, but the bastard was smart. Alongside his pillaging, raping and murdering, he also supplied the Angels in all nations with their slaves, and he was damn good at it. The best in the business. Because of that, the Angels let him do whatever the fuck he wanted, as long as it was away from their precious Divine Ring.

Today was the day that all changed.

The small, cozy cabin swayed gently with the swell of the ocean as she examined her wall littered with claimed bounties. Those were Konstantin's men—his power—and Lorelei had taken them out. Konstantin was weak now. It was time.

She had their mission planned; every little detail mapped out. She had the exact size of the ship, a count of how many men he would have and their ranking. She had everything she needed to take him out.

Then why was she shaking?

"Are you freaking kidding me?" *James. Always so nervous.* "You really think all four of us can take on one of Konstantin's ships? It will be swarming with pirates."

Lorelei waved him off. "Konstantin will have sent out his best fighters to clean up the mess we left behind. All that's left on his boat are pawns—cannon fodder."

"There's still a lot of them!"

Yuri let out his booming laugh, clapping James on the back. "Don't worry so much, James! I can take out ten men with one swipe. You just worry about your job."

"My job takes me right into that awful ship!"

Yuri laughed again, looking down upon his best friend. There was no other option for him. Yuri was huge. Not a giant, but damn close.

Lorelei sighed. "Alright, do we need to go over the plan again?"

"Yes!" James insisted.

Lorelei grumbled under her breath, but brought back her shoulders and stood tall. "I greet Konstantin's ship. While we discuss how I'm not dead, the rest of you get into position." She indicated to the map on the wall. "When all the bastards come out to kill or capture me, seriously underestimating how much I've grown, Xin and Yuri will start hacking away from the outside. While they're distracted, James sneaks into the ship and releases the prisoners... Like he usually does."

"But they'll kill me if they see me!" James whined. "And what if Konstantin sees me?"

"Don't worry, he'll be more concerned about me. Besides, Xin will be there to take his head in no time."

"But—"

Yuri gripped James' shoulder. "Come on, James, you need to relax. How about a round of cards?"

James gave a familiar groan and ultimately agreed. The two strode out of the room, and Lorelei turned back to her wall. All these men had fallen to her plans. Konstantin would be no different.

A familiar pair of muscular arms wrapped around her waist. "Are you sure we're ready for this, Lore?"

She turned her head up to look at Xin, and, as always, those steel-blue eyes calmed her racing mind.

"Yeah, yeah I'm sure. All our work has led up to this moment. This plan will work."

"You know, as soon as we do this, he'll know you're alive. There will be no going back."

There was so much worry in his voice. Why did he care so much?

"I know, but this is important. Konstantin has way too much power for one man. There are so many people suffering because of him. I can't let him keep going on." There was something else, but she couldn't tell Xin. She couldn't tell him about that other man, the one far worse than Konstantin... to her, anyway. He was the one she had to face down herself. She needed to take his life to properly continue hers.

She was sure her plan would work.

It didn't. She paid for that mistake for five years.

Xin's comforting touch turned to throbbing pain as Lorelei slowly came back to consciousness. She heard Astrid's voice calling out to her, but all she could manage in reply was a loud groan.

Astrid gave a loud sigh of relief, fiddling with her braid. "Thank the gods you're awake. How are you feeling?"

"Like I got fucking blown up. What do you think?"

This time, she gave a resigned sigh. "Guess you're fine. I was worried about you, you know."

"Ah, don't worry. You should know by now the gods hate me too much to let me die."

Lorelei looked around. They were still on their little cutter ship they had taken to ambush that pirate ship. Injured people filled the cabin around her. Most she knew, some she didn't. With another groan, Lorelei sat herself up on the makeshift bed. As she did, she noticed the redhead, Trisa, standing at attention in a salute to her other side.

"What in Helheim, Trisa?" exclaimed Lorelei, clutching at her heart. "How long have you been standing like that?"

"Just since you woke up, ma'am."

"For fuck's sake, stop with the formality already."

"Yes, ma'am," Trisa replied, standing at ease, though still like a soldier.

Lorelei shook her head. "Alright Trisa, what's the report?"

"Of the fifteen that came, we have five critically injured, three confirmed dead and two unaccounted for."

"So five dead."

"Y-yes, I suppose."

"Who?"

Trisa listed off their names, and Lorelei's stomach twisted. Most of them had families. She was going to have to break the news to all of them. All because that fucking bastard tricked her.

"How long are you going to do this?" growled a man's voice in her ear. "Your idiocy is just getting people killed."

She closed her eyes and tried to ignore it. She knew what it was. She knew he wasn't there, but that didn't stop her from hearing him.

"What about the prisoners we came for?" she asked.

"All eight were rescued and are safe, thanks to Astrid."

Astrid beamed at the praise.

"Well, there's that at least," sighed Lorelei, then she looked around again. "There's more than eight fresh faces here."

Trisa fidgeted. "Right, well, we found a few pirates still alive."

"And you rescued them?"

"Yes..."

"Get rid of them," Lorelei growled, trying to stand up from her bed.

"What? No!" Astrid cried. "We can't just kill them like that! They're injured."

"They had no problem trying to kill you earlier. Besides, they'll just be a drain on resources."

"Lorelei, please. They're not all bad. Please, don't do this."

Lorelei sneered as those big, shimmering, green eyes bore right into her soul. Finally, Lorelei gave a roar of frustration. "Tchah, fine! But they are the last to be treated, and they are going straight to the brig when we get back, understood?"

Astrid gave a wide smile. "Yes, yes, of course. Thank you." She motioned to hug her, but stopped. She knew the rules, and Lorelei was definitely not in a hugging mood. Astrid bounced off to help treat the rest of the injured as Trisa continued to stand beside Lorelei.

"How is she still so naïve after everything she's been through?" Trisa asked.

"I don't know," Lorelei sighed. "But I suppose one of us should be. Monitor the prisoners. If they try anything, you know what to do."

"Yes, ma'am." Lorelei knew Trisa wasn't comfortable killing without purpose, but she wouldn't hesitate to protect her own at any cost. That was a necessary survival instinct to live out in the Forsaken Ring.

"Land ho!"

Lorelei heard the call and managed to painfully pull herself out of bed. She pushed the pain aside, positive all her aches were mere bruises, and set out to the deck. As she came out, a few hands gave her a quick salute, which she waved off, then demanded a spyglass.

They placed a small tube in her hand, which she gave a twist. With a bit of grinding and clicking, the tube sprang open into a long spyglass. First, she checked on the homing pigeon, flapping just ahead of their boat. They had been at sea for a couple weeks, and not even she knew where her home had docked at the moment. That was an important safety precaution.

She gave the spyglass another twist, zooming in on the horizon where she spotted the land ahead of them and recognized the towering, golden structure jutting out in the middle of a small island. Wrastan Island. That wasn't quite where they were aiming, though. That was just a temporary dock. What was important was the massive, five-masted vessel anchored offshore.

Home. Also known as *The Oasis*.

That was Lorelei's baby, her creation, though not entirely by choice. After five years of tracking down Konstantin's crews, his trade lines, and his underground connections, Lorelei had come across many souls in need (currently just over two-hundred). That led her to create one of the largest ships on the seas. The only vessels that could match its size were the battleships owned by the Angel families, and those rarely left the Divine Ring. It wasn't as pretty as an Angel vessel, however, being constructed with mismatched parts she had traded and bargained for.

Cannons lined the hull, exactly fifteen on both sides. They ranged in age, size and effectiveness, and ended up being whatever Lorelei could get her hands on. She had plenty of contacts and resources, but there was still only so much she could get out in the Forsaken Ring. What was important was that they had the firepower to defend themselves from the scum that crawled these oceans.

The homing pigeon flew off to its aviary, a small hut atop one mast, adorned with a buzzing orb of glass with streams of electricity reaching out here and there. That was where its homing signal came from.

As the tiny cutter ship pulled up to that mismatched hull, helpful hands immediately greeted them. Doctor Hina and her assistants were the first to greet them, and quickly hauled away the injured to their large, recently well-stocked sickbay.

As they loaded up the last of the injured onto a stretcher, Hina, a middle-aged, tall, slender woman, looked Astrid over. "You did well, Astrid. We have it from here."

"What? But I can still help."

"Astrid, what is my first rule?" Hina asked with that unbendable sternness.

Astrid sighed and started pulling on her braid. "I can't help others if I don't help myself first."

"That's right. Take care of yourself, Darling. We have it from here."

"Thank you."

As they walked off, Astrid looked over and spotted Lorelei speaking to one of the crew about the supplies. Their stores were stocked and ready to go. That meant they'd be leaving soon. They never stayed in one spot long. They couldn't risk Konstantin finding them. Their defences were good, but the Angels supplied Konstantin. A surprise battle with him was not one they wanted to test their mettle against.

As the report ended, a familiar, ecstatic, childish voice called out to them. "Miss Lowelei! Miss Lowelei! You'we back!" Sure enough, bouncing across the wide deck was Jack, his bleach-blonde hair sparkling as it bounced with every step.

"What do you want, Jack? I'm busy," Lorelei snapped with a frustrated sigh and dismissed the report giver.

"Look, look! I made you a dwawing!" he declared, his dazzling violet eyes sparkling with excitement as he held up an adorable drawing of what appeared to be a woman in red and black on a murder spree.

Lorelei looked down her nose at it, her face suddenly twisting into a smile as she snorted out a quick laugh. With a clearing of her throat, she regained her composure. "Tchah, blood is red, not orange. And it looks too forced. Keep trying." Done with the conversation, Lorelei turned on her heels and headed toward the cabin.

Little Jack's eyes brimmed over with tears and Astrid came over to lay a supportive hand on his shoulder. "Oh Jack, don't worry, it's lovely. She's just had a terrible night."

He turned to her with a huge grin, tears running down his face. "Did you see, Miss Astwid? She smiled at my pictwer. I'm gonna make mowe so she will smile mowe!" he declared and sprinted off happily inside.

Another sigh escaped Astrid's lips as she watched the boy run off. Frustration bubbled up inside her and she stormed over to Lorelei's side.

"What?" Lorelei growled, clearly noticing Astrid's ridgid body language.

"Can't you at least try to be nice to him?"

"I told him to keep trying. Besides, he's just another orphan tagging along. Why should I care?"

"An orphan we've had since he was a baby. You aren't nearly as critical with the others."

"Do you have a point? Or are you just trying to piss me off more?"

Astrid sighed. There was no point in pushing that subject any further. "About tonight… Are you alright?"

"Tchah. I'm fine."

"It's just… last time Konstantin got the better of you… you kind of stranded some important people to you."

Lorelei stopped in her tracks, glaring at the floor, jaw and fists clenched. Normally in the past, any mention of that accursed day five years ago would lead to instant and violent threats. Luckily for Astrid, she had grown past that. At least a little. Still, she refused to talk about it, and it continued to drive Astrid mad.

"I… I just want you to talk to me," Astrid pleaded softly.

Through the intense silence, a bird came barrelling at them. Astrid noticed at the last minute and ducked, while Lorelei grabbed it out of the air without even looking.

In her hand sat a pigeon. Not one of flesh and bone, but of metal, gears and beady glass eyes. A comm-pigeon. It was only available to those with money and power. Lorelei owned five. With it, people could communicate over long distances. It was a similar design to the homing pigeon, made to let it blend with the more common comm-pigeons. This one was one of the older models with a dark bronze hue and a few fraying parts here and there.

"Oh! That must be James' update," squeaked Astrid excitedly, suddenly glad for the distraction. Lorelei held it out in her hand and pushed the tail feathers down. Its eyes lit up, its mouth opened, and the familiar voice of James came out.

"Hello, ladies! The Oasis is all stocked up and ready for your return. I also ran into someone very interesting, but it's a surprise! We'll be at the casino whenever you get back. Later!" With a click, the bird's mouth closed, and the eyes went dim.

"I wonder who he found," pondered Astrid.

"I don't give a fuck. I'm going to blow off some steam. Go check on James for me." She threw the pigeon in the air, letting it fly off to its electric aviary. Without waiting for a reply, Lorelei stormed off into The Oasis, leaving Astrid to watch her go with a sigh.

It really had been one hell of a night. Astrid looked around the ship suspiciously to see if anyone else was around. Deciding the coast was clear, she shoved her hand in one of her bags, pulled out a joint and lit it happily, taking a long, calming drag. She held it for a moment and exhaled, releasing all the negative events of the day with it.

Astrid gazed off onto the horizon, where dark storm clouds flashed with light crept ever nearer.

How appropriate, she thought with another sigh. *I'd better get to land before that storm hits.*

3

Old Friend

Half a century ago, the three gods shattered the Earth, decimating the lands and leaving only a handful of livable islands in the world. This incident became known as the Calamity.

The remainder of this world centred around the Ancient Holy Lands, the origin of the Calamity, a barren land surrounded by a lethal fog that no one, human or Angel, could even touch. No one knew why or how it worked. All anyone knew was that a weekly pulse would originate from that source and protect them from the endless storms on the edge of their world.

From that centre point lay the expanse of ocean known as Purgatory, which was surrounded by the mighty Divine Wall. That wall, originally constructed to protect the outside world from the war between the gods, now served as a prison for the worst criminals.

Beyond that lay the Divine Ring, consisting of the three fortresses of the Angels, descendants of the gods, and the bustling cities that were protected by the Angel families. Next was the Rustic Ring, where humans farmed or gathered resources.

The last ring was where Lorelei called home. The Forsaken Ring, aptly named by the complete lack of any interjection from the Angel families. These lands were barren, scattered, and crawling with outlaws, namely pirates, since there was more ocean than land. Resources were slim, and survival was hard.

While it was an awful place to live, the Forsaken Ring had its gems. Places of refuge. The island of Wrastan was one such place. The mighty casino, which desperate people would flock to, lay in the centre of the island, a shimmering beacon of hope to all that could sail to its shores.

Wrastan's saviour, the founder, owner, and manager of the casino, Nickolas, strode across the floors of his casino in a fine, neatly pressed suit, his salt and pepper hair neatly slicked back. People all around him stopped to wish him well, trying to be his friend. He just smiled, returned the well wishes, and continued on his way. He had no need for fake friends. One particular voice caused him to pause as he saw the familiar limping figure of James, his copper skin and shining bald head sticking out amongst the sea of whiteness between them.

"Nicky! Buddy!" gushed James, thumping Nick on the back with a large appreciative smile on his face. "You are the best, as always. These supplies should last us a good while."

"Anytime, James," he replied with a prideful smile. It wasn't easy being as successful as Nick was, but he loved to show it off. Nick's eyes wandered as a satisfied grin snuck onto his face. "Seriously. Tell your boss to come back anytime. She must be pretty crazy to work for. Say, have you ever had a go with her? She's quite the wild ride."

The smile faded from James' face as Nick nudged him in the ribs, and an annoyed grimace replaced it. "No, and I don't exactly want to talk about my boss and friend that w—"

"Thief! They took my jewels!" warbled the sound of an elderly lady within the crowd.

"What in Helheim are you talking about?" yelled a gruff man's voice from the same direction. "I didn't take these. It was that little thief over the—gods dammit, where did he go?"

James craned his neck toward the commotion, getting that gnawing, familiar feeling from the gruff man's voice. "What is going on over there?"

"Sounds like someone's stealing," replied Nick with a yawn, motioning James to continue to walk with him. "Happens a fair bit. Lots of refugees from Ratum show up here. We have a hel of a time with those orphans. Don't worry, the guards will take care of it."

"Oh yeah," said James. "We've been keeping an eye out for those kids, but they keep pretty well hidden. Why would that be?"

Nick scoffed. "Probably because they're a pack of thieves."

"They're just hungry kids. Couldn't you feed them?"

"Sometimes I do, but this is a business, James. I can't survive on good feelings. I need something in return, and those kids have nothing. Besides, if I start giving handouts, they'll just expect more and more."

James couldn't help but send him a disgusted look.

"Now, don't look at me like that. It's not like I'm rounding them up and selling them to slavers. They are still far better off here than in Ratum. Bloody Konstantin has his men scouring every inch of those seas. Ever since Lorelei's been kicking ass in Yggdria, things have gotten quite cushy."

James gritted his teeth. "Then feed the—"

Surprised screams burst out from the rowdy crowd, and a curious sight caught James' eye. An orange-haired man, strapped with what looked like a simple glider (laced with bedazzlement) flew up over the crowd, laughing all the way. It couldn't be that simple. Gliders didn't work that way. Still, that wasn't what really caught his attention. It was the man hanging below him that interested James. Few people strapped swords to their back—even fewer wore them that way.

"What the fuck? Stop them!" shouted Nick to the dumbfounded guards, who all looked around at each other, unsure how to continue, being unequipped to deal with airborne issues. One innovative guard pulled out his sword and aimed to throw it at the flying thieves.

To the guard's relief, his plan need not happen. James threw open his trench-coat, revealing a firearm arsenal, and pulled out a worn, bronze revolver from its holster.

Bang, bang, bang.

Three shots were all it took to rip apart the glider and the pair to come hurtling back to the ground.

Moments earlier, two men stood on guard, back to back, as the angry crowd surrounded them. Gold and jewels lay strewn at their feet. The younger looking man, with dazzling orange hair wrapped with a red bandana, couldn't seem to stop himself from laughing at their situation.

"Would you stop it already?" grumbled Xin, the gruff sounding man, who looked as he sounded with a tattered fur-lined leather coat, and a pair of long swords strapped to his back to form an 'X'. He tousled his already unkempt chestnut brown hair in thought. "Argh! I can't exactly slice our way out of this one, Chase. Any ideas?"

"Of course!" Chase proclaimed, grinning madly. With a grand flourish of his long, eccentric coat, he shouted, "Sorry lads, but you won't get the better of Chase the Ace!"

The crowd looked around in confusion, unsure of what the man had said with his odd accent.

"Chet the ace?" asked one patron.

A guard scratched his head. "No, I think he said 'cheat the ace'."

Chase's grin faded, and his shoulders sank. "What? No! Are you thick?"

"Not only are they thieves, they're cheaters too! Get them!" screamed the elderly, hoity-toity lady.

"Oh, for the love of—" he moaned, shook his head, then smiled that boyish grin again. With a turn of his belt buckle, gears clicked into motion. A string of metal sprung out from the buckle, wrapping itself first around Chase's belt, then along his back. Through his jacket, a pair of fabric gliders, embroidered with designs of diamonds, popped out.

He held a hand out to Xin and beckoned him in. "Come on, mate."

Xin's eyes grew wide in horror. "What in Helheim are you planning with that?"

Chase laughed and ran toward Xin. A pleasant breeze with a hint of citrus scent filled the room, though all the windows were closed tight. A sense of calm filled the room until the breeze turned to a breathtaking gust, scooping up an exuberant Chase. As his feet left the ground, he hooked onto Xin's bulky arms.

"Hold on tight!"

"No, no, no!" cried Xin, but his pleas fell on deaf ears.

Up they went, nearly crashing into the tall ceiling and levelling out to glide toward the large windows. Freedom seemed well in their reach until—

Bang, bang, bang.

Suddenly, their flight was not so level. The now holy glider was useless, and the pair went spiralling to the ground.

"Shit!" cried Chase, unable to stop their descent.

"By the fucking gods..." Xin twisted his way out of Chase's grip and landed in a rolling dive on the ground. Chase, on the other hand, did a lovely belly flop, slowed only slightly by a last-minute gust of wind.

"Ow."

Xin plopped cross-legged upon the ground with a grunt and rummaged through his pockets to pull out a toothpick to roll distractedly in his mouth. "Remind me why I decided to join you again?"

Chase coughed and laughed, looking weakly up at him. "Cause I'm lucky. I told you I'd find that Konstantin guy for you."

"How are we going to do that if we're in jail?"

With a deep breath, Chase pushed himself up to sit across from Xin, once again finding that mad grin. "Then that's what's meant to happen. The gods—"

"Tch... The gods don't decide anything. They're dead and gone. They have no power... anymore..." Xin's annoyance trailed off as he noticed a familiar man pushing his way through the guards. As he locked eyes with James, both of their faces warped in surprise.

"Xin?" asked James, squinting his eyes in disbelief.

A soft smile found its way to Xin's face. "James."

"Xin!" James cried out again, this time with a huge grin. He ran clumsily toward him and dived into the open arms of his long-lost friend.

After some persuasion with Nick and the guards to let them go, James sent a quick message back to the Oasis, then took them to the glorious showroom and bar to catch up on times past.

A plethora of shimmering, pure white, round tables with a few scattered patrons lined the showroom. Above their heads, little mechanical bugs known as fireflies shone their blue-hued light. These round, winged gadgets were smaller than their more common, torch-like brethren, and drifted about the ceiling, following their commanded path, setting a nice, calming effect on the patrons below. Electricity was not a common commodity in Yggdria, especially not in the Forsaken Ring, but Nickolas had his share of contacts within Ratum that helped him set up his entire casino.

On the dazzling stage was a well-dressed man softly playing the piano, while the hum of people's chatting voices filled the air.

James came limping over to their table with a round of drinks for them.

Chase wrapped an appreciative arm around his shoulders, that boyish grin on his face. "Fair play, mate! You're the best! You cleared our names, you brought us drinks… We were fecken lucky to run into you, eh, Xin?"

"Would have been luckier if we hadn't gotten mixed up in that, anyway. If I ever find that little thief again…"

"Then we might not have found your old buddy!" Chase cheered, rubbing James' bald head affectionately, causing James to finally shoo him away. With a sigh and a shrug, Chase slouched back in his chair. "Come on, you gotta admit that was lucky. How do you know each other, anyway?"

"We used to bounty hunt together," said Xin simply.

"Oh, come on, buddy! You're selling us short," trumpeted James, standing proudly on his chair and heaving his rather heavy-sounding leg onto the top of the table. "We were the best bounty hunting team on these seas! No one, pirate, bandit or Angel could defeat our mighty band."

Chase gazed up at him, his sky-blue eyes shimmering with excitement. "What? No way! Deadly!"

Xin gave a dejected sigh. "Except we were defeated."

Like puncturing a balloon, James' chest deflated, and he dragged his leg off of the table. "Right…" He sat back down, his shoulders now slumped in despair.

"What? Why? What happened?" asked Chase, the curious excitement still radiating off of his face.

Xin sighed. "Things didn't go as planned. Our mark got the better of us. End of story."

"What? Oh, come on. I love a good story."

"End of story," Xin stressed with a glare.

Chase pouted. "Alright, fine. But why didn't you mention you were a bounty hunter?"

"You never asked, didn't seem important."

"Ah, Xin's never been the best at talking, especially not about the past," said James with a smile, and a renewed confidence in his knowledge. "Poor little Xin was just an angsty teen when me and Yuri found him, and completely clueless. Didn't even know what to do with the bounties he collected. Just goin' around chopping heads off. Kid was all murdery and broody after losing his family to Konstantin's crew."

"Like you wouldn't be," growled Xin.

James shot him a soft smile. "Just wish we had found you sooner after you escaped that bastard. No kid should go through that alone."

"Tch…" Xin replied, trying to hold back a smile of his own. "When did you get all mature and shit?"

"Ha! What can I say? I've done a lot of growing in the last five years." James laughed, then punched Xin in the arm. "And apparently, so have you, muscles. Ah, but you still got nothing on Yuri."

"Tch…" The hidden smile melted into an intense sorrow, which seemed to infect James as well. The two sat just staring at their drinks.

After a few long and awkward moments, Chase asked, "So… why did you guys stop bounty hunting?"

The sorrowful silence turned anxious as James' eyes darted toward Xin, unsure how to answer the question. Xin, however, continued to stare at his drink, but this time as if it were something to slay.

"Does it have something to do with that Konstantin fecker? Is he the one that defeated you?" Chase prodded, looking anxiously between the two.

"Uh, yeah," James said uncomfortably.

Chase regained his toothy grin. "Bang on! Right then, what do you know about the guy?"

James snapped his gaze to him in disbelief. "Wh-why… What?"

"That's how my luck works, you know," Chase explained, thumping a prideful fist to his chest. "I told Xin I'd help him find Konstantin, and here you are. Obvious, really."

"Well then, your luck has run out," sighed Xin, finally giving up the staring contest with his drink. After a long swig, he continued. "Why would James know about Konstantin? That's the last guy he'd want to find again."

"Haha, yeah… That's ridiculous. Why would I have anything to do with hunting down Konstantin? You're a funny guy, Chad," stammered James, a little too eagerly, sweat beading on his bald head. It didn't take a genius to catch the awkwardness.

"Argh! It's Chase! C.H.A.S.E," shouted Chase, his freckled face turning red.

"Right, right. Sorry, Chase. Anyway, I don't know a thing!"

"James," Xin growled, leaning forward with a scowl that could make a lion turn tail and run. "Why are you lying?"

"Well… you see…"

Before he could explain himself, a pair of fair, small arms wrapped around James' neck in a big hug.

"There you are! I am so glad I found you," Astrid chirped. "You will not believe what Konstantin pulled on us this time!" With a sigh, she flopped down on a chair next to a shocked and confused Xin. Even though James was eagerly trying to motion to their company, she was completely oblivious to anyone else but James and continued to ramble on. "So we were doing great. We got all the slaves freed, and then this big meanie pulls out an explosive and blows up the whole ship! Lorelei was furious. I'm a little worried—"

"What?" uttered Xin, his face dropped in panic. He hadn't heard that name in casual conversation in over five years.

Astrid jumped in surprise at the voice at her side. She examined the unexpected company with a small tilt of her head. "Oh, when did you two get here?"

Chase grinned, reached over an annoyed James, and gently grabbed Astrid's hands. As suave as possible, he said, "The real question is, where have you been all my life, fine thing?"

"You're very silly," she giggled. She wasn't usually the one to be flirted with. Even if he wasn't her type, it was still a little nice.

"He's an idiot is what he is," grumbled Xin. "Now, is anyone going to explain what the fuck is going on here? Why is Astrid here?"

Astrid glanced over at him with surprise, pulling her hands away from a disappointed Chase. Those tiny hands and soft face got right close to Xin, pushing his mess of hair from his face. As realization dawned on her, she let out a frequency that should not have been capable of a human, an excited vibration running through her whole body. In pure self-defence, both James and Xin covered their ears, scowling at the screeching woman. Not Chase. He found the whole thing quite amusing, apparently unfazed by her inhuman noises.

"Xin? Xin! By the gods, James! It's Xin! Oh my goodness! I'm so happy! Look at you! You look amazing, if not a little scruffy. She's going to be so excited! Or is she… Oh, I don't care right now. I'm excited!" she squealed, bouncing up and down in her chair.

After a few painful moments, James laid a hand on her arm. "Astrid, breathe."

She looked a little surprised, then did as she was told, taking a deep breath, and settled into her chair, still keeping a very firm posture. "Sorry, it's been a stressful day. What are you doing here? Who's your friend?"

"The name's Chase the Ace, beautiful woman, and we are on the hunt for the monster known as Konstantin," Chase announced with a flourish, spreading his arms out wide, almost smacking an annoyed James in the face.

"Chaz the Ate? That's a very silly name," tittered Astrid as she started fiddling with her braid. As Chase's face fell once again at the misunderstanding, Xin leaned in and corrected her. She gasped and apologized, then continued on with her interrogation. "So you're hunting Konstantin? Is that why you're here? Are you going to ask Lorelei for help? Are you going to be a team again?" she asked, getting increasingly excited and shrill as she went.

"What? No," Xin insisted. "Chase said he could find Konstantin. The last thing I plan to do is ask Lorelei for help."

"Huh? I think you misunderstood." Chase leaned back in his chair again. "I said I have the ability to help you find Konstantin, and that ability is to find people that know things. If you want to find Konstantin, sounds like this Lorelei lass is the one to talk to."

"What?" Xin growled. "That was not the deal. If I wanted to ask my ex for help, I would have found her myself."

"Nope. No way you would have been able to find her on your own," said James, a prideful smile on his face. "Konstantin's been hunting her non-stop. He came close three years back when he burned down headquarters, but since then we've been on constant move. No one could track us." James sat back and laughed. "Besides, you know none of us were very good trackers to begin with."

"Plus, I'm pretty sure she's been actively avoiding you," stated Astrid, a thoughtful finger pressed up to her cheek.

"Astrid," James scolded.

"Wh—Oh, right!" she giggled sheepishly. "I mean, she totally is not avoiding you."

With a grumble, Xin rifled through his pockets to retrieve another calming toothpick to place in his mouth.

"So who is this Lorelei, anyway?" Chase asked. "She seems important, and not just because she's Xin's ex."

James cocked his head. "Have you not heard of Lorelei the Siren?"

Chase's eyes grew wider than should have been possible, and that grin spread even wider. "What? You know the Siren? *THE* Siren? The deadliest, sexiest women in the Yggdrian seas? She's like the main reason I left Gaia! Why didn't you tell me you dated the Siren?"

Xin glared. "Because it's personal."

"So you've seen her naked? I need every juicy detail between you two."

"Good luck with that…" mumbled James.

"You are not getting anything juicy out of me!" exclaimed Xin, a pink hue colouring his cheeks.

"Oh, but I would love to hear about you and Lorelei," Astrid sighed dreamily. "Every time I mentioned your name, I would get in trouble."

"And that's exactly why I'm leaving." True to his word, Xin hopped to his feet and headed for the door.

With a little gasp, Astrid jumped in front of him, her tiny hands pressed up against his massive chest. "No, no, no! You can't leave. Please stay! Lorelei is different now. She's been through a lot. I'm sure she'll be happy to see you! Please!"

As Xin glared dangerously down at her, a distant roll of thunder sounded the imminent arrival of the storm. Unfazed, Xin just growled, "Out of my way."

Astrid shook as those rage-filled eyes bored into her, but she knew she couldn't just let him leave.

4

A Breath of Fresh Air

Hearts raced and resolves were pushed to their limits as the towering man stood over the tiny blonde girl. The plan, in Xin's mind, was to simply pick the tiny woman up by the shoulders and set her aside. As he went to do that, he found one of her needle-like fingers jabbed into his armpit. A tingling shot down his arm and it went completely limp.

"Argh," he growled. "Lorelei's been teaching you shit. Great."

"That's right!" she crowed, head held high. "And if you don't stay, I'll just make your whole body go limp."

That blood-freezing scowl returned to Xin's face as he grabbed for her a second time. This time, as she went to attack, she did not find a connection. Instead, her body completely twisted around, her arms crossed and pinned against her chest with Xin's massive arm wrapped around her. She tried to squirm free, but found absolutely no give from the man.

"Let me go!" she demanded, uselessly whipping her head back and forth.

Setting his scowling face right by her ear, in a growling whisper he said, "Don't think just because Lorelei taught you a few tricks that you could take me in a fight."

The blood completely ran out of Astrid's already very fair skin, and her body shook. *It's been so long since I've seen him,* Astrid thought. *He wouldn't possibly hurt me, would he?*

"Now, you're going to stay out of my way, right?" he asked, still with no kindness in his voice. Astrid nodded shakily, and his bulky arm loosened its grip. Taking in a quick gasp of air, Astrid stumbled away from him. She turned her teary eyes up to him.

"Don't even…" Xin grumbled, though a hint of guilt streaked across his eyes.

Once again, Xin motioned to leave, but this time found James' firm hand resting on his shoulder. "Come on buddy, it's been five years. Give it a chance… for Yuri."

"There's that damn maturity again." Xin sighed and stared at the floor briefly. "It's just… I don't think I'm ready yet. Just… let me get some air."

With a defeated sigh, James lowered his hand, and Astrid scrambled out of the way, her teary eyes keeping a firm gaze on him.

One step, two steps… The music coming from the stage changed, and Xin's feet stuck in place. Wide eyed, he looked at the stage.

"So that's what she meant by blowing off steam." Astrid giggled, also turning her gaze to the stage. "I thought she was going to go punch things."

All around them, a man's smooth voice excitedly announced, "Ladies and gentlemen, tonight we have a very special guest. The deadly, the enchanting, Lorelei the Siren!"

The room filled with gasps and excited whispers. Lorelei may have been a pirate's worst nightmare, but to anyone else in the Forsaken Ring, she was a hero—a legend. For them to be fortunate enough to hear her sing was a blessing. This became obvious as the curtains opened, and the room erupted into a roar of applause like waves crashing on the shore.

Lorelei's enchanting voice filled the air, singing her favourite song. A song she sang time and time again. A bouncing song from ages past about a deadly siren ruling over the oceans.

There she was, the woman who tore Xin's heart out just standing on stage, oblivious to his presence. Oblivious to his heart twisting and his gut wrenching. Five years he had worked to get over her. Why was she still so gorgeous?

That auburn hair was longer now, flowing all the way to the small of her back and neatly to one side to cover half her face. Her shimmering silver two-piece left her almost perfect olive skin open for the world to see, which meant the two faded, but noticeable scars were also visible. One upon her right arm, the other along her abdomen. What surprised Xin most was the lack of coverings on her wrists.

Maybe things really have changed. He smiled softly, and with a sigh, returned to sit at the table.

"Got that breath of fresh air you were looking for, mate?" chuckled Chase, but Xin was completely oblivious to him.

"I've seen that look before," beamed James. "Looks like things haven't changed too much."

Astrid couldn't help but giggle excitedly.

Chase watched his pal giddily, waving a hand in front of his face, having a grand time with his obliviousness. "By the gods, he really is out of it, isn't he?"

"Yup," chuckled James. "Takes quite a lot to snap him out of it at this point. At least, that's how it was when we first met Lorelei."

"Hey… Do you think I could land a hit on him like this?"

Astrid gasped. "Chase! Why would you do something like that?"

"Nothing hard, of course. Just want to see if I can."

"Oh yeah, you totally could," prodded James with a grin.

"James!" Astrid scolded, slapping him on the arm. As she was about to talk Chase out of it, she realized she was too late as he had already wound up and sent a punch flying to his chin.

Smack. Though not on target. Without his eyes leaving the stage, Xin had grabbed Chase's relatively small wrist and turned his flying punch into his own chin. With a small smirk, Xin gave him one more punch in the face for good measure and returned to his own bubble without a word.

James burst at the seams laughing, bent over and slapping the table repeatedly. "I can't believe you fell for that!"

A sour Chase, rubbing his sore chin, replied, "Aw, man. I was hoping to be pinned like Astrid, not hit in the face. Bollocks."

James's laugh stopped abruptly. "What? You wanted him to react?"

"A bit." He chuckled, nudging James in the ribs. "Come on, tell me you don't want to be wrapped in those arms."

"What? No!" James pushed Chase away from him. "What is wrong with you?"

"Ah… I see," said Chase, a small smile curling on his lips. "Oh, well."

"You two are ridiculous," giggled Astrid, bouncing in her chair along with the beat. Finally, she twirled up out of her chair and pulled James' arm. "Come on, James! Dance with me before the song's over!"

With a look of pure exasperation, James replied, "Oh, come on, you know I can't dance anymore, and I especially can't keep up with you."

Her lip stuck out in a pout. "You big fuddy duddy." She turned to Chase and asked, "You'll dance with me, right?"

"Well, I really would love to, lass, but I'm not a great dancer…" he replied with an uncharacteristic forced smile, his fingers now fidgeting with his drink. "I have trouble hearing the beat."

"That's silly," she said, dragging him up to his feet. "You don't hear rhythm, you feel it. Come on, take your shoes off. I'll show you!"

Chase shrugged, kicked off his shining white shoes and joined Astrid on the dance floor. She pulled him in close, looking up with that sweet smile. He looked at her nervously, then around the room, straining his ears to hear the music. She gave him a soft tap on his cheek and he looked straight into those shimmering emerald green eyes.

"Stop trying to listen. Just feel." She started dancing slowly and deliberately to let him feel the beat. As he got more comfortable, the rhythm flowing through him, Astrid pulled him along excitedly in a bouncy dance.

As they danced, Lorelei headed out into the crowd, stopping at different tables, flirting with the patrons. The beat had its control over Astrid as she pulled a happy Chase along with her, while James watched, quite entertained, tapping along with a clunky foot. Only Xin noticed Lorelei coming closer and closer to their table, but in his daze, he didn't realize the implications.

As Astrid did a beautiful spin away from Chase, a firm hand caught and dipped her down.

"Lorelei!" she squeaked, her cheeks tinged pink.

"My, my, Astrid, you've found a cute one. He's not exactly your type. Mind if I steal him?" Lorelei asked, shooting a stunning smile at Chase, her voice still over the speakers as she held the large microphone to her mouth.

"Y-yes! Of course. Go right ahead."

The piano continued its melody as Lorelei picked Astrid back up and walked confidently up to a grinning Chase.

Taking the distraction, Astrid scrambled as fast as she could beside Xin, grabbing his head and shoving it under the table, much to his annoyance. Luckily it was dark and Lorelei hadn't noticed him, yet. Thank the gods. Their meeting needed to be perfect. That couldn't happen if Lorelei was still pissed.

Who is this guy? thought Lorelei, as she strode up to the odd, orange-haired man.

It was not uncommon for Astrid to dance with random people, since she often lost track of the world completely when she danced. There was something different about this man that she couldn't quite put her finger on.

Lorelei slid right up to him, his excited grin inviting her into his bubble. A nice, clean citrusy scent came off of him, making her feel… welcome, comfortable. How odd. The man was well-groomed, obviously caring a fair bit about his appearance. Judging by the clothes he wore, he also liked to be the centre of attention. She could play with that.

"Hmm… that's not a hair colour you see very often in Yggdria," she breathed, sending her hand up to push back his long hair. Before she got the chance, he redirected her hand into his. Smooth. Also, a move she was familiar with. Apparently, he didn't like his hair being touched.

"You must be from Gaia, handsome," she continued with a smile.

"Bang on," said Chase, leaning right into the offered microphone. "Born and raised in Royal Derry. Been traveling here for a few years now."

"Ooh, big city boy has come all the way out to the Forsaken Ring. What on Jord would bring you out here?"

"Adventure mostly. Though I admit, a chance to lay my eyes on the legendary Siren may have been a factor."

"Is that right?" she purred. "And do you like what you see?"

"My imagination couldn't even begin to fathom a fraction of your true beauty," he said, so smoothly and confidently, Lorelei actually felt quite flattered. This man may have looked young, but damn, was he good. She might actually have blushed a little.

An annoyed grunt, followed by a thump, turned Lorelei's attention to the table where a very suspicious-looking Astrid and James were sitting. What the hell were they up to, and what was Astrid hiding?

She turned her attention back to Chase, a flirty smile on her face. "I think I might like you, good looking. What's your name?"

"Chase Burke's the name, but I'm known as 'Chase the Ace'!" he proclaimed with a grand flourish.

Lorelei chuckled at the absurdity. "Chet the Ape? Not as good as Lorelei the Siren, but it's alright."

"It's not—" he began, but Lorelei had other things on her mind.

"Tell you what, Chet, find me after the show and we'll 'talk' some more." She laid a soft kiss on his cheek, which caused the crowd to whoop and cheer.

"It's Chase…" he sighed quietly.

Lorelei continued her song and danced up to the unusually still Astrid holding out her hand, motioning Astrid to dance with her. She stayed where she was, shaking her head.

Alright, she was definitely hiding something. She never refused a dance.

She grabbed Astrid's hand, pulling her up easily and spinning her to the side. The chair behind her fell over, and with it, a man stumbled out toward her. In a single movement, she grabbed onto his hand and pulled him in.

And the light caught those steel-blue eyes.

5

Holy Lands

The words in her mouth came to an abrupt end—her body frozen in place. Lorelei recognized him in an instant, despite the scruffy changes over the last few years. All it took was to see those wonderful steel-blue eyes, and her heart pounded, her mouth became dry. There were no thoughts, just a flood of memories racing through her mind. All the wonderful times they had had sailing and hunting together, growing closer and closer. All to have it come crashing down.

It felt like a lifetime since she had seen Xin, and in that moment, she never wanted to look away. He must have had a similar thought, since as the piano continued on in the background, the two of them just stared into each other's eyes.

The piano man gazed over with confusion, wondering if he should keep playing or not. The room broke out in curious whispers at the odd reaction of the usually glib woman.

A flash of lightning filled the room, and Lorelei's stupor broke before the crash of thunder sounded. Her eyes raced in every direction, taking in all of Xin's face. Thousands of thoughts raced through her mind. How did he find her? Did he find her on purpose? And the most important question, was he mad at her?

In response to her silence, a small smile crept to his face. He leaned into the microphone that was already between them and asked, "What's the matter? You haven't forgotten the words to your favourite song, have you? Or are you expecting me to sing? Because we both know that won't end well."

Voicing a single entertained, "Ha!" she pushed him back into his chair and returned to her performance with renewed energy. Striding and weaving gracefully through the crowd, she reached the stage just in time for the last verse.

Xin stared as she concluded her song with a long, beautiful note and a flourishing bow. All around, the room erupted into a roar of applause. As Lorelei left the stage, he leaned back in his chair and breathed a tremendous sigh of relief.

"Holy Feck!" exclaimed Chase, a mad grin on his face. "You could cut that bloody tension with a knife. You two must have had a deadly sex life."

"Wha— you— I— Dammit Chase, mind your own business," stammered Xin, face bright red.

"Ah hahaha. Oh man Xin, I have missed your awkwardness," said James, giving him a gentle pat on the back.

"Did you see that look?" Astrid squealed, currently unconcerned about Xin, still vibrating as she watched the empty stage. "That went so much better than expected! How exciting!"

"Hey, mate, sorry about flirting with your ex and everything," said Chase, laying a hand on Xin's shoulder. "The way you were talking about her earlier made it seem you weren't interested anymore, but if you want me to lay off, just say the word. We are best friends after all."

Xin gave him a cockeyed look and pulled away. "Wha— you've known me for less than a week. I think 'friend' might be pushing it, let alone 'best friend.'"

Chase's eyes grew dire. "What? But what about all that shite we went through? The wargs, the evil lord, the damsel in distress? I thought we had a connection!" Chase cried, desperately clinging on to Xin's jacket.

"Ak!" Xin grunted, shooing Chase's hands away. "Alright, alright, we're friends. Just calm down."

"Aw, best friend," Chase beamed, wrapping an annoyed Xin in a big hug.

Astrid giggled, watching Xin awkwardly try to remove the clingy Chase.

James shook his head, a small smile upon his face. "I'm going to get another round of drinks," he chuckled, and limped off to the bar. Just as Xin finally detached Chase from his neck, a loud crash sounded from the bar, followed by James wailing, "Wait, wait, wait, I can explain!"

Along stormed Lorelei—now wearing a long jacket over her revealing outfit—dragging a clumsy James by the ear.

"Someone interesting, huh?" She threw James into an empty chair. "You don't think you could have given me a bit more warning than that?"

James' chair wobbled dangerously, but he regained his balance and shot her a pouting glare. "Well, I didn't know you were going to sing tonight! You weren't supposed to find out like that."

"Didn't know I was going to sing? My name is the fucking Siren! Singing is what I do!"

James opened his mouth, taking a deep breath to state his case, but found no words to argue. He gave a great sigh and slumped down.

Xin stood up with a sigh and said, "I'll just go…"

"Sit," she commanded, drawing a menacing glare from Xin. The same kind of glare that had made grown men piss themselves. Lorelei, however, returned the glare, completely unflinching, while the rest of the table sat at the edge of their seats watching the two powerhouses face off.

Finally, and surprising to most at the table, Lorelei was the one to concede the duel with a sigh and a shrug. "I'd like you to stay, but I do understand if you want to leave."

Xin's scowl faded as he searched her face. Was she being sincere, or was she just playing him? Eventually, he decided he wouldn't mind sticking around to find out. With a grumbling sigh, he flopped back down into his chair.

Seemingly quite pleased with his response, she smiled, then leaned back, relaxed in her chair, crossing one leg over the other. "This day just keeps getting weirder and weirder." She looked over to the bar, and as she was about to call "Waiter!" a young, amber skinned man appeared beside her, a pitcher full of golden liquid and five glasses in his hands.

"Good evening!" he beamed with a painfully fake smile, and the table jumped in surprise. All except Lorelei, who shot him a nasty glare.

The man laid the glasses out on the table, poured them full, and handed one personally to each one at the table. In doing so, he also encouraged a small handshake, nudge, or pat on the arm. This guy was touchier than Chase. Unfortunately for him, he did not have the same fresh scent. Quite the opposite. All those he got near tried to kindly pull away, as the man smelt quite ripe.

"My name is Charles," he grinned, "and I will be at your beck and call."

"Tchah," growled Lorelei, downing her drink as soon as he passed it to her. In an instant, the vigilant waiter refilled it. "Charles, huh? You don't strike me as a Charles."

The waiter chuckled and slicked back his wavy black hair. "I get that a lot. Still, if there is anything you need..."

As he laid a hand upon Lorelei's shoulder, a blood curdling scowl settled on her face. Her hand snapped up to her silver hairpin, which held a tiny dagger, and pressed it against his throat. "Touch me again and you lose an eye."

Charles snapped his hand away, his face pulled back in shock. "R-right."

"Don't worry," chuckled Chase, sliding over to Charles and wrapping an arm around him. "Feel free to touch me all you want."

The waiter looked at him apprehensively before forcing a smile back on his face. He chuckled, patted him lightly on the chest in thanks, then slipped from his grip. Lorelei waved him away, and he slunk off with the empty pitcher, allowing the awkward group to continue their conversation.

Lorelei studied them intently, looking each one of them in the eye. "Alright, so James knows Xin, Astrid knows James..."

"And Xin," corrected Astrid.

"Tchah, barely. Anyway, still doesn't answer where Chap the Ass comes in."

Astrid started giggling uncontrollably while Chase sighed, defeated, chugging down his own glass.

"Uh... Lorelei, his name's Chase the Ace," said James, trying to hold back his own laughter.

"Chase the Ace? Well, that's a hel of a lot better. Why didn't you say that in the first place?"

"I did!" cried Chase, almost knocking over his filled glass as he leaned in. He looked at it with mild surprise, shrugged, then drank some more.

"Whatever," she declared with a wave of her hand. "What brings you to this group?"

Finding his second wind, Chase puffed up his chest, a huge grin on this face. "I'm the one that recruited Xin to be a part of my crew. Together we're going to find the best crew in all the seas and enter the Holy Lands!"

Lorelei, James and Astrid stared at him slack jawed, while Xin attempted to hide in his drink.

Slowly, Lorelei laughed, followed by James and Astrid.

"The Holy Lands? Are you fucking drunk?" bellowed Lorelei, barely able to contain her laughter. "No one in over five-hundred years has set foot in those lands. Even if they did, it would be completely desolate. It's the focal point of the Calamity. Nothing could have survived there."

"But what if it did? And what were the Gods fighting over? No one knows for sure. That power is strong enough to keep us safe from the storms. What if the stories are true and there is a magic so powerful there that it can grant any wish? Wouldn't that be worth finding it?" he said, as if he had rehearsed this argument many times.

"Even if it were true, you would still have to accomplish the impossible," scolded Lorelei, now leaning at the edge of her seat, using her finger to draw out on the table what she was talking about. "First, you'd have to make your way past the Divine Wall, a wall that survived an Earth shattering calamity, and is impossible to scale. The only way you could possibly do that is to use one of the Angel's portals, which would mean storming an Angel fortress, which seems just as impossible as scaling the wall itself. Sneaking in may be the best way, but you'd need a small and talented crew to pull that off. Plus, someone that knew the inside well enough to lead you to their portal room."

Lorelei continued on her rant, the table listening intently, sipping away their drinks, not even realizing that their glasses appeared to be bottomless. It didn't take them long to feel a little tipsy. Still, Lorelei continued.

"Assuming you miraculously got past that, you would have to make your way through purgatory, which is devoid of any land or resources and crawling with the worst criminals this world has. You would need a talented crew with the best navigator and engineer you could find just to survive the ocean, plus the greatest fighters to defend you against the denizens."

Lorelei slumped back in her chair and scratched her head as she continued. "Then, if you somehow manage to do all that, you would have to pass through the death fog, a fog that no one, human or angel, has been able to touch without dying…"

She trailed off as she noticed Chase's goofy grin. "What?"

"Well, I thought we were here for Xin's thing with Konstantin, but I'm starting to think you're meant to help me with my mission, too," he chuckled, those sky-blue eyes sparkling with excitement.

Xin slapped a hand on his own forehead. He didn't want Lorelei knowing he was looking for Konstantin.

Lorelei's face dropped at the new information, giving Xin a cock-eyed look. He just gazed down into his empty… no, make that full glass, unable to make eye-contact. She growled, downed her own glass, and flicked her gaze back to Chase, who was still staring at her with bubbling excitement. She looked between the two in contemplative silence until—

Splash.

The ever vigilant waiter, coming to refill Lorelei's empty glass, had tripped and soaked Lorelei in booze.

"What the fuck, Charles!" she cursed, flicking the liquid off.

"Apologies, most patient one. Let me assist you," he insisted, taking the cloth from his belt and wiping down her shoulders and chest.

"Get the fuck off me, idiot!" she growled, pushing him away. He gave a quick bow, apologized profusely, set the cloth on the table and slinked away.

"Fucking imbecile," she cursed under her breath, dabbing away the liquid.

She pointed a finger at Xin. "We are discussing the Konstantin thing later."

Xin gave her a small nod, which turned her attention to Chase. "Everything in your stupid adventure is technically possible, except for one thing. How do you plan to get past the fog?"

"Simple..." he said with a cunning smile.

As Lorelei stared at him, waiting for him to finish his thought, she noticed a warm breeze caress her face. It grew stronger. That wonderful citrus smell she had noticed on Chase now surrounded her. Suddenly, her hair flew about as well as her jacket as the breeze turned upwards, and her chair rocked, then hovered. She gripped the side of her chair, her heart racing in fear and confusion until her chair set gently back down to the ground without a sound, and the breeze vanished as quickly as it came.

"I'll just blow the fog away," Chase finished, that smile still on his face.

Her breath quickened, her eyes darted around the room. She focused on Chase, looking him up and down with wide eyes. That was impossible. An impossible power. No one had ever controlled the winds. It had to be a trick.

Everyone focused on Lorelei, waiting for her reaction. It wasn't often she was left speechless. As that was happening, Xin noticed his lap becoming cold and wet. He snapped his gaze to the table, where an amber hand was overfilling his drink and making it pour onto his lap. He looked at the gawking waiter, then realized the man's other hand was in Xin's jacket pocket.

The waiter smiled sheepishly as he realized the jig was up.

Xin grabbed the man's shirt, pulling him in, giving him a death glare as he pulled the man's hand out of his pocket and took back the silver lighter in his hand. The thief shook, his eyes wide, terrified of what the man would do to him. Just as Xin was about to bring attention to the thief, a loud shattering sound broke the air. Xin snapped his gaze back to Lorelei, who was looking at the shattered glass in her hand with horrified surprise.

"Uh... I didn't do that," said Chase. "Did I?"

Lorelei threw away the broken shards in her hand and started pawing at her chest in a panic. "My necklace! Where's my necklace?" Xin snapped his glare back at the waiter, but discovered he was now only holding a shirt.

Lorelei threw things around in a mad panic, looking for it. Overhead, the buzzing blue fireflies faded in and out, fluttering off course. The air felt heavy, energized.

6

The Thief

The energy turned chaotic. Chairs flew, tables overturned, and people scrambled over each other to get out of the room.

Xin leapt atop his chair, searching the crowd for that damned thief. It was the same guy that stole from them earlier. He was sure of it. How could he have missed that?

Lorelei continued searching frantically on the ground for the necklace, the panic clearly rising in her.

"Lore. It got stolen," snapped Xin, still searching the crowd. "Panicking isn't going to help."

"No. It can't be. I need it. I need it now!" she screamed.

The fireflies above them exploded with energy. The deafening sound of thunder cracked outside, accompanied by multiple lightning strikes right above their head.

Xin stood unflinching, and just as the lights faded to nothing, he spotted him.

"East exit," Xin announced, jumping from the chair, grabbing his swords and sprinting through the crowd.

As soon as the words left his mouth, Lorelei snapped from her panic and sprinted close behind. Astrid attempted to join, but found Chase clung tightly around her arm.

"Chase? What are you—"

"Please don't leave me alone. I don't do great in the dark," he whimpered.

Astrid gave a dejected sigh, and with the help of James, the three slowly made their way to the east exit.

Gods be damned, why did I go and push my luck? cursed Emir, the true name of the fake waiter and actual thief. He raced into the storming city, the rain beating against his naked chest, chilling him to the core.

Emir took a glance behind him, sure that he would have lost them in the casino. A flash of light struck, and lit up the two very dangerous people he had just robbed sprinting after him. He couldn't see their faces, but he was pretty sure they were out for blood. With a little whimper, he forced his scrawny legs to go faster.

Kaboom!

Once again, the lightning struck nearby, almost as if it was following him. That was ridiculous. He may not have experienced many storms growing up, but he knew lightning didn't do that.

He thought he heard a whistle to his right. Shit. There she was.

Off he went to the left, his heart threatening to explode. He turned down an alley, only to almost run into the hulking brute. He slid to a halt and dashed another way.

Another whistle sounded.

He was being hunted.

What was he doing? This was his city. He could lose them. He turned down every side street he knew, the rain washing away any tracks he may have left. There was no way they could find him.

He slowed his sprint, looking cautiously around him. Another shot of lightning rang a little further off. Perhaps he was in the clear. He jogged a few more blocks. He needed to get home before he got completely chilled.

Taking one last look around, he gave a sigh of relief, and leaned against a door, its awning protecting him from the storm. Finally, he could look at his prize—the legendary Siren's necklace. The thing she was never without. It must be worth a fortune…

His face dropped in despair as he pulled out the simple chain. He had expected a huge gem on the end, a diamond, maybe a sapphire or ruby, not this. It was just a tarnished silver pendant with two crossed swords. He couldn't buy food and medicine with this. Was this really what he risked his life for?

Emir glared up at the casino through the haze. That stupid casino, with its stupid stone walls to keep out the riffraff. People came here to make a new life for themselves, to be saved by the luck of the casino, but in reality they got conned and shoved outside. They didn't even bother to supply them with decent housing.

They made all the houses out here of corrupted wood, the wood already on the island when they started colonizing it. It was weak and offered little protection from the elements. The Forsaken Ring was about the only place they actually needed it. Storms barely touched the inner rings, but were plentiful out here.

Then there was that casino, made of perfect wood and stone, just sitting there, mocking their squalor. The rich only cared about one thing, and that was themselves.

All at once, there was a blinding flash and a deafening boom of thunder. The pressure shook his body from the inside out, and he was almost sure he was just struck by lightning. As his senses came back, he saw the house beside him with a large, smouldering hole in its pathetic attempt of a roof. Emir thanked his luck that he didn't live there.

His luck didn't hold out long.

A vicious scream of rage pierced the air.

Emir snapped his gaze up to see the fury-filled face of Lorelei diving at him. She crashed into him. They flew through the door and tumbled to the dirt floor. The necklace flew across the room. The woman pinned him down, an odd heaviness about her, with a dagger poised in the air, ready to strike.

"You fucking bastard!" she screamed. "No one steals from me, you fuckin—"

Thunk.

A rock went flying into her forehead. She snapped her snarling face up, peering into the inky blackness of the room. She was looking for what Emir already knew was there.

"Leave Emir alone!" yelled a youthful voice, followed by another rock flying at her head. It struck hard, leaving a slight cut upon her cheek.

Lorelei growled bestially and glared down at Emir. "Emir? For fuck's sake. I should have known."

Emir looked at her in shock. She knew his name? How? Why?

"Attack!" called the child's voice, and from every angle rocks flew at Lorelei. She tried to catch or block them, but more than a fair few broke past her defence.

"Fucking brats! Stop that!" Lorelei roared, but the rocks continued to fly. Another roll of thunder and a flash of light filled the room. This time a striking shadowed figure of a large, chiselled man with an "X" filled the room.

The room broke into small, terrified whispers as the man towered at the door, flicking a lighter on and off in his hand. He strolled in, grabbed a lantern by the door, and lit it up. The room filled with a faint glow, revealing a handful of children, all different ages, pressed against the crumbling walls of what could only be described as a hovel.

With an annoyed grumble, Lorelei stepped off of Emir.

After Xin tossed Emir's shirt at him, he strolled towards one trembling, sickly looking child against the wall. She whimpered as he neared, trying to sink into the wall, all the while suppressing a cough.

Emir motioned to confront him, but found Lorelei's strong, toned arm across his bony chest.

Xin gave the little one a quick scan, sighed, and bent down to pick up the necklace. His face momentarily streaked with surprise, then faded back into flat seriousness. He strode back to Lorelei and handed it back with only a sliver of a smile.

Lorelei snatched it away and returned it around her neck, uttering a small 'thank you'. After a relieved sigh, she looked around the room, sending an annoyed look at the fearful children staring at Xin.

"Are you freaking serious? You're scared of him? You know I am way more dangerous than him, right?" said Lorelei, a vicious scowl on her face, her arms crossed. Still, the children continued to stare at Xin.

"In all fairness, he did make a far grander entrance," stated Emir, sending a glance her way as he returned his shirt to its rightful place. His eyes widened at the sight of her face in the light. Her previously perfect hair had been soaked, windswept, and pushed to the side. "By the gods! What happened to your face?" he exclaimed, pointing at the horrid, blotchy scar all along the right side of her face.

"I got it saving fucking puppies from a tree. What happened to yours?" she snarled, sending him a sidelong glare.

"Mine?" He pawed at his face. "There's nothing wrong with my face."

"That's a matter of opinion," she said, causing Xin to snort out a small laugh, and Lorelei couldn't help but smile a little herself.

Emir grumbled some very unsavoury curses under his breath at the woman.

"Tchah, whatever. Come on," she barked, motioning to the door, where the storm had apparently calmed.

Confused whispers filled the room. An older, pockmarked child spoke up. "Are you taking us to Purgatory?"

"Ha! Seriously? For trying to survive? No, I'm taking you to the Oasis," said Lorelei, not even looking at the children. "Been trying to do that for a while now. Now hurry it up."

A few curious, even excited, whispers filled the room. Many people had heard tales of The Siren's Oasis. It was a paradise. No one would ever turn down an invitation.

"Wait, wait, wait, wait, wait," interrupted Emir, waving his hands back and forth. "The Oasis? The magical paradise whispered in the streets? No way. This is clearly some sort of trick. People don't help thieves, they chop off their hands or take them to Purgatory. Or worse, they sell them to the Angels, where they make them sex slaves or experiments. No. These children are staying with me."

The children looked around and nodded, whispering their agreement.

Lorelei sighed, tapping her finger on her thigh with annoyance. "You're not in Ratum anymore, Emir. I'm not saying child traffickers don't exist here, but they're not nearly as common. Odin hates them. And I hate them, which is why they are the first ones I seek out and kill."

"That proves nothing. All your so-called triumphs are only hearsay. Who is to say you do not secretly work for Arch-Angel Set?"

In an instant, Lorelei pulled her silver tiny dagger from its hairpin sheath and pressed up against Emir's neck. "Say anything like that again, I will slit your fucking throat."

Emir whimpered, and Xin's hand came to Lorelei's arm.

"Lore, you're trying to convince them you're not dangerous, remember?"

"Tchah," she spat, and pulled away her dagger, placing it back in her hair. "I am dangerous, just not in the way he thinks."

Xin motioned to the children, basically telling her to convince them, not him.

She turned to them and sighed. "Look, the Oasis isn't exactly a paradise. We're attacked a lot, and we sometimes run out of supplies, but we all work together to make the place work. We have all sorts of people that are professionals in tons of fields like engineers, writers, musicians, scientists, you name it. The kids will get to learn from everyone. We're basically a big family full of people who have been fucked over. You're not the first thieves to board the Oasis, and you won't be the last."

The smallest girl interrupted with a deep chest cough.

"And we have trained doctors and medical supplies for everyone. We can make sure the little one lives to see her next birthday."

"She is not dying," insisted Emir as the little one cried.

"Well, I'm not a doctor, but I've seen grown men die from an untreated cough like that."

"But why? Why would anyone go out of their way just to protect people they don't know?"

Lorelei quirked a brow at him, and he realized the irony of his words.

"My situation is different. We are all poor and starving, just trying to survive together. You are rich and powerful. Surely there must be a catch."

"It is a selfish reason, actually," she sighed, sending her gaze to her worn-out boots. "I'm doing it to try and make amends for my past. I did horrible things, and I allowed horrible people to prosper. Men who abused and raped me, I called crewmates because I thought that's how the world was. I want to make sure people understand that the world can be better. I want a safe place for them."

"That is… honourable," said Emir with a smile.

"Thank you." She looked around at the children with a soft smile. "Come on. If you don't trust me enough to come to the Oasis yet, at least take a night off at the Casino. Get a proper meal and a warm night's sleep."

Emir looked back and forth from the children to Lorelei. The poor little girl's deep cough broke his thoughts, and he sighed. "And medicine?"

"Of course."

"For free?"

She gritted her teeth. "Yes."

"Very well," he sighed. "Lead the way."

Not long after leaving the hovel, they ran into the ragged, breathless trio of Astrid, James, and Chase.

Astrid saw them and broke out into an excited squeal. "Lorelei! Xin! There you are! And you found Charles! And… a bunch of children. Wait, does that mean you're actually Emir?"

"That's right," he sighed.

"Oh my goodness, Chase! You weren't kidding about your luck. We've been looking for these kids!"

Chase chuckled knowingly.

Lorelei continued walking, unfazed by the new arrivals. Chase and Astrid caught up to her with a light jog, while James hung back around Xin and the ogling children.

The group continued on their path down the puddled streets. The children still stared at Xin as they walked, but this time with more intrigue than fear.

"Are you Xin the Executioner?" asked the pockmarked boy.

"Yep."

"How many people have you killed?" whispered the little dark-haired girl.

"Lots."

"How strong are you?" asked a tan skinned young boy.

"Very."

"Strong enough to carry all of us at once?"

"Easily."

"...Would you?"

Xin smiled, looking down at all the exuberant faces watching him. He gave a small nod, and they all squealed with excitement, climbing on top of him. Eventually, all the children climbed aboard and rode the muscle man down the street with gleeful giggles.

James gave a hearty laugh at the sight.

At the head of the group, Astrid and Chase caught up to the striding Lorelei.

"I was so worried about you," squeaked Astrid. "That storm was insane, even by Forsaken Ring standards."

"Just a thunderstorm," grumbled Lorelei. "It is Stormday, after all."

"Not like any thunderstorm I'd seen," added Chase. "And I've seen a lot. Might have been able to help you out more if it weren't for that. I could have flown around and..." Chase's face fell at the remembrance of his torn glider. "Oh... never mind."

"Doesn't matter. It worked out."

Chase caught the action behind them, grinned, and went to join in the fun.

Emir jogged up and kept pace with Lorelei, holding himself tall and proud. "I have a query for you."

Lorelei rolled her eyes. "What?"

"Is it true that you were a pirate before you became..." He motioned generally at her. "...This."

A dark grin spread across her face. "What? A pirate's worst nightmare? The queen of the dark oceans?"

"Not the words I would choose, but yes."

"Yes, I was," she concluded with a shrug.

"Ah yes, that would explain it."

She looked at him apprehensively. "Explain what?"

"Your taste in clothing and overall… what would you call it… sluttiness?"

Her teeth clenched together as she growled, "What?"

"Perhaps sluttiness is the wrong word… Easiness, perhaps?"

"There had better be a fucking good point to this."

"Oh, there is! See, I have had the privilege to grow up as a noble in the Divine Ring."

Lorelei snorted. "Is that right?"

Astrid gasped. "Really? Then what are you doing here?"

"Well, you see…" Emir began, a smile across his face as he pulled his shoulders back. "My island was ruled by a beautiful family, with an elegant and beautiful Princess. Princess Vira. The two of us, of course, fell in love. Unfortunately for me, my brother also loved her and became jealous. He betrayed me and framed me for a crime that I did not commit. When my beloved and I tried to run away together, a severe storm tore our ship asunder.

"I know not of her fate, and I dare not return to the island of my birth for fear of my brother's wrath. I can only pray to the gods that my beloved was kept safe.

"When I washed up on these shores a year ago, these children took me in with no hesitation, sharing their meals with me and nursing me back to health. In return, I taught them… some skills in the stealth department."

Astrid giggled. "You taught them how to be thieves."

"I suppose, but it was only for the sake of survival, I assure you."

Lorelei couldn't help but laugh. "So that's the story you're going with? Why on Jord would a nobleman have any skills in thievery?"

"I… It was a hobby of mine."

"And what about the ship destroying storm? Those don't exist in the

Divine Ring."

"It can too, if a pulse is missed."

"Those are rare and you know it."

"Oh, give him a break," giggled Astrid, giving Lorelei a light slap on the arm, then turned her sparkling eyes back to Emir. "I believe you, Emir. That is the most beautiful story I've ever heard! I am so jealous. I wish I had a love like that!"

"Ah, you believe anything, especially if there's romance," teased Lorelei.

Astrid crossed her arms and pouted with a, "Humph."

"Thank you, blonde one. But back to my original query. I would like to train you in exchange for taking us in."

"Train me?" quizzed Lorelei. "In what? Stealth? I'm actually pretty good at that as it is."

"Oh, no, no. I mean in properness. You see, a proper woman does not have to worry about foul men taking advantage of them."

Lorelei glared viciously at Emir. "What?"

"Please, hear me out. You see, men differ from women. When they get… the urge… they become very different. They have trouble thinking straight. Therefore, it is very important to dress modestly in public."

"Emir, stop," Astrid urged softly, seeing Lorelei's clenched fists and teeth.

Emir either didn't hear, or didn't care. "Look at your lovely friend here. She dresses quite well, even if she has seemed to have forgotten her shoes. I bet you she is always treated with respect."

Astrid sighed, her shoulders slumped. She suddenly didn't feel the need to protect him any longer.

Lorelei stopped in her tracks, bringing the entire group to a sudden halt. The children and Chase (who had also taken the chance to ride on Xin) jumped off and watched the scene ahead with growing concern.

The Casino was right there. They were almost inside, but Emir continued his… 'explanation', oblivious to the warning signs Lorelei was putting out.

"I am just saying you are a very attractive woman. It would be in your best interest to cover up to prevent men from forcing themselves upon you."

"So it's my fault," Lorelei said, a twisted smile on her face. "It's my fault that when I was eight years old, my father forced himself on me every night? I suppose my dress did show a lot of ankle. I guess it's also my fault that my first boyfriend took advantage of me whenever he felt like it, even though I wasn't ready or willing. I suppose those oversized men's clothes did show off a lot of collar bone…"

"I… that's not. Certainly… there were other factors," stammered Emir.

"Oh yes," she sighed sensually, getting close and personal to Emir. He took a few uncomfortable steps back. "I've been told I am quite irresistible. Clearly that means that those men had no choice but to have their way with me."

"Surely there were things you could have done. People you could have gone to. You could have fought."

That was it. The final string snapped. Lorelei grabbed his boney wrist and pulled him in close. He tried to pull away, but her hand stayed strong. His eyes grew wide. Before he knew it, she twisted him around, pinned his arm behind his back, and shoved his face against a wall.

"What are you doing?" he cried. "Release me!"

"Aw baby, don't be like that," she sighed in his ear, pulling his shirt off of his shoulder. "I saw you running around town topless. I know what that means."

"No, no! It means nothing!" he exclaimed, straining against her. He couldn't budge. "This is ridiculous! There were circumstances—"

"Then you go and leave your top undone as we're talking. I get it. I know what you want."

Suddenly, Emir's legs felt the cool breeze as they became revealed to the world. She dropped his pants? What the hell? "No! No, no, no! I do not want anything!"

"Don't lie to me, baby. I saw it in your eyes. I know what you really want."

"Okay, Lorelei, I think he gets it," urged Astrid. "You're scaring the children."

"Good," Lorelei hissed, still pinning Emir to the wall. "They need some education, too, in case this idiot passed any of his morals on to them."

Lorelei twisted Emir around once again, somehow pinning both of his hands to his chest. Still, he couldn't overpower her. He had never felt so helpless.

She poised a fist in the air. "Now, since there are children present, I will keep this part a little less graphic. Now just imagine my fist is a dick, and your face is your ass."

Before he could argue, her fist descended upon his face with a sickening crunch. The metallic taste of blood filled his mouth and pain shot through his whole body.

The children screamed out.

"That hurts!" cried Emir.

"Yeah. Keep talking dirty. That's how I like it," she said, raising her fist again and connecting with his face.

Over and over she went, ignoring his pleas, Astrid's pleas, the children's pleas for her to stop. She was zoned in.

The children cried and shouted, hiding behind their new, muscled friend. The littlest one looked up at Xin. "Please stop her! She's going to kill him!"

"Nah, she wouldn't. She only kills people that deserve it. Emir is just an idiot."

"Please!"

He looked into those watery eyes, sighed, and walked up to Lorelei. He leaned in as close as he dared with her current anger level and whispered, so only she and Emir could hear. "Hey Lore, this seems like a pretty weak punishment for you."

Emir's desperate, dumbfounded eyes looked at Xin as blood poured down his face. "What the fuck?"

"And what would you suggest?" asked Lorelei, her fiery eyes still burning in Emir's rage-inducing face, not letting up in her torment.

"Remind me again, what did you do to the child molester, Cole Greyhate?" asked Xin.

Lorelei's fist stayed poised in the air for a moment. "Honey and fire ants on his balls."

"Nicolas Bones, the man who experimented on pregnant women?"

"Disembowelment," she replied, turning a wide smile up at him.

"Roland the toothless, the bastard who murdered your teacher?" he asked, with far more intensity, though still quietly enough that the children would not hear.

"I made him fuck himself, then let him bleed out," she replied darkly in the same lowered voice as Xin. They locked eyes for a moment, the bloody memories of their past written on their dark smiles.

Finally, with a happy sigh, she released Emir's arms and took a step back. Astrid immediately ran to Emir's aid as Lorelei stepped away from him. "Oh, the good old days. I don't torture nearly as much as I used to. Astrid gets so twitchy about it."

Astrid glared. "Torture is inhumane!"

"The ones I torture aren't human," she replied with a wicked scowl.

"You are crazy," Emir whined.

Lorelei lunged at him, pulling her hand back. Emir flinched fearfully, raising his freed hands to protect his face.

Unexpectedly, Lorelei came in with a gentle pat on his cheek. "And don't you forget it. What else have we learned?" she asked, as a teacher would a kindergartener.

Emir honestly thought it through for a moment. The only thing he really remembered was the fear, the pain, the helplessness. He didn't think he did anything to deserve it.

Perhaps that was the point.

"Anyone… can be a victim," he replied softly.

Lorelei's eyes widened, apparently a little impressed by his epiphany. "Good boy," she grinned, then looked around at the children's fearful eyes on her.

The scowl returned.

"Tchah. I told you I was more dangerous, didn't I? Don't forget it."

The kids nodded fearfully.

"Xin, James, get the kids cleaned up and fed. Chase, help Astrid get the idiot somewhere to get patched up. I have some things I need to do."

7

Razin

Somewhere in the vast ocean, a massive battleship heaved, the roll of thunder growing closer. A pirate flag with the symbol of a skull atop the North star flapped eagerly upon the mast. Below it, a menacing man sporting a worn tricorn, with striking blonde hair beneath, sat atop the deck in his self-declared throne.

Konstantin Razin.

His chiselled face wore the lines and determination of a long time captain. His large body and poor complexion a testament to the countless amounts of rum he consumed. A battle-worn jacket covered a very crude, metallic peg leg from his right knee down.

As the ship swayed gently with the swell of the ocean, a sleazy, dirty man strode up to Konstantin, an excited grin on his face. "Cap'n. We've successfully captured one of The Siren's ships. The homing pigeon is primed and ready to fly."

Konstantin's wicked, violet eyes gleamed with excitement, and in his deep, chilling voice said, "Time for this game to end."

8

Storytime

"I'm sorry again about Lorelei," sighed Astrid, as she, Emir and Chase walked the dim, stuffy hallways of the Casino.

Emir, who had been cautiously pressing his stitched up nose, wincing at the self-inflicted sting, sent her a sadden look. "Honestly, do not apologize. I had no idea that people had suffered that way. I was fortunate enough to grow up in the Divine Ring, so things were not so terrible. We never had things like that happen there." Though his tone was serious and sincere, it sounded absolutely ridiculous with his nose completely stuffed full of gauze.

Astrid turned her sad green eyes to Emir. "Is it that it didn't happen, or that you didn't see it? Sure, bad things tend to happen more often in the Forsaken Ring, but that doesn't mean it doesn't happen in other places. I was raised in the Rustic Ring and I…" she paused, furrowing her brow, her eyes shimmering with withheld tears. "Never mind."

"Oh no… do not tell me someone as sweet and innocent as you was—"

"I'd rather not talk about it," she interrupted with a sweet, but obviously forced smile.

"Of course."

She stopped at a door. "Here we are. The kids should be in here."

The door opened into a wonderful, clean smelling room. A waft of warm, inviting steam rolled out of the doorway, and revealed a sparkling bath

58

house. As they stepped inside, they saw only Xin and James relaxing in the tub.

Emir bursted in and looked around. "Where are my children?"

"Calm down," sighed James. "You were taking too long, so we got Nick to get them set up in the VIP suite with a ton of food. Figured we'd relax here and wait for you."

"We did not take that long," Emir insisted.

"Well… you were quite resistant to the stitches." Astrid held back a smile. "We could have been a lot quicker if we didn't have to wait so long for the painkillers to kick in."

"It hurt!"

"I'm sorry," she replied, still biting back that smile. "Anyway, I'll go check on the—Chase! Where are your clothes?"

Chase, now standing in nothing but that red bandana, looked back at her with confusion. "What? We're in a bath. I'm going to have a bath!"

"You're supposed to leave your underwear on, dumbass," sighed Xin, his bare, chiselled arms up on the edge of the tub, showing off his tribal tattoo going all the way up his right arm and onto his chest. A few scars adorned his arms, chest, and back, but only one really stuck out. A large, rounded and jagged scar on his back shoulder.

"What? But that's so uncomfortable!" Chase sighed. "But I suppose if it makes you uncomfortable…"

"Oh, just get in the tub, I'm leaving right away anyway," Astrid said with a resigned sigh.

Chase grinned and jumped happily into the water, somehow keeping his head dry, while completely soaking a no longer relaxed James.

Astrid giggled and shook her head. "Anyway, I'll go check on the kids and get the little one the medicine she needs." She turned to Emir, laying a hand on his shoulder. "You… really should have a bath, too. It smells like you haven't bathed for months."

The boys all broke out into a roaring laugh as Emir's shoulders dropped. Astrid giggled, gave a brief apology, and left with a wave.

"This is ridiculous," Emir grumbled as the laughter subsided. "Not only have I been beaten today, you all mock me as well? I have half a mind to—"

"Yup, that sounds about right," cut in Xin, a smirk on his face. "Hey Chase, sounds like Emir might need a hand into the tub."

"On it!" exclaimed Chase, and with a sweep of his hand, a gust of wind blew Emir into the tub with an "ak!" and a satisfying splash.

Emir came up, gasping for air, a deep anger in his dark brown eyes. "How dare you dunk a prince of—"

Xin's powerful hand grabbed his head and dunked him back underneath. "You still stink." Xin smirked as he held him down for a moment, then let him up.

"You stupid, hairy, uncivilized brute! I will steal every last gold from your cold dead fing—" Under he went again.

"Good luck with that," grinned Xin.

A cheerful silence filled the room of the steamy bath. The only noises were the dripping of Emir's wet clothes, hung to dry, and the occasional satisfied sigh from one of the four men present.

Emir gave a contented sigh, winced, and sighed again with a smile. "I could get used to this."

Xin chuckled. "Which? The bath or the beating?"

Emir shot him a nasty scowl, causing another wince of pain which entertained Xin immensely. Emir ignored him as best he could and looked over at James. "So, what is it like on the Oasis? I cannot believe it is just a paradise as many have claimed."

"No, I definitely wouldn't say it's paradise. Just a safe haven," he replied, rubbing his bald head in thought. "Everyone has to pull their own weight and work together to make the place work. You're given jobs at what you're best at. For me, I'm good with people, so I deal with trades. Lorelei is good at fighting, so she goes and takes out pirates and brings back any gold they might have. It works out pretty good."

Chase's big blue eyes were right up close to James. "But weren't you a bounty hunter? Why aren't you off killing pirates?"

"Well, I was never the best at the fighting part… and after our fight with Konstantin…" He pulled himself out of the tub, causing Emir and Chase to gasp. His right leg was missing from just above the knee. "...Things became a bit more difficult."

"What? No way! I'm so sorry, mate."

A dejected sigh escaped his lips. "Yeah well, it could have been way worse."

"Hey James," said Xin, his face furrowed. "How... no, when... no, why did you start working with Lore again? She left us both high and dry after everything. Did you find her or..."

"No. She found me. Or rather... Trisa made her find me. I was in a pretty dark place," James explained, gazing into the shimmering waters.

"Trisa is here too?"

"Yep, she left the Gaian army about three years ago to help Lorelei. Guess she finally decided Yuri was right," James said with a scowl before smiling at Xin. "Anyway, I went back to Niflheim after everything that happened, but turned out Liza had found and married someone else. She put me up for a while, but she was happy and about to start a family, so I didn't bother her too long. After that, well, I didn't know what to do. I just kinda wandered around going from bar to bar until Lorelei kicked my ass and dragged me to the Oasis."

"I'm sorry, James. I shouldn't have left you alone on that island."

"Don't worry about it, buddy. You had your own shit to deal with."

"What about Astrid? When did Lorelei find her again?"

"Well... actually," James began, but before he could explain, Astrid's voice sounded from the other side of the door.

"Can't it wait? They're still bathing!" she pleaded, but obviously to no avail as the bath door slammed wide open, revealing a proud-looking Lorelei with a rough-looking guitar strapped to her back and an enormous book of fairy tales in her arms. Astrid trotted close behind, giving the boys an apologetic look.

"Not you again..." moaned Emir.

Ignoring the whining of the infuriating man, Lorelei set herself up on the floor, towel laid out, book spread open. "Alright, here's how it goes, boys. Normally, a plan to find the Holy Lands is just dumb. Chasing a fairy tale, a children's story, but after seeing your power it started to click."

The boys came to the edge of the tub, and when Chase spotted the book on the floor, his eyes shimmered with excitement. "Hey, I know this book!" He reached for it, but received a slap on the hand.

"Don't touch, you'll get it wet."

"You're the one that brought it into the bath!" he pouted, rubbing his injured hand.

Lorelei ignored him and continued. "As you should all know, the gods created the three nations. Before the Calamity they created places of power for the humans." Everyone nodded. Of course they knew.

Lorelei flipped the book to one page, showing a shimmering golden city on it, and an immense library on another. One that stretched for ages. "In Ratum, Ra created the library of Alexandria, filled with knowledge of technology far beyond our capabilities."

On the next page, she flipped to lay a massive forge filled with shimmering weapons and armour. "In Yggdria, Ymir created the forges, where enchanted weapons are crafted and gifted."

The next page was a picture of a flowering, enchanting garden with a grand tree, larger than any other in the world. "Gaia created the sacred gardens, filling the life there with her power in order to imbue any human with a Blessing. These are usually mild increases to one's own natural ability, such as increased strength or speed. Occasionally a person will show an affinity with an element, but only have minor control over it. Usually Angels are the only known people with an impressive control over a certain element.

"However, there hasn't been anyone with the power of the air element," continued Lorelei, now pointing to the very attentive Chase. "At least not in recent history. It was in the back of my mind and I couldn't quite remember where I had heard about it before."

Once more, she flipped the page, this time laying it out perfectly, flattening the book so it would stay open on its own. That page held a simple drawing of a world being torn apart, with a poem written beside it. Lorelei swung about her ivory white acoustic guitar, which was covered with wear and multiple repaired breaks, cracks, and possibly knife wounds. She started strumming out a lovely, wistful melody. She sang:

Where our makers did clash, you find the gods' wrath.
   The earth shattered, the oceans raged,
   The lands burned, we faded away.
   Then came the air, so clean and so fair
   It whispered the song of great times to come.
   Oh, bring us the treasure, we will thrive again
   Grant us our wishes, we will thrive again
   Pass through the fog and battle your foes
   And find us the treasure, we will thrive again.

The room remained in complete silence through the whole song, each one enjoying Lorelei's rendition of the ancient verse.

"That's the song my ma sang to me every night," Chase said with a reminiscent smile as Lorelei strummed her last chord. "It's the reason I started on this mission!"

"Everyone knows that song," Astrid added. "Plenty of people have had the same idea as Chase and died in the process."

"That's true, but there was something they didn't know," Lorelei revealed, leaning closer to the group, a cunning smile on her face. "Most people don't realize there was a fourth god, one who disappeared before the Calamity Wars. No one knows for sure if that god is still alive, but the fairy tale of the godslayers suggest that they did."

Astrid fiddled with her braid in thought. "I've never heard of that fairy tale."

"It's a fairy tale told to Angel children of the scary godslayer human that hunted angel children in search of the lost god they failed to slay. What if Chase has been Blessed by the power of this god? What if Chase is the missing piece of the puzzle?" Lorelei paused for a moment, letting the thought linger in their minds.

She continued, "The land of Gaia, ruled by descendants of Gaia herself, has an affinity for the earth. The land of Yggdria, ruled by the descendants of Ymir, has an affinity for the sea. The land of Ratum, ruled by the descendants of Ra, can harness fire and lightning. It makes sense that the fourth god's elemental affinity could be of the air, just like in the song," Lorelei explained, becoming more and more excited as she went.

"What would that mean?" asked Chase, completely enamoured by Lorelei's story.

She spread her arms out wide, a grin on her face. "It would mean that your crew might actually be able to find the Holy Lands. To make the world thrive again. To find the treasure the gods fought over."

"Really? You think so?"

"What happened to 'just a fairy tale'?" asked Xin, his arms crossed over his chest.

Lorelei smirked. "You're not still worried about what Odin said, are you? That was like seven years ago."

"Tch. Being called a godslayer by the arch-angel does tend to stick with you."

Chase looked giddily between them. "Seriously? Is Xin a godslayer?"

"Well, I thought it was Odin just being his usual asshole self, but if Chase is the proof that the Lost God exists… then maybe?"

Xin's face went pale. "Don't even joke about that, Lore."

"I know… I know it's all a stretch," replied Lorelei with a sigh. "But fairy tales, legends, they're always based on some sort of truth, some sort of event. And now with Chase here… it just makes too much sense. It all works together."

"So what does that mean?" Xin asked.

Lorelei's lips parted into a large grin as she announced, "It means I'm going to join Chase on his adventure."

9

Gold is Good

"Yes! Bloody fantastic!" cheered Chase, jumping up and down in the tub in celebration. "I would've never dreamed The Siren was going to join me! Praise the fecking gods!"

Everyone else present didn't seem to share in Chase's exuberance. Instead, they stared at Lorelei in disbelief. She gave a quick glance around at their faces and chuckled.

"Alright, alright, the flattery is lovely, but don't get too excited yet. I can't leave the Oasis unprotected while that bastard Konstantin is still hunting us down. That's all I need is another Leyuan to burn to the ground."

"Leyuan? You mean paradise? The home of Lin Siliang and the Dragon Ladies? The island of the whores that fight? Konstantin burned it down?" Chase rambled, growing more and more distressed.

"That's right. A few years ago. I made the mistake of making the island my home base and he tracked it down while I was away. Luckily, my right hand lady Trisa was there and got everyone out safely."

"That bastard! I wanted to visit that island! At first I was doing this for Xin, but now it's personal!"

"Well, all the ladies that were there are aboard the Oasis. I'm sure they'd love to meet you…" chuckled Lorelei, making Chase grin huge. "Assuming you have gold."

His face fell flat. Gold was something he had little of.

Lorelei noticed Chase's downtrodden look and laughed. "Well, if you're lucky, the Holy Lands will be filled with treasure, and not just of the wishing nature."

"Wait, wait, wait," Emir interjected, waving his arms back and forth. "I must get this insanity clear. You are actually trying to get to the Holy Lands? For the treasure that will grant any wish?"

"Bang on!" said Chase, resting an arm around Emir's shoulders. "There a wish you want to make?"

"There is indeed," replied Emir, a wistful look on his face.

"Grand! Then you can join us, too!"

"What? Seriously?" Lorelei fumed. "You want to make the guy that just stole from all of us become part of your impossible mission? You should only have people you trust going on this mission."

Chase laughed. "But I do trust him. He has a good soul, I can tell. Besides, we could use a talented thief like him."

"And weren't you going to bring him aboard the Oasis?" Astrid asked.

"Yeah, but I have people that can keep an eye on him there, then slit his throat if he tries anything."

The two glared at each other.

Emir scoffed. "Perhaps it would be best for me not to join."

"Aw, don't be like that," Chase pouted. "Come on, mate. I don't really care about the gold. I just need enough to pay some ladies. Figure you can take ninety percent of the gold we find."

"Really?" Emir squeaked excitedly.

Xin shook his head. "Tch… don't be stupid Chase. What about the rest of us?"

"Not to mention paying to keep your boat afloat and the store room stocked. You really do need me along, don't you?" sighed Lorelei.

"Hmm… Alright fifty percent, then," declared Chase, slamming a fist in his hand.

"Yes, yes, yes!" squeaked Emir excitedly. "I will join you. I will not let you down!"

"We'll work out the details later," Lorelei said with an annoyed wave of her hand.

Emir gazed wide-eyed at Lorelei. "Wait, will the children be safe without me? You just said the last place you had as headquarters burned down."

"Well, that won't be an issue if Konstantin no longer has a head," she grinned.

"Right! So it's agreed," said Chase, holding his hand out. "We take out Konstantin, then find the Holy Lands!"

"Perfect," said Lorelei, putting her hand on top of Chase's.

"Works for me," said Xin, putting his hand on top of Lorelei's, a small smile coming to both of their faces.

Emir looked at their hands for a moment, scratching the stubble on his chin, and sighed. "Alright, as long as I get my share of the treasure," he decided, putting his hand on the pile.

Lorelei looked over to Astrid and asked, "Well, what are you waiting for?"

"What? You want me with you?" she squeaked, her cheeks flushed.

Lorelei smirked. "Don't look so surprised! How many times have I ditched you and you found me again? I just figured I'd save you the hassle. Besides, I can't go anywhere without my left hand. It's far too important." While Lorelei was right hand dominant, her right arm was damaged years ago, so her left hand was the one she used to fight with.

Astrid grinned madly at the unexpected compliment. "Alright," she stated, throwing her hand on the pile. "I guess you're going to need someone to patch you up when you inevitably try to get yourself killed."

The only one left in the room was James, still sitting on the edge of the tub. As all eyes turned his way, he shook his head, letting his gaze fall to that stub of a leg of his.

"Thanks, but no thanks," he said with a sad smile. "I've had enough adventure for one lifetime. I think I'm better served staying and keeping the Oasis safe."

"Alright then, here we go, team Ace!" cheered Chase, lifting everyone's hands in the air as they let out their own unique cheer.

"We'll also talk about our name later," said Lorelei. "But for now..." Lorelei started unbuttoning her coat.

"What are you doing?" scolded Astrid.

"What do you think? I still reek like booze. I'm having a bath," she said, kicking off her boots, then looking over at the guys in the tub. "Unless there are objections?"

"Definitely not!" Chase said excitedly.

"Definitely yes!" said Emir, quite offended by the idea.

"Oh, well, I don't care about you," said Lorelei with a teasing smirk, "you're the one that spilt on me in the first place."

"There's a bath on the Oasis," sighed Astrid.

"I wasn't planning on going back there tonight. I need my feet on dry land for a while after almost getting blown up. You're welcome to join us if you want," said Lorelei, sending a teasing grin her way.

Astrid gave her a pouting glare. Lorelei looked her straight in the eye, a knowing smile on her face as she removed her top, leaving her now only in her underwear, and her whip-scarred back open for the entire room to view. Emir opened his mouth, clearly about to mention it, but Xin flicked him on his bandaged nose. A grumbling, sore Emir got the point and kept his mouth shut.

Astrid turned her head away from Lorelei, cheeks tinged pink. "Oh, I give up. She's your problem now."

Lorelei snickered as she stormed out the door, then shrugged. She motioned to unclip her bra. Chase watched eagerly, but Emir cut in with, "You will at least leave your underwear on, yes?"

"What? But that's so uncomfortable," she whined, pausing her undressing.

"Right?" agreed Chase, trying to downplay his eagerness.

"Ugh, and you don't have to worry about bras," she groaned. "Those things are torture devices. And believe me, I know torture," she concluded with a wicked laugh that made Emir slink to the furthest edge of the tub.

"Why do you wear them?" asked Chase. "Those things are pretty rare and pricey. Why bother if they're not comfortable?"

"I only wear this one for special occasions, like performing in front of a crowd. Have you seen how good it makes my boobs look?"

"Heh heh, yeah," Chase snickered. "Though natural is good, too."

"My thoughts exactly."

As the two of them discussed Lorelei's breasts, Xin played the staring game with the tiles on the bottom of the tub. He couldn't help but smirk at the comment about torture, knowing full well what she was capable of, but most of the time, he'd just let his eyes roll in annoyance, sounding a soft 'tch' at them.

After one of these moments, a sprinkling of water splashed his face. He snapped a snarling face at James, but softened upon seeing his old friend's supportive smile. He was glad to see that smile again. After everything that happened, Xin thought he might never see it again.

With a small chuckle, Xin leaned back in the tub, trying to let himself relax again. "You're enjoying this, aren't you?"

"Immensely, though I have to say, after working for the woman for three years, on top of the two years we were bounty hunters, I'm just not as attracted to her as I used to be," James sighed, and Xin just shook his head and chuckled.

By this time, Lorelei, still in her bra, had turned back to Emir. "Look, I know you were raised in Ratum, where seeing a woman's ankle is taboo, but you're in Yggdria now. The body and desires are what people worship here, not the mind. You'd best get used to seeing naked women, especially around Spring."

"What? Why?"

"The Spring Festival, of course. A time to celebrate love and fertility. Of course you know what that means."

"No…"

Lorelei laughed. "It means orgies abound! Men and women roaming the streets indulging in their basic desires."

"Are… you serious?"

"Deadly. Wrastan rarely partakes at such an extreme level, since there're so many people from Ratum. Not every island celebrates the same way, of course, but it's what the Angel Freya demands every year."

"That… is disgusting."

"Says you, mate!" chimed Chase. "It's fecking beautiful. First time I found myself in one of those festivals I thought I'd died and gone to Elysium."

"It's not everyone's cup of tea," Lorelei said with a grin, "and it can sometimes end badly, but, for the most part, people have fun."

Emir just shook his head in disbelief.

"Tell you what, bashful, I'll leave my panties on. We're all grownups here. It's not like you've never seen boobs before." Without waiting for a response, she unclasped her bra, causing Emir to quickly cover his eyes and Chase to grin wide. As she gently slipped into the water, Emir started blindly searching for a towel.

"This is quite inappropriate," he grumbled, obviously trying to hold back even further scolding.

"Wait…" smiled Lorelei. "Have you never seen boobs before? Are you a virgin?"

"Of course I am a virgin. I am unwed. I am saving myself for my love, Vira. Not that someone like you could understand," he grumbled, receiving disbelieving looks from the rest of the boys.

James passed him a towel before he could say anything else.

Lorelei gave a hearty laugh, sending a wave of relief through everyone else present. "No need to get defensive. I just think it's cute."

"You do?" he asked, quite confused, almost looking over at her, but quickly covering his eyes.

"Sure. Usually, it's all on a woman to be virtuous. Don't get me started on what I think about that. I find it funny, though. Weren't you the one saying men can't control the urge? Are you trying to tell me you've never been turned on?"

"That… is personal information. Also, I told you that *some* men are like that. Not I."

Her smile faded away. "Well, joking aside, I actually think it's nice that you're waiting. I never really got that option."

"I am sorry," sighed Emir, back still turned, but standing tall. "I suppose I should inform the children. What room are they in?"

"I'll come with you," said James. "Think I've pruned up enough, anyway. Give me a hand…" he snorted out a laugh. "or a leg, rather." He motioned to a spot where a towel hung. Emir removed the towel, revealing a large, gear filled prosthetic leg leaning up against the wall. With a grunt and a few wheezes, Emir dragged the leg over.

James swung it about easily and set it in its rightful place. With a grin, he gave it a couple knocks, and showed off how it could bend on its own. "Good ol' Kari. It's like nothing ever happened after she built this for me. Those crutches were a real pain." His grin was still firmly in place, but a sadness lay behind it. "Well, see you guys later!"

James heaved himself to his feet, slung his clothes over one shoulder, and wrapped the other arm around Emir, guiding him to the door with his still averted eyes. The metallic clunk of his leg rang throughout the room without the boots and clothes to dampen it.

Lorelei's gaze followed the two with a snicker, then stopped as she noticed the lingering gaze of Chase. She grinned slyly as she slid herself closer to him, once again getting right into his personal bubble, letting his crisp scent envelop her. She walked her fingers up her chest, then rested her gaze on his excited, grinning face.

"And what would you be looking at, *Captain?*" Lorelei asked with a knowing grin.

Chase's face absolutely lit up at the sound of her calling him Captain, even if it was with severe sarcasm. He chortled a little, then said, "Would you believe I was checking out the tattoo?"

Just above Lorelei's left breast lay a small, dark tattoo. A silhouette of a nightingale in flight. It was a tattoo to cover up the mark of Konstantin's crew that once adorned her chest. Now it was her own symbol. A symbol of hope and freedom.

It was also not what Chase was looking at.

"Nice try," she quipped.

"Ah, well. What can I say? Sometimes when you see something of absolute perfection, it's hard to look away."

"Ha… Ah hahaha. Damn Chase, you do have a way with words, don't you? I might just be falling for you."

A huge, hopeful grin spread across his face. "Really?"

With a huge, exaggerated sigh, she said, "Perhaps… But unfortunately, I have a rule: I don't sleep with crew mates."

"Bollocks."

"Hope that wasn't the only reason you asked me to join."

"Of course not!" he exclaimed. "You're the most bad-ass chick I've ever met. I'd be an idiot not to have you on my crew."

"Damn right."

"So… that's a definite no to sex, then?"

"Yep."

"Oh, well," he sighed. "I had found a few other people that seemed up for a good time earlier. Think I'll go find them, especially after all that talk about the Spring Festival." With that, he hopped out of the tub, once again unabashed by his complete nakedness.

"You're… not going to try and convince me otherwise?" she asked, with a tilt of her head, giving his pleasantly toned body a quick glance over.

"Huh? No, why would I? Wait… was I supposed to?" he asked with a furrowed brow as he attempted to get dressed.

"No, no. You were perfect. Go have fun."

"Aye aye," he said with a salute. "And if you do happen to change your mind, I'll be in room 224," he concluded with a flourish, throwing on his shirt and dashing out of the room.

Lorelei watched him go with quiet respect.

"So he passed your test, did he?" asked Xin from the far corner, making Lorelei jump a little. Bastard was so quiet, she almost forgot he was there.

Without looking back, she said, "With flying colours. Impressive. You sure know how to pick them."

"I do, don't I?"

Lorelei looked back at him with a smile. Suddenly, she realized they were completely alone. Her face fell a little, and she crossed her arms over her chest, dipping deeper into the water. "Sorry, I guess that was a little thoughtless of me. It's just…"

"You had a plan," Xin concluded for her.

"Yeah… I can leave if you want."

With a shake of his head, he said, "I don't mind. I'm glad you've gotten more comfortable with your body. Quite different from the girl I first met."

"Yeah well… I've come to decide that those who mind don't matter, and those who matter don't mind."

They smiled at each other.

A long silence filled the room, and it became increasingly awkward as time moved on. There was so much to say, but neither of them knew how to start. Maybe it was best not to say anything at all.

"You know what, I've been here longer. I'll let you have your bath," said Xin, motioning to get out of the tub.

"Why?" she asked. He stopped, looking back at her, a bit confused.

"Uh… 'cause you said you needed a bath?"

"Why are you going after Konstantin?"

Xin sat upon the edge of the tub with a dejected sigh, now staring at his folded hands. "I don't know. Revenge I guess."

"Don't give me that shit," she scolded. "Like you're some kind of mindless swordsman."

"Aren't I?" he asked, sneaking a narrowed glance at her.

"Tchah! What happened to 'revenge was pointless?' That we should look to the future?" she asked, a stern seriousness on her face.

The weight of the past seemed upon his shoulders as he silently stared at the water. He wasn't avoiding the question—she knew that—he was finding the right words.

"The only future I cared about left that day," he replied softly. "So after that… I don't know. I guess it felt like revenge was the only thing I had left. Like it was the only thing that could make things right."

Silence once again filled the room. Lorelei had expected something like that, but to hear him say it twisted her heart into a knot. She caused that. She caused that pain… that doubt.

Xin gave a halfhearted chuckle and looked at her once again. "But at least you seem to have taken it to heart—the whole future thing—at least a bit. Even if you are still hunting Konstantin down, it sounds like you've made a proper home, helped a lot of people."

Lorelei smiled, shaking her head. "Ah, well, that was mostly Astrid's fault. She was so damn needy I had to set down some sort of roots."

"Ha! That sounds like her," Xin exclaimed, a proper smile now rooted on his face. "Why did you go back for her?"

With a burst of laughter, Lorelei replied, "Go back for her? The little cunt was stowed away on my ship the night I took off. She's been glued to me ever since, insisting that I train her to be stronger, so she'd never be a slave again. I thought I could just dump her off on Leyuan, but she was fucking persistent."

"Good for her," he laughed.

"Tchah," she scolded, splashing Xin, and for a moment, through the laughter, it felt like old times.

But it wasn't.

Lorelei's face fell once again as she rubbed her arm absentmindedly. "After that, I just kept finding people that needed help. It started with one or two here and there, but then there were more and more. A fucking village's worth. Eventually, I ended up leading some sort of crazy haven full of people that hated the way the world worked. I got so many people willing to fight and die for me… and I don't know why. That was the last fucking thing I wanted was more people dying for me," she quavered, tears filling her eyes.

"Lore…" Xin sighed, slipping back into the warm, welcoming water. He came in close, gently laying a hand on her shoulder, her skin just as soft as it always was. He had planned to continue with some soothing words, though he wasn't sure what they would be. It didn't matter. As soon as his hand touched her, she dived into his chest and wrapped her arms tightly around him with a shuddering breath.

In an instant, the shield he had put up around his heart melted away as her shoulders quavered in his hands. He hugged her tightly, burying his face into her damp hair. It still had that sweet, inviting scent she always had. By the gods, he missed that smell.

"Fucking Konstantin," Lorelei choked, gripping Xin tighter and tighter. "He killed five more people, all because he was trying to get at me. Why did

I start this? We should have just kept bounty hunting. I should have never confronted him. I should have just let them keep thinking I was dead. Now this will never be over until he is fucking dead."

He brought his one rough hand to her face, gently nudging her up to gaze into those golden eyes. "Then we take him out," he said with such intensity, his heart alight with a hope he thought had long gone. "We started this together. By the fucking gods, we're going to end it together."

She leaned in closer, as did he, gently running his hand over the side of her face, pushing her hair back, revealing that one accursed scar she would never talk about.

10

The Mark

Every inch of Xin's body burned with exhaustion, his body was littered with cuts and bruises. Every breath he drew felt like daggers, but no matter what, he couldn't stop. His feet ran as fast as they could, sprinting up the rickety stairs of the old lighthouse. The creaks and groans were suddenly overshadowed by a sound he had heard many times, but never from Lorelei.

A blood-curdling scream.

The sound rang through his whole body, and he no longer felt any pain. The only thing that mattered to him was going faster. Even the solid oak door that blocked his path wouldn't hinder him.

The door went flying from its hinges, resting at the feet of that scrawny, violet-eyed bastard, a fresh, gruesome gash along his face. He barely even noticed Xin's entrance as his awful pale hands shoved Lorelei's face into the wildfire in the middle of the room.

Without a thought, the sword drawn in Xin's hand went flying off to impale that monster right in the shoulder and pinned him to the wall opposite with a satisfying roar of pain.

Xin dashed towards Lorelei, pulling her from the flames and inspecting the damage. There she was, usually so powerful, so strong. But now her body was bloody and battered, her battle outfit torn to shreds, and the fire in her eyes had completely faded. Fear and despair now filled those golden eyes—that awful burn covering the whole right side of her face.

Five years later, that heart-wrenching burn had healed well, but it still marred her beautiful face. The scar didn't matter to Xin, of course, but he couldn't help that the memories of that horrible day came flooding back into his mind.

Lorelei jerked away from him. "Tchah, don't give me that look."

"Wha—" he asked, not even realizing he had a look.

"That pity. I don't want your fucking pity."

"I-I'm sorry… It's just… The scar. I haven't seen it since it healed," he admitted, feeling ashamed of making her self-conscious about it.

"Right…" She looked down, bringing her left hand up to cover that horrible mark.

"I-it's not that it looks bad. I barely even noticed it. I just… I couldn't help but remember…" He motioned to grab her hand from her face, but it quickly received a stinging slap.

"This… this is stupid. What are we doing here? What, I just spout a couple of tears and you're just going to forgive me after everything I did? I'm not sorry, you know? I'm not sorry about any of what I said. I was just frustrated with what happened last night. Nothing has changed."

"Fine."

"Fine? Are you serious? Why can't you just be mad? Yell at me, fight me, something!" she screamed.

He gazed at her, eyes narrowed, then leaned back on the tub wall, arms crossed. As calm as he could muster, he said, "What point is there to be angry? It doesn't change anything."

"That doesn't mean you can't be angry!" she cried, throwing her arms up in the air. "I'm angry all the time. I'm angry about what happened last night. I'm angry about what happened five years ago."

"So what? I should overreact to everything like you do? What would that accomplish? I'm not going to make up emotions to make you feel better about your own."

"You're not angry about what happened? Because of us, James lost his leg and Yuri fucking died!"

"I don't like what happened, but being angry about it changes nothing. Besides, what was I supposed to do? Just let him take you?" His voice was getting a little louder than he would have liked.

"Yes!"

"I couldn't," he said with dead seriousness.

She looked him straight in the eye. "How do you think that makes me feel? That my life was more important than our friends?"

He stared back at her, but had no response. How could he argue with that? His gaze fell back to the steaming water below them. She gave a frustrated grunt. Then he heard the water slosh as Lorelei pulled herself out of the tub. As he looked back up at her, she was drying off and slipping on her long jacket.

"Where are you going?" he asked.

"To see Chase. He seems like fun. By the gods, I could use some fun right now," she replied flatly, buttoning up her jacket.

"So, is he your next mark? Are you just going to use him, too?" Xin growled as she headed for the door.

"That's what I do," she said coldly, her gaze still focused forward. "You'd be wise to remember that." She left the room without a single look back.

Xin took a few steps forward, contemplating going after her. He stopped and stood just staring at the closed door. His breath quickened, his fist clenched. With a single roar of rage, he punched a massive hole in the stone wall of the tub, and splashed down with a sigh of frustration.

Lorelei stormed down the hallways, frustration flowing through her. Five fucking minutes with that man and he has her bawling her fucking eyes out. She was better than that—she was stronger than that. How did he make her so weak? She was strong. She didn't need him.

Lorelei stopped at room 224 and paused for a moment with a raised fist as she heard laughing and giggling voices coming from inside. With a stifled growl, she rapped on the door. Some confusion within occurred, followed by Chase opening the door, presently only in his pants.

"Lorelei!" Chase exclaimed. "I really didn't expect you to actually show up."

"I'm impressed, Chase. You found this many people this quickly?" said Lorelei, examining the handful of men and women sitting in the room, goofing around.

"Huh? Oh sure, this place is full of sexually repressed people." He leaned in and whispered, "A lot of failing marriages."

Lorelei attempted to hold back a laugh.

He turned back to the group, a grin on his face, and said, "Still, they are all beautiful souls that need love, isn't that right?"

They all giggled and agreed.

"Uh… yeah, sure," muttered Lorelei, though she believed beautiful may be a strong word. A couple were attractive enough, but most of them were pretty plain, bordering on ugly.

"So what's the deal? You going to join in?" asked Chase.

Lorelei crossed her arms and leaned against the frame. "I don't do orgies. It's them or me."

"Wait, what? You're serious? What about the crew thing? And I did promise them…" said Chase, looking back at the group.

"Not really in the mood for discussion, Chase. This is kind of a limited time offer," snapped Lorelei, tapping her fingers impatiently.

Chase scratched his head, then with an apologetic smile, turned back to the group. "Sorry mates, the party is over."

A portly man came up to Chase, hugging him and kissing him on the cheek. Chase smiled.

"It's alright," said the man. "We can go somewhere else. I think this one might need you more than us, anyway."

"I don't need…" Lorelei started, her teeth clenched, but that wonderful citrus scent coming from Chase seemed to calm her.

"Alright," said Chase. "You crazy kids go have some fun. It seems the Siren could use an Ace in her hole."

Lorelei couldn't help but snort out a laugh. "Seriously?"

Chase shrugged with a smile. "Sorry, couldn't pass that one up."

One by one, Chase's posse left the room, giving some affection as they went, and turning a knowing smile at the frustrated Lorelei. She was starting to regret this course of action. As the last one left, Chase invited Lorelei inside with a sweep of his arm. She abided, stepping in a little cautiously. This man was certainly different from what she was used to, and that was saying a lot.

He closed the door and leaned against the wall with a sigh. "So, what's up?"

Her face scrunched up. "Wh— what do you think is up?"

"Well, *I* certainly am," chortled Chase. "But you seemed pretty sure about the 'no sleeping with crew mates' rule earlier. I thought maybe something else was up."

"You… got rid of an orgy, 'cause you thought I wanted to talk?"

Chase shrugged, "Sure. You're my crewmate. You're important."

"Ha…" she said, getting right up close to look him in the eye. As she searched his face, she realized he was actually serious.

"In-fucking-credible," she breathed. "But I actually *do* want you to fuck me." Without waiting for a response, she pressed her lips against his.

His eyes grew wide, but he embraced the kiss, pulling her right into him.

"Oh!" he exclaimed, pulling away for a moment. "Hang on, I never did get the go ahead from Xin about this. It seems a little strange sleeping with his ex. I wouldn't want to make my new best mate mad at me."

"Don't worry. I can assure you he won't be mad at *you*."

"But he'll be mad at you?" he asked suspiciously, catching her emphasis.

She shrugged and removed her jacket, revealing her nearly naked form. "Maybe, but let's not worry about that right now, hmm?"

Chase grinned, coming in close and lightly kissing her neck. "By the gods, you smell amazing. What did you do, bathe in vanilla?"

Lorelei just smiled, letting him kiss her as she worked her hands down to his belt.

"No, wait!" he blurted, quickly pulling away, but too late. Out popped his ripped glider, sending Lorelei falling to her ass in surprise.

After a moment of intense, confused silence, she started bursting at the seams, laughing. "By the gods. I've been with a lot of guys, gotta say that is a definite first for me."

"Sorry," he said, clicking the buckle back the other way, returning it to its rightful spot. "It's my glider. I use it to fly around with my power."

She stood up and slid in close to him again. "You are definitely showing me that later. But for now, where were we?"

Chase took off his belt and put it gently on the table. "I think you were working on taking my pants off."

She smiled and pulled on the hem of his pants slightly, glancing down. "I don't know. Are there any other surprises in there?"

"No surprises." He picked her up, and threw her in the bed. "Just pure pleasure."

11

Stuck in the Past

Five Years Ago

Their fight with Konstantin failed. *Yuri died, James lost his leg, and Lorelei lost her mind. There was nothing Xin could do now. He had already failed. Two weeks had gone by, and still they remained on that accursed island. There was no choice. Yuri needed to be buried, and everyone needed to heal.*

Xin sat upon their home, the small sloop ship, trying his best to find his meditative state. His wounds had recovered physically, but flashes of that cursed day flowed through his mind.

He had Konstantin—could have taken his head, but something was wrong. He couldn't find Lore on the battlefield. What had gone wrong? Why didn't Lorelei's plan work? Everything was going perfectly. She should have made it to that ship while he was fighting Konstantin, but she didn't.

Konstantin's words rang in his mind. "How do you not know about my useless son and his obsession with her? Bloody kid would never let her out of his sight for more than five minutes. Had her bloody trained, too. She wouldn't do a thing without his say so. If he wasn't around, she was that wild bitch you're accustomed to, but he had her wrapped around his finger. Never did figure out what he had over her that made her so obedient."

Part of him didn't want to believe it. He wanted to believe it was a trick so Konstantin could escape his blade, but he just couldn't ignore his warning.

"I'd act quickly if I were you. Knowing Mikhail, he's probably already had his way with her and is looking for a way off the island with her."

Mikhail. The man that hurt Lore. For years, he abused and raped her on that ship, then again during their fight. Mikhail had almost taken her from him. Xin wanted so much to slice that man's head from his body, but Lore wouldn't let him. She wanted him alive. Why? Did she actually love him? After everything he did?

He wouldn't be finding out anytime soon. After learning that Konstantin had killed Yuri, she became completely catatonic. She wouldn't talk to anyone, not even Xin.

"Please Lore. I can't do this without you."

Xin shook himself out of his moment of weakness. Nothing was bringing her back to him right now. He had to get stronger. He had to kill Konstantin quickly when they found him again.

That all so familiar longing for a cigarette crawled through his body so he rooted around in his pocket. Of course, true to his promise, he instead pulled out a toothpick and placed it in his mouth, rolling it around distractedly. As he tried to relax his mind once again, a familiar "ahem" sounded from below, causing him to sigh with frustration.

"Hello, Astrid," *he grumbled without opening his eyes, knowing full well the strawberry-blonde teenage girl they had rescued off of Konstantin's ship stood below. Over the last couple of weeks, she had been very helpful and caring, but she was also quite needy and didn't seem to understand when he wanted to be alone.*

"Hey Xin," *she chirped.* "What are you doing?"

"Trying to be alone."

She nodded. "Mhmm, it's good to be alone sometimes. I know I need it now and then." *Apparently, she did not catch the hint, or did not care as she continued to stand where she was, tilting back and forth on her bare feet, hands behind her back. He had no idea why, but she refused to wear shoes.*

Xin sighed. "Is there something you wanted?"

"Hmm... nothing really. Just came back from the hospital."

Xin snapped to attention. "How's Lore?"

Astrid frowned. She let him know Lorelei had healed physically, but still wasn't speaking. There was a councillor in town to talk with all the slaves that had escaped Konstantin's ship, and they hoped it would help Lorelei as well. It seemed like a stretch. Lorelei hated talking about feelings. Still, he was willing to try anything.

Astrid also let him know James had escaped the hospital, so while Astrid went back to the hospital, Xin went on the search for his friend. He had a pretty good idea where he would be.

Sure enough, he found him in a bar, drinking his sorrows away, still wearing a simple dressing gown and sitting in a wheelchair. His curly hair, usually so perky, laid limp and greasy against his face.

"Come on, James. You're still not healed enough for this shit," insisted Xin, trying to coax him away from his drink.

"Fuck off, Xin. I'm grieving. This is how I grieve," he slurred.

"Well, you can grieve when you're healed. This shit is only going to end up killing you right now. Do you really think that's what Yuri would want?"

"I don't know what he fucking wants!" James roared in his face. "He's fucking dead! It's not like he can fucking tell me!"

Xin threw his arms up in the air. "Argh! Fine! Be that way. Fucking stubborn ass."

Suddenly, Astrid barged in, gasping for air, snapping a wide eyed look at Xin. "Astrid? What's wrong?"

"Lorelei... talking... packing..." she managed to say through gasps.

Xin's mouth hung open. "Lorelei is talking again?" He looked around the suddenly silent bar, all eyes on him. The reality sank in. A grin crept over Xin's face as excitement filled his body. He looked back to James, who waved him on.

"What the hel you looking at me for? Go get her."

Without a second delay, Xin sprinted out the door, a warmness in his heart he hadn't felt in weeks. She was talking. Thank the gods.

Xin came bursting into the familiar hospital room, a room once littered with Lorelei's items now only held Lorelei (with half of her face bandaged), a full bag, and her guitar. As he entered, she looked him over with her one tired eye, and with a sigh, continued to pick up her things.

"Lore! How are you feeling?"

"Fine," she replied, her words as flat as the pancakes she loved so much. Xin didn't care about the tone, though. All that mattered was that she spoke to him. By the gods, he missed her voice.

"So the group worked? I wasn't sure it would."

"It was stupid. All that whining was getting on my nerves," she grumbled, pushing past Xin and going to the door. "It made me realize something, though. I can't just sit around here moping. I need to get out there again."

Xin followed closely behind her. "Yes, that's exactly what I was thinking. I'll go get James and we can be out before nightfall."

"No."

"No?" he echoed. "I know James is still in rough shape, but I'm sure he'll be good to go. I really think he needs to get off this islan—"

"I'm going alone," she snarled, quickening her pace as they strode out into the crisp, clean night air.

"I... What?" Xin asked, jogging ahead and stopping in front of her, trying to make eye contact.

She swerved around and continued on her path.

"Look, I know a lot happened, and that bastard really messed with your head, but we're better if we stick together," he said, quickly catching up.

Lorelei continued to ignore him.

Over and over, he prodded her as they walked along, gravel crunching beneath their feet to their ship. "Lore, don't block me out again, please just talk to me."

Finally, Lorelei stopped, laying a hand on their ship. The ship she had bought with their first bounty together. Their home. It rocked gently with the swell, the night so calm and still. Nothing at all like the mood in the air.

Lorelei took a deep breath, and let out a growling sigh. "We're not better together. We're weaker. We rely on each other too much. How can either of us become stronger that way?"

"Fine, then we're weaker. I don't care!" he bellowed.

Lorelei spun around and slapped him full force in the face as she sent him that vicious glare. "What happened to that fighter on Lofoten? The one that swore he would get his revenge—that would kill all the bastards who wronged him and his family? You think you'll get there this way? You think you're strong enough to defeat your Master? How many people have died on your island since we've been playing bounty hunter? It's time to get serious."

He met her searing gaze, unflinching, though it still twisted his gut. He was no stranger to her anger, but it had been a long time since she had taken it out on him like this. Her breath quickened, her chest heaved up and down. She wanted to scream at him more, he could see that, but she turned back to the boat instead, throwing her bag upon it.

"I don't care about revenge any more, Lore. Living in the past, it doesn't fix anything. I just want to look to the future, and that future is with you. I'm better with you. You make me better. Lorelei, I lo—"

"Don't say it... please don't say it," she growled intensely, freezing where she was, her hands gripped on the railing.

"Gods be damned, Lorelei, I love you!"

The railing beneath her hands cracked from her grip, her teeth grinding together as she stood in complete, intense silence.

"I know you don't like that word," he continued with a softer tone, "and after meeting him, I think I understand why, but I can't deny it. I love you and I want to be with you. The rest of the world can fuck itself."

It started small. Just a small little chortle. It grew bigger, louder, crazier until she was in a full out howling laughter.

"Lore!" Xin cried, completely baffled by her behaviour.

Lorelei finally turned to him, her face twisted up into an evil grin. "You think you love me? You're fucking delusional. All I am to you is a damsel that needs saving. You couldn't save your family, so now you have to save me."

"That's not true!"

"Well, guess what? It's too late. I'm too far fucking gone."

"Stop it."

"It doesn't fucking matter how you feel. You know what you were to me? A fucking mark."

"What?" he asked weakly, a pit opening in his stomach. His mind raced. What was she doing? Why was she doing this?

"You idiot, I don't love you. I never have and I never will," she proclaimed, arms raised up in the air. "I told you when we first met that it was just bodies, that I have my way with men, then leave them. I used you for a purpose and you failed. It's time to find someone who can actually do the job I give them."

His mind was buzzing. He couldn't believe the words that came out of her mouth. She had to be lying. There was no way. Two years... two years they all spent together. They were friends. No, they were family. There was no way all of it meant nothing, that they were just marks. That he meant nothing...

"Idiot," growled Xin as he stormed down the dark, rocky roads of Wrastan. "Idiot, idiot, idiot. What is wrong with you? You finally just got over her, now you're just throwing yourself back at her? Idiot! I should have left when I had the chance."

Every little wood house was quiet, the lights snuffed out for the night. No one was around to hear his rant. At least that's what he thought.

A deep laugh sounded from the shadows. "Sounds like someone had awful night."

Xin jumped and looked over at the hefty man, his face lit up by the cigarette in his mouth. Oh gods. A cigarette. He could really use one of those. He didn't give a fuck about his promise at the moment.

"Yeah, sorry. Didn't realize I was talking so loud. Hey... I don't suppose I could bum one of those off of you."

The man smiled. "Sure thing, friend. Sounds like you could use one."

Xin walked over as the man flicked out a cigarette from its pack. As Xin came in close to grab it, he got a good look at the man's face.

"Wait... do I know you?"

A gaped, yellow smile spread across his face as the man jabbed Xin with something. Xin's body tensed as electricity coursed through him. He couldn't fight it. The world went dark.

12

The Songbird

"Damn woman, that was fecking amazing," sighed Chase, naked amongst the scattered sheets of his soft bed.

"You weren't so bad yourself," teased an equally naked Lorelei, shooting a half-hearted smile his way. It was difficult to find a sincere smile. Now, within the clarity of post-orgasm, she was feeling guilty about the events that brought her there. Rather than dwell on the thought, she put on her necklace.

Chase rolled to his side, looking her up and down with that huge grin. "So glad you decided against your rule."

"Well, don't expect that to happen again," she quipped. "I just figured since we weren't technically sailing together yet, we weren't technically crewmates."

Those long, gentle fingers of his found their way sliding down her thigh, sending a tingle through her as his warm body pressed up behind her. "Really? You don't think you might want some more of this sometime?"

"Hmm… maybe." She turned herself into him, motioning to run her hand on the side of his face. Just like earlier, in one swift and almost undetectable movement, he redirected her hand, this time to his chest.

She smiled knowingly. "Why do you do that?"

"What?"

"You won't let me touch your hair."

"Wha, I don't… I don't know what you're talking about."

With a cock of her head and a raised eyebrow, she motioned to sweep his hair back, which caused him to violently flinch away. "Like I wouldn't notice that? Do you have any idea how much fun hair pulling is?"

"Well then, why didn't you mention it before?"

She shrugged. "Had other things on my mind. So are you going to tell me why?"

"Are you going to tell me about saving puppies from a tree?" he teased, nodding to her scar on her face.

"Tchah…" She thought for a moment. Perhaps she could tell him. She was curious enough. Most of the time she made up bullshit because people were dicks about the scar, or she didn't trust them, but there was something about Chase that seemed safe. Comforting. Maybe it wouldn't be too bad to tell him. "I tell you about the scar, you tell me about the hair?"

His eyes widened, sitting in stunned silence at the offer. After a long moment of Chase's eyes scanning the room in thought, he sighed, "Alright, but you first."

"Alright," she said, pushing the hair back from her face. She took a deep breath. "I was burned so that men would find me disgusting, so no one would ever want to sleep with me…" It was strange for her to finally say that out loud.

"Well, that backfired, 'cause you are still absolutely stunning," Chase grinned, and she gave him a thankful smile. His face suddenly turned dire as a thought struck him. "But… who did that? Why would anyone do something like that?"

"It was…" she began, snapping her gaze to a corner of the room, then back at Chase, "… just a jealous ex."

"Hang on. Did Xin do that? That whole unspoken fight between you two?" Outrage filled his face, and without waiting for an answer, he jumped out of bed. "That fecker! He is in for an ass kicking." With a flick of his hand, his jacket flew to him. He headed to the door, wearing literally only his jacket, completely unaware of Lorelei yelling at him to stop.

Before he could reach the door, Lorelei's surprisingly powerful hand grabbed his arm. Instantly, Chase was lying on his back gasping for air, looking up at the woman with betrayal in his eyes.

"Alright. We need to get a few things clear," she said, sitting on his chest, looking him in the eye. "First, you need to take more than one second to think about something. Second, I do not need anyone's protection, especially not your scrawny ass. Third, Xin could kick your ass in an instant, no matter how many magic tricks you have. Last, and most importantly, Xin has been nothing but sweet and caring with me. He is the most trustworthy person you could have in your crew. The last thing in the world that man would do is hurt me." With all of that in the clear, and being sure that he actually heard her, she unpinned him and sat beside him.

"Oh," said Chase, sitting back up. "That's good. I really like Xin."

Lorelei laughed, then prodded him to tell his story with, "Alright, your turn."

"I uh… It's just…" He started twiddling his thumbs. "Well, people always treat me differently when they find out. It's not exactly something I want everyone knowing about."

"Oh, come on. It's not like talking about this is the most comfortable." Lorelei smiled, rubbing at her scar.

Chase sighed and removed his headband. He pushed his hair back, revealing a pair of hearing aids, one in each ear. "I, uh… I was born mostly deaf. I can hear a bit with my hearing aids, but I usually need to actually see people's mouths to properly understand them, and if I'm focused on something else… it's easy for me to miss different noises."

Lorelei looked at him with shock. "Seriously? That was why you were so twitchy about your hair? Damn. I thought it was some funky birthmark or something, not a serious disability."

Chase sighed. "Yeah… my whole childhood I couldn't hear. The kids always treated me like some sort of disease. Once I got my hearing aids and learned to talk properly, I made sure no one knew about it so I would just be treated like everyone else."

Lorelei broke out into a loud laugh.

Chase frowned.

"S-sorry. I'm not laughing at you. Well, I kind of am. I just find it funny that you want to be treated like a normal person. Normal people are fucking boring. Things like this—" she tapped his hearing aids. "—they make you wonderfully unique. Everyone on the Oasis has something different about them, and we always find a way to use it to our advantage. You'll fit in quite well."

Chase visibly relaxed, and that wide grin returned to his face. "Really?"

"Absolutely. Now then, since there's nothing to hide anymore…" She ran her fingers through his hair. He flinched a little, but let her. "…how do you feel about a little hair pulling?"

He grinned and leaned in to kiss her, only to be interrupted by the door flying open.

Astrid barged in. "Chase! Have you seen…" She stopped in her tracks, her mouth agape as she saw the mostly naked two on the floor. "Lorelei? What? Why? Chase? What about…"

"Tchah! Enough. What's going on?" Lorelei asked, jumping into action and scrounging up her clothes.

"There's some men at the gate asking for you. They say they send word from Konstantin. They only want to talk with you."

"Fuck," she growled, striding out of the room. Chase went to follow along, but found Astrid's fair hand gently pointing out he had no pants. He grinned sheepishly and blew the rest of his clothes over. The two caught up to the storming Lorelei, Chase lagging behind awkwardly trying to get dressed.

"How did he know I was here? Is this because of one of those prisoners we took in?" Lorelei added with a glare at Astrid.

"I… I don't know. I haven't heard from The Oasis. I was busy taking care of the kids."

"Where's James?"

"Out at the gate. He was the one that found them while he was looking for Xin."

"Where is Xin?"

"Not sure."

"So it's just us and James… That might not be enough for a fight here. If we could get back to the Oasis…"

"We also have Emir," chirped Chase. "I bet he would help."

Lorelei snapped a glare at Chase, but considered his words. With a sigh, she said, "That's right… He's an ass, but he is quite talented. Astrid, go get him and bring him along."

Astrid nodded and hurried off in the opposite direction.

"So what's the plan?" Chase asked.

She shook her head. "I don't know yet. First things first, I need to know what Konstantin wants. I can't make a plan with no information."

The two of them headed straight for the south exit. The casino was dark and quiet, except where Nick and a handful of guards were waiting for them by the doors, a couple of orange fireflies buzzing around them.

"Well, hello there, Nicky. Fancy meeting you here," she grinned with a nudge on Nick's arm.

"Are you kidding? This is the most action we've seen here in over a year. Well, battle-wise anyway." He smiled, running a thumb over her cheek. His smile turned serious. "Are you really going out there? It's not too late, I can get you out of here before he attacks."

"I'm not going anywhere. If Konstantin knows I'm here, it means he's probably not far away. I can't turn up this opportunity to kick his ass."

Nick sighed. "Alright, if you're sure." He nodded to the guards, who unlocked and opened the large metal doors. As the three of them stepped out, the guards and Nick followed behind.

A couple more guards were standing by the gate, weapons drawn and pointed at the four men waiting patiently. The click of a revolver sounded beside her, and she looked to see James at the ready.

"Lorelei." His gaze stayed focused on the four at the gate. "I've got your back."

She smiled. "I know. Chase, stay back here."

"But—"

"No arguments."

Chase looked worriedly at her.

Before she walked off, she moved her hands in a familiar motion. Sign language. She signed, "Watch carefully for instructions."

He smiled and nodded at her.

Nick passed her a round object, with metal on the bottom and glass on the top. She gave it a twist, and the internal gears ground. A dim yellow light lit up the dark night. The little firefly buzzed and fluttered above her head.

Lorelei strode to the gate, not a hint of fear in her step.

"Ivan," Lorelei sighed as she neared, noticing the balding old man at the head of the group. He was a man she was all too familiar with. Konstantin's close friend and quartermaster.

"Ibby. Long time," he said with that curt accent, smiling a toothy, yellow smile at her.

"Not long enough. What does your fat ass want?"

Ivan laughed. "Just as personable as ever. What if I just missed your singing, hmm? It was always highlight of my day."

"I don't have time for this."

Ivan shrugged. "Captain just wants to talk. He figured you might be least violent with me."

"Tchah," she snapped, not wanting to admit he was probably right. Ivan was one of the least horrible men on that ship, and he had taught her a lot of things over the years. "What does he want to talk about?"

"To come to an accord."

Lorelei scoffed. "Yeah, right. Seriously."

"I am serious! He is getting old, you know. He's tiring of all dis fighting."

"Say I believe you, what would this 'accord' entail?"

"Ah, dat's not my place to tell you. He wants to talk to you himself."

"Alone I assume."

"Of course."

"Why the fuck would I do that?"

Ivan laughed and pulled a metal pigeon from his jacket. He held it up for her to see.

Her heart sank. It had the telltale markings of one of her crew. That was one of their homing pigeons.

"Where are they?" Lorelei growled.

Ivan laughed. "Some dead, most are back on the ship."

She growled at him.

"Oh, and that's not all. You never mentioned your dear soldier boy was back in the picture. I figured I'd send him back to Captain as well."

Lorelei's eyes went wide and her gut twisted. "What?"

Ivan chuckled as he lit up a cigarette. "Tut, tut, tut. You really should treat your men better. Poor little soldier boy was quite distraught, you know. Took him too long to recognize me. Though, I suppose it was mostly you he saw back then, not me."

"Bastard," she growled, clenching her fist so hard her nails bit into her flesh. "How? No way an old man like you took out Xin."

He laughed and pulled out a small box. A taser. "It was supposed to be for you if you didn't cooperate, but I just couldn't pass up using it on him. So I guess you'll just have to cooperate with me. It only gets one use."

Lorelei took a few deep breaths, clenching her jaw. Of all the rotten luck. Behind her back, she signed to Chase. Hopefully, they could figure it out.

"Alright," she snapped, looking Ivan in the eye. "I'll talk to him, but I have a message for him first."

"Aye, of course."

13

Romo

"*Rawr! I'm a hug monster!*"

The little hug monster jumped on young Xin's back, tackling him to the floor with uncontrollable giggles as Xin cried out his defeat. "Oh no! The hug monster! My one weakness!"

"Me too!" cried an even smaller hug monster, jumping onto her brother with a fit of giggles. The girls pinned their young teenage brother to the floor with hugs and kisses. Just as he feigned death, he grabbed them, sprung to his feet and tossed them in the bed.

"Ah hahaha! You still have much to learn, young monsters. One day, perhaps you will be able to defeat me. For today, it is bedtime."

"Aw! I don't want to go to bed," whined the elder girl, Jia, crossing her arms in a little pout.

"No bed, no bed!" chanted Ren, the younger sister, hammering her fists on the bed.

Xin crossed his arms, and with as much sternness as a fourteen-year-old could muster, said, "Time for bed. All little monsters need to sleep."

The girls whined some more, then demanded bedtime stories and songs, and with a sigh, Xin agreed. Eventually, all three children passed out on the tiny straw bed, snuggled up with smiles.

Their slumber didn't last long.

The door of the room slammed open as their mother came charging in, a crying baby strapped to her chest. Xin snapped open his eyes and immediately saw the panic on her face.

Before he could ask, their mother whispered urgently, "To the cellar. Pirates."

They sprang to action, having prepared for this eventuality many times. Xin turned up the worn, dirty hempen rug and opened up the creaky trapdoor. The smell of dirt and mold wafted up. He hurried them all down and, as his mother beckoned him down, Xin shook his head and smiled.

"Dad's not here. Let me protect you."

"Xin. No."

Before his mother could climb back up the narrow stairwell, Xin shut and locked the trapdoor. She banged on it a few times, and Xin silenced her urgently, warning of the oncoming voices. He flipped back the old rug and grabbed his swords. So far, he had only trained with his father and master. He had never actually seen a proper battle. Still, he was the best in his class, and his father was a master swordsman. He was sure he could win any fight.

Terrified screams drew nearer to his home. He snuffed out all the candles and lamps, keeping to the shadows. Hopefully, they would just pass them by. Baby Emi had gone silent, thank the gods. Hopefully, she would stay sleeping until the danger had passed.

"Is this the one?" It was a raspy voice from outside.

"Looks like it," replied a rough voice. "Cap'n paid Master Hotaru good money for this one, so make sure he stays alive."

"Aye, Viktor."

Xin's blood ran cold. His master sent these goons here? Why?

Rhythmic thumps sounded at the door. It only took a few blows to break down that rickety old thing. Xin stood at the ready as six grown men sauntered into the door, reeking of body odour and booze. It didn't take long for them to see him.

"Ah, there he is. Already dressed an' ready to go." Viktor, the man with the rough voice, smiled at him, his long, wiry hair hanging past his shoulders. His dark eyes scanned the room. "Now what's a boy like you doing home alone?"

Xin just scowled, gritting his teeth and tightening the grip on his swords.

"Ah, strong silent type, eh? That's alright by me. Now come along, your new home awaits."

All he had to do was go with them? Maybe that was best. They were only here for him. He could lead them away from the house and fight them when he was sure his family was safe. Would he have to kill them? He had never killed anything before.

He lowered the swords, and Viktor's smile widened. "There's a good b—"

A baby's cry broke the man's thought. Xin's heart dropped, his eyes wide as the man turned his wicked grin towards the old rug, then back at Xin.

"Ah ha. I knew you wouldn't be here alone. Let's go see what's under the carpet, eh, boys?"

The men laughed and took slow, purposeful steps towards Xin's family. He wouldn't let them. Before he even realized it, Xin slashed out to the man closest to him, embedding the sword in his arm. The solidity of the body caught him off guard, and he let go of his sword as the man cried out in pain. Their eyes were back on Xin now. He needed to fight smart, just like his dad taught him. Maybe if he ran, they would just come after him. He could get to better ground, find help.

Xin sprinted to the door, only to be grabbed by Viktor, his long arms wrapped around his chest.

"Argh! Get off of me, you disgusting bastard!"

He laughed, and the smell of his breath was even worse than his body. "Someone get the other sword off the kid."

One of the smaller men came to grab it from him, but Xin slashed out, and the blade cut into the man's neck. He gurgled, clutching at the wound. There was so much blood. He fell to his death in an instant, and Xin felt an odd mixture of sickness and pride.

"Fucking brat!" Viktor grabbed Xin's head and slammed it on the kitchen table. The world spun, and they swiped the sword from his hand. He tried to grab it back, but found a solid strike to the gut, sending him coughing to the floor.

He heard the trapdoor opening, then the screams of his sisters. The men were laughing, but shifted to cries of rage as another man gurgled his last breath. A large piece of wood stuck out of a scrawny man's throat as he stumbled back and fell into the kitchen table.

Xin smiled and whispered, "Go mom."

Viktor was shouting out angry orders and walking toward them. Xin grabbed the man's ankle, causing him to stumble to the ground. He twisted around and kicked Xin hard in the nose. His eyes watered, and the world blurred.

He heard his family screaming again and heard the thumps of someone being hit. He hoped it was his mom beating on the pirates, but judging by the cries of his sisters, that wasn't the case. Baby Emi was screaming at the top of her lungs. Then there was a deafening silence. Xin got to his feet and charged just as his mom started screaming at the top of her lungs.

Viktor caught Xin again and pinned him against the wall. He heard Jia cry out to let go of her. His mom begged them not to hurt them, that she'd do anything. They liked the sound of that too much.

Viktor's sickening sour breath sat by his ear and said, "You see, boy? Mommy is being cooperative. How about you play nice for a while, and maybe we'll let your family go?"

Xin relaxed and gave a small nod. He wasn't strong enough to take them all on his own. He wasn't his father. Still, he had a duty to protect them, even if that meant giving himself up.

His mother came up the stairs, tears streaming down her face, the wrap around her chest no longer holding his baby sister. Next, a bulky man came up the stairs, wrangling his other two sisters as they pulled and screamed against him.

"Shut up you little brats, or I put a bullet through mommy's head."

The girls went completely silent.

"Good girls," chuckled Viktor. He looked at the two dead men on the ground. "Well, this was certainly not expected. What do you think, boys? Do ya think they owe us for sending our comrades to Valhalla?"

The men laughed darkly, agreeing with the sentiment.

"Alright. You can have your fun with those three. I think I'm going to have my fun with this one."

"No!" Xin exclaimed, once again trying to squirm free.

His mother begged them again not to hurt her children, but they all just laughed.

"Now, now, if you are all very good, I might just feel compassionate enough to let you go..."

So, they let them have their way. They had to believe that something would come of it. That their lives would be spared.

They weren't.

Back and forth, his body swayed with that familiar sensation. He was on a ship. As his senses came back to him, Xin felt like his whole body was on fire, each muscle tingling with pain. He wanted nothing more than to curl up into a ball, but his hands were being held firmly above his head.

For a moment, he tried to strain against it, but quickly recognized the cold hard steel around his wrists, then the cold air against his skin. He was completely naked. His eyes opened, slowly adjusting to the dimly lit room. It didn't take him long to recognize the place. He had spent nearly a month here after his family was murdered. That was over thirteen years ago. Still, those screams haunted his nightmares.

Those thoughts wouldn't help him now. He needed to focus. He looked around. It was definitely Konstantin's brig. It was even the same cell his younger self had stayed in. With some immense effort, Xin looked up to examine his shackles. Those were new. Apparently, Konstantin wanted to make sure he had fresh, strong chains to keep Xin in place. Not that it mattered right now. Whatever that guy had hit him with felt like it fried his whole body.

The door creaked open, and in came that violet-eyed bastard looking fucking smug.

"Ah, little soldier boy, you're awake. I'm glad."

Xin just growled.

"I was so 'appy to hear you were in the area. I thought Ibby gave ya the boot after our last encounter."

"Tch... Ibby. You know damn well that's not her name, anymore."

"Ah, yes. What is it now? *Lorelei the Siren?*" he asked with seething sarcasm. "Fuckin' pompous, if ye ask me."

"I didn't."

Konstantin laughed that guttural laugh and clunked his way over to Xin with that crude peg leg.

Xin chuckled.

"What's so fucking funny, you little bastard?" snapped Konstantin.

"Your leg!"

"Ah haha, that's right. You get your laughs from the last ditch attack that killed your friend," Konstantin mocked, bringing a vicious scowl to Xin's face. Now it was Konstantin's turn to chuckle as he went through a table of torture tools.

"It really was kind o' ye to show up when ye did. I wasn't sure these other little pawns here would be enough to draw her out here."

Xin looked around at the other cells. There were at least six others chained, battered, and beaten.

"Waste of time capturing me. You said so yourself. She gave me the boot ages ago. She doesn't give a fuck about me."

"Aw, did our little Ibby break your heart? I warned ya, didn't I? I told you she knew how to use men."

"Tch..."

He chortled, examined a long, hooked tool with some appreciation, then set it down again. "Either way, I am certainly glad for this chance. If it weren't for you, Ibby wouldn't have gotten all those grand ideas of escape all those years ago. Spoutin' on about a warrior spirit." He stopped his search through the torture tools, glaring at the table, shoulders hunched. "Do ya know how long it took me to break that girl? I shoulda never taken that deal with yer Master. That gold was not worth this headache."

"Oh, poor you. I'm so sorry the death of my family was a fucking inconvenience to you."

Konstantin ignored him, continuing on with his woe. "I thought for sure she woulda kicked the bucket after finding out that her friend died, but all that 'appened was she became a bigger pain in my ass. I almost regret letting you take care of Mikhail for me. At least he knew how to control the bitch."

"The sympathy you have for your son is overwhelming. No wonder he turned out so fucked up."

Konstantin waved his hand in annoyance. "Ah, that boy was already fucked up before I had anything to do with 'im. Then after he brought that fucking bitch along, he was nothin' but a pain in me arse."

"She has really pissed you off, hasn't she?" Xin asked with a satisfied grin.

A small chortle escaped his lips. "Aye. She's taken over most of my trade routes, stunted my main revenues, and destroyed 'undreds of my fuckin' ships."

Xin studied the man. "You… don't seem upset."

"I was, for quite some time. After a while, however, I realized somethin'… She was becoming me."

A twist of disgust flowed through his body. "What?"

"Do yeh have any idea what she's accomplished these last few years? The connections she's made? She's got more control of the underworld than I do! All within five years! It took me over ten years to get even close to where she's at."

"And you're… happy about that?"

"I guess we'll see once Ibby arrives how 'appy I am about it."

Xin shook his head. "She won't come. She's smarter than that."

A soft cooing sounded from the porthole. There stood a com-pigeon, its metal head clicking side to side, waiting for it to be answered. Konstantin smiled and clunked his way over to it, clicking down the tail-feathers.

"Konstantin," it said with Lorelei's voice. "I'll listen to your stupid alliance idea, but I will warn you now, for every dead and injured crewmate I find, that is how many limbs I am going to take from you. That counts for Xin, too."

The pigeon's eyes darkened, and Konstantin laughed. "Aw, well, would ya listen to that? Maybe she does still like ya." He laughed again. "Or maybe she just wants to use ya again. What do ya think?"

Xin growled.

"Now, now, don't worry. I know Ibby didn't want you harmed, but we can always say I just got her message too late. We all know what a rowdy spirit you are. Obviously, I had to try and keep you in place."

"Tch…"

Konstantin pulled out a long whip, a dark smile spreading across his face. "You know what this is?"

"A whip," Xin replied flatly.

"Not just any whip. I saved this one especially for Ibby," he smirked, receiving a glare of utter hatred from Xin.

He cackled, now clunking his way behind Xin, coming in close, but not quite close enough for Xin to strike him with his head, though he certainly tried. "I know you still care for 'er. I saw it in yer eyes. I'll tell you what, since you like 'er so much, I'll give ya some matching scars. I know exactly where 'ers are, since I saw to 'em personally."

"Why? You know it will just piss her off."

Konstantin sighed. "I know, but I am still pissed off at her. I need to get my frustrations out before she gets here. So do me a favour, boy, give me some good screams like she used to."

The whip struck Xin's naked back. The pain shot through his body, but Xin withheld the cry of pain. He wouldn't give Konstantin that pleasure. Instead, he thought about back then, when he was first on this ship. After what those bastards did to his family, there was no way he was going to cooperate with anyone. He fought tooth and nail at every turn.

There was only one girl on that ship, and she was slightly younger than him. She watched him, but didn't mock or tease him like the others. She just studied him. When it had come time for him to be sent to the brig to be tortured and broken, Ibby had requested to watch and learn.

The girl looked rough. Her hair was short and unkempt, her clothes were too big and meant for men, not a little girl, and when she looked into Xin's eyes, her golden eyes were hollow and far away. At least for the first while. As the quartermaster had given her permission to torture Xin, her eyes found a spark. At the time, Xin thought it was cruelty, a desire for pain. It wasn't until years later when he found her again that he found out the truth.

Her plan to help him escape was working.

She would beat him, mock him for not being able to save his family, and leave the key to freedom just out of his reach, until one day, it wasn't. Back then, he thought she slipped up, but that wasn't the case. She left it close on purpose. She let him escape, to the risk of her own hide, and he loved her for it. For that, and so much more.

A wave of emotion came over him as realization dawned. He still cared about her. No… he still loved her. Even after everything she said and did, she had been, and always would be, a person who wanted to help people. She was coming out here, despite the obvious threat to her safety, in order to save her crew.

Could Konstantin be right about her using him again? No… No, that thought didn't sit right. Perhaps everything could point to that, but then he remembered that necklace. The one she still wore. It had a different chain, but it had the same pendant he gave her all those years ago. The only reason she would wear that was if she still cared. She may not love him like he loved her, but she still cared. That thought filled him up and made that awful whip feel like an unpleasant mosquito sting.

"Ah, you're no fun," Konstantin finally growled after a while of silent beating, hanging the whip back in its cupboard. "Couldn't give me anything. Oh well, Ibby should be here soon. You just sit tight." He cackled as he clunked out of the brig.

Xin watched him go, trying his best to break the chains, but it was no good. They were solid. He stared out the open door. Lorelei was coming here, and he was terrified for her. He didn't want her to go back to this life, not for him. Still, he couldn't help but smile a little.

She still cared.

"Why on Geb are you smiling?"

Xin jumped at the nasally voice behind him. "Emir?"

"By the gods, I have never seen so much blood… I—" Emir gagged.

"What are you doing here?"

"All part of the plan," Emir assured him, walking in front of Xin, trying not to look at his back. With a smile, he continued, "The woman may be unpleasant, but she is quite clever. She sent a pigeon out here for us to follow ahead of her."

Emir pulled out a ring of keys, and a wave of relief flowed through Xin. As Emir reached up to undo the chains, Xin caught movement from behind him.

"Emir! Watch—"

Too late. A fist struck Emir in the jaw, and he went sprawling to the ground. Xin snapped his glare up to a sickening familiar face.

Viktor.

As soon as Xin laid eyes on him, every inch of him wanted to snap that scraggly haired head off of his fucking neck. No matter how hard he tried, however, the chains wouldn't give way.

"You! You bastard! I'm going to fucking kill you!" Xin screamed out in pure fury.

"Funny, it don' look like you're in a position to do much killing. You do look like you're in a position for sumthin' else though." Viktor laughed. "You're hairier than the last time, but I'm not picky."

The grotesque man sauntered up behind him and ran an awful dirty hand down Xin's raw back. Disgust and pain coursed through his body as he tried, unsuccessfully, to writhe away from his touch. He let out a vicious roar, and Viktor just laughed.

14

Decisions

Clouds sprinkled the sky as another storm lurked in the distance. It was still Stormday, after all. These clouds wouldn't clear until tomorrow after the pulse.

Lorelei looked up, catching a glimpse of the moon as it peeked out. *First crescent moon. Time for decisions.*

She sighed deep, burying her face in her hands as the little ship tossed up and down against the waves, spraying her body with a cool mist. *An alliance with Konstantin? What would that even mean?* Was it something she could actually do? There was no way that was actually what he wanted. He wanted her out on that ship alone. She was sure of it. Hopefully, Chase had gotten her message, and the rest had come up with a plan. She could not do this alone.

She needed everyone safe. She needed Xin safe.

"You look worried," said Ivan, the stink from his cigarette wafting over her.

"Of course I'm fucking worried. Last time I properly talked to Konstantin, I tried to put a dagger through his heart. He put one in me instead. You really think he's going to want to talk?"

"Oh, I know he will."

They pulled up along that familiar galleon ship. The hull was getting older, filled with wear and a few too many barnacles. It was a gigantic ship,

105

not as big as the Oasis, but could easily house over a hundred men. Lorelei was sure it would have as many men as it could hold if Konstantin was bringing her onboard.

They threw a ladder down, and two of the men went up ahead of her.

Ivan held out his hand, telling her to go ahead. Her hand touched the ladder and dread overtook her. She didn't know what was going to happen. She didn't like not knowing.

Ivan urged her onwards, and she complied. As soon as she stepped on deck, a few voices drunkenly cheered out her old name. That was unexpected. Ivan seemed to have the same reaction as he climbed aboard.

"Ibby!" slurred a familiar man with a bulbous nose and rosy cheeks. She knew him, but fuck if she could remember his name. "Are yeh really gonna come back to us? No more killin'? Aw man, all the men have missed your singin' somethin' awful." He started to wrap an arm around her shoulders, but found himself twisted into an armlock.

"The lack of killing has yet to be determined," she growled in his ear. "Touch me again and you won't live to find out."

Ivan laughed. "You have not changed bit."

The door that led below deck opened wide, and the familiar violet-eyed Konstantin stepped out with a smile. "Ibby, so glad you could make it."

"Cut the shit. Where's Xin?"

"Oh, don't worry. He is safe and comfy."

Lorelei's eyes locked onto the blood splatter on Konstantin's coat. Rage bubbled from deep down. "I warned you not to hurt him."

"Ah, yes, well, the pigeon came a little late. You know how that boy is. Would have gone around chopping off heads if I didn't put him in his place."

"I'll fucking kill you," she growled, taking a step towards him.

"Now hold on, don't you at least want to hear what I have to—"

A group of men belted out a song, cheering out for Ibby to join them. Lorelei couldn't help but chuckle as Konstantin's face twisted into rage, his pale face turning beat red.

"What the fuck is yer problem?" he roared, clunking over to the group. He grabbed the smallest one by his collar. "What the fuck is wrong with you lot? Have you been in the rum already?"

The little one hiccuped. "Aye, Cap'n, but we only had one drink. Just to celebrate the accord!"

"Idiots! She hasn't agreed to anything yet."

"Wha? But the orange-haired kid said—"

"I don't give a fuck! Sober yerselves up right now or I'll keelhaul the lot of yeh."

"Aye- *hiccup* -aye Cap'n."

Konstantin turned a glare back at Lorelei. "Did you have sumthin' to do with this?"

"Me?" She pointed to herself, looking amazed. "You must really think highly of me. I just found out you were here and haven't spoken to anyone since dear Ivan told me what was happening. Right, Ivan?"

"It is true, Captain."

"And even if I did, how would they have gotten out here before us? It's not like people can control the wind."

He gave a small growl. "Fine. Come along, girl. We'll talk in private."

"Fuck no," she snapped, staying firmly along the railing. "You want to talk? Here I am. I am not going into your room with you."

He chortled. "Quite the change from before you left. You would've done anything to get in there before."

"Yeah, so I could kill you. I will not give you that opportunity."

With a shake of his head, he sighed. "Very well." He snapped his fingers, and one man brought over a chair. Konstantin sat down with a sigh, stretching out his gimped leg. Another man brought one to her, but she waved them off and stood cross armed.

"Talk quick," she snapped.

"It's simple, really. I want an accord. I want to join our powers and rule the entire underworld. You've done well, girl. I am quite impressed."

She scanned him over. He actually seemed serious. Still, she scoffed.

"Really," he insisted. "How is it you've gotten so many allies?"

She smirked. "Well, you know how persuasive I can be."

"Aye, that I do. Even so, your body can only get you so far. Dear Lin learned that, didn't she?"

Lorelei snarled, gripping the sword on her hip. She hated hearing her name from his lips, but he wasn't wrong. Her teacher, Lin, had gotten a lot of things using her wiles, but in the end she only led a small group on a small island. She didn't have what Lorelei had.

"I'm not here to trade secrets with you," she snarled. "Why the hell would I make an alliance with you? After everything you've done?"

"What I've done? Woman, you have taken out far more of my men than I have yours. Although I suppose, to be fair, I didn't care much for any of them."

"Even Mikhail?"

Konstantin laughed. "Oh, no. If anything, my life was better with him out of it. I'm sure he's happy enough with his mommy in Purgatory."

A small smile cracked on Lorelei's lips. "So, basically what I'm hearing is that I'm doing better than you, and you're getting scared."

He sat forward in his chair, glaring Lorelei down with those piercing eyes. "That's not what I'm sayin'. I'm giving you an opportunity. I've got yer crewmates and boyfriend prisoner, yer home surrounded, and you here all alone. If I don't like what I hear from yer mouth today, everything you love will die."

"And if I do agree? What happens then?"

"Then you get everything back and more. We stop these pointless sea battles and people stop dying."

"Just your people, or are you saying you're going to stop raiding islands?"

"I'm saying we refine our methods. I'm getting old and tired. Running around kidnapping people just ain't that fun anymore. But, if we join our contacts together, we can round up anyone that causes trouble, then use those as our… 'sacrifice' to the Angels. It keeps us out of Purgatory and keeps our power throughout all three nations. Tell me that don't interest you."

Lorelei furrowed her brow, finally taking a seat in the chair beside her.

Konstantin smiled. "Then, when I get the urge to retire, which I imagine won't be too long from now, I give yeh everything I have."

Shock surged through her. Was he serious? The look on his face said he was. "Why?"

"Who else am I going to give it to? You sent Mikhail to Purgatory, and everyone that works for me is either too old or too stupid."

Lorelei sighed, leaning back in her chair and looking up at the moon that had peeked out again. *Time for decisions.* Could she really make this deal? It actually seemed beneficial. Konstantin would stop hunting down innocents and they would still take out bad people. The Oasis would be safe, Xin would be safe… but she would work for the people she hated the most in this world. The Angels. She would supply them with people, making her no better than the people she had been hunting down for the last five years.

But was there any other option? While the Angels controlled the world, they needed to be satisfied. It would be impossible to take them out of power, even with all the contacts she had. Maybe if she took this deal, she could get enough power to take them out, but something like that would take years. A few human lifetimes, for sure.

A glint from the crow's nest caught her eye. Beside it waved the figure of someone with bright orange hair. A smile came back to Lorelei's lips. Chase's mission was far-fetched, and a little crazy, but it could make her dream come true in just a few years. That impossible man with the impossible power. Perhaps he could help her make the impossible happen.

She stood and stretched, signing *'ready for action'* at the crow's nest. She gave Konstantin a flirty smile and sauntered over. "I have to say, it is a very tempting offer."

He grinned at her as she slid herself onto his lap, but before she could get any closer, he placed a dagger to her throat.

She smiled. "I can't help but wonder what else you want from me. This ship absolutely reeks of testosterone. So what? Are we going to rule the seas side by side, king and queen?"

"Oh, that is tempting, but I tried the relationship thing once before. Didn't work well for me." His free hand came up to her face and pushed back her hair, and a smile flickered on his lips. "Nor you, it seems. I'm guessing Mikhail did that to you."

"What? This old thing? Nah, it was a cooking accident." She placed a hand on his dagger'd hand, and slid her other down his chest to his belt. She leaned in close and whispered in his ear, "I got so distracted thinking about your tiny dick that I went and burned myself."

His body tensed as he screamed, "Fucking bitch!" and attempted to slide the dagger across her throat. Instead, she jabbed it into his shoulder and leapt off him, doing a backflip onto the railing.

"So, Konny baby, I have a counteroffer for you. I'll let you retire now if you disband all your ships. Do that and I'll let you live."

"Not fucking likely." Konstantin nodded at Ivan, and before she realized it, a com-pigeon flew out from Ivan's jacket and out of her reach. "Say goodbye to your Oasis, Ibby."

As the man sat laughing, the sound of a bullet pierced the night air, and that little bird crashed to the deck.

Konstantin's eyes went wide with rage. "What the fuck? Dammit. Kill her, kill her now!"

The crowd of pirates dispersed, and a massive pirate with an even larger gun set its sights on her.

"Big gun," she squeaked.

He pulled the trigger. She heard the blast and leapt towards the dark ocean below. The deck exploded into shards of wood and fire and she thanked the gods she wasn't standing there. As the water drew nearer, a streak of orange flew by, and she found herself sailing upward instead of down.

With a laugh, she pulled herself in for a tight hug and close to his ear so he could hear her. "Best rescue ever! Thanks, good lookin'."

"Told you I'd take you for a spin. Sorry it wasn't under better conditions." To stress his point, he wobbled a bit to one side, almost crashing them into a sail. "Had to do a quick repair on the glider."

As the night air whipped against her cheeks, they drew closer and closer to the crow's nest, where James and Astrid were waiting for them. Lorelei looked at Chase and asked, "Any luck releasing the prisoners?"

"We sent Emir to get them, but they should have been out by now. I don't know what happened."

"Well, it's a good thing I got these." Lorelei dangled the ring of keys she had swiped from Konstantin's belt. "Put me down by the door there. Keep everyone safe until we're back."

"Are you sure?"

"Absolutely."

Chase set them down at the same door Konstantin had come out, and with a nod, took off again. The pirates were busy searching for her over the edge of the railing. No one had noticed her set down, so she gave them a loud whistle.

All eyes snapped to her.

"That was quite the explosion," she said with a grin. "Quite the gun you got there."

Konstantin glared at her. "What in Helheim? How'd ya do that?"

She winked at him. "Magic." In one swift motion, she opened the door, stepped inside, and locked it closed.

Konstantin hammered on the steel reinforced door, trying to break through, to no avail. "Let me in, you bitch!"

"What's the password?" she sang.

"Fuck you!"

"That's not right," she quipped. "You think about it. I'll be back in a bit."

Konstantin laughed maniacally. "That's right, lil' girl, you run away to yer big strong man. Ya really can't do shit on your own, can you? It's alright, I know yer afraid of me."

She could almost feel that knowing smirk on his face. She knew he was playing her, but the anger within her was winning out. With a cry of rage, she turned around and smacked her fist on the door.

"Fuck you, you bastard! I'm not afraid of anything!"

"Come out here and prove it."

Lorelei stood staring at the door, her whole body shaking with anger. Her hand shakily reached out towards the doorknob as she thought, *I'll show that bastard here and now who should be afr—*

"Get away from me, you sick bastard! I'll fucking kill you!" bellowed Xin's uncharacteristically panicked voice.

Lorelei's hand snapped away from the door, the shaking ceasing in an instant.

"Sorry, Konny baby," she said in her usual glib tone. "I have a much more important person to see first. You'll just have to wait your turn."

With that, she sprinted down the hall, not waiting for Konstantin's angry reply.

"Get away from me, you sick bastard! I'll fucking kill you!" bellowed Xin.

Viktor's long, nasty hand once again ran down his back, purposefully digging those unclean nails into the whip wounds. The pain seared through his body, but no matter how much Xin writhed, strained and flailed, the chains would not give in. All those years working on his body, becoming stronger, and here he was, still fucking helpless. The screams and twisted faces of his mother and sisters rang clearly in his head just as the day they took them from him.

Viktor's awful laugh rebounded off the cell walls. Soon, his bile-turning voice got right into Xin's ear and whispered, "Relax boy, it will be over soon."

Xin's heart threatened to explode from his chest as he heard the man's pants drop. "Don't touch me you fucking—"

A flash of silver flew by his head, followed by a wet *thunk* and a satisfying scream of pain.

"I believe the man said no," growled the oh-so-sweet and familiar voice of Lorelei.

A wave of relief washed over him as he looked up. "Lore."

"Fancy meeting you here," she teased, striding up to him, keys in hand. "We really need to stop meeting like this."

"Why did you come here?" Xin asked, rubbing his freed wrists.

Lorelei had no time to answer as Viktor removed the dagger from his eye with a mighty roar.

"Ibby! You fucking bitch, you'll pay for that!"

The rage returned to Xin's eyes at the sound of Viktor's voice.

Lorelei smiled knowingly. "Oh, I don't think I'll be paying for anything today, Vicky babe. You, on the other hand…"

Xin twisted his head around, glaring the pantsless, ugly bastard down. "You have a lot to pay for."

He charged, punching Viktor square in the face, breaking through the pathetic attempt of a block. Viktor fell to the ground. Xin put a knee to his throat and smashed his fists into Viktor's face mercilessly.

As Xin beat the man to a pulp, Lorelei went around unlocking the cells of her grateful crewmates. She gathered Xin's clothes and gear and cleaned her dagger, whistling a merry tune over the screams and pleas of mercy from Viktor, pausing at the torture table to look over a few of the pieces with reminiscent appreciation.

As Viktor's cries of pain simmered to a whimper, Xin stood the man up, holding him easily out at arm's length by his scraggly hair.

"You… you're letting me live?" he asked hopefully, straining to look at Xin through his one puffy eye.

Without breaking eye contact, Xin held his hand out to Lorelei. Understanding perfectly, she passed Xin one of his swords.

"Ask for mercy one more time," Xin growled.

"M-merc—" was all he could muster, as he found his vocal chords as well as the rest of his body severed from his head with one swift slice of Xin's sword.

"No," said Xin, a dark, satisfied grin on his face.

As Viktor's body fell limp to the ground, Xin took one disgusted look at the face that had haunted his nightmares for years. He tossed the head to the ground and turned to Lorelei, who held his clothes out to him, a small, caring smile on her face.

"Feel better?" she asked.

"A bit," he replied, throwing on his pants. "Not as much as I'd hoped."

"It doesn't change what happened," Lorelei replied sadly, recalling their conversation years ago.

"Lore… What are you doing here?" asked Xin, gingerly throwing on his shirt and jacket.

"Rescuing the damsel in distress, obviously."

"Har, har. Come on Lore, were you really thinking about making an alliance with him?"

She sighed and scratched her head. "I thought I'd hear him out at least. Might not have been a terrible offer, you know, if it didn't cost my soul."

They smiled at each other.

"You know he's probably got a ton of men and gear on this ship," said Xin. "Think we'll be able to do it this time?"

"I do, and do you know why?"

"Why?" he asked, strapping his swords to his back in their usual "X" shape, wincing from the pressure on his back.

She grinned and tapped him on the chest. "Because this time we're fighting together," she sang, bringing a large, confident smile to Xin's face.

"We'll do what we can too," said a woman with pigtails and a toothy smile as the rest of Lorelei's crew stood behind her.

"Oh, what about him?" Xin asked, pointing to the unconscious Emir in one of the other cells. Lorelei chuckled and unlocked it. She threw a bucket of water on him.

Emir gasped awake, screaming in pain as he clenched his bruised jaw as he glared up at Lorelei. "Why do I keep getting hurt around you?!"

A small smile flicked across her face and she pressed a finger to her lips to silence his whining. "I need you to do another job for me, thief. Think you can handle it?"

He grumbled, and gave a small nod.

15

Deadly Duo

Atop one of the large masts, Astrid, Chase and James watched the scattering pirates below. James had his sniper at the ready, but wasn't firing yet. They hadn't figured out where they were, and he needed to keep it that way. A group with a battering ram rhythmically crashed against the door, though not as well as they could have been, were they actually sober.

"Damn Astrid. What was that stuff you got me to put in that rum?" asked Chase, balancing perfectly on the edge of the nest.

"It's actually a really powerful poison, but in the right doses can make a man instantly drunk," she explained, ensuring the bind on the struggling pirate lookout was secure.

"Think you could've poisoned them all if we had the time?"

"I would not, even if I could! I'm not a killer, and that is an especially dirty way to kill someone."

Chase laughed. "Well, I am quite impressed either way."

Astrid giggled. "Oh please, you did all the work. All I did was give you the right stuff."

"Ah, well, getting people to party is one of my specialties."

Astrid looked below. "Do you think they're alright? They've been down there a while."

"I don't know, but Konstantin is still out here, right? They're probably fine." Slowly, a goofy grin spread across his face. "Maybe they're getting reacquainted."

Astrid punched him on the leg, sending a slight numbing sensation through it, which he desperately tried to shake off.

"Don't even joke," she scolded. "Lorelei may be promiscuous, but she would never put us in danger for sex."

With a chuckle, Chase replied, "Alright, alright, just trying to lighten the mood. Do you really think we can take all these guys out?"

James laughed. "Oh definitely. Lorelei and Xin together again? They probably don't even need us here."

Just then, the pirates burst down the door and went streaming in. Almost instantly, the wave slowed, followed by angry yelling. Lorelei's familiar song floated out of the doorway, followed by a symphony of screams and panicked voices.

"Oh! That sounds like Lorelei!" chirped Astrid.

The screaming hoard tried to clamber out of the doorway, but came out in a spray of blood instead. At least three heads rolled separately from their bodies.

"And that's definitely Xin's handiwork," smiled James.

Side by side, the confident warriors stood observing the nervous, stinking crowd. With a laugh, Lorelei did some light stretches, a giddy smile upon her face.

As the crowd surrounded them, Xin cracked his neck and knuckles. "So what're you thinking? Tactic Beta?"

"Nah, I've been itching for Tactic Omega with these guys."

"Perfect."

Lorelei grinned and cocked her head back to the loyal soldiers behind her. "Stay back for a bit guys and enjoy the show."

"What are you standing around for, you cowards?" yelled Konstantin. "Attack!"

Obediently, the crew attacked the two calm, smiling warriors. At the very last moment, with perfect timing, the two sprang into action. Xin swung his swords wide, decapitating all in range. Lorelei ducked, disembowelling three enemies with one swift slice.

She held up her hand as Xin took both his swords into one. He grabbed her hand and easily tossed her up into a graceful flip in the air. As the enamoured crowd watched her, Xin sliced through their ranks, herding them into a condensed group.

Descending, Lorelei sheathed her sword and readied a punch. She crashed down in the middle of the herded group.

The deck buckled beneath her.

With Lorelei on the inside, and Xin on the outside, they easily dispatched the stumbling attackers. They locked eyes, and with a smile, fought back-to-back. Though their styles differed, they could make them work flawlessly together.

Above, Chase and Astrid watched the duo in complete awe. James grinned, finally opening fire on the surrounding pirates as the rest of their crew had taken action. He wasn't about to make it easy for the bastards. Unfortunately for him, Konstantin wasn't in sight.

"Look who's fucking useless now, Konstantin, you fucking bastard," growled James, popping another enemy in the head. "I hope Xin and Lorelei make you die a slow, gruesome death, you motherfucker. For Yuri."

"Incredible," breathed Astrid. "You told me they were amazing together. I never realized just how much. They look so happy."

"Creepily happy," shuddered Emir. "Why are they so happy killing people?"

Astrid gasped and squeaked in fear, then relaxed upon seeing the new arrival. "Emir! You're alright."

"That's a matter of opinion," he grumbled, rubbing his sore chin. "Anyway, Lorelei has a request. I have done my part. The rest is up to the bright-haired one," he said with a thumb jab at Chase.

Konstantin watched the fight from the safety of the cabin wall with a seething rage, wondering how the hell she had gotten the better of him. She had help. That was obvious by the sniper in the crow's nest, but how did they get here so quickly? All of his careful planning was undone. This was not how he wanted things to end, but clearly, she was just as foolish as ever.

The bitch had to die, along with all her little friends.

Konstantin turned his attention to the idiot holding the bazooka, who was just gawking at the scene. "You, idiot. Take out the sniper in the nest."

"Aye Cap'n," he said, turning the gun upward. Before he could pull the trigger, a sweet gust of wind blew in, throwing his aim off and sending the bullet into the air and off toward the ocean to the opposite end of the battle. As it exploded, Konstantin saw an unfamiliar boat sailing at them. He grinned wickedly.

"All hands not in combat, below deck and man the cannons to the port side. Take out that ship!"

A swarm of men disengaged and did as ordered.

Konstantin waited eagerly, watching that bitch as she hacked her way through his men. He couldn't wait to see her face when he took out her reinforcements.

Boom, boom, boom.

The port side of Konstantin's precious ship now had a gaping hole, and any of his crew near it were dead. All Konstantin heard was Ibby's fucking mocking laugh. The world turned red. He didn't care about his life anymore. All that mattered was killing that fucking bitch.

He sprinted out to his man with the bazooka, zigging and zagging as the bullets from above concentrated on him. He grabbed his man and held him like a shield as a bullet pierced him right where Konstantin's head would have been.

As the sniper was reloading, Konstantin aimed for the crow's nest and pulled the trigger.

Astrid screamed as she saw the huge bullet coming their way. Before it struck, she felt herself pulled upward, and saw Chase struggling to hold all three of them as he glided into the air. The flames licked up and caught his glider on fire, sending them hurtling down to the deck.

Chase gave them a non-fatal landing, but poor Astrid fell right in front of the grinning Konstantin. His fist came down upon her head, just slow enough to block with her staff. He pressed down, boring those violet eyes into her soul.

"Well, hello there, little flower. You look awfully familiar. Have I beat you before?"

It was true. The memories came flooding back in a wave of pain, fear, and disgust.

Cold iron dug into her wrists.

Fists collided with her delicate form—broken ribs.

Konstantin's vile, pale body pinning her down—powerless to his urges.

Tears streamed down Astrid's face, and Konstantin laughed, his sickening belly jiggling laugh. "Ah, it would seem so." With his one meaty hand, he snatched the staff from her hand and snapped it like a twig. He took a swing at her with the shattered piece, but hit only air. His violet eyes narrowed at the bold, orange-haired boy that had taken her place.

"Sorry Astrid, I know you're a badass and all, but I couldn't help but notice you don't like this guy," grinned Chase. "Think I'll take care of him if that's alright."

Astrid nodded, wiping away the tears and turned to face the hoard coming their way.

Konstantin looked him up and down. "Orange hair… Are you the boy that got my crew drunk?"

"Bang on, fecker. It was pretty easy if we're being honest. These guys have some serious issues. I think you may need to work on your captaining skills."

Konstantin sneered at him.

Chase sighed, shrugged, and continued with a flourish, "Anyway, you can call me Chase the Ace."

"Case the base? That's an odd name," Konstantin replied, of course making Chase's face fall with frustration.

"No! Chase! Argh, never mind," Chase conceded, throwing a punch Konstantin's way. He easily stepped back from the attack, but the gust of wind that followed blindsided him and sent him flying into a wall.

Astrid stood, now recovered from her moment of weakness. She was unarmed, but not useless. With ease and efficiency, she sent her opponents flopping to the ground with paralyzing strikes.

From the crowd came a heavily armoured pirate.

One, two. She tried to hit within the armour's gaps, but found only metal. She shook out her hand and smiled sheepishly at him.

"You wouldn't hit a girl, would you?" she asked sweetly.

The armoured man laughed and reached for his weapon. It was not there. He looked around confused and saw Emir standing at the edge of the boat, smiling and holding his weapon.

"You little brat!" he yelled and charged at him, not seeing the caltrops before him. The screaming pirate slid uncontrollably into the railing and overboard.

Astrid looked at Emir, quite impressed. "Nicely done."

Emir scratched his head and grinned.

James fell straight into a group of angry pirates. He tried to stand, but found his leg wasn't quite on right. No time to fix it as the pirates dove in for the kill. Out came his trusty revolver. Six shots, six dead. The rest paused, aghast at the sudden kills, but quickly came in, realizing he was out of bullets.

His heart raced as memories flooded his mind. He felt completely useless again. He reloaded as quickly as possible, but a rapier came straight toward his eye and he flinched away. Rather than his flesh tearing, he heard metal on metal. There was Lorelei smiling down at him, the attackers around him dead on the ground.

"Looks like you could use a leg up," she said.

"This is exactly why I like to stay home," he grumbled, fixing his leg.

"Well, I appreciate the help. Feels a bit like old times, huh? You know, except you're actually useful now." She shot him a teasing smile as she ran another pirate through.

"Haha…"

The battle between the experienced and inexperienced captains raged on. Chase held his own, but was clearly untrained and untested compared to the old captain. Luckily for Chase, his odd power kept Konstantin on his toes.

After another large gust, Konstantin took a moment to catch his breath. "What power is this? I've never seen it before."

"I am an air master! Hmm, no, that doesn't feel right either. Bender maybe?" Chase pondered, scratching his chin.

Konstantin chortled. "Not like people can control the wind, huh? Fucking bitch planned this whole thing."

A concentrated gust struck Konstantin hard in the gut. "Now that's not a very nice word to describe a lady, you fecking ugly bastard," growled Chase, that child-like glimmer faded from his eyes.

"I am so sick of you fucking kids!" shouted Konstantin. Before Chase knew what was going on, Konstantin reached into his jacket. The next moment—

BANG!

Gun? Chase stood in shock, looking down, expecting to feel a bullet in his gut. There was none. Chase looked back up and saw the gun not pointed at him at all. Xin stood between the two, Konstantin's arm thrown out wide, making the bullet hit an unsuspecting pirate.

"Nice work Chase, but I'll take it from here," said Xin with an eager smile. "You help the others."

"Will do. Kick his ass!" Chase took off.

Konstantin readied himself, shooting Xin a wicked smirk. "So kid, you looking for another beating?"

"It won't be so easy now that I'm not in chains," Xin sneered, though the pain upon his back seared through his body. For now, he let the pain flow through him. He wouldn't let Konstantin have the pleasure of knowing. "And don't think your mind games are going to save you this time."

Konstantin aimed and fired. Too slow. As soon as Konstantin twitched a muscle, Xin was already dodging. The bullet hit another of Konstantin's oblivious men. Lunging in close, Xin swiftly brought his hands together around the gun, breaking the old man's grip. Before it could touch the deck, Xin kicked it overboard. He swept a sword across Konstantin's gut.

The old captain stepped back with surprising deftness for one of his size, gripping the sword tight with his gloved hands.

Xin tried to yank it away, but the sword wouldn't budge.

Impossible. Thought Xin. *He can't be this strong.* To his even greater surprise, the sword bent beneath his grip and snapped in two.

"Well, that's a new one," remarked Xin, examining his broken sword.

"Gift from the lovely Freya from me last load of slaves to the Capitol." Konstantin examined his cut hands. "Mighta preferred invincibility though..."

Xin let out a single booming "Ha!" as he sheathed his broken sword, then smirked at the scowling bastard. "You were hitting me with enhanced strength? And you still hit like a child. That's pretty sad."

Konstantin roared with rage, drawing his rapier from its sheath and swinging it wildly. Perhaps he believed his enhanced strength would win him this battle easily.

An exaggerated sigh of boredom escaped Xin's lips as he blocked each swing with grace and ease. "You know I remember this being harder last time we fought. I guess the last five years have been kinder to me than you, old man."

Down came that rapier on Xin's head, and up went his own longsword to block. Pain shot through Xin's body, and his arm faltered.

Damn those whip wounds.

The rapier came down, taking a small chunk of Xin's jacket as he twisted away. Xin followed up with an elbow to the man's nose.

Konstantin stumbled back, nose running red. He stepped on Astrid's discarded staff and went crashing to his ass. Before he could regain himself, he found Xin's sword pointed at his throat.

"I'd ask if you have any last words, but I'd rather not hear them." Xin's sword snapped up for the final blow, just as Konstantin reached into his jacket.

A brilliant burst of light blinded the unsuspecting Xin.

"Fucking bastard!" he yelled, trying to blink away the spots burned into his retinas.

As Xin blinked away his blindness, Konstantin ran off, clearly not wanting to test himself against the man even in that state. As he ran, he saw the discarded sniper rifle on the ground, picked it up and grinned. He dashed to the upper decks as fast as his peg leg would allow.

"I'm killing this bitch if it's the last thing I do." He aimed his sights on the fighting and oblivious Lorelei.

He pulled the trigger as a flash of orange streaked past his sights.

Bang.

Lorelei snapped her head at the sound. Chase fell from the air and Konstantin held the rifle, looking surprised and confused. She saw Xin catch Chase, and all she could think was that he was dead.

Why did everyone have to die for her?

Overwhelming rage consumed her, and she let it out in a piercing scream that sent the surrounding men stumbling back. She sprinted through the crowd, leapt atop a few annoyed heads, and dove for the upper deck, that violet-eyed bastard in her sights.

His eyes widened as he scrambled to reload the gun, but she would not let him. She grabbed the gun, twisting and turning to get it out of his grip. He wouldn't let go. His grip was stronger than it should have been. Still, his centre was weak. All she needed to do was use his strength against him.

Konstantin flashed that horrid mocking smile at her. "What's the matter, lil' girl? Ya not as strong as ya thought? Or are ye too distracted that I killed another one of your idiotic friends?"

She wasn't in the mood for banter. Another ear-piercing scream left her lips, making Konstantin cringe. Konstantin had a broken nose, so she smashed it again. Then, with a simple turn, the massive man moved to her whim and she tossed him over the railing to the deck below. One hand released the gun, but the other held firm and brought Lorelei down with him.

They hit the deck with an audible *thump*, and the gun flew into the crowd. Lorelei got her feet under her in an instant, but Konstantin was quick, too. He grabbed her left arm, pulling her to her knees.

As she tried to pull free, he squeezed tighter.

That sickening sneer curled on his lips. "I can snap yer arm like a twig."

Lorelei bored her golden eyes into his. No fear, just utter hatred. "You know, I can actually forgive you for the years you made my life a living hell. I've had worse father figures, after all. What I cannot forgive is the pain you've caused my friends and countless other human souls. I've made it my personal mission to avenge them. You think a little strength enchantment is going to stop me?"

With that, she got her feet under her, and easily stood up, lifting the hulking mass of Konstantin with her.

His eyes grew wide.

Her right hand readied, she gave a simple twist and unloaded a gut wrenching punch into Konstantin's gut.

Snap went her arm.

Konstantin folded in pain, releasing Lorelei's now broken arm and coughing up unhealthy amounts of blood. Her useless left arm fell limp as she sucked the air through her teeth, trying to bite back the pain.

Just a little longer.

Her right arm shook. She wasn't sure if it was the adrenaline, the anger, or the memories.

Just one last strike.

Through the tremor, Lorelei gripped her right hand around her sword, drawing it from its sheath with a satisfying, *schwing.* It wasn't her strong arm—not since her tendon had been cut as a child—but it would have to do.

"Burn in hell you bastard."

Her sword thrust straight through his heart. He gasped. Then came that all-so-familiar oozing as warm blood flowed down her sword, then to her hand.

The satisfaction was written on her blood-drenched grin.

His hands gripped her shoulders, trying to push away, but he had no strength left. He was dying. He knew it. Those violet eyes searched her and as the light faded, a look of pride flickered, and faded as his body fell heavy against her.

The bastard was dead.

She let the blood flow a little longer and rolled the huge man off her. His body fell with a dull thud.

A light drizzle fell from the heavens, and the blood on her face dripped down. She watched that lifeless body for a long time as the entire deck became completely silent. With a few deep breaths, she bent over him and snatched that damned hat from his head.

Grinning that vicious smile again, she turned to the gawking pirates, placing her too large prize upon her head.

"Now then, if the rest of you want to keep your life, you're going to haul this ship over to the Oasis."

The pirates looked at their now dead captain, along with the multitude of dead comrades scattered amongst the ship. Most eyes turned to Ivan, who was battered and bruised, but still alive. He nodded, and the crew hauled anchor.

Lorelei sprinted to her friends. Relief flowed through her. Chase was still alive.

"We need to get him home now," Astrid cried, busily trying to stanch the bleeding coming from Chase's gut. "I need to operate and I don't have the supplies here."

Lorelei laid a hand on her shoulder. "We'll be there soon. Keep him alive until then."

Xin sat down cross-legged by Chase, a smirk on his face. "Just had to go and be a hero, didn't you, Captain?"

"Fucking dumbass," Lorelei spat. "I swear to the gods if you die I'm going to Valhalla just to kick your scrawny ass."

Chase grinned up at her. "Totally worth it."

As she readied to give him a punch on the arm, he chuckled weakly and went limp.

16

Angels

A lantern flickered by the bedside as Chase lay bandaged and sleeping. The morning sun peeked in and out of the window as the room swayed softly with the waves. Astrid flattened the downy quilt laying on top of Chase. Her gut still twisted with worry for him, but his calming scent, mixed with the morning sea breeze seeping in from the window, calmed her worried heart. She knew she shouldn't worry as much as she did. His wound was already healing well… but still. She sat in the oaken chair, perfectly poised, but leaned in to watch his slow but sure breaths.

It had been two days since his injury, and would likely be another few days before he woke up. He had lost a lot of blood and sustained a lot of damage. All signs showed he would be fine, but there was always a possibility he would never wake up. A tear came to her eye at the thought of it. Gently, she grabbed his hand and squeezed it, praying to the gods that he made a speedy recovery.

He squeezed back.

She wasn't expecting her prayers to be answered so swiftly. She shot her head up to see Chase slowly opening his eyes. He looked at her and beamed a weak smile.

"Ah, I must be in Elysium. Where else would I find such a beautiful angel?"

Astrid grinned madly, happy tears filling her eyes. "Chase!" she squealed, and hugged him tightly.

"Ow."

Astrid jumped back. "Oh, sorry. How're you feeling?"

"Like I got hit by an elephant," he groaned with a small cough. With a quick glance around the room, he asked, "Where are we?"

She gave him that sweet smile. "You're on the Oasis."

"Everyone's alright?"

"Thanks to you. There were a few minor injuries and Lorelei's pissed about the broken arm, but everyone is fine. Ivan agreed to report to Lorelei from now on, but the rest of the ships under Konstantin's rule have gone rogue. Still, without an organized leader, they shouldn't be as much of a threat."

"Glad it all worked out, then."

Chase's eyes wandered to the nightstand, where beside his bandana lay a familiar hat. It was the tricorn Konstantin had been wearing, though much cleaner and patched up. He gave it a cock-eyed look. "What's with the hat?"

Astrid giggled happily. "It's for you, from Lorelei."

"Wha—? Why would she want me to have that? Wouldn't it be a constant reminder of the guy?"

"That's what I asked! She said, 'Anything that reminds me that the bastard is dead is a good thing.'" Astrid quoted in her best serious Lorelei impression, then continued in her usual sweet tone. "She also said something about it being symbolic. I guess she really has accepted you're going to be her next captain."

Chase smiled, grabbing the hat off of the table. He surveyed it, and placed it upon his head. Perfect fit. They must have done some adjusting while he slept.

"Well? How does it look?" he asked with his boyish grin.

"Fucking perfect," sang Lorelei's voice from the door.

They spun to see the grinning woman balancing a couple drinks in one hand as her other arm was cast and in a sling.

Chase grinned madly. "Lorelei!"

"So, you're finally awake." She smiled and strode over to Chase, passing the drinks to Astrid. He opened his arms wide, expecting another hug, but received a few annoyed punches on the arm instead.

"Never. Do. that. Again," she scolded between punches. "What is with people sacrificing themselves for me?!"

"Honestly… I thought I could catch the bullet with my power," he responded sheepishly, and Lorelei gave him a skeptical look.

"And you needed to be in front of it to do that?"

He grinned again. "No, I needed to be in front of it in case it didn't work."

Lorelei punched him again, a little harder this time.

"OW!" he cried, rubbing his arm. "I'm injured, you know."

"Yes… but not nearly as much as you should be," Astrid informed them, drawing two confused gazes her way. "Well, there's a chance that your power slowed down the bullet enough to not kill you instantly, but the internal bleeding we found when we operated… you should not have recovered so easily from that. You should be dead. At the very least, you should still be unconscious."

"What can I say? I'm a fast healer," chuckled Chase.

"Supernaturally fast," Astrid added.

"Wait, are you trying to say that on top of wind powers, Chase has accelerated healing?" asked Lorelei, her face scrunched up in thought.

"It would seem so."

"No… No, no, no, no," muttered Lorelei as she began pacing the room, lost in thought. "That can't be… I mean, I suppose it is possible, but he would have had to have been blessed directly from a god. Which would actually be good since it would fall into the narrative…" She looked Chase in the eye. "I guess I just assumed and never asked. How did you get your powers?"

Chase twiddled his thumbs nervously, avoiding her gaze. "From the Sacred Garden, of course."

Her fist went flying through the wall right by his head. "Don't you fucking lie to me."

"I'm sorry! My ma told me never to tell anyone!" he cried, flinching away from her.

"If you want me to go on the most dangerous journey in the world with you, you will tell me the truth."

"I... I never ate from the garden." He kept his gaze down, staring at his blanket. "When I was about ten, I started being able to control the wind. Just a little at first, then a lot. When Ma found out, she told me to tell people I snuck into the garden and ate something. It was believable because my mom was a priestess and often took me there. She got in trouble and got demoted. After that, she said she had to go on a pilgrimage. By the time she came back, she was sick and died shortly after."

"Oh Chase, I'm so sorry," said Astrid, giving him a gentle squeeze on his arm.

Lorelei was not so moved. "Your mother, what was her name?"

A smile crept back to his face, and he sat a little taller. "My mother was the beautiful, kind, caring Lilian Rose Burke, but everyone called her Lily. She was a priestess of Artemis, who wandered Gaia, taking care of anyone in need. She was the most caring mother anyone could ask for."

"She sounds wonderful," Astrid said with a soft smile.

"She was. She was always so busy, but always made time for me. My favourite thing was her reading to me about the Holy Lands. She always believed I would be the one to find it."

Astrid smiled softly at him.

Lorelei sat thinking, still unmoved by Chase's emotional moment. "So it's possible you may have received your blessing from an Angel directly. Do you remember anything like that happening?"

"Huh? Uh, no, not really. What is the difference if you receive it directly from an Angel?"

"It is possible for Angels to bestow their blessings on humans directly, but unlike the garden, these blessings will stay within the bloodline, meaning it will be passed down to offspring. Angels obviously don't like the idea of not having control over that, so they usually just stick to giving Blessings from the garden Gaia created, which will only stay with the human it is given to. Plus, you cannot get multiple blessings from the garden. The only humans that have been given multiple Blessings in the past are the Titans of Gaia."

Chase's eyes went wide. "Wha—you mean I'm like a giant?"

"Well… obviously not in size, meaning you might only have a couple blessings. Which is good news. The more blessings a human is imbued with, the shorter their life."

"Whoa…" said Chase.

Lorelei processed the information out loud, ensuring she had her facts straight. "Alright, so you started showing your powers about ten years ago…"

"No, I got them when I was ten. That was over twenty years ago now."

Lorelei flinched. "Wait, what? How old are you?"

"Uh, thirty-three. Why?"

Lorelei and Astrid both looked at him, mouths agape, and he squirmed uncomfortably at the stares. "What?"

"I thought you were like twenty-one, twenty-two at the most!" cried Lorelei.

"What? I mean, I know I look young, but come on. And why did you sleep with me if you thought I was that young?"

"I… well…" Lorelei's ears turned red. "It's not like it was that much younger! I'm only twenty-seven. Plus, you were still technically a man either way!"

Chase just chuckled. She gave him a light punch on the arm, then sat and pondered for a moment.

Suddenly, her face fell into a sick realization. "Who is your father?"

Chase shrugged. "Not sure. Ma never really talked about him. I asked a few times, but she just told me he was a wonderful man. I just figured it was some one-night stand and ma didn't actually know who he was." Chase laughed.

Lorelei did not share in the lightheartedness. She became twitchy. Her eyes darted to one corner of the room, and she bit her lip as if trying to keep herself from yelling.

"What's wrong, Lorelei?" asked Astrid, a nervous concern plastered on her face.

Lorelei just shook her head and smiled. "Never mind. It's probably nothing. I just have something I need to do." Without another word, she left the room.

Chase looked over at Astrid. "Is she alright?"

"Yeah… she does that sometimes," she replied, though the look in her eyes didn't seem to match her words. "Don't worry. You relax here. I'll let everyone know you're up. Maybe if you're feeling up to it later, I could take you for a little tour of the Oasis."

"That would be awesome."

Astrid gave him that warm smile and walked to the door. As she got there, Xin passed by the door and stopped with a smile to see Chase awake.

"Xin? Is that you?" Chase teased, taking a full look-over of his freshly groomed friend. "How long have I been out?"

"Haha, just a couple of days. I was getting tired of the scruffy comments."

"Is that the only reason you got cleaned up?" Chase prodded with a knowing smile.

"Tch…" replied Xin, narrowing his eyes at Chase, who just chuckled. Xin sighed and looked over to Astrid. The annoyance on his face changed to concern. "What's wrong?"

"Nothing," she insisted, watching her bare feet rock back and forth.

"Astrid."

Astrid sighed and leaned close to Xin. She wasn't whispering, but her lowered tone and the fact she was facing away meant Chase had a hard time knowing what she was saying. Definitely something about Lorelei… seeing… him? Who was *'him'*? Xin seemed to have a similar thought as he tilted his head and asked the same thing.

Astrid looked him straight in the eye, her face dire with an immense sadness. That was all Xin needed, apparently.

"Oh… *him*…" he growled, his usual blood freezing scowl amplified ten-fold. Clearly, whoever it was, he was seriously bad news.

Xin took a deep calming breath and turned a small, forced smile at Astrid. "I'll go keep an eye on her." He then looked over at Chase with a nod. "See you later Chase."

Chase snapped him a quick salute, and he left. Astrid gave Chase a last wave and left him to his solitude. Chase sighed, leaned back in the cozy bed, and nodded off once again.

The library—Lorelei's place of escape. She loved the smell, the quiet, and the knowledge that surrounded her. Today, however, it was not a relaxing place, but a place filled with panic.

Striding back to her pile of books, she awkwardly set down another armload, trying her best not to further injure her cast arm, though a sting of pain made her curse out loud more than once. The books slid away now and then with the swell of the boat, but it didn't slow her down as she flipped through page after page.

Her desperation grew more and more dire. Book after book, the pile loomed larger around her until she cried out, "No! That doesn't work either." She leaned back and sighed, pulling at her long auburn hair. "There is only one way, isn't there?"

"That's right. You know what he is," said a man next to her, sharpening a worn dagger. The man resembled Konstantin, sporting the same pale skin, blonde hair and violet eyes, as well as the same air of cocky confidence. This man, however, was far younger, with sharp features and protruding cheekbones, quite unlike the square, soft face of Konstantin.

Despondently, she put the book down, unsurprised by the man's sudden presence. "I know…"

"So what, you're following one of them now? After you worked so hard to escape them?" he hissed, stabbing the dagger into one book.

"I know but…"

"He will be just like them, you know."

"No… he won't," she said weakly.

"All the trouble we did to free you from them. You're just going to throw it all away because, what? He has a cute smile? He seems like a nice guy? He didn't jump you the moment he saw your breasts?"

"Stop it," she whispered.

His pale, sneering face was right in front of Lorelei, locking in with those mocking eyes. "Once he finds out who he is, he'll be no different than the rest of them. We had to fake your death just to escape them the first time. You follow him, you'll end up dead for real this time."

"Stop it, Mikhail! Just shut up!" she screamed, holding her hands over her ears and closing her eyes. It made no difference. It never did. Panic set in her heart, her mind raced, her breath shortened.

All of that came to a slow, as she felt a rough but gentle pair of large hands touch hers. She snapped her eyes open. In front of her were those very familiar, calming steel-blue eyes, his previously long chestnut hair now shortened on the sides, and tied neatly back.

"Xin," she sighed softly, lowering her hands.

"What's going on?" he asked, his eyes warm and full of concern.

"What? Nothing, silly. Just doing some research," she replied with a forced smile.

"Lore."

Lorelei's forced smile faded away, and the panic returned as she rambled. "I… It's just… It's Chase. Things just don't make sense. Or… they make too much sense…"

"Lore… *you're* not making sense."

"Of course she doesn't make sense. She's a fucking idiot," sneered Mikhail from beside her, but Xin didn't notice. His eyes remained on Lorelei, waiting for her answer. Only hers.

She couldn't ignore him. She snapped her head at Mikhail and screamed, "Shut up!" in his stupid, pale face.

Xin grabbed her face, those huge, strong arms ever so gently turning her toward him. Still, her eyes kept wandering to that violet-eyed bastard as he continued to mock her.

"Lore. Lorelei! Look at me, not him," Xin demanded, and she complied.

He loosened his grip, and pushed her hair back from her face to see all of her, even that wrinkled, blotchy scar covering the right side of her face.

"He's not here, Lore. You know that, right?"

Her eyes wandered back to Mikhail. There was a large, bloody gash over his right eye that wasn't there before. She gave him that. How did she forget?

She looked back at Xin. "I… I know."

"How long has it been since you slept?" he asked, lowering his hands to hers, being especially gentle with her cast hand.

"I don't know, a day maybe."

"For longer than a couple hours?"

Her body suddenly felt heavy, as if the realization was all she needed to feel the exhaustion. With great effort, she looked up at Xin, but all she could manage was a sad look. She opened her mouth to speak, to tell him she couldn't remember, but instead that violet-eyed bastard hissed in her ear.

"You do so remember, you stupid slut. Last time you slept was before you went psycho five years ago." Lorelei snuck another glance at him, now noticing the bloody wound on his shoulder. Xin gave him that…

Xin sighed, understanding her silence perfectly. "You need to sleep."

Lorelei snapped her gaze back and shook her head. She looked at her hands, examining the faded scars upon her wrist. They were barely visible now, but she knew they would always be there.

"That's right, sleep. We can have more fun there," cackled Mikhail, coughing up blood, his face battered and bruised.

"Konstantin is dead. Mikhail's in Purgatory. Lore, you're safe here." His voice was so soft, so caring. Despite that, she couldn't believe his words.

She shook her head again, though with less conviction.

"That's right. You know I will find you, no matter where you are," said Mikhail, but this time, a little softer, weaker, more distant.

"Lorelei. You are safe." There was such conviction in his voice now. It had been so long since she felt that comfort, that warmness. She was able to look up to Xin again, a soft, thankful smile on her face, not bothering to look for Mikhail. She knew he was gone… for now.

"Now, it's just you and me," said Xin, his caring eyes locking onto hers. "Tell me what's going on with Chase. Why are you so freaked out?"

She took a steadying breath, taking a quick glance around at the multiple books and papers strewn about the floor. "I… I've looked and I've looked, but… Chase's powers, and everything about his past… the only explanation is that…" she trailed off, uncomfortable by the thought.

"What?" Xin prodded, and after another deep breath, she whispered, "Chase is an Angel."

17

Scars

As the sun set, the tidied library grew dimmer with only a few scattered yellow fireflies buzzing and clicking on their holders. Beside one firefly, Lorelei laid curled up under Xin's leather jacket, dozing peacefully on a time-worn couch that smelled, as the entire library did, faintly of dust.

Xin sat on a chair nearby, contemplating their earlier conversation. They had talked for almost two hours until Lorelei passed out.

Lorelei was positive that Chase was an Angel. Not just any Angel, a descendant of The Lost God. The God that they thought was only a fairytale. The God that Godslayers hunted down. The God that—if Odin were to be believed—Xin should also be hunting. Xin shook his head. It just couldn't be true. Surely his father would have told him if he was descended from legends. He was just a soldier boy from the Forsaken Ring that would have been hired on to the Yggdrian army when he came of age—at least if he hadn't been sold to slavery first. It was impossible that he was a Godslayer.

But if all clues pointed to Chase being a descendant of the Lost God… then the possibility was becoming more real.

Lorelei always needed information on people. She hated not knowing things. She studied and researched everyone she sailed with, so of course, the moment she met Chase, she needed all the information she could get on him. As they were recovering, she got a report from the priests that raised him. She found it odd how detailed the reports about him were. They wrote every detail down from birth until the day he left. Everything except who his father was.

The only clue was Chase's middle name. Chase Lysik Burke. They had never heard that name before, and it wasn't in any other records. There was no one else with that name.

Xin had skimmed through the report as well, not wanting to pry into his past, but Lorelei had insisted he did in case he could see something she didn't.

Mostly, the notes were taken from the head priest of the Saints that raised Chase. The notes became more detailed after his mother's death, but nothing that seemed out of the ordinary. There were basic comments about the young boy's mental state, his sadness, occasional acts of aggression that were common with despair. The notes became disturbing around the time Chase was thirteen. Apparently, he had shown interest in a boy, and the head priest did not like that and for a year after that, the notes were about his various methods to "cure" Chase. Each way was more horrendous than the last. The last entry spoke of Chase disappearing in the night. He would have been fifteen.

Xin's heart ached for Chase. He had no idea he had been through such a shit-show growing up. He was always so happy, always spoke so highly of the wonderful priests that raised him.

Lorelei, with her calculating mind, used this information as an excuse to keep the truth from him. She insisted he needed to be tested, that she needed to understand his mental capacity first before revealing such shocking information. Being an Angel was not information one should take lightly.

Xin wanted to argue against her reasoning, but he couldn't. He hadn't known Chase long enough to speak to his mental health, so, despite his reservations, he agreed to keep quiet.

His attention turned back to Lorelei, who had begun to stir. She took a deep breath in, snuggling up in Xin's jacket with a smile. When she opened her eyes, her smile faded as she took in her odd blanket and surroundings.

"Good morning sleepy-head," Xin teased. "Or should I say, good evening?"

With a large yawn, Lorelei looked around, then out a window. "How long was I out?"

"About ten hours I'd say."

"Huh, didn't know I could do that," she said, standing up and stretching.

"Well, I hope you're well rested. Astrid came in about an hour ago. I guess they are having a party for everyone tonight to celebrate Chase's early recovery. Should be about ready now."

"Oh man… I slept through Astrid being here? Did you make sure I wasn't dead?" she chuckled, throwing Xin his jacket.

He laughed. "Multiple times."

Along the way to the party, Lorelei insisted on stopping by her room for a change of clothes. Xin waited outside her door, then waited some more, absentmindedly rolling a toothpick back and forth in his mouth. Finally, Lorelei came out clean and ready. Her hair hung down, nicely brushed, with her bangs pushed back just enough to reveal some of her scar. Her clothes were nothing special, just a loose tank top and jeans with her usual combat boots, but Xin couldn't help but smile at her.

She noticed his smile. "What?"

"Nothing."

"Oh, come on," she teased as they walked down the hall.

"I guess… it's still weird seeing you dress like a normal person. It's especially weird seeing you gloveless."

"Heh… yeah." Her ears turned red as she scratched her head. "Well, I realized that everyone here has been or is suffering in some way. That's when I remembered someone really wise telling me my scars shouldn't be reminders of when I was weak, but that they are the marks of how I became strong. I figured it might help people if they could see those times. That's why I don't hide my scars anymore."

"Huh…" Xin said with a prideful smile. "This guy, he sounds pretty smart. Probably really handsome too."

"He's alright," Lorelei said with a sly grin. "He got a hell of a lot cuter when he stopped smoking. Can't seem to break him of that oral fixation though…" She slid up close to him, gently reaching those perfect fingers up and snatching the toothpick from Xin's mouth. He couldn't help but smile as she examined it. She looked up at him, her eyes dancing like a golden flame. There was a soft smile on her lips. Those perfect lips. Gods, he missed those lips.

Something flew between them, making them both take a stuttering step back. The object crashed on the wall behind Xin, struggled for a moment, then fizzled, popped and gave up.

Lorelei glared down the dark hallway. "Gods dammit, Kari!"

As Xin followed her glare, a dark, bestial figure bounded toward him, a dull thump with every other step. Before he even considered it was a threat, the beast lunged, placing its front paws on Xin's chest and knocking him to the ground. In an instant, the creature was licking his face enthusiastically.

"Ack!" he cried, trying to defend himself from the multitude of dog kisses. "Is this Kari?"

Lorelei gave a hardy laugh as she pulled it away. "No, this is Chrissy, Kari's dog," explained Lorelei, trying to hold back the dog along with the laughter.

Now, without his face being covered with a tongue, Xin looked at the large, yellow, shaggy dog as it bared its teeth—not in anger, but excitement—its whole body wagging, wanting to give him more kisses.

Another figure came bounding down the hall with an odd clanging and jangling sound. This one flew past the enthralled dog and unimpressed Lorelei to leap on top of Xin's shoulders.

"What the—" Xin cried, looking up at the obtrusive girl standing on his shoulders pulling out the odd gadget from the wall. She was young, not quite in her teens, with ebony skin that was splattered with oil. At least that's what he assumed it was by the smell of her filthy overalls.

"Hey kid! Do I look like a ladder to you?" Xin snarled.

"Well, you're the one just sitting there," she said, blowing a piece of her wild, curly hair from her face, not looking up from the gadget.

"What did I tell you about flying your experiments inside?" scolded

Lorelei.

The girl snapped her head up and turned around slowly with an apologetic smile, jumping down from Xin's shoulders. "Sorry, Miss Lorelei. It got away from me."

"And I told you to train your dog," growled Lorelei, making Chrissy sit and whine.

"She is trained," Kari said confidently, rubbing the pup affectionately on the head.

Lorelei gave a resigned sigh. "For something other than helping you with your tools."

"Oh, come on. Chrissy only does that with people she really likes. Big and broody over there should be happy," quipped Kari, jabbing a thumb Xin's way.

"She's never done that to me."

Kari snickered. "Exactly."

"I'm more of a cat person, anyway," Lorelei replied with a pouty lip.

Xin snorted a laugh and motioned to get up, but a pair of big brown eyes kept him in place as the invasive girl scrutinized him.

"Hmm… big muscles, blue eyes, scary scowl… you must be Xin! I've heard a lot about you!" she exclaimed, then examined him again, more thoughtfully. "Hmm…"

"What?" He did not like this girl in his space.

"You're not as cute as the ladies made you seem. That orange-haired guy was way cuter."

Xin turned bright red. "You… I… what?"

Lorelei burst into a gut busting laugh.

"Come on Chrissy! Let's go fix this so it's ready for tonight," exclaimed Kari, receiving a big excited woof in reply as they sprinted off down the hall.

Xin heard the odd thump sound again and noticed the dog's back right leg was made of metal, not fur. Xin wondered what had happened, but was currently more concerned about Lorelei still laughing at him.

"Alright, alright, you've had your laugh," he grumbled, standing up and dusting himself off.

Lorelei took a couple of calming breaths, shaking off the hilarity. "That was Kari. She likes to say what's on her mind."

"I gathered that."

"Brilliant kid. Just be careful around her experiments, they tend to—"

Kaboom!

"I'm okay!" shouted Kari, followed by a deep, "Woof!" from Chrissy.

"—explode…" concluded Lorelei, looking down the hall, exasperated.

It was Xin's turn to laugh. "You've got quite the bunch here."

"Sure do," she replied with a smile, motioning Xin to follow her down the hall. "We have princes and paupers, farmers and scholars, whores and saints."

"You found all of these people on Konstantin's ships?"

"No, we've been doing more than just taking out Konstantin's ships," laughed Lorelei. She put a finger to her cheek in thought. "Let's see, I took over an assassin's guild, started an alliance with a spy network, got invited to join the Valkyries on multiple occasions and started a couple civil wars."

Xin laughed, and Lorelei gave him a confused look.

"Sorry," he said, wiping a tear from his eye. "It's just… Konstantin said you were becoming like him. I never realized how fucking wrong he was."

Lorelei looked to the ground sheepishly. "Well, I do have a lot of ties in the underworld, and I've done a lot of things I'm not proud of…"

"Which is exactly why you're not like him. You may have a similar power structure, but you did it for completely different reasons. You want to help people, he just wanted power."

Lorelei smiled warmly at him. "Yeah, I guess you're right."

"It is seriously impressive what you've accomplished, though. I've just been doing mercenary work."

"On your own?"

"Mostly. Joined one group once, but the leader turned out to be a real creep. You know, killing and raping innocence when it suited him." He shrugged. "So I killed him."

"That's not fair… I'm the one that wanted to be alone."

"I'm glad you weren't," he said with a smile.

Lorelei gave a soft chuckle. "There you go again. Just can't be mad at me, can you? What have I gotten myself into? We have a promiscuous captain that can't take anything seriously, a virgin thief that takes everything too seriously, and… you." She stopped him in front of an enormous set of doors, giving him a small nudge and a smile. He returned the smile just as an ensemble of instruments started tuning behind the large doors.

"Come on. Everyone on this boat's been through their own personal hell, but damn do they know how to party."

The doors opened wide into a huge, warmly lit room filling Xin's nose with a salivating mix of sweet and savoury scents. He had eaten little after their discussion this morning, so those long tables piled high with food were a welcome sight.

A massive wave of greetings aimed at Lorelei interrupted his hungry stupor.

"Yeah, yeah, keep your pants on," she yelled, waving at the eager people. Through the bustling, excited crowd, James limped his way towards them.

James stopped and looked at Lorelei with a cocked head. "You look different." He looked between the two of them. "Are you two…"

"Tchah. Get your head out of the gutter. I just finally slept."

"Oh, thank the gods. Does that mean you're actually in a good mood?"

Lorelei gave him a playful scowl, then grabbed him and gave his bald head an aggressive rub.

"Ak! Stop that!"

She let him go with a laugh and looked around. "By the gods, you guys have been busy. No Chase, yet?"

"Not yet. I think Astrid was showing him around." He straightened out his jacket. "I'm sure they'll be here soon."

A gaggle of giggling made its way through the crowd, and a gorgeous group of women appeared. The Dragon Ladies of Leyuan, the whores that fight, and the women who helped raise Lorelei.

The giggles turned into excited cheers, and squeals as they locked onto Xin. In an instant, they surrounded him, completely invading his personal space as they clung to him.

"Here you are! We've been looking everywhere for you!" exclaimed Anna, the shortest woman of them all.

Sandy, the most voluptuous of the bunch, pressed up right against him and petted his cheek. "My, my. You have turned into quite a handsome man, haven't you?"

Xin's face turned completely red.

"Not that he wasn't a looker before, right Lorelei?" giggled the willowy Tarla.

"Argh, that's enough out of all of you. Can't you see you're making the man uncomfortable?" Lorelei snapped, drawing yet another round of giggles from the ladies.

Another boom of greetings filled the air, this time directed at a sheepish Astrid and grinning Chase in a wheelchair. Astrid gave a small wave and pushed Chase over to their group.

As soon as they saw Chase, the Dragon Ladies changed their desired target, drawing a sigh of relief from Xin.

"You must be Chase. Astrid told us all about your heroics," giggled Anna.

"Thank you so much for protecting Lorelei," sighed Tarla, drawing a death glare from Lorelei.

"Ladies, ladies, please. There is enough Chase to go around," he said assuredly, with as grand of a flourish as possible. He flinched slightly from the pain, and the ladies doted on him.

"How is your injury?" asked Anna.

"Healing just fine. I'm told it will leave a pretty awesome scar, though," he boasted, drawing a round of giggles from the ladies and a sigh from Astrid.

"You will have to let us thank you properly for your heroics," breathed Sandy, bending down with a grin and a wink.

"Yes ma'am!"

"Oh goodness no," scolded Astrid. "You are not to be doing any strenuous activity for at least another couple of days. This especially counts for sex."

"What?!" cried Chase, shoulders slumped. "That's not fair! You said I was a fast healer."

"But you are still not healed enough. How sexy would it be for you to pop a stitch and bleed out mid orgasm?"

"Well… it would be one of my top ways of dying," admitted Chase, drawing a frustrated grunt from Astrid.

The ladies tittered at Astrid, assuring her they would treat Chase well and stole him away, to his great delight. They rolled him up to the table and began serving him food and drink, each eagerly wanting to help him in any way they could.

Xin chuckled at his grin, and Astrid's scowl. Then he caught Trisa sneaking into the room. It always surprised him that this woman was a soldier when she adorned her formal wear and makeup. She was the picture of properness.

"Xin!" Trisa exclaimed, wrapping him in a big hug, though her short arms could not quite reach around him.

Xin smiled, accepting the hug gratefully. "Hey, Trisa."

James looked between the two, crossed his arms, and pouted. "What? Xin gets hugs? I got a beating when you first saw me."

"You know damn well why you got a beating," Trisa scowled.

James just glared.

Lorelei chuckled and patted James on the back. "To be fair, she also gave me a beating the first time, too."

Trisa's face softened. "I am still so sorry about that, Lorelei. I never really blamed you. You didn't deserve that."

"But I did?" exclaimed James.

"A whole year," Trisa growled, thrusting her finger in front of his face. "A whole year I went without knowing that the love of my life died. How could you not remember to tell me at least once in that time! I thought we were family."

"I… I had my own things going on."

Trisa sighed with a mix of annoyance and defeat. "I know."

After a sorrowful moment of silence in the group, Trisa snapped her gaze back to Lorelei and saluted. "There is something I need to discuss with you."

Lorelei shook her head at her constant propriety. Once a soldier, always a soldier apparently. James and Xin took off to find a seat while Trisa made her report.

"Our friend in high places has sent a message regarding Konstantin," Trisa said. "It's not good news..."

"Shit... don't tell me. Freya got involved, didn't she?"

"That's right."

"How long?"

"She can hold back the verdict for a couple of days, but that's a maybe."

"Shit."

"She urged me to mention the option of taking over what Konstantin left behind. That if you don't do it, someone else far more cruel will probably take on the mantle."

Lorelei sighed. "Yeah, I know, but I just can't. Sure, I could send them the criminals we capture, but what if that's not enough? Do I start raiding like Konstantin? I just can't."

Trisa smiled warmly at her. "I completely understand, but what do we do now?"

"I can't stay here."

Trisa's face went even whiter. "What?"

"If I stay, the Valkyries will have to come after me, and I know what everyone on this boat will think of that."

"We'd defend you till our last breath."

"Exactly. Which is why we'll be leaving."

"Who will be in charge?"

"Well, you of course."

"Are you serious?" Trisa squeaked in fear.

"Oh, come on, how is this any different from leading soldiers for the army?"

"It's a lot different! I know nothing about assassins, or bards, or whoever else that reports to us. Now you have Ivan and his crew. I just don't know."

Lorelei laughed. "I know it's a lot, but I've already got things set up to basically run without me. You just need to let them all know we're still working, so they don't start wandering off on their own. I know you can do it."

Trisa sighed. "I guess I don't have a choice."

"Of course you do. It just makes things far more difficult if you don't agree."

Trisa laughed. "Alright, but you'd better not take long."

"The new ship is ready?"

"Yes, they finished it today."

"Then we leave tomorrow morning. Should only take a couple months if everything goes well." Lorelei gave a prideful smile. "We are working off of one of my plans, after all.

"Well then, I'll see you back here in a few months after the world has changed for the better."

Lorelei looked around to the rest of the room, examining all the people she had met and protected over the years. They were all so happy at that moment. She turned to Trisa with a smile. "Well, no point wasting this party. Let's go have one more night of fun all together."

Trisa got a huge smile and snapped another salute, then stood at ease, looking like she wanted to ask something else. Lorelei sighed, knowing exactly what it was.

"Alright. You get one hug," she conceded, and the tiny woman gripped Lorelei in a strong, happy hug, making Lorelei chuckle.

"I'm going to miss you, Lorelei. You be safe, alright?" said Trisa, a tear in her eye.

"I promise. You'll keep good care of our home while I'm gone, right?"

Trisa finally released her grip. "Of course."

The band started up a wonderful lilting tune and Lorelei beamed. "Ah, they're playing my tune, time to go!" she chirped and dashed to the stage to play and sing along with the band. If this was the last night at her home, she was going to make the most of it.

18

Party time

After a far shorter time than anyone expected, Chase left the Dragon Ladies and rolled himself in beside James, Xin, and Trisa. Chase noticed there was an awkward tension between James and Trisa, and not the good, sexual kind like Xin and Lorelei had. It was more of a frustrated, unspoken anger sort of tension.

As soon as Chase joined them, they welcomed him with smiles and open arms.

"What are you doing back here, buddy?" asked James, giving him a light punch on the shoulder. "Figured you'd be out all night with the ladies."

"Ah well, what can I say? Didn't seem fair to keep them all night, what with the injury and all."

"Oh man, you're missing out. Those ladies certainly know what they're doing," sighed James, lounging back in his chair, a satisfied grin on his face.

"So, you've had the pleasure of their company?" Chase chuckled, giving James' knee a little nudge with his own.

James raised an eyebrow and gave his head a small shake. With a smile, he continued, "Oh yeah. They were quite happy after we rescued them from that slave ship."

"You rescued them?"

"Well, it was a team effort. I did have to fight my way through swarms of pirates to do it though," James claimed, chest puffed out.

Xin chuckled and shook his head.

Trisa scoffed and rolled her eyes, receiving a glare from James.

"What do you know? You weren't there."

"Oh please, James," Trisa sighed, her voice short and curt, just as her whole attitude seemed to be. "Everyone knows Xin and Yuri were the fighters. You were just... you."

James scowled, staring at the table.

"What? But what about all those amazing shots you made?" said Chase. "You may not be good at hand-to-hand, but I've never seen a better marksman."

James sighed. "It's a natural gift... that I discovered a little too late. Our time as bounty hunters... Well, I was pretty useless."

"That's not true," said Xin. "You weren't useless to those kidnapped children. Gods know what would have happened to them if you weren't there."

"You also convinced Lorelei not to kill my lying, conniving, perverted ex-husband. That's no small feat," chuckled Trisa. "You would've all been sent to Purgatory for sure if you hadn't stepped in."

"Ah... I was just at the right spot at the right time."

"You got our asses out of trouble a ton, James. Don't sell yourself short," smiled Xin.

"Mate, you definitely have to tell me these stories," said Chase, grabbing James' hand and looking him in the eyes.

His brown eyes widened, a moment of wonder in his eyes. He gently pulled his hand away, cleared his throat, and found a proper smile as he recounted their many adventures. The stories winded around, jumping from year to year as James thought of different things. He wasn't the greatest storyteller, but he absolutely loved it, and Chase hung on every word.

The pitcher on the table grew empty, and James hopped to his feet, offering to grab them more. He slid past Xin on the way, urging him to join. Xin seemed confused, but as was his way, he just shrugged, and joined. They headed over to the bar, where they stood in silence as the bartender filled their pitcher. Once it was full, James made no motion to head back to the table, so Xin shrugged, grabbed an empty glass from behind the counter, and filled it.

"I think Chase might be flirting with me," James finally blurted, and Xin inhaled the fresh drink in his hand.

After coughing up a lung to clear his throat, Xin laughed and clapped a hand on James' shoulder. "I really wouldn't doubt it. He's definitely not a one-track guy. If you're uncomfortable, just tell him to stop. He's pretty good about it."

"That's the thing… I think I like it," James said in disbelief.

Xin snorted out a laugh. "Well then, why are you here talking to me?"

"But… I like women, I love boobs…"

"You can like more than one thing. Honestly, with how close you and Yuri were, I'm surprised it didn't come up sooner."

"Well, I mean, we were never shy around each other, and we had fun in the same room together… but never with each other." said James, trying to dig a hole in the wood floor with his foot.

"You really don't need to explain," insisted Xin. "Just have fun. Do what feels right. No one will think less of you here."

"But… he seems pretty young. I am pushing forty, you know."

"Apparently, he's thirty-three," said Xin with a shrug.

James' eyes popped open. "Wh— he's older than you? How…"

"Not important," said Xin with a shake of his head. "What matters is that you both have a good time."

"Yeah…"

As James gazed at the counter, the gears in his mind working overtime, Xin chuckled, gave him another sturdy clap on the shoulder, and went to sit back down. He shot Chase a small smile, making the previously nervous man sit a little taller.

With a broad smile on his face, James came over, pouring their drinks, a hand on Chase's shoulder.

Xin couldn't help but smile at the two. Lorelei had mentioned that James had been pretty reclusive since she recruited him. That was odd. He always loved having people around him. Hopefully, being around Chase would help him find his old self.

"Ladies and gentlemen, I would like to thank you all for being so amazing," called Lorelei's melodic voice over the small crackling speakers. Everyone looked to her on the stage, arms wide. The crowd sent her a resounding awe and a round of compliments.

"Ah, shut up for a minute," she scolded teasingly. "As some of you may know, a small group of us have decided to go in search of the Holy Lands." The air filled with gasps and curious whispers, all except their table. Chase sat a little taller in his chair, feeling rather special. "I know, I know, it sounds like a fool's dream, and to be honest, it really is," she continued with a chuckle, looking over at him.

The smile faded from her face, her gaze furrowed as she looked back out at the crowd. "However, if there is any chance I can change the way this world is, I need to take it. Konstantin may finally be dead—" The crowd burst into a small round of cheers, "—but people like him are still out there. It is only a matter of time before the Angels find someone else to gather their slaves."

A sorrowful silence filled the room.

"We've all been through so much together, I am sad to say. We will be leaving much earlier than expected."

The crowd protested, not wanting Lorelei to leave them, being confused why she had to leave. Chase looked over to Xin, hoping for an explanation, but Xin just shrugged, just as surprised as him.

As the crowd calmed, Lorelei continued. "While not completely unexpected, the death of Konstantin has put me in the Angels' sights. Since I definitely will not be indulging their slave quota for them, I will likely be hunted by the Valkyries very soon. Because of this, we will be leaving in the morning."

Cries of objection rang through the air. James let out a sigh, slumping a little lower in his chair. With a small smile, Chase slipped his hand over to his, giving it a light squeeze, and received a pleasantly surprising firm squeeze in reply.

"Now, now, you all knew it was inevitable that I would ditch you all, anyway," Lorelei laughed, receiving a round of agreement.

"So now, let me sing you all one last song. Until we meet again my friends."

Right on cue, the band started playing a beautiful, soft melody, as Lorelei sang a song about friendship, family and times to come.

Chase scratched the top of his head. "I don't get it."

"What?" asked James.

"Wasn't Konstantin a pirate? Shouldn't the Angels be glad he's gone?"

"He wasn't just a pirate. He was the Angel's main supplier of slaves. Mostly in Yggdria, but he's sold everywhere. While he wasn't technically on their payroll, he basically worked for them."

"That's fucked up."

James shrugged. "It's the way this world works, unfortunately. Seems like the only way to actually change anything is to do the impossible. But you must know that. Why else would you be looking for the Holy Lands?"

Chase grinned that excited, boyish grin. "I just want the adventure and the chance to connect with all the amazing people along the way!"

James blinked.

Trisa's mouth dropped.

Xin burst out laughing.

After being bombarded by her loving crewmates, Lorelei could finally sneak away and join the rest of them at their table.

She flopped down beside Xin with a grand sigh. "By the gods, you'd think I was leaving on some sort of suicide mission, the amount of people that want to talk to me."

"Absolutely crazy," chuckled Xin. "It's almost like they care."

"Ah, bunch of softies. They won't even notice I'm gone, I'm sure."

"I wouldn't be so sure."

Lorelei laughed and shrugged, then sent her attention over to James, who was energetically, if not a bit drunkenly, telling a completely enamoured Chase about another tale of his time as a bounty hunter.

"Those two seem to get along pretty well, don't they?"

"More than you'd think," Xin chuckled.

"He's just been dying to talk about those days, hasn't he? Guess now that Konstantin's dead, it's a little easier."

"Yeah," he replied, the smile fading from his face. "How do you feel... now that he's gone?"

She stopped to think for a moment, silently grabbing a few chunks of food off of the table in front of her. After a moment, she replied, "Not that much different. More relaxed, I guess. It's nice knowing the Oasis is safe for a little while, at least."

"I'm glad."

"It was strange, though. The last look he gave me... Almost like he was proud of me. Maybe there was more to his offer than just power..."

"Maybe," replied Xin, unperturbed. He took a long swig of his drink and continued. "I mean, you said so yourself. He was basically like a father to you, as terrible as he was. Makes sense that he might have seen you as a daughter. You certainly accomplished more than his actual son."

She gazed into her drink, almost looking like she was going to throw up. "Did I do the right thing? After all these years... I've never second-guessed the need for him to be dead. Now that he is... I'm kind of regretting it."

"He was a big part of your life, good or bad. Of course it's going to be hard, but try not to regret it. I doubt he would have ever apologized for the people he took from you."

"Yeah..." She stared into her drink for a while, took a swig, and smiled at him. "How about you? Still feeling good about killing Viktor?"

Visions of ripping that man's head off flew through his mind, and he couldn't help but get a wicked smile on his face. He snapped himself out of it with a sigh. "Well, no regret, anyway. But it doesn't change anything, does it? My mom... my sisters... they're still gone."

"No, but it does keep someone else from suffering like we did."

"I guess so," Xin said solemnly, and not knowing what else to say, the two of them listened in on James' tale, instead.

"... So here I am, bandaged and broken, feeling like a right hero getting a kiss on the cheek from the cute school teacher and there's Yuri going to get it on with Freya!" shouted James with a huge laugh.

Chase was in awe. "Freya? The Angel Freya?"

"The one and only," he said proudly.

"I've never seen an Angel," Chase said, wide eyed. "What was she like? I hear the Angels glow. Did she have wings?"

"I didn't notice any glowing or wings, but she was the most beautiful woman I had ever seen," said James, practically drooling.

"Excuse me?" snapped Lorelei.

"Sorry Lorelei, you might be the most beautiful human, but Freya is an Angel! How can you compete with that?"

"How indeed..." Lorelei grumbled.

"Aw man, you shoulda seen Yuri when she was done with him. That was a happy looking bastard," said James in happy reflection.

Trisa, who had been listening to the tale with mild annoyance, stood up and walked away.

James took notice. "What's the matter, Trisa? Don't like my story?" His glare was unsteady and his words slurred. Apparently, the multitude of drinks had finally gotten to him.

"I'm tired. I'm going to rest," she replied curtly.

"What? You surprised to hear Yuri slept with other women? You're the one who dumped him. What, was he just supposed to pine for you?" James' voice grew louder and louder.

She clenched her fists and gritted her teeth. "I don't want to talk about it."

Lorelei placed herself between the two. "Alright, I think you've had enough to drink tonight, James."

James ignored her. "It's too bad. If you had just joined us after that Smuggler fiasco, we would have had no problem with Konstantin the first time."

Trisa twisted around, lunging at James. "What?!"

With her fiercest glare, Lorelei held back Trisa and looked James in the eye. "James. That's enough."

He didn't meet her gaze. He just continued to glare at Trisa. "Come on

Lorelei, like you weren't thinking it? Little Miss Prissy Captain here was so worried about her position in the Gaian army she couldn't be bothered with us little guys."

Trisa slammed her hand on the table. "It was my dream! Yuri understood that."

"I just find it interesting that it took Yuri fucking dying for you to come to your senses."

"You fucking asshole!" She twisted around Lorelei and grabbed James by the neck. She threw him to the ground and wrapped him in a headlock.

Lorelei desperately tried to break them apart.

Xin just watched with a broken spirit. Losing Yuri had affected them all so much and he had just run off on his own.

"'Scuse me, mister. Can you pass me some chicken?" said the voice of a child, gently tapping Xin on the arm.

Xin took a quick glance at the little one, glimpsing his bleach blonde hair. He couldn't have been more than five years old. Jia, the eldest of his three sisters, was only six when they took her from this world…

Xin snapped himself from his memories. "Yeah, sure kid." He grabbed a drumstick off the table. As he turned to pass it to him, he got a full view of the boy's face. Xin froze in his tracks.

Those eyes.

A rage bubbled somewhere deep inside him at the sight of them, but the boy didn't notice. He just looked up at the piece of chicken still out of his reach, then back at Xin, rubbed his chest in a circular motion and said as sweetly as possible, "Pwease?"

"Oh, yeah. Sorry kid," said Xin, snapping out of his stupor and quietly cursing himself for any sort of rage directed at this boy. He handed over the chicken, which the boy gratefully munched on.

As the screaming match continued on a few chairs over, Xin turned his attention slowly back to his still grieving friends.

"Why dey fighting?" the boy asked with concern as he seated himself in Lorelei's chair and helped himself to the food on her plate.

"They lost someone they both loved a lot and are still mad about it," Xin explained sadly.

"Why are you sad?" he asked, those big violet eyes looking caringly at Xin.

"Because I miss him, too," Xin said softly, and to his surprise, the boy jumped on top of him and gave him a great big hug. Memories of his lost sisters assaulted his mind. He embraced the boy tightly, letting the tears of the past silently roll down his face, and after a few tender moments, the boy pulled back and shot him a large, caring smile.

"Thanks kid. I apparently needed that," said Xin with a smile, wiping away the tears.

The boy thought for a moment and said, "You know what makes me feel better when I'm sad? Looking at the stars!"

"That right? Sounds like someone else I know…"

He held his hand out to Xin. "Come! I can show you all the cons… constell… star gwoups!"

"That sounds great."

It was a perfect night for stargazing. Not a cloud in the dark sky. The air was calm, and the waves lapped lightly against the hull of the great ship. A crow cawed nearby, inviting an eager Chrissy to promptly chase it away as Kari ran about in the distance, clearly busy with something.

The little blonde boy had revealed his name was Jack, and now the two of them lay head-to-head, gazing up at the beautiful stars.

"Dat's the big sipper!" said Jack proudly.

Xin chuckled. "I think it's 'dipper.'"

"Oh, yeah!"

"You sure know a lot of these."

"Miss Lowlei taught me. She is super smawt."

"She is." The smile faded from Xin's face. "Hey Jack, thanks for getting me out of there, but where are your parents?"

"I don't have any. Piwates killed them," he said matter-of-factly.

"I'm sorry. How old are you anyway?"

Jack proudly held up four fingers to the night sky. "Four!"

"Very cool," Xin said with a distracted smile.

Jack sat up and looked at Xin's swords lying beside him. "You can fight?"

Xin smirked. "Yeah. Pretty good at it too."

"Then fight!" cried Jack, jumping and tackling Xin. He honestly had not expected that, but he certainly wouldn't argue. That was exactly the kind of thing he and his dad would do.

As they play-fought, a pleasantly plump woman cautiously peaked her head around the corner. One could call her tall but that would be an understatement. She was a giant, half again as tall as the tallest man on the ship. Her wavy brown-black hair ran down just past her chin and she wore a simple flowery dress.

"Jack? Jack, where are you? Lorelei wanted all the kids away from the p—" She stopped short, seeing Xin with Jack in a headlock. Her eyes flashed red with rage.

"Jack!" she cried out in a deep, terrifying voice.

Xin jumped out of his skin, releasing Jack immediately, but it didn't matter. She charged, lifted him up, and tossed him away like a rag doll. Xin hit the rail hard, leaving him breathless.

"Who are you and what were you doing with Jack?" she growled, looming over the breathless man.

Jack pulled at her dress. "Miss Dana, we were just playing!"

"That's what they want you to think."

Xin coughed, regaining some breath. "No really. I'm—"

"Woof!" Unaware that anything was amiss, a grinning Chrissy came bounding towards the seated Xin and licked his face.

"Argh! Not again," Xin cried, fending off the licks with a laugh. He found his seriousness. "Sit."

Obediently, Chrissy stopped and sat down nicely, wagging her tail. Xin gave a laugh and petted her affectionately. "There we go. That's much better. Your breath isn't that great, you know."

The giggling Jack gave Chrissy a big hug, making her tail wag even harder.

With the beast satiated by the child's attention, Xin stood to his feet and looked up at the towering woman. It was an odd feeling for Xin. Few people were taller than him, especially not this much. He smiled, held out his hand, and she took it apprehensively.

"The name's Xin. Xin Romo."

Dana pulled her hands back in a gasp. "Xin? *THE* Xin?"

"So I'm told," he said with a chuckle.

"Sorry about that," she said, hands folded, staring at the ground. "I get a little protective of the kids."

"Don't worry about it," he assured her, picking up his swords and strapping them to his back.

Kari ran by, an excited grin on her face. "Come on Chrissy! Let's go get everyone else. It's time for the big show!" she shouted, apparently not caring about the rest of them there. Chrissy woofed and bounced off after Kari, that metal leg clanging as she went.

"I should go back with the kids," Dana said nervously. "I don't do great in big groups. Jack, come on."

"But I wanna stay here with Sin!" Jack pouted. Dana looked at Xin with worried eyes.

Xin chuckled. "It's fine by me."

The doors opened wide, and first out was a still fuming Trisa and a frustrated Lorelei. Lorelei's face quickly twisted into surprise—and perhaps a brief panic—as she spotted Xin and Jack standing together.

"Jack? What are you doing here? You're supposed to be with the other kids."

"Sowy miss Lowlei. I was bored and wanted to see you. But then you were in the fight, so the nice man came outside with me"

"That right?" She placed her hand on her hips, trying her best to scowl at him, but she was obviously holding back a small smile. "Have I taught you nothing about stranger danger? Do you even know his name?"

"Yeah! It's mister Sin, and he doesn't feel like a stwanger, and you seemed to weally, weally like him. You were smiling soooo much!"

Lorelei's ears went red as she could not come up with a response.

Xin laughed.

At the front of the crowd, Kari stood ready with a large button in hand, Chrissy patiently waiting beside her with a wagging tail. "Everyone ready?"

Lorelei picked up Jack with her one good arm and swung him onto her shoulders, causing the boy to brim over with happiness.

"Not really, but let's get this over with," sighed Lorelei.

"Here we go!" Kari pressed the button. After an intense moment of silence, a streak of light flew up, followed by a boom and a beautiful light filled the air. Again and again, the fireworks lit up the sky, and everyone watched with oohs and awes. Well, everyone except Xin, who seemed to enjoy the sight of Lorelei's face far more than the fireworks in the sky.

Lorelei caught his stare and shot a knowing glance his way. He looked away as nonchalantly as possible, but still watched from the corner of his eye. How could he not want to watch that smile? She was rubbing Kari's fluffy hair affectionately, congratulating her on a job well done as the final firework went off.

Then came the explosion, and Lorelei's hand met her face.

"Ah, shit," cried Kari. "Chrissy! Fetch the firehose!"

"Woof!" said Chrissy as she ran off obediently.

19

Set Sail

The morning sun peaked out over the still ocean, and Lorelei knocked at Chase's door, ready to go.

Rap, rap, rap.

"Chase! We're burning daylight. Hurry your ass up!" she shouted as loud as possible, unsure if he could even hear her.

"Yeah, yeah, I'm coming," yawned Chase, swinging his door wide open, revealing his completely nude self.

Lorelei scowled. "For crying out loud, Chase, there are children on this ship. Please answer your door with pants on."

"Oh, right!"

As he ran off to get dressed, Lorelei leaned against the door in a huff, then glimpsed James in Chase's bed, yawning and rubbing his eyes.

Lorelei shook her head in disbelief. "James?"

"Lorelei!" he squeaked. "It's not… we didn't…"

She laughed. "It's about damn time you got laid."

James' mouth hung open.

Chase, now fully clothed and sending a small chuckle James' bashful way, came back to the door.

"But you," she scolded Chase, punching him lightly on the arm. "You were supposed to take it easy."

"What? I'm fine. All healed, look," he said, lifting his shirt to reveal his wound, still fresh, but completely healed over.

Lorelei leaned in and looked it over, running a hand over it. She furrowed her brow, but not in an inquisitive way, more of a deep concern. Chase thought to mention it, but before he could, she stood up and looked at him with a grin.

"Damn, that is impressive. Think you could share some of that healing with me? This cast is a pain in the ass."

Chase laughed. "I wish!"

"Well, come on, the others are waiting. You have everything?" she asked, noticing his small bag slung over his shoulder.

"Hmm, I think so…" he contemplated, then his eyes lit up with remembrance. "Oh, one more thing." Dropping the little bag at the door, he ran over to James, who was working on re-attaching his prosthetic leg. With unexpected speed and grace, Chase dived in and gave him a passionate kiss, causing James to grin madly as he pulled away.

"You are an incredible, amazing man, and a beautiful soul. I cannot wait to see you again someday."

James had no words. He just smiled a glowing grin, his eyes sparkling with happiness. With another gentle kiss, Chase said his farewells and left an exuberant James in his room.

Lorelei waved to James, bidding him one last farewell. Before she could close the door, James said, "Lorelei. Bring everyone home safe, alright?"

She looked over at him, knowing full well what he was feeling. A handful of his closest friends were leaving on what would probably be a suicide mission. He didn't want to lose anyone else, but he knew there was no stopping them now.

"I'll do everything in my power to keep them safe. I promise," she breathed, and with another wave, she closed the door.

She took a deep, sorrowful sigh at the door, then glimpsed Chase's supportive smile. She looked into those eyes, full of child-like wonder, and gave him a teasing smirk. "Did you really pass up a night with the Dragon Ladies to sleep with James?"

"Ah haha, I guess I did," he said as they started strolling side by side. "Ah, the ladies were nice and all, but they were all about the fun. It's far more satisfying making a connection with someone, you know?"

"Yeah…" she said, unconvincingly. That was something she hadn't done in quite some time.

Chase chuckled. "Besides, he really needed an Ace in—"

"Don't you dare say that again," she scolded with a laugh, punching him in the arm.

The bright light assaulted their eyes as they stepped into the cheery morning sun on the deck.

"Oh, I almost forgot," said Lorelei, passing over Chase's belt. "We got it all fixed up for you. Should be flying ready."

Chase took it gleefully, equipping the belt, and turning the buckle. As his glider obediently attached to his back, he checked out the patchwork repair job with a grin. "Well, that's a much better job than what I did."

Lorelei chuckled. "That's what happens when you're not in a life or death situation. Plus, you know, a professional at it."

"Well, come on then," he said, nodding to his back.

She gave him a cockeyed look. "What?"

"It's a lot different when you're not in a life or death situation. Plus, you know, it's properly repaired."

Lorelei gave a loud laugh and jumped on Chase's back, wrapping her legs around his waist and her one good arm loosely around his neck.

Woosh came that pleasant, citrusy breeze, sending them up into the air. Chase soared through the masts and sails, dipping and weaving last minute to try to give Lorelei a heart attack. Finally, they got above it all, and Lorelei examined her home with a full heart. She made that happen. By the gods, she was going to miss it and everyone on board.

A tear came to her eye, and she hugged Chase warmly.

Only for a moment. They were in a hurry, after all, and she wanted to have some fun up here. Not needing to be convinced, Chase did loops and twists, making Lorelei's heart race in excitement.

"This is amazing!" Lorelei cheered. "Last time I was up this high was after I pissed off a Valkyrie. This is much better!"

After a few more exciting moments, Chase headed back down to the deck where Astrid and Xin were waiting and chatting, oblivious to the two in the sky. They heard, "heads up!" and snapped their heads up to the sound. Down came Lorelei, right into the surprised arms of Xin.

"Still good reaction time," she praised, patting him on the head.

He cocked an eye, but couldn't keep the smile off of his face.

As Chase touched down, Astrid strode up to him, wagging a finger. "What are you doing? You are supposed to—" She stopped as Chase raised his shirt, showing the mostly healed wound. She gasped and inspected it.

"So, I assume we're not taking this ship on our adventure," said Chase as Astrid continued to look over him, completely astounded. "Though that would be amazing."

"Nope," said Lorelei, sliding out of Xin's arms. "She is way too big to handle the seas in purgatory. I had our engineers recommission one of our ships specially for our journey."

Chase followed her to the rail, where a small, duel-mast, powder white, caravel ship floated happily in the water. On its stern, the outline of a lily held the words, *'Water Lily'*.

"We named her, *The Water Lily*. Just seemed right to name her after the woman that inspired all of this," Lorelei explained with a smile, bringing tears to Chase's eyes.

"You named her after my mom? Oh Lorelei, she's perfect!" he cried, and motioned to hug her.

She held up her hand. "Uh, uh. Rule number one for sailing with me is; no touching unless given express permission. This especially counts for hugs."

"Oh, okay, then. Can I please hug you for being so amazing?"

"Ha! Well, when you put it like that, alright." She opened her arms and Chase picked her up in a big hug, swinging her around happily. After a gleeful chuckle, Lorelei patted Chase to let her down. She dusted herself off and continued. "She's all stocked up and ready to sail and the rest of the crew should be on board. So, by your leave, *Captain*."

She still heavily-ladened the word with sarcasm, but Chase didn't care.

His grin grew wider and wider, his heart threatening to explode from his chest.

"I am so excited!" he finally cheered, pumping a fist in the air and hopping up onto the railing. "Holy Lands, here we come!"

Is this really to be my new home? Emir had arrived upon the Water Lily before anyone else, and he was going to make the most of it.

It was far smaller than he was expecting, but he supposed if their crew was small, that would make sense. Although it seemed strange that even though the ship itself was small, the doorways and stairs seemed oddly large. Still, they seemed to make use of every space. There was a room beneath the helm, which Emir would guess was the Captain's quarters. It certainly had the essence of their captain.

Below that was the kitchen, which was once again oddly large. The counters were almost as tall as Emir, and he would have to climb in order to reach the upper cupboards. In the same room was a large table, clearly where they would spend their meal time. Attached to that was a modest sized bathroom, with a gigantic shower and regular-sized bath beside it.

The rest of the rooms he discovered seemed to be properly sized. One was clearly the infirmary, filled with medicines and other such objects, as well as an examination table, and a small bed that folded up into the wall. Likely for the healer to sleep upon.

Next to it was a room that Emir initially thought was the arsenal, filled with different swords, spears, and things he wasn't even sure were weapons but certainly looked deadly. Then he noticed the small bed and vanity and realized it was a bedroom. Must be the Siren's.

The last room was a simple room with a few hammocks hanging about and simple dressers. He supposed this was where the rest of them slept.

Not quite.

At the last level, which he had only expected to be the cargo hold, a large section seemed to be dedicated to an oversized bed stuffed away in the corner. It was easily twice the length of a normal bed. How odd. Other than that was just a small workshop with another small bed hidden in the wall.

Well, he had explored the ship, and now his stomach was rumbling. Still no sounds up on deck, but he caught the occasional whispers coming from the bathroom. He did not recognize the voices. Apparently, the rest of the crewmates were not very punctual. He hoped that wouldn't be an issue in their journey to come. Still, it gave him a chance to… 'explore' the kitchen.

By explore, of course, he meant loot. He went through all the cupboards and drawers he could find to fill his pocket. Most of the food, of course, was in the cargo hold, but he spied a large cookie jar on one of the upper cupboards. Eagerly, he climbed up to reach it, and as he stretched, he suddenly floated up and could reach the jar. It took him a moment to realize the oddity of the event. He turned around slowly, seeing the giant face of a plump woman smiling at him, her massive hand holding him up by his vest.

"You must be Emir," she said. "My name's Dana."

Emir's hair stood on end. "Oh, most wonderful of giants, most gracious of creatures, please do not eat me."

"Why would I eat you?" Dana asked in confusion. "You'd taste horrible. I just thought I'd help you reach the cookies. Don't tell Lorelei you took those, though. She's pretty protective of her sugar."

"You are… not mad that I was stealing?"

"Stealing? You're part of the crew. This food's for everyone," she explained with a small smile, and Emir relaxed.

Now there were voices coming from above and footsteps descending the stairs. The giant gave a small gasp and swung Emir behind her back.

"Oh, there you are, Dana," he heard The Siren say with sickly sweetness. "I see you've met Emir. What was he stealing this time?"

"Nothing…" said the gentle giant.

"Dana…" Lorelei said, a clear warning tone to her voice.

With a sigh, Dana brought Emir in front of her as he innocently clutched the cookie jar.

"You little—Those are mine! No one touches my cookies," Lorelei growled, grabbing the cookie jar from him and bonking him on the head. Unpleasant, but far more gentle than their first encounter.

Chase stood, slack-jawed, gawking at Dana. "A giant! You're a giant!"

"Only part. My mom was much bigger than me."

"So how does that work exactly?" asked Chase giddily, and Dana just looked at him with confusion, not understanding the question at all.

Astrid shot Chase a nasty look. "Chase, that is not an appropriate question to ask someone you just met!"

"Alright, alright, I'll ask her later," he said, drawing a frustrated sigh from Astrid.

With a sweep of her hand and a renewed smile, Lorelei said, "Everyone, I would like you to meet Dana. She's our cook, and the sweetest person you will ever meet."

Dana blushed. "Aw shucks, Lorelei, you're too nice."

"We have a giant on our crew? This is amazing," cheered Chase.

"Guess that explains the size of the kitchen," said Xin.

"Seems like it would take a lot of resources to have a giant with us," Emir pointed out, making Dana's face fall in embarrassment.

"You're not wrong, 'insensitive one'," Lorelei growled, "but Dana is the best cook in these seas. Plus, it's good to have a giant on board in case we run into any of her kin. Giants aren't exactly friendly to humans, but they're not bad people. Just been treated like shit for generations. So Dana talks to them."

"And beats them up if they don't listen!" exclaimed Chase.

"Oh... no. I don't fight," Dana said abashedly.

"A giant... that doesn't fight?" Chase's shoulders dropped. "Aw man. I was hoping for bone crushing."

"I suppose I could crush some bones... If it makes you happy," she mumbled.

"Really?"

Lorelei sighed. "Dana... What have I told you about things like this?"

Dana dug her foot into the floor as she gazed down. "My thoughts and feelings come first."

"That's right."

"So no bone crushing, then?" Chase asked sadly.

Xin smirked. "Ah, you can leave that to me."

Lorelei started looking around, then asked, "Where's Bobby?"

"...In the... bathroom," said Dana

"Ah, he'll be in there a while. We might as well set sail."

"Wait, wait, who's Bobby?" asked Chase.

"Oh, the engineer. He'll take care of repairs to the ship. He's a bit on the old side, but he's pretty talented. He just... has some bowel problems. Come on, let's go out on deck."

They all complied.

All except Dana.

She watched the crew leave, her eyes nervously darting around the entire room to ensure no one else was around. Once she was sure, she went to the bathroom door and knocked. "We're taking off now Kari, won't be long now."

"Thanks Dana, I owe you one!" said Kari's excited voice on the other side of the door, followed by an excited "woof!"

"Shh, Chrissy."

"Well, well, seems like we have some stowaways," said Lorelei in a lighthearted voice. Dana's blood ran cold as she slowly turned around, but Lorelei wasn't there.

"We didn't get a chance to say goodbye!" said a young girl's voice from up above, and Dana sighed in relief and went to join the crew on deck. She got up to see the small group of children that had been living aboard the Oasis, as well as the children that had come with Emir watching eagerly to the side.

One of the older girls announced, "We prepared a song for you!" to Lorelei, who gave them a small smile.

"Did you? Well, let's hear it!"

The children began singing an adorable little song as Lorelei watched with a small smile.

As they sang, Astrid slid up beside Xin, an innocent smile on her face. "She acts like she doesn't care, but she's actually great with the kids. Whenever we weren't out hunting, she was teaching them stuff. She's pretty amazing, huh?"

Xin sent her a suspicious smile. "You still have a pretty active imagination, don't you? Are you trying to get us back together?"

"What? No..." she replied unconvincingly, as she continued to rock back and forth.

"Don't bother," Xin sighed. "Lorelei made herself pretty clear five years ago. I'm not going down that hole again. We're just friends."

Astrid looked sadly down at her feet. "I know your fight was really bad, but—"

"That's right. Lore said you were on the ship that night. I guess you heard everything then."

"Yes..."

He sent her a small scowl. "Then you out of everyone should know why it won't work."

Astrid looked up at him, those shimmering green eyes locking on to him. "I was there. Before, during... and after."

Xin's eyes widened, then narrowed. He searched her face, trying to figure out exactly what she meant by that. What did Lorelei do afterward? He had never really dwelled on that fact before.

Astrid just giggled at Xin's dumbfounded look, then sent her sweet, knowing smile over to Lorelei once again, as the kids gave a grand finale.

"Not bad!" beamed Lorelei. "But your timing was off, and the Altos were flat..." The kids' faces fell flat. "I guess I have no choice..." she sighed, causing the kids to look at her with confusion. "...I'm just going to have to make it back as fast as possible so I can keep teaching you."

The kids cheered, started coming in for a hug, but stopped.

"I suppose you're all going to want a hug." The kids nodded enthusiastically. She sighed and spread her arms out wide. "Alright, you get one."

With a full round of cheers, the kids came at her in a big group hug. "Oh, no! Ambush! Argh!" cried Lorelei as they swarmed, making the kids laugh excitedly.

They broke off, stopping by Astrid as well to give her a farewell hug.

All except Jack, who stayed with Lorelei, tears flowing down his face.

"Jack. What have I told you about crying? You'll get nothing from me with the waterworks show," Lorelei scolded softly.

"I'm sowwy Miss Lowlei. I can't help it. I don' wan' you to go!" The well of tears broke completely, drenching the boy's face and shirt.

Lorelei's face softened. She gave him a soft hug, drawing a look of confusion and surprise from Jack. "I need to go, Jack. I need to try and make this world a better place, for you… for all the kids. If I can really find the Holy Lands, and the treasure it promises, then I can do that."

Jack pushed away and stood tall. "I want to go too! I can fight!"

She clapped her hands on his shoulders. "Ha! I know you can, but I need you to train more first, alright?"

"Otay!"

"Good boy." She gave him an appreciative rub on his head and motioned for him to join the other kids off the boat.

He started, then stopped and looked back with wide eyes. "Miss Lowlei, can you make a wish for me?"

Lorelei smiled. "Sure Jacky, what do you want?"

"To see my pawents!" he declared, punching his fist in the air.

The smile vanished, and Lorelei snapped her gaze to the ground. "Some things are better left unknown. True family is what you make of it, Jack. Don't worry so much about who your blood is."

Jack just looked at her with confusion.

She looked back up at him with a strained smile. "Be a good boy while I'm gone, alright Jack?"

"Yes, ma'am," he said with a quick little salute. He trotted off to join the rest of the children.

Lorelei looked back to the group, where Xin was giving her a small smile.

"What?" she snapped.

"Looks like you've gotten better with kids."

"Tchah, well when they keep hanging around you all the time, you tend to get used to them." She looked around. "Where's Chase?"

Xin pointed down to the bow of the ship, where Chase was kneeled, head bowed and eyes shut.

"What's he doing?"

Xin shrugged. "Praying I think."

"Aw, that's so sweet," chirped Astrid. "It's been so long since I've seen someone do that. Everyone is so jaded on this boat."

"For good reason," Lorelei sneered.

"Oh, please don't give him trouble!" Astrid pleaded, but Lorelei did not slow. She strode right up to Chase and gave him an aggressive nudge.

He snapped his eyes open and looked up at her with that boyish grin. "Hey Lorelei, what's up?"

"What are you doing?"

"Praying to the gods for a safe trip," he grinned. "Gaia for good health, Ymir for calm seas, and Ra for good weather. I always do it before a journey."

"You know they don't actually care, right? They're not going to listen to you."

"What? Of course they listen. How do you think I found all of you? They've been helping me out for years, ever since mom died."

"Seriously?" she exclaimed, honestly taken aback. Of course, he didn't know what she had found out about him, and she wasn't about to give up that information, but how could he be so devout after all the things those priests did to him?

Chase laughed, stood up and set his tricorn back on his head. "Yep. There were a few rough years, but they always led me to the people I needed to be around. And here I am. So, I think I'll keep doing what I'm doing."

"But... our quest literally goes against the gods' wishes."

"No, it goes against the Angels' wishes."

Lorelei looked Chase over. "Aren't they basically the same?"

"Not really. The gods are pure, perfect. The Angels, while super powerful, are still part human, which means they can't be perfect."

"No one's perfect…" Lorelei grumbled under her breath. Chase cocked his head, unsure of what she had said. She shook her head. "Never mind. Do what you want. Just keep it to yourself."

"Right. Well, I'm done now, anyway. Shall we set sail?" Chase looked around. "Wait… is there enough of us here to sail this big of a ship? This looks like at least a ten person vessel."

Lorelei snapped her head back in a huge laugh and grounded herself with a smug smile. "Alright everyone, time to set sail, let's get this tub underway! Xin! Haul in the anchor. Astrid, Dana, clear the lines and sails. Emir, to the helm and on the steering wheel."

Just as they were about to spring to action, Chase shouted, "What? No. Emir! Haul the anchor, Dana to the helm… Xin… Clear the… sails?"

The crew looked around at each other, and as they slowly backed away, set to the tasks given to them by Lorelei. Even Emir, though with some confusion.

Chase's shoulders slumped as he looked around with defeat and betrayal.

Lorelei laughed, patted him on the shoulder, then opened a panel on the mast. Within were a few different buttons and levers.

"Chase, prepare to be impressed." With that, she pulled the largest lever, and after a few moments, the sounds of grinding gears filling the air, all the sails unfurled and snapped into place. Chase's mouth dropped in amazement as the sails filled, and the ship was underway.

Lorelei turned to Emir at the helm. "Set our heading for South-southwest. Chart a course for the Gaian's border checkpoint in the Rustic Ring."

Emir stood, hands on the wheel with a completely baffled expression. "I… what?"

"Don't just stand there looking useless—navigate. That's your job."

"It is?"

"Well, it is until we get to the border. If you can prove yourself until then, then I won't replace you."

"But, why?"

"Because, unlike everyone else here, I know who you are, Emir Kaur," she said with a deadly grin. "And I am curious if your father's skills have transferred to you."

Emir stood, looking at her with his eyes wide, mouth agape.

"So, can you do it, Kaur boy?"

He gathered his wits, nodded, adjusted their course, and began pouring over the maps.

20

Basic Training

In no time, the Oasis faded off on the horizon. The crisp morning sun glistened off the calm seas in front of them as the ship cut through. The seagulls above squawked their farewells, and Chase snapped himself from his amazement.

"Alright, that was cool, but we need to get one thing absolutely clear," said Chase, arms crossed. "I am the Captain. We already agreed to that."

"Yep," she said with a smile.

He flicked his arms open wide in frustration. "Then what in Tartarus were all those orders you were giving?" He looked around with a pouty glare. "And what was with everyone taking her orders over mine?"

"The anchor is quite heavy," said Emir.

"I didn't know what 'clear the lines' meant," said Xin.

"I've never steered the ship before…" said Dana with her head hung low.

Chase gave an exasperated sigh, then turned to Lorelei. "Well, you could have briefed me before we took off."

"Tchah. Where's the fun in that? Besides, we're in a hurry, remember? On top of that, you're new and untested. I am not giving you full rein over my crew until you prove yourself."

"Your crew? I invited Xin and Emir."

"Ha! Alright then, boss them around to your heart's content. The rest of them are under my care."

Chase stared her down for a moment, eyes narrowed, lip stuck out. Finally, he dropped his shoulder and gave a defeated sigh. "Alright, fine. What about our heading? I thought we were going to storm an angel fortress. Shouldn't we be going south?"

"We are going to enter an Angel fortress and borrow their portal, yes, but not in Yggdria," Lorelei explained. "We're keeping our crew small, so we can hopefully just sneak in unnoticed. No one in their right minds would enter an Angel's fortress uninvited. However, Odin knows my face, so it will be difficult to sneak in there."

Xin chuckled as he leaned against the rail. "Are you sure your boyfriend won't just let you use his portal?"

Lorelei scoffed with a small smile. "Again, with the boyfriend thing. By the gods, a guy gives a girl a silver hairpin once and suddenly he's my boyfriend."

"Wait, what? Did you sleep with Odin? Arch-angel Odin? Leader of all angels in Yggdria, Odin?" asked Chase, suddenly clinging onto Lorelei's loose t-shirt, his eyes sparkling.

"I did not! I would not." She slapped Chase's hands off of her. "That guy is an asshole. He uses humans as he pleases. He has no regard for life, hiding out in his fortress for three hundred years, thinking he's better than everyone else."

Chase's eyes glazed over. "Yeah, but I've heard he is drop dead gorgeous."

Her ears turned red. "Tchah… Alright, yeah, he's pretty good looking." Her shoulders relaxed and a small smile spread across her face. "And by the gods, he smells good."

Chase grinned and Xin regretted he brought it up.

With a shake of her head, she continued. "Anyway, it doesn't matter. He may have been entertained by me back then, but I've done quite a lot to piss him off since. Obviously, he won't be letting us anywhere near his fortress if he is willing to make me a wanted criminal. So, we go to Gaia."

"But Ratum is closer…" chimed Astrid, drawing a vicious scowl from Lorelei.

"We are never, and I mean never, going anywhere near the Ratum fortress."

Astrid put her hands up in the air. "Alright, alright."

"Besides, the Gaians focus so heavily on defending their borders, their fortress will be the least guarded."

Chase sighed and shrugged. "Alright, so to Gaia."

"Miss Lorelei, I have a question," said Kari from the back of the group, arm raised, Chrissy sitting happily beside her. The crew turned and looked at her with a mixture of surprise and confusion.

Lorelei, however, didn't seem to click with the oddity.

"Yes Kari?"

"Well, I was just wondering, why did you agree to let Chase be captain? You have more experience and clearly have more of a plan..." she listed, counting each on her fingers.

Lorelei sighed. "Well, first, if we're being honest, I've never been a fan of titles, and the Captain is only as good as the rest of his crew. For another thing, this is Chase's dream. Without him, we wouldn't be doing this. That and honestly, I'm sick of leading. I could use a break from deciding everyone's lives. I'd rather just give a guiding hand and..." Lorelei trailed off as she realized what was going on. Her twitching eyes focused on the girl.

"Kari..."

"Yes, Miss Lorelei?" Kari asked innocently.

A vein popped on Lorelei's forehead as she screamed, "What the fuck are you doing here!?"

Lorelei grabbed Kari by the ear. "Turn the ship around now, Emir. Kari is going back."

"Wait, wait! We can't go back. We already made our dramatic exit!" complained Chase.

Chrissy growled and whined in circles around them.

Lorelei glared. "And you brought your dog? Do you have any idea what we're even doing?"

Kari pulled herself away from Lorelei's grip. "Of course I do! That's why you need me and not Bobby! That guy would keel over halfway and you know it. Besides that, I can fix circles around him. I created this ship, not him. You know I'm the better engineer!" Kari proclaimed, standing proudly.

"You're twelve!"

"I'm almost thirteen! You were only eight when you started sailing!"

"On a ship of bloodthirsty pirates that kidnapped and raped people."

"Exactly! I'll be much safer with you guys."

Lorelei's shoulders fell in thought. "Tchah!" She threw her hands in the air. "You realize there is a very high probability that we will all die, right?"

"Of course I do," said Kari solemnly. "But I want to help change the world just as much as you. I don't want anyone else to suffer, either!"

Lorelei sighed in defeat.

"So am I turning around or not?" questioned Emir, ready to turn at a moment's notice.

Lorelei turned a finger at Chase, looking him straight in the eye. "You're the Captain now. You decide."

"Huh?" said Chase, thrown off guard by her decision. "Oh, okay."

Chase came right up to Kari, looking her over. Kari stood at attention, acting uncaring, but the sweat on her brow and nervous fidgeting told another story.

"So, you're an engineer? I saw your handy work at the party last night, but how good are you at ship repairs?" he asked, hand to chin.

Kari grinned. "I'm the best!" she proclaimed, then told Chase a ton of engineering mumbo jumbo, mostly about how she came up with the system that rigged the sails to unfurl, but Chase mostly just glazed over it.

After about five minutes, Chase said, "Alright, alright, you're definitely smart. What about fighting?"

"Well, Miss Lorelei taught all the kids a bit, but I wouldn't say I'm a fighter. I do have a lot of gadgets that can help in a fight, though."

"Really? Alright, I'm convinced. She can stay," Chase replied, his eyes sparkling.

"Yes! Thank you, thank you!" cheered Kari, wrapping him in a big hug, then made an odd nervous squeak and ran below deck.

Chase watched her run off with a chuckle.

"Don't look too pleased with yourself," said Lorelei, arms crossed. "Keep in mind her life is in your hands now."

"Man, you're such a downer. Just like Xin," pouted Chase.

Lorelei looked over to the observing Xin, who also had his arms crossed as he leaned against the rail. She uncrossed her arms as nonchalantly as possible and shook her head in annoyance. "Life isn't all smiles and jokes, especially in our line of business. You need to always be thinking ahead."

"But sometimes even the best laid plan can fall to shit. Sometimes you just have to roll with the punches and enjoy the small things life has to offer."

Lorelei glared at him for a moment and laughed. "Not bad, *Captain*. Not bad. Well, enjoy the small things for one more night. Tomorrow we start basic training."

Chase grinned wide. "You're going to teach me to fight?"

"That's right. Everyone here has already learned the basics, except you."

"Really? What about Emir?"

Emir sent a curious, hopeful glance over to them.

"Ah, he's special." Lorelei said with a grin. Emir's ears perked up, his shoulders held high until she concluded with, "I don't care about him."

Emir completely deflated with a sigh, grumbling multiple rude curses under his breath.

Lorelei just laughed.

The first beam of light cracked through the window of the Captain's quarters, and within his modest sized bed, Chase laid strewn out softly snoring. Upon his bedside table laid his bandana and hearing aids, which was why he did not hear Lorelei's insistent knocking at his door, nor her loud entrance to his room. He did, however, notice the sudden chill of the toasty blankets being torn from his naked body, his morning glory at half-mast.

His eyes snapped awake to see Lorelei's narrowed golden eyes glaring down at him, probably telling him to get up. He was still a little groggy. Lip reading took a lot of effort. His suspicions were accentuated by Lorelei throwing some clothes in his face and motioning him to follow.

With a moan, he rolled over, grabbed his hearing aids and put them in place.

"What time is it?" he asked the restless woman waiting at his door.

"Dawn. That's all that matters. I told you, training starts today. Get dressed."

"Or, you know, you could get undressed and we could do some warm-ups here," he grinned, patting the bed beside him.

"You've had better pickup lines," she scoffed, though a small smile lurked beneath.

"Ah, it's too early to think of good ones." He stressed his point with a yawn.

"Training. Now. And new rule: no flirting when we're training. Got it?"

"Alright." He looked at the clothes she threw at him and wrinkled his nose. "You want me to wear these?"

"That's right. You need something you can move around in. I figured your wardrobe might be lacking in that department."

"Where'd you get these?" he asked, throwing on a pair of his own underwear, then the loose pants, that disgusted wrinkle still on his face. They didn't do too much to hide anything in the morning wood department.

"They're mine. Figured we were about the same height, so it should work."

"These are girl clothes?"

"No. Well, not in the sense that they are designed for women."

Chase gave her a look over, examining her outfit of the day. Her shirt was so loose it covered down to her elbows and revealed most of her shoulder, as well as the chest wrap beneath. It also ran down so far past her backside that he hardly noticed the tight fitting shorts underneath. Was that a man's shirt as well, he wondered.

"Why do you have these?" he asked.

"Cause I don't always like to dress girly," she strained as her foot tapped a hole through the ground. "Now, if you want to keep talking fashion, you'll have to find Astrid later. For now, hurry your ass up."

After a quick stop at the washroom for a piss, and to make the pants fit a little better, Chase stepped out onto the deck, taking a moment to adjust his eyes to the glaring morning light.

A quiet calm filled the air as the ship swayed gently with the swell of the ocean. Only two of his crew were on deck at the moment. Xin, who was out on the bow, legs crossed and eyes closed, and Lorelei, who was busy stretching out in a full split that made Chase really glad he had already gone to the washroom. No flirting during training may prove to be an arduous task.

"What is wrong with you two? Why would anyone get up so early?" Chase whined as he trudged up to Lorelei.

"Xin is always up at the crack of dawn to start his morning meditation. Something his dad always got him to do. For me, I just don't sleep."

Chase looked at her with concern.

She didn't notice. She just jumped up to her feet straight from her splits and continued as if she had done nothing impressive. "Besides, being that we're on the run from Valkyries, we should all be up at this time. For today, I'll just pick on you."

Chase's shoulders dropped. Apparently, this would not be the only early morning wake up.

"Right, first things first. Horse stance." She stood tall, her fists at her side, and Chase attempted to copy. She made a large circle with one foot, then the other, widening her stance, and Chase did the same, just far less graceful.

"Like this? This isn't so bad," he said with pride, though the stance looked nothing like Lorelei's.

"Good, now stay there." She rose up and made her way behind Chase and forced his body into the proper place. "Toes forward, knees bent and over the toes. Good, now down."

"By the gods! Why!" cried Chase, his legs shaking almost immediately.

"Good, now hold it there."

Chase strained to hold, his legs shaking harder and harder. After about five seconds, he collapsed to the ground. "Okay, I'm done. I've decided I don't want to be a fighter."

"Up," she commanded.

"But—"

"Now!" Lorelei roared, and Chase complied with as much attitude as he could muster.

"Why can't Xin train me?"

"Horse stance," she commanded.

Chase obeyed.

She smiled. "You don't get the nice teacher until you pass basic training."

"So are you admitting that Xin is the better fighter?" Chase asked with a shit-eating grin that made Xin crack a smirk from his perch.

Lorelei came up close, an evil grin on her face, and forced his stance lower, bringing a fire to his legs. "You really want to piss me off? Just think about that for a minute."

"Sorry," he squeaked in pain. "Won't happen again."

After about a minute, Lorelei showed him the next stance.

After Chase complied, he asked, "Why are we doing this? Isn't fighting the best way to learn how to fight?"

"You can learn to fight that way, sure, but that way is trial and error. Besides, if you throw a punch the wrong way one hundred times, you'll just get better at a bad punch.

"Contrary-wise, if you learn techniques from past warriors, people who already went through the trial-and-error process to refine their skills, then you can become a better fighter far faster. This is how the world advances, by learning from the past, and building on what we know.

"For example, my style has been around long before the Calamity, even the arrival of the gods. The art has been refined to move your body in such a way that a simple flick of your finger can bring down a grown man. It does not rely on strength of body, like simpler arts."

"What?" Chase understood most of it, but the last part just did not make sense.

"Perhaps a visual. Oh, Xin…" she said sweetly, tilting her head back to the still perched meditating man.

He sighed. "You're not going to poke me, are you? That's the worst."

"Of course not. This is just a simple example," she assured him.

With a resigned sigh, he went up to Lorelei and faced off.

"Now, clearly, Xin is bigger and stronger than me. In a test of pure strength, he will win." To enunciate the point, she pushed against Xin with her one good arm, leaning in, putting her whole body into it. Xin stood firm and pushed her back with no problem.

"But, if you connect your body to work as one…" She placed herself in close, and without leaning or apparently making any effort, she gave a slight push of her hand and sent Xin flying to his ass. "…then you don't need pure strength anymore."

"Whoa," Chase gushed, his eyes sparkling.

"But you need to be able to do simple stances before you can get that advanced. For now, your stances are your base, your strength. A punch can be much deadlier with a proper stance with it," she concluded, giving Xin a hand up off the ground.

"What was Xin saying about a poke?" Chase asked.

Xin's face fell. "No, no, please don't."

"What? It's just a poke." As she smiled innocently, still standing in that relaxed stance, she jabbed a finger into Xin's gut.

Xin bent in half and groaned, "Argh, why?"

"But… What did you do?" Chase asked, cocking his head side to side. "There's no way a poke could hurt that much."

Lorelei strode up close, that same smile on her face, and poked him the same way. As soon as her finger touched him, it was like it didn't even stop. Like there was a drill going right through his gut and out his back. The pain was so great, Chase fell to the ground panting.

"You asked for it," laughed Lorelei. "So, are we ready to continue the basics?"

"Yeah, yeah, alright."

Back on the Oasis, James strode about the deck, whistling a merry tune with a huge grin plastered on his face. A grin that hadn't faded for three days. He waved energetically at the Dragon Ladies, who chuckled knowingly.

A crow cawed nearby, and his attention turned to it immediately. Where was Chrissy? She always chased these things off. Come to think of it, he hadn't seen Kari since the night of the fireworks. His leg was about due for some upkeep. Hopefully, she wasn't too busy.

James followed the cawing and came across the culprit sitting pridefully on the rail. He whipped out his revolver and aimed.

It cocked its head at James and cawed.

"Dammit. Calling my bluff, huh? Odin trained you well," James sighed, leaning against the rail beside it, gazing out at the ocean.

"Well, if you're looking for Lorelei, she's long gone."

"Caw."

"No, I'm not telling you where she's going."

"Caw, caw."

"You can beg all you want. It's not happening. It's your own fault working for a guy like Odin in the first place."

A strange silence filled the air. The chatter disappeared, even the sea seemed more quiet. James furrowed his brow, then felt hot steam against the back of his bare neck

His eyes widened.

Cautiously, he turned around, and the source he feared stood in front of him. A colossal, metal horse with glowing blue eyes, mechanical cogs whirring about its insides and steam pouring from its nostrils. Upon its back, it sported two enormous wings, along with a towering woman.

She looked down at him and smiled. "It's not all that bad."

21

No News is Good News

Over a week later, the crew was still sailing through Yggdria. Tensions grew. They received no news about Lorelei's criminal status, but at this point it was a blessing. Far better than being ambushed by Valkyries, anyway.

It was just after Stormday, but since they were getting further from the Forsaken ring, the storms were just a light drizzle here and there. The last pulse they had must have been a strong one.

Xin sat within the cover of the helm as Astrid looked over the wounds on his back.

"Looks like these are healing well. Probably good to start giving them some air," said Astrid, spreading over the last of the antiseptic cream. "If you're lucky, they shouldn't leave much of a scar. Your tattoos probably won't look quite the same, though."

"Ah, that was bound to happen at some point," he said with a shrug.

Astrid fidgeted and distractedly cleaned up her items. "I, umm... I couldn't help but notice the pattern..."

"Same as Lore's? Yeah. Konstantin said he'd give me some matching scars. Nice guy, huh? Glad he's dead." He couldn't help but sneer at his last remark.

Astrid gave a half-hearted chuckle. She sat with tight lips for a bit, looking at the large, jagged scar on his shoulder.

He glanced at her and laughed. "You know I'm not Lore, right? You're allowed to ask me about my scars."

"Oh… Oh, right," she giggled, visibly relaxing. "What happened?"

"That's where the mark of my school was tattooed. After my master decided to sell me off to slavery for the sake of his early retirement, well… I didn't like the idea of it being on me anymore."

Astrid gasped. "You cut it off?"

"Yup. Hurt like hell, but I've never regretted it."

"Why didn't you cover it up with this tattoo?"

"I like the reminder of why I need to train my body. One day, when I'm strong enough, I'm going back home and giving that man a piece of my mind."

"You're not strong enough now?" Astrid asked, quite skeptical. Xin was the second strongest person she knew, and apparently this master was old enough to be retired. It didn't seem like something to worry about.

Xin laughed. "Maybe… not likely, though. That man killed Arch-angel Burr in his prime."

"What? Why isn't he in Purgatory? Or dead?"

With a shrug, Xin replied, "Some kind of deal with Odin to make him Arch-angel. Not sure on the details."

"Wait, wasn't Burr Odin's father?"

"Yep."

"Odin had his father killed? Oh my goodness… Lorelei's right. He really is an asshole."

Xin burst out laughing just as Lorelei came up from below deck.

"What kind of backwards world did I just walk into? Astrid making Xin laugh? Is that going to be a thing now?"

"Maybe, maybe not," chuckled Xin, standing and stretching up, then motioning to put his shirt back on. He paused as he glimpsed Lorelei doing a quick glance over his body. He held back a smile, tossed his shirt to the side, then went into workout mode.

With a restrained smile of her own, Lorelei sauntered over to the opposite side of the deck and began her own training, standing in a low stance and making circles with her good arm. It looked rather silly, but Astrid knew it was how she trained her centre. What wasn't part of the training was the constantly distracted looks she sent Xin's way. Astrid couldn't help but giggle.

In the meantime, Chase was sitting at the edge of the boat, making small whirlwinds in the water, confusing a school of fish with sighs of boredom. "Emir! Are you sure we're not lost?"

"No way, Captain. I'm sure of our path. It's just a really long journey. It will still be about a week, assuming we don't have to stop for anything."

Chase gave a big disappointed sigh.

Emir walked over to the control panel on the mast to unfurl the sails, but was met with, "What are you doing?"

He looked over to Lorelei with a furrowed brow. "Uh, setting us on course?"

"Idiot. It's Pulseday. We don't unfurl the sails until the pulse goes by."

"What? We didn't do that last Pulseday."

"It happened when you were all still sleeping. You know it happens at random times."

"Right..."

"Are you really sure about him, Lore?" asked Xin, making no secret about his question as he easily did his one hand pushups. "If he doesn't kill us with incompetence, he might just steer us right into the enemy, looking to collect the Bounty on our heads."

"I would not!" cried Emir.

"He really wouldn't," chuckled Lorelei, doing what she figured was another sneaky check out of Xin. A small giggle from Astrid told another story.

Xin sighed and switched hands. "I just don't get it. I thought we were meant to have the best navigator in order to make it through Purgatory."

"I don't like him either, and he's certainly new at this, but he's not incompetent. Before we left, I had my navigator put him through a bunch of tests..."

"You did?" asked Emir.

Lorelei ignored him. "He passed them all with flying colours."

"I did?" Emir asked, now with a prideful smile.

"He knows what he's doing. He's just never done it before. Besides, if he fucks up there are a few others I can call in."

Emir's shoulders slumped with a sigh. Still though, that pride in his chest didn't fade away. He passed a test from The Siren.

Xin laughed and shook his head. "Alright, I trust you. Just don't want us to go and starve 'cause of that guy."

"We will not starve because we are not lost!" insisted Emir.

Astrid giggled. "Well, as long as we don't let Lorelei navigate. We really did almost starve when that happened."

"Hey! It was one time. And what have I told you about telling people about my mistakes?" Lorelei growled playfully.

Astrid sighed. "To be honest, though, I think I would have chosen starvation over your cooking."

"Oh, no. Lorelei cooked for you?" Xin gave a booming laugh. "How are you still alive?"

"I must have an iron stomach," she giggled, giving her stomach a little pat.

"Hey. It's not like you two are perfect." She pointed to Astrid. "You're so trusting you've gotten kidnapped three times..." She turned her finger to Xin. "...and you're completely useless in a sea battle. You literally wrecked all our cannons the one time you tried."

"Yeah, well, no one showed me how. You all just expected me to know," he objected, easily hopping to his feet and standing his ground with a smirk. "Besides, my skills are meant to be up close and personal."

"I suppose you are quite talented at being up close and personal," she purred with a smirk of her own, sliding in close to Xin.

"Damn right," he smiled, leaning in even closer. "I've been told I'm the best, you know."

"That right? By more than one person?"

"Maybe."

They stared each other down for a long moment, locked in each other's eyes with a smile curled upon their faces. The connection was short-lived, as that familiar pulse came upon their boat. It was completely transparent, but they could see it coming from the small wave it created in the waters, and the clouds that were pushed back with it. It rocked the boat, tousled about anything that wasn't strapped down, and went on its way out to the edge of their world.

The sun shone uninhibited, and Xin and Lorelei noticed, almost in unison, that two pairs of eager eyes were watching them. An exuberant Astrid and Chase stood nearby, leaning in and grinning madly at the pair.

"What?" they snapped in unison.

"That smile!" Astrid chirped, looking at Lorelei.

"I…" said Lorelei.

"And Xin's not all bashful with the flirting," chuckled Chase.

Xin's face went red. "You—"

Wide-eyed, the flirting pair snapped their gaze back to the other and took a couple careful steps back. Ever since they started sailing, they seemed to make a conscious effort to avoid each other, and the sudden realization of that unspoken rule being broken caused Xin's face to turn a beautiful shade of red, and Lorelei to scratch her head. They both sounded a respective "tch" and "tchah" then went their separate ways. Xin returned to his workout routine. Lorelei told Emir to set sail before grabbing her guitar.

Disappointment flowed through the previously exuberant pair with a grand sigh. With a shrug to each other, they also went about their own projects. Astrid went up to Xin, apologizing and asking if he would train with her. He agreed readily, being very curious about her fighting style. As the two sparred, Chase slid up to Lorelei as she was frustratingly trying to figure out how to play her guitar with a cast.

"So, you and Xin have some serious history, huh?"

"Yeah, we do," she sighed, flipping her guitar around to use as if it were left-handed.

"What happened?" Chase asked gently.

Lorelei sighed again, Chase's calming scent filling her senses. She looked at him, her cast arm resting uselessly upon the guitar, then looked over to

Xin and Astrid training.

"I took on a fight I couldn't handle. Bad things happened. We lost one of our best friends. I had a breakdown, said some terrible things and stranded Xin and James on an island."

"So… Are you planning to hook back up with Xin now?"

Lorelei snapped her gaze from Xin to Chase and back again, her ears turning slightly red. "I…" she began, unsure of what to say, then let out a hearty laugh, as if she were not just flustered by the question. "No way. That guy is all about commitment. That's not who I am. There are way too many guys I haven't slept with yet."

"Too bad for Xin, I guess," sighed Chase, sliding in a little closer, letting his knee touch hers. She shot him a knowing smile. "It really would be a shame to bottle up such radiating beauty to just one person. A gift such as yours should be shared with the world."

"Tchah, cut it out," she said playfully, giving him a nudge on the knee. "I already told you I don't sleep with crew mates. That first night was the only exception."

"Aw, man," Chase said, his shoulders slumped. "Alright, if that's really how you feel. Keep in mind, we had quite a lot of fun. Plus, there is no commitment required here," he concluded with a grin, motioning to himself up and down.

"Well, that's true," she chuckled, putting the guitar down and sliding in closer.

A little way off, Xin noticed the interaction between the two of them, sending his focus away from his sparring match.

Clunk

"Ouch! Son of a…" Xin cursed, rubbing his head where Astrid's staff had struck.

"Oh, my gosh! I am so sorry."

"Don't be. It was my fault," he assured her with a smile.

Astrid looked over to also see Chase and Lorelei getting friendly. She smiled knowingly at Xin. "You're not jealous, are you?"

"What? Don't be stupid. Lore doesn't take any of that stuff seriously.

Why should I?" he said, but his flushing cheeks told another story.

"If you say so," she said with an exaggerated sigh. "I suppose I could see those two together. They're both really flirty, and Lorelei does like to joke around in the right instances. Maybe she needs a guy like Chase."

"What? No way," Xin snapped. "Chase and Lore wouldn't last. He's way too care-free. She'd get sick of him in no time."

"I don't know. A good sense of humour goes a long way," she chirped.

"I have a sense of humour!"

Astrid started giggling uncontrollably at the comment. "What happened to not caring?"

Xin sighed, his eyes wandered to the floor, and the red hue from his cheeks rescinded. "All I've ever wanted for Lorelei was for her to be happy. If that means she ends up with Chase, then so be it." After a moment of contrite silence, he looked back up to Astrid. Tears streamed from her eyes.

Xin was thrown for a loop. "Are you crying?"

"That… that is so beautiful," she sniffled. "I'm going to hug you now."

"Uh… okay."

True to her word, she wrapped her tiny arms around Xin in a big hug. He chuckled, and she looked up at him with a beaming smile.

"Alright, I'm team Xlor all the way! Hmm… team Lorin?" she said, thinking hard on what their combined name should be while Xin shook his head.

Suddenly, a loud *squawk* sounded from the upper deck followed by, *thunk,* "Ouch!" then incoherent grumblings from Emir.

"Oh, good!" Lorelei clapped her hands together. "A Paper Pelican. Emir! Grab a paper!"

"What? How?" asked Emir, looking at the strange pelican with beady glass eyes and whirring cogs everywhere.

"Bloody land boy," mumbled Lorelei.

Paper Pelicans were sent out around the rustic ring to give merchant sailors the news. That meant they were definitely out of the Forsaken Ring. Emir may not be used to sailing, but at least he could navigate.

"Just put a coin in its butt. It will spit out a paper!"

Emir flinched away from the creature, giving it a look of utter disgust. "I have to do what?!"

Lorelei scoffed. "Oh, grow up, it's just a machine."

Emir pulled out a coin from one of his many pockets and looked at it longingly. "You are going to reimburse me, correct?"

She gave a loud, exasperated sigh. "By the gods, fucking cheapskate. Fine, I will pay you back. Just hurry up before it takes off."

Emir took the coin, studied the bird's rear for a moment, and inserted the coin after discovering the slot. The bird turned its head to Emir and seemed to give him a… look. Could birds smile? Could mechanical birds smile? Were those hearts in its eyes?

"Umm… Why is it looking at me like that?" Emir asked nervously, not taking his eye off the unnerving creature.

"It's a machine, Emir. It doesn't give looks. Now hurry up and throw me the paper!" scolded Lorelei from the lower deck.

Emir looked around and realized no one else was in view of the creepy bird. It spat out a rolled up newspaper, which Emir reluctantly took. With a wink, it flew off.

He shivered with disgust and threw the paper down to Lorelei. "Please never make me do that again."

Lorelei unfurled the paper and laughed. "You got two papers for the price of one? Sorry Emir, I think you'll have to be our paperboy from now on!"

Lorelei passed one paper over to Xin and studied hers, mumbling as she went.

"Shit!" she finally cried. "It's been reported already. 'Lorelei The Siren and Xin the Executioner have been charged with murder of an Angel Representative. They are both to be considered highly dangerous and are now on Yggdria's most wanted. If you encounter them…' blah blah blah… Tchah. Angel Representative." A sneer curled upon her face. She shrugged and let it go. "Still, though, at least he didn't release the name. Means the rest of the nations might not be pissed at me, yet. Thank you,

Odin. Still means we need to hurry. It's going to be really tricky getting past the border with so many wanted criminals on board. Hugo is not going to like this." She continued to mumble more and more as she walked off below deck.

Chase watched her go with growing concern. "Uh…"

"Don't worry, she does that when she's thinking. She'll be back and tell us about the plan eventually," Astrid assured him.

"So, who's on the most wanted list? The way Lorelei was talking, it's more than just Xin and her." Chase got a glimmer of hope in his eyes. "Am I on the most wanted list?"

Xin just chuckled and held up a newspaper article, mentioning another mispronunciation of Chase's name, with a small blurb about him being a cheater. Nothing more.

"You're barely a criminal."

"What? Oh man. This is not going to be good for my bad boy reputation," Chase sighed, making Xin and Astrid laugh at his misfortune. "Alright then, who else is wanted?"

"Not me! I've been a good girl. They haven't given me any trouble, yet," giggled Astrid.

Xin shrugged. "Not sure about anyone else. Didn't see anything."

"Kari is… Well, she's not a criminal," said Astrid. "I don't know much about Dana though… She's usually not one to come along on the adventure, especially if it requires going to Gaia."

Inside the cabin, Lorelei continued her mumblings while examining the paper. She looked up to see Dana staring out the porthole, taking deep exaggerated breaths and wringing a washcloth repeatedly.

"Dana."

Dana jumped in surprise, nearly hitting her head on the ceiling. "Lorelei!

I didn't hear you. Are you alright? Can I get you something?" Dana rambled on, still wringing that washcloth.

Lorelei smirked. "She asks as she's having her own meltdown."

"I... I'm sorry. I just... I don't know if I can do this, Lorelei. It's been almost ten years since I've been to Gaia. It's not safe for you all to have me along. This was a ridiculous idea."

"Don't worry, Dana, I have a plan to get us all across. We'll be fine," said Lorelei with a soft, reassuring smile.

"N-no," Dana stammered. "I should just go. Or you should just turn me in at the border. You'd all be better off—"

"You listen and you listen good, Missy," cut in Lorelei, grabbing her nose and pulling her down to look her in the eyes. "You are no less important than the rest of us. There's more than one wanted criminal on this boat. It was your decision to help us make the world better. And what about that wish you wanted to make? It's too late to back out now."

Dana's lip quivered. "Right."

Lorelei released Dana's nose and stood tall, finding her best commanding tone. "Now, you know I don't like making you do something you don't want to do, but dammit Dana, I will not let you turn yourself in. Is that understood?"

Dana gave her head a nod, a small smile creeping on her face. "Yes ma'am"

Out on deck, as the rest of the crew discussed the paper and their reputations, an odd noise pervaded the air. As it grew louder, it seemed to be that of flapping, as well as gears and hissing.

Emir took cover under the table and groaned, "Aw man, don't tell me there's more of those weird mechanical birds."

Xin snapped his eyes to the sky. "No. That's—"

A shimmering figure dove from the heavens, landing with such force that the entire ship heaved to one side, and the deck cracked beneath it. The crew stumbled around as the ship swayed back and forth.

A great, steaming, mechanical, blue-eyed horse stood towering above the crew, its giant wings stretched out as it reared up on its hind legs, letting out an ear-piercing, unnatural whinny. It rescinded its wings and kneeled down, letting the armoured woman on top slide off.

She sauntered to the crew, her perfectly formed, shining silver armour clinking with each deliberate step. She stopped a few paces away from the recovering group and removed her winged helmet. The woman with neatly tied silver hair and lightly lined facial features glared down at the crew.

Chase looked her up and down with doey eyes. "Wow, talk about an entrance. And such beauty."

"Where is she?" the woman asked with unbendable sternness.

Chase dusted himself off, and with a flourish said, "I don't know who 'she' is, beautiful angel, but by all means you can have me."

"Do not test me, boy. I am looking for The Siren. Tell me where she is now."

"Lorelei? What do you want her for? I don't think she's into women," said Chase, scratching his head.

Finally, Xin had had enough of his ridiculousness. "By the gods, Chase, you are such an idiot. That's Sigrun, the leader of the Valkyries."

Sigrun looked him over. "Oh, Xin. It's good to see you again. I will deal with you later. First, tell me where she is."

"Not here. You have the wrong ship," Xin insisted, his hands hanging by his side, itching and ready for action.

"I don't have time for games."

Chase looked back and forth between the two as dawning finally fell. "Wait… Have you come to take Lorelei? No way! She's one of my crew now. You can't take her already."

With desperation, not malice, Chase reached out to the woman. Before Xin could warn him otherwise, Sigrun punched Chase in the gut, sending him into the air. She roundhouse kicked him into the rail, leaving him stunned.

Xin drew his one good sword (the other still broken from his battle with Konstantin) and stepped between her and Chase, ready for combat. They stood eye to eye, just waiting for either to make a move, until a loud "Ha!" sounded from behind him. Within the doorway leaned Lorelei, munching on a cookie.

"Oh Xin, darling, you're not really thinking of fighting Sigrun, are you? Even with the both of us combined, I doubt we'd stand a chance."

"Tch…" He sheathed his sword.

Lorelei finished her cookie, dusted off her hands, and went right up to Sigrun. As she looked up at her, staring unflinchingly into Sigrun's hazel eyes, she asked, "How in Helheim did you find us so fast?"

"I have my ways, and I know you well," Sigrun replied with a stern seriousness about her.

"So what now?"

Sigrun didn't say a word. She just glared down at Lorelei, and Lorelei returned the glare, unflinching. The entire ship sat in tense silence.

22

The Valkyrie

Sigrun was the first to break their staring contest. She broke out into a huge smile, unable to contain her joy any longer, and scooped Lorelei up into an enormous hug.

All mouths fell open.

"Argh! Not more hugs," complained Lorelei.

"I'm so happy you finally killed him!" Sigrun cried in a far more relaxed tone of voice, squeezing Lorelei harder and harder.

"Can't… breathe…" wheezed Lorelei, and Sigrun dropped her to her feet.

"Sorry," she said with a chuckle. "It's just been so long since you started this. Lin would be so proud."

Lorelei gave her a thankful smile. "Thank you, Sigrun. That means a lot."

"Wait, wait, wait," interrupted Chase, still attempting to catch his breath from his beating. "So you're not here to take Lorelei away?"

"No," said Sigrun, still looking at Lorelei. "I do suggest you leave Yggdria as soon as possible. You've pissed off a lot of the other Valkyries, and they will jump on this chance to take you out."

"I know, I know. We're working on it." A smug grin crept over Lorelie's face. "First though, I've gotta know. How pissed were the Angels about Konstantin?"

"Ha! Immensely. They absolutely hate change, and Konstantin had been around longer than I have. Plus, now they have to talk to other dirty humans to find their next supplier. So, yes, they were not impressed."

"Good," said Lorelei, her head held high.

"Oh, but Odin did tell me to tell you he hopes you haven't reached your peak with this stunt, and that he quite enjoys watching your shenanigans, as annoying as they are."

"Ha, well then he'll love my next trick," said Lorelei, drawing a raised eyebrow from Sigrun. "Tchah, never mind. You can tell Odin that if I catch any of his crows spying on me, they will become a dog toy."

"Alright," she replied with a laugh, followed by a soft sigh. "Well, I suppose I should be off. I just wanted to congratulate you."

"What? No way! You can't leave yet," Chase objected. "I've never met a Valkyrie before. I have so many questions. Surely you can stay for supper! Dana is an amazing cook. We'll have a party!"

"I really should go. I am a busy woman…"

"Which is exactly why you should relax!" said Chase.

"Chase's right, Sigrun," said Lorelei, nudging Sigrun's arm. "You just got here. You have to be exhausted from flying all this way. Besides, it's been ages since we've talked."

"I suppose…" said Sigrun.

"Great! Chase here will show you around his ship. I'll let our cook know to expect one more."

"Absolutely!" Chase said, shooting a charming grin up to Sigrun, then offered an arm out to her. She took it with an unsure smile and he led her off, fist bumping with Lorelei behind his back as he went by.

"So you're Chase's wingman now, huh?" Xin said to Lorelei as the two walked off.

"Well, I didn't see you stepping up to the plate. Unless you were hoping Chase would flirt with me some more."

Xin turned a frown.

Lorelei chuckled. "Besides, Sigrun works too much. She could use a break. I think Chase will be good for her."

Xin shot her a smile, and they stood in an awkward silence for a moment.

The silence broke when a distracted Kari came up on deck and almost fell into the hole Sigrun and her mount had made.

"Ga! What the hell?" Kari shouted, followed by a "woof!" from Chrissy. "Xin! Did you put another hole in the deck?"

"I did not!" Xin looked at Lorelei. "I did that one time. Is she going to blame me every time now?"

"Probably," laughed Lorelei.

Kari looked up to see the magnificent mechanical beast standing completely still, the steam no longer flowing, its eyes dark. Her face lit up with excitement.

"Is that… is that a Valkyrie mount?" she squeaked, practically vibrating.

"Don't you even think about tampering with that, Kari," Lorelei scolded.

"No! No, no. I just want to look at it. That's all!"

"Look with your eyes, not your hands. Got it?"

Kari's shoulders slumped with a big sigh. "Yes, Miss Lorelei."

"Emir!" shouted Lorelei, and the thin man peaked out from behind the mast.

"Yeah?"

"Keep an eye on her."

"What? Why me?"

"Were you planning on spending time with the Valkyrie that takes wanted criminals to Purgatory?" she asked knowingly.

He gave a great defeated sigh. "No."

"Then that's why. Come on Xin, we have a party to put on."

Xin cocked an eye at Emir, shook his head, and followed along behind Lorelei.

Later that night, the crew (minus Kari and Emir) sat together with Sigrun at the dinner table, the fantastic food from Dana sitting happily in their guts. Now the table was filled with a variety of drinks, the crew a little tipsy from the celebrations.

Chase sat on one side of Sigrun, with Lorelei on the other. Sigrun had removed her armour, and now sat in the simple black clothing that was underneath, her body broad and muscular. The crew laughed and joked, telling tales of their adventure with Konstantin, and the events that led to his demise. After some time, Sigrun placed a strong, caring hand on Lorelei's shoulder.

"I stopped by your Oasis before I came to find you. I can't believe how much it's grown. You have done so many good things. I was so worried about you after poor Yuri died. I'm so glad you found your own path."

Those words brought a smile to Lorelei's face.

Sigrun took a large swig of her drink, and leaned in, trying to whisper, but ultimately failing. "And I saw the boy. He's gotten so big. What did you end up naming him?"

Xin's ears perked up. Lorelei glanced his way, unsure if he had heard Sigrun's comment. He looked deeply into his drink.

Lorelei sighed and said, "Jack."

"It's a good name," said Sigrun, leaning back.

Lorelei leaned over to look at the infatuated Chase. "Hey Chase, how about you grab us some more drinks?"

"Yes ma'am," he said with a salute, and ran off.

"So, what do you think of the *Captain?*" Lorelei asked with a nudge. She still wasn't able to say it without a hint of sarcasm, even when she really tried.

"He confuses me. He is clearly the most inexperienced, yet you follow him."

Lorelei let out a frustrated sigh. A sly smirk slid to her face. "Alright, I'll tell you a secret, but don't tell Chase. Way I see it, Captain is just a fancy title. The Captain doesn't really have the power over the ship. The quartermaster, yours truly, decides how to divide up the bounty, decides punishment, everything like that. Why would I give up the actual position of power for a fancy title?"

Sigrun burst out into laughter. "Oh, you are too much like Lin, Lorelei.

Always have some sort of trick, don't you?"

Lorelei shrugged. She leaned into Sigrun, giving her forearm a squeeze. "Anyway, that's not what I meant. I mean, what do you think of him, you know, as a man?"

"Oh… I'd rather not say," said Sigrun, her fair cheeks turning a slightly pink hue.

"Aw, come on. You don't need to be shy."

Sigrun looked over at Chase, thoroughly examining him as he poured their drinks. "He is interesting… And quite charming. However, he is a bit young."

"He's older than he looks, but either way, you should give him a chance. Talk to him. And don't worry so much about properness, especially not on a ship of outlaws."

Sigrun sat in consideration.

As Chase returned with the drinks, Lorelei quickly downed hers, stood up, and said, "I need some fresh air. You two kids have fun." With that, she headed up the stairs and onto the deck.

Without missing a beat, Chase passed Sigrun her drink with a charming smile, and she flushed once again. This sort of attention wasn't familiar to her, but she absolutely loved it.

As the sun sank lower, Kari was still examining the amazing feat of engineering in front of her. She had never gotten the chance to examine one of these up close and was going to use every second she had. As she laid underneath the creature, examining the inner workings as best she could without touching, she sighed with amazement.

"Oh, that must be the power core," she said, seeing a faint blue glow within its chest cavity. "I wonder what they use. I always thought it was coal, but there is no way coal would last as long as these things can fly. Fossil fuel maybe, but there's no exhaust, plus it is super rare. Hmmm... Maybe I could just..." She reached her hand inwards, and Chrissy put a paw on her lap. She looked at the worried eyes of her pup and sighed.

"I know, look, don't touch. I suppose it's for the best. We don't want to accidentally blow up Sigrun."

"That would be very bad for all of us," confirmed Emir.

Kari jumped so high she conked her head on the horse's belly. "Dammit Emir! Why are you so damn sneaky all the time?"

"I am sorry! I can't help it."

Kari growled. Then her stomach growled. "Oh. I've forgotten to eat again, haven't I? I suppose I should grab something."

"Please bring me something, too."

"Couldn't you just sneak in?"

"Perhaps... but I'd rather not risk it," he sighed.

"So you're a criminal, huh?"

"Y-yes, well... When my love and I ran off together, an enormous bounty was placed on my head. I—"

Kari shrugged. "Whatever. Don't really care. I'll bring you something back, I guess."

With that, Kari and Chrissy ran off into the cabin, passing Lorelei by on the way. With assurances that they touched nothing, Lorelei let them go and made her way over to her training dummy.

She started with light drills, working on her accuracy and technique. With each strike she became increasingly frustrated, and her dummy turned into that violet-eyed bastard Mikhail, mocking her, calling her useless, stupid. Harder and harder until the dummy threatened to shatter. Suddenly the dummy changed into that violet eyed little boy back on the Oasis, and she stopped in her tracks, fist still poised but unwilling to continue.

A soft cough from behind her snapped Lorelei from her mind. She glanced back to see Xin leaning against the cabin, watching her train, and a small smile crept to her face.

"Still got that smoker's lung, eh Xin?"

"Tch..." he replied with a smirk, rolling the toothpick in his mouth back and forth.

"Well, are you just going to stand there and stare, or are you going to join?"

"You sure you're up for that, one arm?"

"Ha! I could take you on with no arms. Bring it big and broody," she chided, bringing up a taunting finger.

He rolled off his jacket, tossing it against the mast, leaving him in just a t-shirt. "Thought you'd never ask."

Together, they started some light punching drills, which continued to escalate into something more complicated, each trying to throw the other off until it turned into a light sparring match. They had each learned new things over the years, and the absolute giddiness in each of them learning to overcome their new techniques made it feel like old times again.

Lorelei went to knock Xin over, but he didn't budge. "Oh! Looks like someone's been working on his centre..." She adjusted in the other direction, sending him falling to his ass. She pinned him to the ground, a smile on her face. "...but not quite good enough."

Xin returned the smile, kicking one of her legs out and reversing the pin, successfully getting her underneath, while avoiding landing on her broken arm. "Or maybe I still know the best way to sweep you off your feet."

Lorelei bit back an excited smile. "Tchah. Smart ass," she breathed. He leaned in a little closer, accidentally pressing on her cast, making her wince with pain. He pulled away, standing to his feet, leaving a mildly disappointed Lorelei on the ground alone.

"Sorry," he said, though he wasn't sure if he meant for the arm, or for something else.

"Don't worry about it," she sighed, sitting up. She took the hand he offered her, but as she stood up, she flipped him onto his back with a twist of his wrist.

Xin laughed as he recovered from his winding. "Not done yet, huh?"

"No way," she said with a mocking smile.

Below decks, only Sigrun and Chase remained, still happily chatting away over a few drinks. Sigrun gazed toward the stairs, hearing the clear sounds of Xin and Lorelei's sparring.

She smiled softly. "I'm quite impressed you had the power to bring Xin and Lorelei back together. I don't think I have ever seen such a powerful… no, such a perfect team."

"What can I say? I have a tendency to bring souls together that are meant to be," he said, running a hand over to hers.

She pulled back and looked him over with confusion. "Why… Why are you interested in me? I am far older than you, and far stronger. Does… does that not intimidate you?"

"Intimidate?" he asked in disbelief, then laughed. "No way. If anything, it's a turn on. The strength of your body and spirit, it's incredible. And age? Age is just the number of years of experience we've had on this Earth. I don't believe it should necessarily be a blockade for mature, consenting adults."

Sigrun laughed, that pink hue turning red. She shot him an appreciative smile. "Thank you. Few men seem to think the way you do… And if I were to be honest, it is quite draining some days. Obviously Lorelei recognized that," she said with a sigh. "I almost never take time to myself."

Chase slid his hand a little closer to Sigrun once again, and this time, she reciprocated, a bashful smile on her face.

"I think the more we end up taking on in life, the harder it is for us to go back to simplicity," said Chase. "I think we all need that sometimes. To let the weight of our everyday life melt away." His fingers entwined with Sigrun's and came up to his lips to kiss them softly. "I'd like to help you with that, if you'd allow me."

He spoke so softly she needed to get in close to hear him, and she didn't mind. As she searched his face, examining every detail, she found herself completely enamoured and baffled by him.

"I think I would like that very much," she whispered, bringing a smile to his face.

He kissed her hand again. "Well then, beautiful angel, would you care to join me in the Captain's quarters?"

"Aye, Captain," she said with a warm giggle.

After about an hour of sparring off and on, Lorelei and Xin sat side by side against the mast.

"I forgot how much fun it is to spar with someone your same level," panted Lorelei. "The past five years I've just been training beginners and killing."

"I've just been killing," said Xin, and they both had a small chuckle. Xin thought for a bit and asked, "Have you really not sparred with anyone? There has to be someone on that ship that could take you on."

"Ha, not really. Even if there was, they were all too… I don't know, intimidated, I guess."

"Even Trisa?"

Lorelei burst out laughing. "Well, I guess after tricking her, kicking her ass and tossing her in the ocean, she never really seemed too keen about fighting me again."

"You did what?"

Lorelei sighed. "Not long after I left, Astrid told me she was abducted from the Rustic Ring. Of course you know what that meant."

"Jace was up to his old tricks."

"Yep. Trisa had been promoted, and was doing border patrol. Jace got his nice cozy position back as captain and continued his transactions with Konstantin as the Smuggler. So, I convinced Trisa she needed to seduce her wonderful ex-husband to trick him into revealing himself to the Angels, knowing full well she wouldn't be able to…" Lorelei shook her head and sighed. "I had just told her about Yuri… and she still wanted to help. I knew she wouldn't be able to, but I did it anyway. I used it to my advantage. I betrayed her, beat her up, tied her in chains and threw her in the ocean, all to gain Jace's trust."

Lorelei glanced over at Xin, his mouth hung wide open.

"Oh… she was fine. The chains were tied to a small boat with a couple of my… 'employees'. Anyway, I got Jace's trust, managed to figure out all his contacts and got a nice shipment of Blessings from the garden for my… 'employees'."

"You gave black market Blessings to people? Isn't that dangerous?"

"Very. The garden is supposed to pick the fruit for you. Eating something random can really fuck you up. But everyone knew the risks. I didn't force anyone into it. A few went mad, one died on the spot… but it worked out in the end… I guess."

"Your plans usually do."

"Yeah…"

Silence filled the air, broken only by the small waves crashing against the hull. A chill wind blew, and Lorelei shivered.

"Still not used to the cold, huh?" asked Xin, stretching over to grab his jacket.

"Guess not," she replied, rubbing her bare arms. Xin's all-so-familiar jacket appeared around her shoulders. She pulled it around her, a small smile on her face as she breathed in. It had no particular fancy smell, it just smelled like leather and Xin, and to her, it was the best smell.

Xin relaxed back against the mast, glanced over at her, then back at his knees. He started fiddling, making circles with his fingers, then took a deep breath.

"Hey… Lore?"

"Yeah?"

"Will you tell me about Jack?"

Lorelei's face fell, and she pulled the jacket tighter around herself. "There's nothing much to tell. I found him on a pirate ship after I killed the whole crew. We took him in. That's it. There's a bunch of other kids on the Oasis. You don't seem concerned about them," she said, a hint of annoyance in her voice.

"None of them have his eyes."

Lorelei sat in stunned silence.

Xin glanced at her and sighed. "It's alright. You don't need to tell me. But I'm here if you need to."

A soft smile crept to her face, and she laid her head on his shoulder. "I know," she whispered, then slowly drifted off to sleep.

The crisp morning breeze lightly caressed Lorelei's cheek as the first rays of the morning sun lit her face. With a happy sigh, she opened her eyes, only to be confronted by two faces, one furrier than the other.

"Argh! What the fuck?" Lorelei cried, starting the sleeping Xin awake beside her, and sending Kari and Chrissy jumping back in surprise.

"Sorry Miss…" Kari said abashedly. "It's just, I don't think I've ever seen you sleep."

Lorelei looked over to Xin, who was now stretching and yawning, then looked at the jacket still wrapped around her shoulders. Kari and Chrissy watched her expectantly.

"Well, I do sleep, obviously. I just…" She trailed off as she glanced back at Xin. "Ak, why am I even trying to explain this?" She stood up and threw Xin his jacket and stormed off inside the cabin. Xin slipped his jacket back on, watching her go with a small smile. Now, however, the curious eyes of the two young ones watched him.

"So what? Did you drug her?" Kari spat, causing Xin to snap his gaze to her in confusion.

"What? No! Of course not. We just fell asleep after training. She… I… never mind," said a flustered Xin, who also stormed off without further explanation.

"Adults are weird," decided Kari with a sigh, and Chrissy gave her a woof of agreement.

The morning sun reached into the Captain's quarters where Sigrun laid nestled up against Chase's naked chest, a soft smile upon her lips. As the light caressed her eyelids, her eyes shot open, and she leapt out of bed.

"Shit! I overslept. I need to go," she said as she scrambled up her clothing off of the floor.

Chase yawned, rubbed his eyes, and watched the woman with a smile. Slowly and calmly, he made his way over to her, holding out her shirt. She paused, and took it from him slowly, looking his naked form up and down multiple times. He ran his hand along her arm, causing her to bite her lip.

"Are you sure you need to leave already?" he asked softly.

"I really should… You should all be leaving as well. It's not safe for you here."

He pulled her in close, running a hand through her silver hair, and every muscle in her body relaxed. She gently dropped her clothing to the floor and let herself come in closer.

"Are you sure you're not going to get in trouble for not taking us in?" he asked, those sky-blue eyes sparkling with concern.

She shook her head gently. "I should be fine. No one needs to know I was here. I can lead them off your scent and—"

Chase kissed her gently, and as he pulled away, a small sigh of pleasure escaped her lips.

"I guess you should get going then," he said.

"Well… I am already late…" she whispered, leaning into him for another passionate kiss, gently urging him back to the bed.

Later, the crew met up to send Sigrun off. She stood centre deck, once again dressed in her shimmering armour, this time accompanied by an unbreakable smile upon her face.

Lorelei nudged her knowingly. "Did you have a good night off?"

"The best…" Sigrun sighed dreamily, sending another smile Chase's grinning way. "Thank you for convincing me to stay."

"Well, I'd say any time, but we actually have some important business I'd rather not get you involved in."

"Still not going to tell me what?"

"Still working for the Angels?"

"Ha! Well, just remember, next time we meet I will have to take you in." Sigrun's face turned serious as she said, "I'll do my best to mislead the rest for now, but make haste to the border. Thank you all, and I hope you fare well on your quest, whatever it may be."

In one swift motion, Sigrun swung her leg over her mount and clicked her sabatons into the stirrups. The creature flared to life and steam poured from its nose.

Kari watched in awe.

Sigrun sent them all a farewell wave, sending an especially warm smile to Chase, and took off into the sky.

Chase looked to Lorelei, wanting to thank her for her help with Sigrun, but found a surprisingly serious face instead. Before he could say a word, Lorelei started barking orders again.

"Right, the party is over, everyone. Let's get a move on. We were fucking lucky with Sigrun. We can't be here any longer than we need to be. Emir, make sure we are still on the best path. Kari, I need constant tabs on the ship to ensure we are at full sailing capacity. Chase, I need as much wind as you can make to keep us at full sail. If we do this right, we should be able to make it there before next Pulseday, understood?"

All the crew agreed and ran off to their jobs. All except Chase.

"Lorelei! I thought…" He stopped as he looked into Lorelei's serious eyes.

"I know Chase, but right now, you need to trust the experience your crew has over you. Your time will come, but for now, we can't piss around. Understood?"

"Yeah, alright." He glided up to the crow's nest, where he filled the sails.

23

Into Gaia

A few more days went by, the crew working almost flawlessly together day and night to move things along. By the time they reached the border, they were so exhausted the crew could hardly appreciate the majesty of the sight in front of them.

The Angels of Gaia almost all had some sort of power to control the Earth. For some, it was controlling plants, for others the dirt and rock. With this power, they were able to create their border. This border consisted of a sheer cliff face, reaching as far as the eye could see and stretching up at least twenty ships into the sky. Within the wall lay a huge gate surrounded by a large barracks woven into the cliff face and multiple battleships lying in wait.

"Ah, there she is," sighed an exhausted Chase, leaning up against the mast. "Home sweet home."

Over the last few days, Chase had by far taken the brunt of the workout. He never had reason to constantly use his power so much, and it burned him out to the core.

"Wow, are you sure this isn't the Divine Wall?" asked an awe-inspired Kari. "It's massive!"

"Ah, this has nothing on the Divine Wall, but it is still quite impressive, I'll admit," said Lorelei with a tired smile, then turned a concerned eye to Chase. "Are you sure you want to do this Chase? You've been working really hard, why don't you let me handle this one?"

Chase turned a scowl and pushed himself off of the mast. "No way! You agreed to let me do this one. I want to prove myself already. I know I can do it."

"Alright, alright," she chuckled. "Do you remember what I told you?"

"Of course! Something to do about a kinky power and something else..." he replied with a yawn.

"You listen and you listen good," spat Lorelei, pointing a threatening finger at Chase. "I have brought my very best crew and I expect you to keep them safe. You wanted this test. You are going to use it to prove you are worthy to be Captain, do you understand?"

"Yes of course," he said with a teasing grin. "I was just codding you. I know this is important. Gaia takes their border defense insanely seriously. Because of that, only the best soldiers are sent out to guard them. In the Rustic Ring there is only one entrance to Gaia and it is guarded by Gaian soldiers who have all received Blessings. Most of the soldiers will only have mild Blessings to increase their strength or speed, but the man who leads them is General Markham and his Blessing allows him to control ropes."

Lorelei shot him an impressed smile. "That's right. Well done," she said, rubbing the back of his head appreciatively, consequently knocking off his hat.

"Argh! Not the hair," he whined, then diligently returned everything to its rightful place. Though they had been sailing together for a couple of weeks, Chase still was not very comfortable flaunting around his hearing aids.

"Speaking of..." said Chase, giving Lorelei a sudden appreciative look-over. "Your hair looks amazing."

"Uh... thank you," she replied uncomfortably.

"Hang on. What are you wearing?"

Lorelei gave him a cockeyed look. "Uh, clothes?"

"No... you're wearing sexy clothes. Cleavage shirt, tight pants, and do those boots have heels?"

"Tchah. Barely."

Chase got up closer, his once tired eyes now alive with curiosity. "And you waxed your eyebrows." He gave her a look up and down, his grin growing wider as his eyes travelled downwards. "What else did you wax?"

Lorelei growled and pushed his face away from her. "Would you stop? Do you have a point? Am I not allowed to get dressed up? We're supposed to look like we're crossing the border, not preparing for a fight. You're not judging Xin for not having his swords."

"I know, and that makes sense, but I happen to remember you mentioning that you only wear a certain lovely lacy bra on important occasions," he grinned, pointing out the ever so subtle but noticeable bra peeking out of her shirt. "So who's the lucky bloke?"

"Tchah. Never mind that. This is supposed to be your plan, and it better be good."

"Of course it is!"

"And it would be?"

"A secret," he grinned, finger to his nose.

Lorelei sighed. "Alright. I'm only going to say one more thing. Keep in mind these men aren't evil bloodthirsty outlaws like Konstantin's men. They are soldiers doing a job. And with that in mind..." She climbed her way up into the crow's nest. "...I will be a silent observer today."

"WHAT?" Chase cried. "But you're one of my best fighters!"

"But I've come down with a terrible sickness," she snivelled, accentuating her point with a fake cough. "Hope fighting wasn't your only plan. Good luck, *Captain!*"

Chase sighed with defeat. "Set course for the entrance."

Xin leaned over and whispered, "So do you actually have a plan?"

"Nope. Totally just winging this," he replied with a grin.

Xin smirked. "Oh, this will be fun."

As the crew approached their target, the gate opened to make way for a large battleship. As it came closer, the crew saw it was swarmed with neat and orderly soldiers standing at attention along the rail. Their white and green uniforms were a simple soldier outfit, not necessarily meant for combat, but for looks.

The ship slid along next to them and laid the boarding planks down onto the tiny *Water Lily*, canons aimed and ready. An important, but young looking man stepped down the boarding plank, his jacket looking as if it had come straight from the tailors. He stood in front of the crew, shoulders back, and asked with a stern and condescending tone, "State your name, and your business coming to Gaia."

"My name is Chase Burke, and I'm returning home to Royal Derry," he announced with his typical flourish.

Standing slightly behind the leader was a smaller man, with thick glasses and a slight hunch to his back, a huge book hugged to his chest. Upon the revelation of Chase's name, he promptly opened the book, filled with the tiniest of writing, and thumbed through until he got to one page. He showed it to the main man, the man Chase assumed must be General Markham.

"Hmm… Chase Burke. Ah, here you are. Also known as Chase the Act? That's an odd name."

"Are you codding me? They even wrote it down wrong? It's Chase the Ace!" he cried, exasperated.

"Well, whatever the case, it looks as though you have some criminal charges. This means you will not be granted access across the border."

"What? They're minor annoyance charges, nothing serious."

"Apologies, but our job is to keep criminals from entering our borders, whether they're born Gaian or not." With that, they started to head back to their ship.

"Please," Chase said intensely, his head lowered. "It's been so long since I've been home. After my ma died, I wanted to explore the world, and I know I got in some trouble while I was doing it, but I really just want to go home. I want to see my ma's grave again."

All eyes soften onto Chase. Even Xin looked over to him with some care, not sure if he was pretending at this point or not. The man holding the book pushed his glasses up in thought. He whispered something into the important man's ear, who furrowed his brow and looked at Chase with a tilt of his head.

"Are you Lilian Burke's son?"

Chase's eyes lit up, that usual toothy grin returning to his face. "Yes! That's right. Lilian Rose Burke, priestess of Artemis."

The leader's eyes lit up, and a scattered handful of soldiers broke into large smiles. "Really? I knew Lilian! She was the one that inspired me to join the army."

"She saved my life when I was a baby," said the bookman with a soft smile.

The other scattered soldiers gushed about how Lilian had helped them or their families before she passed away, and Chase couldn't help but tear up. Xin gave him a little nudge, and Chase looked up to see a small smile upon his face. With a nod of his head, Chase snapped out of it and continued on with his half-cocked plan.

"I'm really glad my ma helped so many of you. If I could..." he started, but they were already way ahead of him.

"Alright, I'm sure we can make an exception for you."

"Really!?" Chase exclaimed. "Thank you!"

"We would need to do a full search of your ship and your crew. Any illegal items will be confiscated."

"R-right, of course!" Chase said, his nerves starting to get the better of him.

The important man gave out orders to different soldiers while Chase stood nervously. He really didn't think any of this through. Well, he had gotten by with luck so far.

At least Lorelei was hiding, but what would he do about Xin, and he knew nothing about Kari and Dana, nor Emir, for that matter. Lorelei knew all these things, not him. Why didn't he just let her do this? He took a look around at his crew. Xin and Astrid seem quite amused by the situation, while Dana looked like a nervous wreck, with Kari supportively holding her hand. Emir was... nowhere to be seen. Well, that was possibly good, he supposed.

Things seemed to go smoothly for Dana and Kari. Apparently, their papers were all in order. The book-wielding soldier came up to the hooded

Astrid, cocked his head, then gave an excited smile. She giggled and gave him a shushing finger. With a smile, he moved on to Xin.

"What's your name?" the book man asked.

"John Smith," said Xin without missing a beat.

"John? What kind of ancient name is that? Sheesh," he said, adjusting his glasses, then examined the ledger. "Hmm… I don't see anyone by that name," he muttered, continuing to thumb through.

A soldier beside him with a spear strapped to his back, dressed in white and green leather armour, (as was common amongst the flora and fauna heavy nation of Gaia), examined Xin up and down. "Say… you look familiar."

"Uh… he's just got one of those faces," Chase assured him, making Xin crack a small smile.

The book man also gave him a thorough examination. "You know, I think you're right… Feels like he's missing something, though."

"Now, now lads," Chase laughed nervously. "You keep looking at him like that, you're going to have to buy him dinner."

Xin sent Chase a nasty scowl, which was apparently all the men needed to identify him.

"That's it! You're Xin the Executioner!" exclaimed the spear man.

"Wh— no way! You're right. By the gods, we are big fans, Mr. Executioner. We've heard so much about you!" cried the book man, making Xin blush a little.

The man with the spear leaned in, eyes wide, and in a hushed voice asked, "Is it really true that you ate a man?"

"Tch… well, yes, but not 'cause I wanted to. It was for survival," he stated, and their curious eyes bore into him.

"What happened?"

Xin sighed. "Well, I was out hunting this mark and got caught in an avalanche in the process. It killed my mark and broke my leg, so I was stranded on the mountain for three days. Seemed stupid to go hungry with the guy right there, so I cooked him up. Would have been fine if a group of hikers hadn't shown up just as I was chowing down on his leg like a drumstick."

The soldiers who were listening intently burst out in laughter.

Chase nervously joined in the laughter, clapping the book soldier on the back. "So, since we're all good here, we'll just head on through the border, aye?"

As the men calmed their laughter, the book soldier wiped a tear from his eye and said, "Sorry, Mr. Burke. We can do a lot of things to push limits, but Xin Romo is one of Yggdria's most wanted. Not only can we not let you pass, we're going to have to report you to the Valkyries and hold you here until they arrive."

"What?" cried Chase. "But… What about my ma?"

"Well, if you play your cards right, we might be able to keep you from being taken by the Valkyries, but trying to smuggle wanted criminals is a serious offence. It's a shame you didn't follow closer in her footsteps."

Chase furrowed his brow, the carefree smile gone and replaced by an uncharacteristic anger about him. "Xin. Plan B."

"What's Plan B?"

"Force."

"Aye Captain," Xin replied, that bloodthirsty smirk about him.

Spear guy grabbed for his weapon, but Xin collided the two soldier's heads together. Both went down.

Chase gave a cry of frustration, sending a whirlwind punch to the suspected General. Into the ocean he went. Another sweep of his arm conjured a plow wind, forcing the battleship away from theirs and upheaving their cannons.

"Dana, Kari, Astrid, get the sails unfurled," Chase commanded. "Xin, hold them off until we get through the border."

All hands snapped to attention following orders. Kari released a few gadgets from her bag, which flew up to the top of the mast, untying the ropes. Chrissy bounded about doing what she could do to help, tripping up confused soldiers. Dana worked on reaching the lower level mast, Astrid ready at the controls, and Xin went around knocking out any soldiers trying to interrupt their work.

Chase flew up to the wheel and aimed the bow to the gate. As soon as the sails were ready, he conjured a gale, sending them flying away from the battleship.

Only for a moment.

The *Water Lily* lurched to a standstill. Above them, Chase saw thick, winding ropes reaching out and engulfing their sails, tying them to the mighty battleship. From its source stood a grouchy, gruff looking soldier, his green and white jacket hanging off his shoulder, rather than done up nicely like all the rest. The shirt underneath was unkempt and the buttons were not properly done up. Wrapped around his one shoulder was a ring of rope.

A rope lifted the uptight soldier, who Chase had assumed was the General, out of the water and beside the gruff, terrifying man.

"Thanks General," coughed the fake General, wringing out his jacket.

"That's General Markham?" squeaked Chase.

Astrid giggled, "Yep."

"Wait, you knew that other guy wasn't? Why didn't you say so?"

Astrid shrugged. "You never asked, silly. How was I supposed to know?"

Chase let out a frustrated cry. "This isn't over. Xin, cut the rope. We can still get out of this."

Xin shrugged, pulled out his swords from a barrel, and got to work.

Astrid gasped a small "Oh, I wouldn't…"

Up went the sword. It tried to strike down, but Xin's hands were completely immobilized. As he tried to squirm away, so became the rest of his body. He grumbled then slumped in defeat.

Another cry of frustration escaped Chase's lips as he sliced at the biggest clump of ropes with his hand. A sharp gust flew out, fraying a few of the ropes, but not enough. No chance to try again. Ropes slithered around him, wrapping him up tight.

A makeshift rope staircase came down from the battleship, and with it, the gruff General, lighting up a cigar. He glared about the deck, ordering those not tied up to sit, and they complied. He sneered as he walked up to Chase.

"You've interrupted my nap, kid."

Chase put on his best puppy dog eyes. "Look, I really don't want any trouble. I just want to visit my ma's grave, that's all."

"Mhmm, and for that you need Yggdria's bloody mercenary Xin Romo, huh?"

Chase looked from the cockeyed Xin, to the skeptical General, and back. "Well… He… We… We're in love! We can't go anywhere without each other."

Xin's face turned beet red. "What?!"

The soldiers stared skeptically between them. They all burst out into laughter, except for the still grouchy General.

"Take them all in. I don't care if they're criminals or not," he growled, still staring Chase in the eye while the soldiers got to work arresting the crew.

Chase's eyes became desperate, sweat pouring from his every pore.

"No, no, no! I've just started. You can't take my crew from me already! I won't let you!" From that scream, the winds whipped around violently, knocking soldiers from their feet and overboard. The continuous gale coming from Chase twisted above and to the horror of all aboard, a funnel cloud formed.

24

General Markham

e's lost control. Fuck. Why... Why did I push him so hard? This is way too much power. I hope I'm not too late, thought Lorelei as the looming funnel cloud grew closer to their ship.

Chase seemed oblivious to the screams and pleas from his crewmates, his focus now solely on the General. Soldiers darted about, trying to flee back into their ship to sail away from the destruction that awaited them. General Markham, however, had not flinched from his stare-down of Chase.

"Call it off," he growled, the smoke from his cigar billowing about them.

Chase didn't respond, he just continued his glare.

The General wrapped a rope around his neck, pulling it tighter and tighter, but still the rage in his eyes refused to fade. The tornado grew ever closer, the winds still whipping about the ship in pure chaos.

Through the screams, a soft, calming melody floated down from above. The soldiers stopped in their tracks, looking up to the voice that they all knew well. Lorelei slid down on a rope from the crow's nest, coming between General Markham and Chase.

"Lo—"

Lorelei held up a silencing hand to the General. She looked straight into Chase's eyes, forcing his gaze to hers and removing the rope around his neck. "Chase. Look at me," she demanded over and over, both in voice and sign language. After an intense moment, Chase seemed to finally click that she was there.

"Lorelei?" The funnel cloud began to recede.

"You did good, Chase, but I think I'll take it from here," she said, once again both in words and sign language, a soft smile on her lips.

His lip quivered. "But… the test."

"I have some notes," she teased, "but all in all you did good, Captain." Finally, there was not a hint of sarcasm at the word and Chase beamed. With that, the tornado dispersed and the clouds cleared away.

Now that the real danger was out of the way, Lorelei turned her flirty grin to General Markham. "Hugo, Baby, could you please let my boys go?" she asked sweetly, running her hand through his ashen brown hair. He scowled, looking at the two tied up, then over at the other three watching intently. His eyes lingered on Dana, a scowl forming ever larger.

With a large, annoyed sigh, he turned his attention back to Lorelei. "You can't be serious. You've done some pretty fucking crazy things before, but this takes the cake. You can't possibly think I'll let this man go. He's a menace."

"Hey, Xin might be grouchy, but I wouldn't call him a menace," quipped Chase, apparently unaware of the chaos he had just caused. All eyes looked at Chase in disbelief, and he returned a confused look.

Lorelei shook her head and tried to find that flirty smile again. "Tchah, he's a puppy that needs some training, that's all," she assured the General. "Everything is fine, and everyone is calm. Let's talk in private, and we'll get everything figured out." Her hand ran gently up his chest, then to his mouth, where she snatched the still burning cigar and put it out on the mast. She tucked it gently in his front pocket.

He gave a small scoff. "I am not taking my eye off of—"

Lorelei laid a soft finger on his lips, making him look her dead in the eye. "Please, Hugo," she said with a stern seriousness. "I want to talk with you. Chase will stay here, sitting very nicely, not moving a muscle. Right, Chase?"

"Huh? Oh, yeah, sure," he replied, still very confused.

Hugo sighed and released Chase and Xin from their binds. He glared at

Chase, glanced over once again to the ever silent Dana, and back to Lorelei.

"We definitely do need to talk," he conceded, wrapping his arm around her shoulders. Before they left, he turned his head and said, "But if I get any word of funny business on this ship while we are gone, I will not hesitate to burn it to ashes. You are all to remain on deck. Is that clear?"

The crew nodded.

Away the two went up into the huge ship, while the crew watched with mixed reactions.

Chase chuckled giddily as he watched the two walk off. "I knew she was dressing up for someone. Damn though. First that Nick guy, now this general, it looks like she has a type, and I'm not it," he concluded with a nudge in Xin's ribs.

This drew both a red-faced scowl from Xin, and some very nervous weapon drawing from the guard.

Chase looked around at them wide eyed. "Why is everyone looking at me like I'm Xin?"

"You made a tornado, dumbass," scolded Xin, cuffing him on the head. "By the way, not impressed by the 'lover' comment. Do you have any idea how many rumours there are about me already? That's all I needed."

"Ow. Sheesh, I'm sorry. I thought it would work." His face dropped. "Wait, did you say I made a tornado?"

Inside the Gaian ship, Hugo led them back to his all so familiar office, which also happened to connect to his bedroom. Lorelei smiled a little, recalling the first time they met here before it was Hugo's. She had done a lot for him in these last four years.

He was just a regular soldier, grasping for grandeur, when she showed up. Together with Trisa, they took out The Smuggler, a man who had been stealing fruits from the Sacred Garden and selling them for a profit.

Arch-Angel Demeter was so impressed by Hugo, (not knowing Lorelei had a hand in any of it), that she gave him the highest ranking a human could receive and sent him out to the toughest border patrol.

It was Hugo's dream-come-true.

As they stepped inside his office, Hugo locked the door behind them, sighed, and smiled. "So he's actually dead, isn't he? Konstantin."

"You bet your sweet ass he is. Of course, he is still a pain in my ass putting me on the most wanted list like that."

"So then you're going to Gaia for sanctuary? I doubt you'll find it. You're a criminal here, too, and that will become even worse once they find out who you killed."

"I know," she sighed, clearing off a spot on the desk and sitting atop of it. "Look, Hugo sweetie, I've had a very stressful few weeks. You think we could talk after?"

A smile crept to his face as he came right into her, letting her wrap her legs around his waist. The rope around his shoulder sprang to life, tying her good hand and pulling her in even closer.

"Alright," he said, setting his hands around her waist, "but we are talking afterwards. No sneaky Lorelei schemes, deal?"

"Deal," she whispered, inviting the man's rough mouth onto hers with a sigh of delight.

After an extended session of de-stressing, Lorelei and Hugo lay relaxed in his bed, Lorelei's naked body covered in soft red lines. Lorelei sighed and sat up, returning the necklace gripped in her hand to its rightful place.

Hugo rolled to his side, watching her thoughtfully.

"Thanks Hugo, that was much needed," she sighed, reaching for her underwear.

He grabbed on to her hand, pulling her back into bed.

She chuckled, looking up at him. "What? Not done yet?"

"I just don't want you to go anywhere before we have a chance to talk."

She shrugged. "I figured we'd talk once we were dressed, but I suppose this works, too. So, then, where do we stand on crossing the border?"

Hugo let out a huge sigh, flopping back down onto the bed. "Most of your crew I can handle, even Xin, since he's never committed a crime in Gaia, but... Lorelei, I can't let that man through."

"Who, Chase? I told you, he just needs training, and I'm working on it. I promise he won't cause problems."

"Not him, though I do have my reservations about him as well."

"Then... who?" she asked, though she was getting the sinking suspicion she knew.

"David. That traitor is not passing this border," he growled, baring his not-so-white teeth.

Lorelei sat up, an innocent curiosity on her face. "There is no David on our ship, Hugo baby."

"Oh, please. You think I wouldn't recognize a former soldier? Even if that bastard deserter does wear dresses, now. Pretty sad that he's so afraid of the army that he needs to pretend to be a woman."

His sneer caused a fire to burn in Lorelei's eyes, and a snarl to form on her lips. She jumped on his chest and pinned him down by his throat.

"SHE is not pretending to be anything. She's finally living how she always wanted and she's become a greater person because of it. It has nothing to do with the army. This is who she is. She is Dana, not David anymore."

A satisfied smile formed on Hugo's face. "Thank you for confirming. That's all I really needed."

Lorelei's face dropped as she loosened her grip on his neck. "You wanted me to admit it," she breathed, amazed that she had fallen into his trap.

He smiled. "Sorry Lorelei, it's just work. You know you'd do the same thing."

She returned the smile, snuggling up, kissing his neck and running her hands up his arm. She set her lips right up to his ear and whispered, "You're right, I would."

Snap, clink.

She snapped a pair of handcuffs onto Hugo's wrist and the headboard. A moment of shock crossed his face, followed by a boisterous laugh. "You think this will help you get away?"

"I don't think so, I know so," she grinned and began getting dressed.

"Not so fast," he demanded, and waved his hand, expecting the ropes to react to him.

Nothing happened.

Again and again he tried while Lorelei calmly got dressed. He pulled against the handcuff, a panic setting in his face. "What the hell?"

"What's the matter? Powers not working? Too bad. I do love being tied up by you. Well, no time to chat, we have a border to pass. Thanks so much for giving me your permission."

"Wait! No, you can't! They'll take my head for this! Or worse… My title!" he begged, still pulling against the handcuffs.

"Sorry, Hugo baby, it's just work." With a teasing smirk, she headed for the door.

"Lorelei! You can't trust him. Do you even know what he's done?"

"Of course. She sold national secrets in exchange to get away from her abusive life."

"That's not all, Lorelei. That's just the official report. I have the full report. He's dangerous. If he loses control, none of you can stop him. Just let me take him in, and the rest of you can go. Please."

Lorelei stopped in her tracks. She didn't realize there was more. She assumed the report she read would have had all the details. He could have been lying to keep her there.

Hugo noticed her hesitation with relief. "In the filing cabinet—David Brooth. Take it if you don't believe me. There are things he's not telling you, Lorelei."

She strode over to the filing cabinet, thumbing through the files. There it was, 'Brooth, David'. She snatched it out and skimmed over it, her eyes growing wider as she went. She snapped the file shut, a panic in her eyes.

"I told you. You can't possibly still want to protect him after learning the truth," he shouted, still trying to figure out how to get the handcuff off.

Lorelei forced a weak smile. "Sorry, Hugo. I can't just betray her like that. Not without knowing her side of the story. I have things to do, can't sit around and chat. Later, sexy."

She left the office file under her arm, striding purposefully towards the deck. The soldiers came excitedly up to her, praising her, asking her to sing for them again.

She chuckled. "Sorry, boys, I would love to stay and put a show on, but we're on a tight schedule. The General has requested that you leave him be so he can finish his nap, and that we are free to go through."

"Sure thing, Lorelei. You'll come back and sing for us soon, won't you?" asked one young soldier.

She smiled that beautiful flirty smile at them. "Definitely. I'll be back as soon as possible and put on a great show for you all."

The men beamed with excitement.

As she arrived at the *Water Lily*, they all helped her down, and called out to the men on board that they were free to go. The soldiers headed back to their ship, still wary of the now dozing Chase.

The crew cautiously watched as the soldiers left the deck. Chase had passed out on Xin's shoulder, and was, to Xin's great annoyance, drooling all over him. He didn't have the heart to wake him, though.

Lorelei's gaze lingered on Dana, but she shook her head. "Come on, we need to move quickly."

"Uh, what about sleeping beauty?" Xin asked.

"Wake him. He can rest when we're clear of the border."

Xin shook Chase awake as the rest sprung up to get the ship ready to sail.

"Huh, wha?" said a groggy Chase.

"We're leaving. Time to get up," said Xin.

Chase jumped to his feet. "Seriously? Feckin' hell Lorelei, you sure know how to rock a bloke's world don't you?" Chase bellowed, making Xin scowl a little.

"No time to discuss. Let's get a move on," she urged.

In no time, they were carefully sailing through the grand gate.

As soon as they were through, Lorelei breathed a sigh of relief. "Chase, I know you're tired, but we need some wind to get us away from here as fast as possible."

Chase nodded.

"Emir, we need the fastest path to the city," said Lorelei, making everyone look around in confusion. None of them had seen Emir the whole time they were at the border.

"Ah, so I am still to be our Navigator? That is good. I quite enjoy it," said Emir, appearing from the shadows, making everyone except Lorelei jump. He headed quickly to the helm and adjusted their course.

"How do you do that?" asked Astrid, still trying to calm her beating heart.

Lorelei laughed. "What? I became headmaster of an Assassin's guild. Be pretty pathetic if I couldn't notice one little thief, especially after he already stole from me once," she added with a scowl.

Back on the ship, Hugo exited his bedroom in just his underwear, a broken pair of handcuffs in his hand. The soldiers noticed him and stood at confused attention.

"Where is she?" he bellowed.

"Uh, Lorelei and her crew have set sail already, sir," replied a soldier.

"Contact headquarters. Tell them to send my replacement. I have a personal mission I need to take care of."

"Yes, sir," the soldier replied with a salute, and hurried off.

Hugo looked thoughtfully at the handcuff, pulling out a small piece of blue-silver chain link.

"What have you discovered, Lorelei?"

25

Dana and David

The border disappeared on the horizon. Dana breathed a sigh of relief and softly announced she would make them some food. As she walked to the stairs, Lorelei interrupted her path, punching a hole into the wall. Dana looked at her, wide eyed and bewildered while Kari voiced an annoyed "AK!", quite concerned about all the holes they insisted on putting in her ship.

Ignoring Kari completely, Lorelei glared up at Dana, throwing the report at her chest. The papers scattered, revealing a picture of an overweight, unhappy looking man, who happened to look remarkably like Dana, with the name David Brooth underneath. Dana saw the report at a glance, and the fear she had earlier seemed a speck to now.

"Lorelei… I can explain," she squeaked.

"You had better fucking be able to. Five years we've known each other. I trusted you! I let you care for m—the children, and only now do I find out about this shit?" Lorelei screamed as Dana carefully studied her own feet.

Meanwhile, Emir had gathered the papers and was studying them. "Who is this David man? Why is he so upsetting? I suppose he does look an awful lot like you Dana. A brother perhaps? Oh… familicide? That is an awful crime."

Upon the revelation of that nasty crime, both Astrid and Kari looked at Dana in shock.

"Dana… how could you?" whispered Astrid.

"No, no," insisted Emir. "It was this David man that did that, not Dana."

Lorelei let out an annoyed growl at Emir's idiocy. "That is Dana."

"But… this is a man," said a confused Emir.

"She was a man, now she's a woman. Try and keep up, would you? Now shut the fuck up so Dana can kindly tell me why the fuck she murdered her wife and two children."

"I… it was… I didn't…" Dana tried to explain, her breath becoming quick and shallow.

"Dana. Think, then speak."

Dana took a deep breath, stopping for a moment to collect her thoughts.

"I was married, but it was a forced marriage through the Angels to make better warriors for them. One without… giant problems. My wife was very mean, always treating me bad, mocking my brains, my looks, my… ability in bed, anything to make me feel terrible. She'd do it in front of the kids all the time. I don't know if it was meant to make them hate me, but it did. As soon as the children were able, they would mock me as well. Of course… I didn't blame them. They didn't know any better. I was just too afraid to teach them otherwise. I was so weak… I am still so weak." Tears started to well in her eyes and Kari came up to her, squeezing her giant hand compassionately.

Dana looked at her with a quivering smile, took a big shuddering breath, and continued. "Then… one day, I just snapped. They were all being so mean, the berserker in me—it just snapped. I didn't even know what I was doing. When I came to, they were all dead." The tears now freely fell down her face.

Kari hugged her close.

Astrid's lips pressed tight as she held back her tears.

Lorelei was unreadable. She looked Dana up and down, and started walking away.

"Lorelei," Dana called. "Lorelei, I'm sorry. Please forgive me."

"It's not your fault, Dana. It's the Angels. It's always the fucking Angels," she growled. "Just… keep doing your job."

With that, Dana nodded and went to the kitchen. Kari shot Lorelei an unimpressed glare and joined Dana, a whining Chrissy following close behind.

"Astrid, bring me some burn cream to my room. I need to be alone for a while," said Lorelei.

Astrid looked as though she wanted to say something, but thought better of it, hurrying off to her room to gather the medicine.

"Burn ointment, eh?" slid in Chase as he followed her down the stairs, a grin on his face, hoping to lighten the mood a bit. "So I guess you did more than talk, then. Come on, you gotta tell me about it."

"I am definitely not in the mood for you right now, Chase. Go get some rest before you kill us all with another tornado." She stormed off to her room.

Chase stood there dumbfounded, and a little heart broken. He felt a firm, reassuring hand on his shoulder, and he looked over to see Xin.

"Don't let it get to you. It's not really your fault what happened. She doesn't actually blame you."

"No… she blames the Angels, apparently. What's with that?"

"Oh, I wish I knew," Astrid chimed in, stepping out of her door, salve in hand. "She's always had such an utter hatred for the Angels. I mean, I know they're pricks and all, but she's on another level."

Xin sighed, thought for a moment, and held out his hand. "Here, I'll take her the ointment, just in case she's in an attacking mood."

Astrid was about to hand it to him, but gave him a suspicious look. "Do you know something about it?"

He looked her dead in the eye. "Even if I did, it would be up to Lore to tell you about it, not me."

Astrid's face dropped. She handed the salve to Xin, and he went off to Lorelei's room. Astrid watched with watery eyes as he went to Lorelei's door, knocked, then entered.

"I've been with Lorelei for five years, yet he knows so much more about her than I do."

Chase laid a hand on her shoulder. "Souls connect differently to each other. Just because Xin knows more doesn't mean Lorelei doesn't care about you."

She couldn't hold back the tears anymore as she turned and gave Chase a big, teary hug.

Xin opened the door to Lorelei's neat, tiny room—or arsenal with a bed. Lorelei sat in front of the mirror in her bra, examining the fresh burn marks on her body. A smirk came to her face as she saw Xin's reflection.

"My, my, Astrid, you're looking quite manly tonight," she quipped.

"Ha, sorry, guess I should've said something. You're not going to take my eye, are you?"

Lorelei laughed. "Still remember the rules, do you?"

"Rule Number One: No touching without permission. This especially counts for hugs. Rule Number Two: Public areas are to remain spotless. Rule Number Three: No spying or peeking. If caught, you lose a body part, starting with the eye. Rule Number Four: No one touches your sugar. Though that one was more implied than stated."

"That's right," she smiled. "But I think I still might make some exceptions for you."

Xin brought over the salve, placing it on the table, then stood there in silence as Lorelei applied the cream.

With a sigh and an eye-roll, she said, "If you're going to just stand there and brood, you might as well make yourself useful." She passed the ointment to him.

He took it with a shrug and did as he was asked. "Do you want to talk about it?"

Lorelei scowled. "About which? The fact that my friend kept an awful secret from me, or the fact that our Captain has far greater power than I thought he was capable of?"

"I haven't known Dana long, but I think you can probably understand why she held back. You are the master of mystery, aren't you?"

The scowl faded away, turning to concern. "Yes, but... I knew she could snap, but I never imagined she could snap on children. I suppose I shouldn't be surprised. They may be cute and innocent, but damn if they aren't the most frustrating things in the universe."

"Well, that's true. I had plenty of fights with my sisters when I tried to help mom. Though, I imagine things are a little different with your own children."

The sentiment was innocent enough, though there was something prodding about the tone. She sent her gaze to Xin's reflection, studying him for a moment as he continued to apply the cream.

"I'll need you to take over training Chase," she stated, deciding she had had enough of the previous conversation.

Xin stopped and gave her a confused look in the mirror. "What? Why? He's barely even started the basics."

"Because clearly he has some anger issues, and I am not the person to teach him how to control those. If anything, I just make it worse. We need him level-headed like you in order to control that power."

"You think you make people angrier?"

"I know I do. Look at Astrid. She was such an innocent, sweet teenager before she started tagging along with me. Now she feels the need to scold and yell at anyone, especially me," she added with a grumble.

Xin laughed. "You think that's a bad thing? Astrid was an abused, secluded girl that didn't know a thing about the outside world. You taught her to come out of her shell and be herself, not just to be angry."

Her face furrowed in thought as she looked through the table in front of her. "Maybe..."

"We'll do it together. Train Chase, I mean. We make a good fighting team. Why wouldn't we make a good teaching team?"

Lorelei smiled. "Alright. You win. We'll do it together."

"Good," he said with a nod, then continued to apply the ointment. As he ran his finger down her back, he paused at her bra strap. He couldn't help but think how easy it would be to unclip it, to run his hands all over her body, to kiss her neck. Apparently, Lorelei might have been having similar thoughts as her breath deepened, and that wonderful sweet scent filled his senses.

He set down the ointment, shaking his head. "I should go," he said, then walked to the door.

"You… don't have to," she said softly, those golden eyes shimmering at him through the reflection. So much of him wanted to stay, but the one phrase kept coming back to his mind, and it was only accentuated by the rope burns on her body.

You were just a mark.

Xin sighed and swung the door open. "If you need to talk, you know where I'll be," he said flatly, leaving Lorelei to her solitude.

Alone once again with only her thoughts, she glared at her marked body in the mirror. Right on que, those pale hands rested on her shoulder, those grinning violet eyes looking into her soul.

"You really thought he was going to stay and fuck you? You're fucking delusional. Why would he want to be with you, you stupid, ugly slut?"

Xin stood outside Lorelei's door, clearly hearing Lorelei cry out in rage, then the shattering of the mirror. He sighed, the guilt welling up inside him, but the decision was already made. Going back now wouldn't help anything. Besides, she had made herself clear on multiple occasions what she thought about their relationship. Instead, he decided to join the rest of the crew in the kitchen.

As he walked over, he found the odd sight of the crew awkwardly gathered at the table while Dana cooked and Emir paced the floor in an odd, confused panic.

"You are a man?" Emir seemed to be asking over and over.

"Was," sighed Dana, apparently not for the first time.

Emir stopped in his tracks, looked her up and down, then asked quietly, "But you still have your manhood?"

"Emir! That is not an appropriate question to ask someone!" scolded Astrid as Dana looked abashedly to the floor.

"But it is important to know!"

"Why?" asked Chase. "Were you hoping to sleep with her?"

Emir's eyes went wide, and his whole body winced. "I- wha- No! Of course not! I told you I am saving myself for my love, Vira!"

"Then why do you need to know what's in her pants... er... panties?"

"I..." he began, but had trouble thinking up a reason.

"Exactly. Had no one said anything, you wouldn't have been any the wiser and nothing would have changed. She's a woman. Just stop overthinking it."

Emir noticed Xin had returned, and looked to him for support. "Xin! Mighty Swordsman! You are the most manly of men. Surely you agree that this is strange."

"Huh? Oh, no, not really," said Xin. "I mean, I guess it was a bit surprising, but I agree with Chase, it doesn't change anything. She still makes amazing food." He accentuated his point by taking a large, drooling sniff of the air.

Emir sighed, clearly outnumbered. He glanced over at Dana, who was actively avoiding his gaze. "I... I need to go," he said, then ran out.

Dana slumped even further, a tear in her eye.

"Don't worry about him, Dana," said Xin. "This is the same guy that thought he could teach Lorelei how to dress properly. I'm sure he'll wrap his head around it, eventually."

"Wait... he did what?" exclaimed Kari, and Dana perked her attention up as well.

"Yep, where do you think that scar on his nose came from?" With a laugh,

Xin proceeded to tell the uncut version of their not-so-kind first encounter.

26

Halftime

U p and down, up and down. By the gods, Chase loved sleeping on the open sea. It was so relaxing. Only thing that was missing was someone to share his bed. Oh, well. Over the last couple of days Chase had been given the privilege of sleeping in while the rest of the crew charted their course. He really needed it after the last exhausting week.

Apparently, that changed today.

He wasn't even completely sleeping. He just had his eyes closed and his hearing aids out, enjoying the swell of the ocean. Then suddenly—*splash*—he was drenched with a bucket of cold water.

He gasped, flung his eyes open and sat right up, glaring at his torturer. "Dammit Xin, what in Tartarus?"

Xin held out a towel and Chase's hearing aids with a small smirk.

He snatched them away, grumbling under his breath, and as the hearing aids were in place, he sent Xin another 'what the fuck' look.

"Lorelei warned me how you like to sleep," said Xin. "Figured I'd avoid the awkwardness of taking the covers off like she does. Also figured I'd take away the invitation to join you in your bed at the same time."

Chase looked down at his soaked mattress and pouted. "That better be dry by tonight. And that still doesn't answer what in Tartarus you are waking me up for."

"Training."

Chase's frown turned into a beaming grin. "With you?"

"That's right."

"Yes!" exclaimed Chase, jumping out of bed and getting dressed in a hurry.

Xin waited for him on deck, where the rest of the crew had already gotten the ship underway. Soon enough, Chase was out and about, vibrating in excitement beside Xin.

"So what's first? Push-ups? Sit-ups? Squats? Are you going to teach me how to use a sword?"

Without a word, Xin walked to the bow of the ship and sat down, cross-legged, hands on his knees.

Chase's whole body dropped in disappointment. "Wha— what are we doing?"

"Meditation."

"But... Why?"

"A strong mind breeds a strong body," said Xin. "You need to be able to keep a level head in the middle of combat. This is how you get there. Sit."

Chase complied with a "humph". He felt a familiar small but strong hand ruffling his hair and looked up to see Lorelei smiling at him.

"Look at it this way, Captain," she said, "if you can master this, you'll be better than me at something."

"Really?" he said with an eager smile.

"Yep. I do not have the patience for this shit. Have fun!" With that, she strode off. To where, Chase didn't find out as Xin motioned his attention back to him.

"First thing's first," said Xin, "Close your eyes."

"Uh... but then I won't be able to understand what you're saying."

"Oh right... Well then relax your gaze, try not to focus on your surroundings. Just pay attention to my voice, and your own body. Go through your body with your mind and feel every little inch of it, and relax."

For a moment, Xin stayed quiet, just steadily breathing in and out, so Chase tried what he was told. Breathing deep, feeling his body, and letting it relax. It felt good.

Crash.

Chase snapped his gaze over to the noise, seeing Kari standing over a pile of scattered scraps.

"Sorry!" she called with a wave, and Chrissy gave her obligatory, 'woof'.

"Focus, Chase," said Xin, his voice still calm and even. "Ignore the outside world. Now, go into your mind, and let it go blank. Address any thoughts that come to you, then let them go until you find that calm—that stillness."

Again silence, just breathing in and out.

Address my thoughts, then let them go? So like this one? I just... let it go...

Silence.

This isn't so hard. Oh, let it go...

Calm.

By the gods, Xin is hot. Not sure I can let that one go.

Chase giggled to himself.

Xin sighed with a small smile. "Alright, that's good for today."

"What? Already? I was just getting the hang of it... I think."

"It's already been a half hour. That's a good start. We'll do it again tomorrow morning."

"Wait, seriously? I thought it'd been like five minutes."

Xin laughed. "Nope, guess you found that stillness faster than I thought. Well done. You've already done better than Lorelei."

"Ha!" exclaimed Chase, jumping to his feet. "Did ya hear that, Lorelei? I'm better than you at something!"

"I can still kick your ass," she called back in reply, accentuating her point with a deadly punch on her training dummy.

Chase sighed. "Yes... yes you can."

Xin laughed and patted him on the shoulder. "You'll get better. Though aiming to get better than Lorelei may be a bit ambitious. Start small, like beating Emir. That should be easy enough."

"Hey! I heard that, you brute," growled Emir from the shadows.

Xin smirked. "Good."

"Right. So what's next in training?" asked Chase.

"I told you, that's it for today. I'm going to do my own training. You can relax."

"What? But what about strength training?"

"Not today. It's still possible that the General guy could catch up to us. We need you at your best in case we need a quick getaway."

"But I'm fine! All rested, really!"

"Lore will do some basic drills with you after lunch. For now, just take it easy."

Chase frowned, letting his head hang. "So I won't try to kill my own crew again?"

Xin sighed, gripped Chase's shoulder a little tighter, and wrapped Chase in a hug.

Chase's eyes grew wide, his heart raced. A hug? He was so excited. Confused, but mostly excited.

"We all make mistakes. The trick is learning from them. We trust you Chase. I trust you. I will literally follow you to the end of this world because I am sure you can bring us back. Trust in yourself like I trust you."

Chase's lip quivered, and he let the tears fall. "What kind of swordsman are you?" Chase sobbed. "You're not supposed to be all wise and shite."

"Tough luck, Captain. That's what you got," said Xin, pulling Chase away from him and giving him a supportive smile. "Strength training will start tomorrow. For now, relax and get to know your crew. That's more important than being able to fight anyway."

"Right. Thanks, mate. I really needed that. Think I could have one more hug?"

Xin smirked, patted him on the head, said, "Nope," and walked away.

Chase sighed, shrugged, and with a beaming smile, went to check out what Dana was doing.

As usual, Dana was in the kitchen, and by the looks and smells of things, she was getting lunch prepped.

"Hey Dana, that smells amazing," said Chase, getting up close to check out what was on the menu. Mmm, fish and chips. His favourite.

"Oh, hello Chase," said Dana. She was never super excitable, but she seemed even more morose today. Actually, for the last few days.

"You alright, Darling?"

Dana's lip quivered. She shook her head. "I'm fine."

"Ah, I think I might get it. Are you feeling a little unsure of yourself, since we all found out about your past?"

Dana sighed.

"I get it. To some degree anyway. I had to pretend I was something different for a while, too. Not as much as you, though."

"Thanks Chase, but… I'd just rather not talk about it, alright?"

"Alright, lass. You just say the word and I'll be there for you. Mentally or physically," he added with a laugh and a nudge.

Dana snapped her wide eyes at him. "What? Why would you…"

"Are you kidding? People like you are absolutely wonderful. Becoming the person your soul wants you to be? It's the most beautiful thing in the world."

Dana blushed something fierce. "I… Well… thank you… but I don't think I'm really interested in… that."

"Not a problem, gorgeous. You just keep being you," said Chase with a flourish, then headed off down the stairs once more to find Kari's little workshop.

He rapped on the door lightly and heard something that didn't sound like "go away" from inside, so he opened the door. Inside sat a greasy, grimy Kari, hard at work at her workbench. The room was filled with objects, half of which Chase had never even seen before. There were gears, both small and large, tools of every shape and size, and barrels of powder that made Chase a little nervous.

Kari, with her little magnifying glass and tiny circuit board, had not looked up to see who had entered her domain. In fact, she was so focused, she may have forgotten someone came in at all. Chrissy saw Chase and came up and licked his hand lovingly, her tail working in a whirlwind fashion. He gave her some affectionate scratches and stood over Kari's shoulder, hoping to get a closer look at her project.

After a moment, Kari took a long, deep breath, her shoulders relaxing, a small smile on her face. Suddenly, her already magnified eyes grew even larger as she realized who was standing behind her.

"Chase!" she squeakily exclaimed, spinning around on her little stool and looking up to see his grinning face.

"Heya, Kari, I wanted to see what you were up to. You're always down here working."

Beads of sweat formed on Kari's brow as she wrung her hands. "I… Well, I like to keep busy. I was just… working… on…" She looked down at the item in her hand. With an "eep!" she jumped to her feet and pushed Chase out the door. "It's not ready yet! You can't see it!" She slammed the door in his face.

Chase looked at the closed door and scratched his head. What a crazy girl. Why did she never seem to want to talk to him? He thought it might be because he was a new person in her life, but she seemed to talk to Xin easy enough, though that was mostly giving him shit for wrecking things. He shrugged and headed back up to the deck, where he spied Astrid hiding in the shade, painting a picture.

Chase sauntered over to check out what Astrid was up to. In front of the woman was a gorgeous painting of Xin and Lorelei, back to back, but giving each other that familiar look. They also appeared to be a little less clothed than they were in reality, though it was tasteful.

"Wow, Astrid. That's amazing," said Chase, looking over her shoulder.

"Chase!" she squeaked with a small jump. "Don't you know it's not nice to sneak up on someone painting?"

"Sorry, Gorgeous. I certainly didn't mean to." Chase laughed. "Now I know how Emir feels."

Astrid giggled.

"Those two really got a lot of shite going on, don't they? That is some serious sexual tension, and I've seen a lot."

Astrid sighed. "Yeah." She looked over at Chase, an inquisitive look on her face. "Have you two been… you know…"

"Fucking? Nah. Lorelei made it pretty clear that was a no-go anymore. Figured I'd let her come to me if that changed. Still, she likes to flirt, and that's fun, though I can't help but feel it's to make Xin jealous."

Astrid grunted in frustration. "So stupid. If she would just apologize, explain everything, things would be fine between them. She's so damn headstrong. I just don't get it."

"Have you tried asking her about it?"

"I've… hinted."

"But nothing direct?"

Astrid crossed her arms, her lip out as far as it could go. "Do you know how hard it is to ask her things directly? You never know if she's going to laugh at you or yell at you."

Chase shrugged. "Never know if you don't try, right?"

"I suppose…"

"Hey, I don't suppose you know why Kari is so weird around me."

"Hmm… I didn't really notice, though now that you mention it, she's not her usual snippy self around you, is she? Hm, well she was always uncomfortable around men when we first took her in, but after she found Chrissy, she seemed fine." Astrid furrowed her brow in thought for a moment, pressing the back of the paintbrush against her chin. "Unless… Oh, maybe. She is the right age for it."

"What?"

Astrid giggled. "She might have a crush on you, Captain."

"A crush?" Chase grimaced. "Oh no, no, no. She is way too young."

"Oh, don't worry, I'm sure she'll end up losing interest eventually. You're just new and exciting." She gave him a sweet smile and continued painting.

Chase sighed frustratedly and wandered off again.

As Astrid continued her painting, Lorelei came and joined her in the shade, once again trying to figure out how to play guitar with a cast. Placing it in a left-handed position, she thought carefully, then successfully made a proper chord and started carefully plucking out a tune with a prideful smile. She glanced over to Astrid's picture and plucked a rather sour note.

"What the crap is that?"

"I- wh- oh! Oops, I umm… I call it 'unspoken words'," Astrid replied with a giggle as she fiddled with her braid.

"I… we don't… we don't look at each other like that!"

Astrid laughed. "You do so! All the time. How do you think I drew it so well?"

"Tchah…" She looked back to her guitar, grumpily trying to figure out a different chord. "Well what do you expect? We're both sexy. It's hard to ignore."

"Oh don't give me that. I've seen men you're attracted to and this is different."

Lorelei scoffed.

"I just… I don't get it. You clearly both still care for each other. I would die to have someone look at me like that. Why don't you…" Astrid stopped, unsure of how to finish the sentence.

"Get over myself?" Lorelei finished.

"Your words, not mine."

Lorelei sighed as she continued plucking out a tune, sending a forlorn look at Xin. "I thought it was obvious… But I suppose not."

"What?"

"He's too good for me," she said simply.

Astrid's jaw dropped. "What?"

"He deserves better. He deserves someone that can give him everything he wants. Commitment, family, lo—." She bit her tongue on the last word, cringing from the thought of it. "I'm not capable of those things."

"What?" Astrid exclaimed once again. "Lorelei! Don't be ridiculous. Of course you're capable of those things!"

"Nah…" she said with a smile. "Tried it out already. Didn't suit me."

"Lorelei…" Astrid sighed sadly.

Lorelei shook her head and continued with her guitar. Apparently, that conversation was over. Astrid wished she could believe that's what she really wanted, but she knew there was more to it. The only time she ever saw true happiness in Lorelei's eyes was around Xin, she couldn't just ignore that.

"Ak!" cried Emir from the helm. "Get off of me, foul beast!"

A soft cooing and flapping combined with Emir's newest bout of curses.

Lorelei cocked an eye, set down her guitar, and looked at the upper deck where Emir was fending off a metal pigeon flapping around his head. Instead of helping, she decided to watch and laugh.

Astrid sighed and rolled her eyes, moving to help Emir. She found, however, that the bird was quite evasive.

"What—the—heck?" she cried in between swipes. "Why won't this thing stay still? Lorelei, would you *please* help?"

Lorelei wiped a tear from her eye and sauntered up. She watched the thing as it flapped around their heads, and just as Astrid was about to plead for help again, her hand snapped out and caught it mid-air.

Astrid sighed with relief. "Thank you."

"Ah, the show was starting to get old, anyway," she chuckled.

Emir grumbled some curses at her.

She ignored him and examined the sparking, struggling creature in her hands. "The crap is wrong with this thing?"

As if being summoned, Kari poked her head up in front of Lorelei. "Oh, that thing's been heavily damaged, probably in that last storm. Could explode any second."

Lorelei dropped it, and Kari promptly snatched it and examined it further, unfazed by her own warning. "Hmm. Looks like it has a message, though. We should… probably listen, right? In case it's important?"

Astrid crossed her arms. "What if it's private? We can't just listen to someone's personal messages."

"Yeah… who knows?" Lorelei said with a small smile. "It could be a love letter to someone across the oceans finally telling their soul mate how they feel." Astrid's eyes went wide, and Lorelei continued. "But, it is personal. We should probably just put the thing out of its misery."

"No, no, no!" cried Astrid. "We have a duty to listen and pass along the message for it."

Lorelei chuckled. "Of course we do." She nodded at Kari. "Alright, let's hear it."

Kari pressed down the tail-feathers, and everyone took a nervous step back. It ground, popped and sparked, then a woman's buzzing voice spoke from it.

"Help—*bzzt*—'re ambushed—*bzzt*—" Sounds of screams crackled through. "Please s—bzzt—elp. The island of—" The bird twitched and repeated the last few words, not continuing on.

"Oh, no, you don't," said Kari, plopping down on the deck crossed legged. Out came a screwdriver from one of her many pockets as she fiddled with the gears on the inside.

"The island of Sasfierm," it concluded. The eyes went dark.

Kari gave a sigh of relief, and—

Boom!

The bird let off a big cloud of smoke and crumbled to pieces.

Kari coughed, fanning the smoke from her face. "I'm okay."

As Astrid looked over Kari's hands and face, Lorelei turned to Emir. "How far off is Sasfierm?"

Emir pulled out the map, laying it on the table, promptly examining and measuring. "It's out of the way, but it should only take us a few days off course."

"Then set course for Sasfierm."

Emir looked around. "Um, should we not ask the Captain about this course change?"

Lorelei scowled. "If Chase isn't okay with helping people in need, then he's not the man I thought he was. Just do it."

"Right."

$$27$$

Sasfierm

"Alright girl, this is it, just like we practiced," said Kari to her dog, who was eagerly jumping up and down in the crow's nest. "Ready?" She took a deep breath, and shouted, "Land Hoooo!"

As she dragged out the "O" Chrissy howled along, her tail thumping back and forth on the wood.

There on the horizon lay the island of Sasfierm. As they sailed to its shores, they could see the town nestled along one edge, while the rest of the island was filled with tracts of full, colourful crops. There were farms sprinkled out as far as the eye could see, but no other obvious townships. That was common in the Rustic Ring of Gaia.

What wasn't common was the odd mountain sticking out of the middle of the island. It seemed completely devoid of life, and not structured as mountains usually were. It instead looked like waves of stone colliding together. Oddly enough, according to Emir's maps the whole island should have been flat. Mountains didn't typically pop up out of nowhere.

Chase couldn't keep his eyes off of that mountain. "What in Tartarus happened here?" he asked, but more to himself than to anyone nearby.

Still, Lorelei replied, "I don't know, but I sure as hell intend to find out."

They docked at port, flying the Gaian flag proudly atop their mast. No need to mark themselves as pirates just yet. As soon as the anchor heaved and the ropes were secured, Astrid leapt off the boat, down the docks and practically dived head first into the sand.

"Oh, land. So wonderful. I missed you," she chirped, a large smile on her face.

As soon as she had ensured her whole body was covered in sand, she leapt to her feet and started dancing, though there was no music to be heard.

"Kari! Dana! We have a land dance!" Lorelei exclaimed, readying her guitar and strumming along to the beat of Astrid's dance.

Kari hurried down from the crow's nest, Chrissy tied safely to her back. As she landed, she released the excited dog and pulled out a contraption from one of her many pockets. It transformed into a gold and silver saxophone that was nearly the size of Kari. She gave it an energetic, but slightly ear piercing blow, but after warming up, she was eagerly playing along to the beat.

Xin stepped in beside Lorelei, a smile on his face. "What are you doing?"

"It's a game the crew plays. Astrid absolutely loves being on solid ground and she almost always does a dance when we land. The longer at sea, the longer the dance. The game is to make a song to go with the music she apparently has in her head."

Xin gave a laugh and watched the show with a smile, drumming his fingers along to the beat. Chase leapt off the ship to join the joyful Astrid in her bouncy dance, while Emir stayed looking nervously about the island.

"Should we not be a little more cautious? There was supposed to have been a battle here."

"Ah, let them have their fun. There's no fighting right now, and I think they need to relax. We'll investigate when they're done," Xin said, grabbing Emir by the vest and throwing him into the dancing pair. They happily dragged him along to the dance, despite his objections.

Lorelei took a look around, still no sign of Dana. She sighed, and headed into the kitchen, where Dana was needlessly peeling potatoes.

"Dana. Come on. Astrid's doing a land dance and then we're off to town to figure out what happened. You can work later."

"I'm... just going to stay here," she replied, grabbing another potato.

Lorelei sighed. "If this is about me getting angry, I'm sorry. I realize that must have been really hard for you. I can't imagine…"

"No…" she said, shaking her head, then thought for a moment. "Well, maybe a little, but honestly, this island gives me the shivers. I'd really rather stay here."

"Alright, if you're sure," said Lorelei with a smile, and Dana nodded.

As Lorelei came back on deck, she saw Astrid's dance had been cut short by an unfriendly-looking welcoming committee. There were six all together, most well past their prime. Chase was busy talking to a hook-nosed old man at the head of the group, so Lorelei slid in beside Xin.

"What'd I miss?" she asked, her voice lowered.

"Apparently they're not in the habit of taking in tourists. They want to send us on our way," said Xin.

Lorelei watched Chase for a bit as he tried his best to turn on his boyish charm. A couple in the group seemed to be eyeing him with some appreciation, but the head man was unmoved.

Xin gave Lorelei a little nudge and motioned to one of the other ships docked. It was huge. Far bigger than theirs, which had been designed with a half-giant in mind. The doorways were twice as tall as their own and clearly designed for long travel. Lorelei cocked her head, thinking for a moment.

She strode up beside Chase and looked the hook-nosed man in the eye. "You don't like tourists, huh? So what's with that ship?"

The group looked over. A few faces went pale, but hook-nose wasn't fazed. "It's one of our supply ships."

"That right? It doesn't look like one. What's with the doors?"

"For transporting large equipment and animals," he replied without pause.

A skeptical smile slid across her face. "I see."

"Don't you worry your pretty little head about it." The man looked back at Chase, apparently done with speaking to Lorelei, but Lorelei was far from done.

"The fuck did you say?"

The man glared back at her, looking her up and down. Before anything further could be said, Chase cleared his throat and came in between them.

"I apologize for her—she's a bit short-tempered." Chase chuckled, and Lorelei shot him a death glare behind his back.

The man smiled. "I admire your grit for being able to put up with such a wild woman. How'd she get that scar?" He gave a gut busting laugh as he said, "Did she forget which end of the frying pan to use?"

The rest of his group joined in the laughter.

Lorelei took a step forward, hand on hilt, ready to run the man through, but found a puff of wind in her face catching the air in her lungs. It was only for a moment, but the message was clear enough. For the first time since they had been sailing together, Chase was asking her to remain silent. He had no idea how much he was asking of her at that moment, but she decided to respect his wishes... for now.

Chase joined in the laughter, though not his usual care-free laugh. This one was clearly fake, at least to those who knew him. He wrapped an arm around the old man's shoulders and gave them a squeeze. "Nah, mate. See, a few years back her house caught on fire—you know how corrupted wood can be. Her husband rescued her from the flames but..." Chase gave a huge sigh. "...unfortunately he lost his life." All the eyes in the group looked at Lorelei sympathetically.

She squirmed in place.

Chase continued. "So you'll have to forgive her for being a little testy."

"Oh..." The man was certainly no longer laughing. "Right, of course. I am sorry for your loss."

"Yeah... Well... It's in the past," said Lorelei.

Chase gave the man his usual boyish grin. "Now then, mate, it would be grand if you'd let us into your darling city for a while. We are low on supplies and we're not sure we'll make it to our destination if we leave now."

The man sighed. "Ah, alright. I suppose we can let you stay for a bit."

"Brilliant!" Chase exclaimed with a grin. "And I insist on buying you all a round tonight. You do have a bar here, right?"

The men grinned and nodded. As they set a time and place, Lorelei just watched in confused awe. The committee left, and Chase turned his smile back at Lorelei, which faded as he caught her slack jawed stare.

"What?" he asked.

"What in Helheim was that?"

Chase's face became serious. "They're hiding something, that's obvious. Unfortunately, that means playing nice until we can figure out what. If that ship is any indication, it might have something to do with giants, and if they can take out giants, we don't want to get on their bad side."

"Wha–How?" Lorelei was amazed. She never realized Chase was so perceptive.

Chase gave a small smile. One that wasn't quite sad, but also not happy. "We're in Gaia now, not Yggdria. I know how people think here. I travelled all around these islands with Ma when I was a kid, then again through most of my twenties with Captain Brown."

"Wait, who?"

"Captain Brown, Captain of the Merchant ship I sailed on for… hmm…" He counted on his fingers. "Oh, wow, thirteen years." He shot a boyish grin. "Time flies, huh?"

"I… had no idea you spent that much time on a ship."

"Of course. It was the best way to meet plenty of new people. Then when he retired a few years back, I decided to do the travelling bit on my own."

Lorelei gawked, and Chase waved his hand. "Anyway, back to the issue at hand. I know how to blend in pretty well. If we want to keep a low profile, you'll have to trust me on this one, alright?"

Lorelei sighed. "What's the plan?"

A proper smile spread across his face. "Well, I might be able to get the lads to spill over a few pints, but I think our best bet for some information lies in your hands." He motioned to Lorelei and Astrid.

"Why?"

"Well, this is a… err… we'll call it a traditional island, meaning women are meant to be at home, and in many cases, seen and not heard."

"I do not get it," said Emir, appearing beside Chase. "I thought Gaia was a matriarchy."

"It is," said Chase as he calmed his racing heart. "But that only seems to matter in the cities. Out in the Rustic Ring, women take on household roles because it is easier for them to take care of the children than tend the fields. Why that garners them little respect, I have no idea, but it happens on some islands. Old ways of thinking I suppose. Back before the Calamity."

"What does that have to do with us?" asked Lorelei.

Chase grinned. "Because people who are forced to keep quiet, tend to want to do the most talking."

As planned, Lorelei and Astrid went to gather the supplies that they didn't really need in hopes of running into some caregivers along the way. Kari decided to tag along as well, never having been on a Gaian island before. She was quite enthralled.

As they travelled down the gravel roads, she found the small wood houses very quaint, but she was not a fan of the constant stares her way. They passed by a red-haired girl around Kari's age who waved eagerly at the sight of her. As Kari waved back, however, the girl's mother hurried her inside.

"What's their problem?" Kari asked, trying not to sound as sad as she really was.

"You're different," said Lorelei. "You don't look like them, so you're something to be feared. Simple as that."

"What? Because I'm from another island?"

Lorelei sighed. "Because you're black."

Kari's mouth hung open. Then she snapped it closed. "Haha, very funny."

"I wish I was joking. Don't worry, it will get better the closer we get to Olympia. It's further south, so the skin colours vary a lot more."

"But Yggdria's not like that and it's way up North where people are white as fuck."

Lorelei chuckled. "Yggdria draws strange and unusual people to it like a moth to the flame. Strange people tend not to mind other strange people. Why do you think I made Yggdria my home nation?"

It was Kari's turn to chuckle. "I always figured it was 'cause you secretly had a crush on Odin."

"Tchah!" Lorelei flicked her on the nose. "Not funny."

Astrid and Kari laughed the whole way to the little grocers. They managed to gather themselves as they roamed the cramped aisles filled with dusty packaged goods, looking for things they could take along. Dana gave them a list of things they could use, so they divided up and met back up at the cashier's with their loads. As they exited, they saw a young woman with a babbling toddler in a stroller.

Astrid broke at the sight of the thing. "Aww! Oh my goodness. He is so cute! How old is he?"

The woman gave her a small smile. "Thank you. He's thirteen months old."

"Aw, such a big boy, aren't you? Aren't you?" she cooed as the boy giggled and babbled.

Lorelei did her best to suppress an eye roll, and Kari tried not to giggle. Finally Astrid stood up and looked the woman in the eye. The big smile on her face dropped in an instant.

"Oh. Sorry. Your eye… what happened?"

The woman gasped a little and turned away from Astrid, which is when Lorelei got a look at her face. She was sporting a large black eye that was diligently covered with makeup.

"Sorry," Astrid continued, placing a hand on her arm. "I know it's rude to pry, but I'm a doctor. I guess I'm just naturally curious about injuries."

The woman seemed to relax at that and sent Astrid a forced smile. "It… It's nothing really. Just me being clumsy. Ran into little Georgie's room when he was crying and hit the door in the dark. It's silly."

Lorelei's fists clenched, her breath quickened. She saw Astrid shoot her a pleading look, which sent the woman to look at Lorelei.

Like turning a switch, Lorelei's face stretched into a wide smile, her eyes lighting up with excitement.

"That is *so* funny." Her words were so honey-filled she almost didn't sound like the same person. The girly giggle that followed made Kari's mouth literally hang open. Still Lorelei continued. "I get hurt like that *all* the time! See this?" She pulled back her hair to reveal her burn. "I got this trying to get our stupid oven to work. And this:" She held up her cast arm. "Fell down the stairs trying to do laundry. Such a ditz! My husband bugs me about it all the time." She gave that giggle again.

The woman relaxed a little and gave her a worried look. "That must have hurt a lot."

She giggled, but this time a little less energetically. "Yeah, it did. Not as much as having one of these, though." She ruffled the little boy's hair and he started to whimper.

Astrid and Kari looked at each other wide eyed.

"Oh," said the woman. "Do you have kids?"

Lorelei's face went a little pale, but still that smile remained. "Coffee. We should totally get some coffee. Me and the girls were just about to grab some, how about you join us?"

The woman smiled. "I'd like that, but I really have to get home to put Georgie down for a nap. Why don't you come over in a little while and I'll put a pot on."

"That sounds wonderful," Lorelei chirped. "My name's Elizabeth, by the way." Lorelei held out her hand.

The woman shook it. "Rebecca," she replied with a small smile. She gave them her address, then hurried off.

Lorelei waved at her energetically until she was no longer in sight. The sickly sweet smile faded from her face, and that far more familiar scowl rested once again. She forcibly closed Kari's still agape jaw and growled, "Not a word."

"Lorelei…" Astrid looked at her friend with deep concern. "Are you sure about this?"

"Chase may know how people think here, but I know a fucking abused woman when I see one." She sent the girls a small smile, resting her gaze on Kari. "Besides, I'd rather be wrong and sorry, than right and have done nothing."

28

The Mountain

A booming cheer filled the air, along with the overwhelming scent of smoke and booze. Glasses clinked and the group of men downed their drinks and slammed them down on the table.

"Hey, darlin'!" Chase called to the husky waitress standing at the bar. "Another round for my new mates!"

The men cheered as she balanced over a plate of fresh drinks for them.

Chase shot her a stunning smile. "Thank yeh, gorgeous. You are an angel."

She tittered as her face grew red.

One of the men slapped Chase on the back and laughed. "Be careful who you're flirting with, there. That there's Carl's niece." He pointed over to a man with a long, thick beard.

Carl laughed. "Don't be stupid. Poor girl's so homely, she could use a good husband like you. Flirt away."

Chase gave a half-hearted laugh while the rest of them burst into a roar of laughter. The girl laughed along, playfully punching her uncle in the arm. As she shuffled off back to the bar, her forced smile quickly faded away.

Xin, who had opted to sit away from the very loud group of men to sit at the bar by himself, caught her look and gave her a smile. He leaned in a little closer and murmured, "This coming from the guy who looks like an ape."

She snorted out a laugh. "By the gods, does he ever."

"The name's Xin, by the way, what's yours?"

"Jessie," she said with a warm smile.

As Xin chatted away with Jessie, Chase continued to schmooze the men, buying them a few more rounds, and keeping them entertained with stories from his travels. Eventually, he decided it was time. "Alright, alright, enough about women." Chase took a swig, and so did everyone else. "I am awful curious about that crazy mountain you got going on here. I've never seen anything like it!"

A sudden silence filled the table. No one met his gaze.

"Oh, sorry mates, did I hit a chord? I was just asking since it seems like a thing that would bring in some tourism. It certainly is odd."

"Never mind that," said Richard, the hook-nosed old man from earlier that day. "Just a strange phenomenon. It won't be here long."

"Oh… is that right? Seems a bit odd, a mountain coming and going out of nowhere."

Richard gave a deep scowl. "I said never mind."

"Alright, alright, I just—"

Crash

The bar door came flying off its hinges, broken in two splintered pieces. Behind it stood the furious face of Lorelei, with the timid Rebecca's arm in her good hand, and Astrid lagging close behind. Xin stood at the ready, while Chase looked at her cockeyed. Well, not quite at her, but around her.

"Lorelei? What's that stuff flying around you?" Chase asked, though from everyone else's eyes, there was no such thing.

Lorelei ignored him. "Which one?" she growled at Rebecca.

Rebecca cried and shook her head.

Astrid begged Lorelei to stop.

One of the younger men in the group, sporting sleek, black hair, stood up. "What the fuck are you doing with my wife?"

Slowly, a dark grin spread across Lorelei's face. She released Rebecca and strode to the man, shoving her way through the group. She pinned the man to the wall by his throat.

The men yelled and swore at her, a couple moving to pull her off of him, but all stopped at the sound of a sword being drawn. Xin didn't say a word—he walked over to stand back to back with her, one sword drawn and at the ready.

Those golden eyes bore into the dark-haired man. "So, Ricky, is it? Richard Junior? You think you're a big, tough man, do you, Ricky?"

Ricky tried to pry her hand off of his throat, but it wouldn't budge. "What the fuck is wrong with you?" he wheezed. "Put me down."

"Oh, did you listen to your wife when she asked you to stop beating her?"

"What?"

Lorelei elbowed him in the nose and a sickening crunch sounded. Blood poured.

"What the fuck?!" he cried.

The men started to step in again.

"Come a step further and I will snap his fucking throat."

She spoke the words with such conviction that everyone in that room believed her. No one moved a muscle.

"You think you have the right to tell your wife what to do with her body? Is your dick so fucking small that you have to control every little thing in your life? You like having that power over a woman, huh?"

Ricky glared at Rebecca. "You told her?" Rebecca apologized profusely, and Ricky looked back at Lorelei. "Did she also tell you what else her selfishness caused?"

"Don't you dare," the elder Richard growled.

"It was her, wasn't it?" asked Xin. "The one everyone thought was kidnapped."

Everyone stopped and gawked at Xin.

Xin looked over at Jessie, who was hiding behind the counter. She gave a small nod, and Xin sighed. "Jessie told me a small group of giants came to visit the island a few days ago. One night, someone in the village went missing, so they decided the giants were to blame..."

"What in Gaia's name, Jessie?" Richard scowled.

"What you did was wrong," Jessie shouted. "They didn't deserve any of that."

Rebecca came up to Lorelei, softly pulling on her arm. "Please, let him go. This was all just a big misunderstanding. I don't want anyone else to get hurt because of me. Please, this is all my fault."

Lorelei's eyes went wide, her teeth clenched. The words 'my fault' bounced over and over again in her mind, and her eye started to twitch. "Your fault? All you wanted was someone that would listen to you, someone that would take away your pain. You know that baby inside of you is going to kill you, but no one on this fucking island will do a damn thing to help you."

"She's just being hysterical," said Ricky. "There's nothing wrong with that baby. I won't let her murder my baby!"

"Oh, I'll show you murder." Streaks of pure darkness swirled around Lorelei. This time, everyone could see it.

Before anyone could do or say anything, Lorelei lifted the man up by the neck once again and threw him through the window. Shards of glass and splatter of blood flew out along with Ricky, who skidded along in the grass. As he coughed and groaned, Lorelei walked through the now open window.

"Lorelei, please stop. This is too much!" cried Astrid.

Lorelei ignored her, still glaring at that man. "What fucking right do you have to say what that woman should do with that baby? All you did was put your fucking seed into her. You don't have to carry the squirming thing around inside of you for months while your whole body stretches and warps into something completely different. You have no idea what a woman goes through to bring a child in this world. I don't give a fuck if that baby is hurting her or not, if she wants to get rid of it, that is her fucking decision, not yours. Never fucking yours."

The darkness grew thicker as she gripped at her sword and drew it from its sheath.

The man tried to scramble to his feet to protect himself, but wasn't fast enough as the sword descended.

He screamed.

The blade stopped short of running through his chest.

"Lore, that's enough." Xin had his arms wrapped around her shoulders and pinned back.

She struggled against him, teeth clenched as the darkness grew denser, flying and weaving around both of them. "Let me go! He deserves this!"

"Come on, Lore. I know this isn't just about them."

"Of course it's about them. This whole fucking island needs to learn a thing or two about the power of a woman. Let me teach them!"

"I know, Lore. I wish violence was the answer here, but it's not." He put his lips close to her ear and whispered, "Please, just talk to me, alright? I know this reminds you of Jack and—"

"Shut up!" Her scream pierced through the night, sending everyone stumbling back in pain. Xin's grip weakened. She grabbed his arm, threw him over and slammed him into the ground. As he tried to regain himself, Lorelei focused back on Ricky, that blood-thirsty grin on her face. "Murder time."

Everyone screamed at her, begging her to stop. A couple of the younger men tried to restrain her, but found themselves tossed to the side like ragdolls. One threw a punch, but found her fist in his gut before he could even get close. Once again, Xin was the only one to break through her focus.

"Hey, idiot!"

Lorelei stopped in her tracks and immediately turned her glare at Xin. "What the fuck did you just call me?"

Xin stood up, dusted himself off and gave her a smug grin. "Idiot, moron, stupid. What are you going to do about it, dummy?"

That did the trick. Lorelei charged straight at him, a new-found rage in her eyes. Luckily for Xin, she still only had one good arm, otherwise he would have been a goner in her first attack alone. She wasn't pulling any punches with him today, and it caught him completely off-guard.

Punch to the head, dodged. Another fist to the gut, blocked. That was a mistake. She grabbed his arm and threw him to the ground again. He rolled away from the crushing foot aimed at his neck and leapt to his feet. She came in again with a flurry of strikes. He was getting into the rhythm, but he didn't want to hurt her. That meant holding back when she wasn't, and for someone on the same skill level as him, that was dangerous.

He needed to get her outside of town. Maybe if they were alone, she would actually talk to him.

As Xin lured Lorelei away from the group, Astrid ran over to the injured man, looking him over. As she concluded he was in no serious danger, she gave him a firm slap across the cheek.

The men yelled out in outrage and Richard glared at Chase. "What the fuck is wrong with your wom—" With a simple move of his hand, Chase silenced Richard. The man fell to his knees, gasping for air.

Chase walked over to Astrid. "Would you like to say something, Astrid?"

She glared at Ricky as he rubbed his sore cheek. "I absolutely hate killing and death. I would do anything in the world to avoid someone dying, but sometimes there is no right answer. Have you taken Rebecca to see a doctor about the pains?"

"No. I told you, she's just being dramatic. She had a hard time with the first kid and she's just scared. I know—"

Astrid slapped him again. "Never ignore a woman when she says she's in pain, especially with a baby. Even if it is just in her mind, these things should never be ignored. I am a trained doctor, and everything Rebecca told me could be signs of serious complications. If you let this go on, Rebecca and your child might die."

The man's face went white. "Wh-what?"

"I would like to take her back to our ship and give her a proper examination, but she refuses to do anything without you."

"No chance in Tartarus," Richard growled, now recovered from his winding. "We have our own doctor that can look her over. We're not trusting strangers."

Ricky stood to his feet and looked at Rebecca. "Wh… What do you want to do?"

She stared at him wide eyed for a moment, clearly unused to being asked her opinion. She looked from Astrid, to Richard, then back to Ricky. "I want to go with her."

Richard took a step towards them, his face beet red. "You can't be serious. She—"

Ricky strode to his wife, wrapping an arm around her shoulder. "No, Dad. No more. There's been enough death with you in charge. I can't risk losing Rebecca. Not again."

"You idiot! They know what we've done. We'll all be sent to Purgatory for this. Is that what you want?"

"No, of course not."

"Then we need to kill them now, before they can report any of this."

Ricky's face fell with disbelief. "What? Dad, no."

The rest of the men agreed and circled Chase and Astrid.

Astrid glared, but Chase just gave his jubilant laugh. With a swipe of his hand, a massive wind rose up and threw them all away.

"You good on your own, Astrid?" Chase asked.

Astrid nodded. "Yes, I should be. What are you going to do?"

"They want to act like criminals, I'll treat them like criminals. I'm going to take care of them, then head over to that mountain."

"What? Why?"

"Because that's where that weird black stuff was coming from."

"So… are you attracted to men or women?" asked Emir as he dried the dishes in the rack.

Dana jumped, almost dropping the dish in her hand. "Emir! When did you get back?"

"Only a moment ago. The Captain had some plans that did not involve me, so I thought I would come try to understand you better."

"Oh… alright." She thought for a moment, then said, "I'm not really sure, to be honest. I spent so long hating myself, I wanted to be able to love myself before I started worrying about someone else."

Emir laid the plate on the counter and set his hand on Dana's arm. "Oh... oh my Habibi, I am so sorry. I never imagined..."

"Habibi?"

"It is what we call a good friend on my home island."

"I'm... your friend?" Dana said with a confused smile. "But I thought..."

Emir folded to his knees, giving Dana a deep bow. "I am sorry, I was so confused and angry. I may not understand, I may not even agree completely, but if it is what makes you happy, then I will accept you, my friend."

Dana chuckled a little. "Well, that was a quick change of heart."

Emir stood to his feet and straightened out his shirt. "Yes, well, you are by far the kindest person I have ever met. It would be foolish of me to treat you otherwise."

"Thank you, Emir. That means a lot to me."

They gave each other a warm smile and continued on with the dishes.

After a while, Dana asked, "So, what are the others up to?"

Emir shrugged. "Something to do with getting the villagers to tell them why there's a giant ship here."

This time, Dana really did drop the plate in her hand. "There's a giant ship here?"

"Y-yes..."

Without another word, Dana turned on her heel and strode up the stairs.

Emir followed close behind. "What is the matter, my Habibi?"

Dana's eyes locked onto the ship nestled in the dock and slowly slid to the towering mountain in the distance. "I need to find them." With that, she began lowering the lifeboat.

"Wait, wait, wait. What are you doing?"

"I'm going to that mountain. I know that's where my kin are. I need to see them."

"But if these people took out full-sized giants, what would they do with you?"

"I'll sail around the town then go to the mountain by foot. It's getting dark. I should be able to make it there without anyone noticing."

"I am coming with you."

"No, I need you to stay here. If I don't come back... you can tell everyone where I went."

"Dana..."

She smiled and lowered herself down to the dark waters below.

Dana reached the mountain just as the sun had set. She examined it close, feeling the stone beneath her hands, feeling that faint connection with the Earth all of her kin had. Eventually, she came to an opening which would have been too small even for a regular sized human to fit through. Still, it gave Dana an opportunity. She gripped the stone and pulled it back as if it were a door on a rusty hinge and a massive chunk broke away. She couldn't control the Earth, but her strength more than made up for that.

One step at a time, Dana made her way into the newly made cave, letting her eyes adjust to the darkness within.

She heard a woman's voice mumbling, "Dolomite; Dumortierite; Ekanite; Emerald..."

The voice continued to list off precious stones in order, occasionally pausing to let out a small sob, then resumed with urgency. Dana followed the voice and in no time was standing before a giant woman, halfway twice the size of herself, balled up into the fetal position.

A sickening smell came over Dana as she neared, and she knew it in an instant. The smell of death. She looked around the room and her stomach dropped. It was hard to say for sure in the darkness, but there looked to be at least four dead giants lying around the mumbling woman.

Rage bubbled within Dana, but she managed to press it down long enough to whisper, "What happened here?"

The woman gasped and snapped her head out from between her knees. She raised her fist in the air, but stopped as she laid eyes on Dana.

"You... you're not from this village. You're... one of us?"

"Uhh, sort of. Half, anyway. My name's Dana."

"Byrnetha."

Dana gasped. "Princess Byrnetha?"

She gave a teary laugh. "That's right."

"Amazing." Dana looked around. "What happened here?"

Tears spilled from Byrnetha's eyes. "We have been going around to different islands trying to create relations with the humans again—To show everyone we have our beast under control…" She took a shuddering breath. "We decided to camp in the fields, getting sick of being on that boat all the time. I thought we were far enough from the town to keep people's minds at ease. I thought things were going well. One of the women even came to our camp one night to ask for our help, hoping we had some healers amongst us. I agreed to look her over and realized the baby within her was causing serious issues. I was going to help her, but then… they tricked us."

She began to sob again, and Dana came close, gripping her hand in hers. It was such an odd feeling being near someone larger than her. She had never been to the land of Titans before. The only giants she had met were her mother and a few other half-giants in the army.

After gathering herself, Byrnetha continued the tale. "A strange gas filled the air. We all became so woozy. Then they ambushed us, and there was nothing we could do."

"What were you doing before I got here?" Dana asked.

"Hmm?" She sniffed back her tears and wiped her face. "Oh, it's a trick we learn early in the control process. When we feel the beast start to take over, we concentrate on something that makes us happy. For me, I've always loved precious gems."

"So… you really can control it?" said Dana, the hopeful excitement clear in her tone.

"Yes… At least, mostly. I… I never had to test it against such… extreme circumstances before." She looked around again. "I made this mountain around me to protect the villagers from my wrath. I can't afford to kill any humans. It would set us back generations."

"How did you learn to control it?"

"With this." She pulled out an onyx gem hanging around her neck. "It is an ancient Relic of the Gods. It washed upon our shores a few generations ago and whispered the secrets of our inner beast."

Dana cocked her head as the gem seemed to shift about on its chain. "Is it… supposed to move like that?"

Byrnetha snapped her eyes on it. "What? No. I've never seen it do that."

"Maybe we should get out of here. It's not good to be in an enclosed space around… um… bodies."

Tears welled in her eyes again, but she held them back. "Y-yes, I suppose. But… but what if they're waiting for me? Waiting to finish the job?"

Dana shook her head. "They're not. Don't worry, my friends will help take care of you. We won't let any more harm come to you."

Byrnetha looked Dana over and slowly nodded. She pressed her palms against the Earth, and slowly the top of the mountain shifted and opened. Just as the moonlight peaked through, a cry of surprise rang out, which came closer and closer, until a clean, crisp breeze flowed around them. Dana smiled, and after a minute the orange-haired man she had expected came gliding down.

"Oh. Dark, very dark," said Chase as he touched lightly down. Dana laid a hand on his shoulder, and he looked up at her with surprise and relief. "Dana? I wasn't expecting to find you here."

"When I found out there were giants, I had to come and see. What are you doing here?"

"I took care of some rabble rousers and thought I'd come to see what was up with… that… darkness…"

Chase trailed off as they both looked up at the giant woman, now with swirling dark around her. It flowed into her ears. Her face furrowed in rage and with a vicious roar, screamed, "Traitor!"

She swung a huge hand down at Chase, who leapt out of the way. With a twist, his glider popped to his back, and he took off into the air.

"Traitor, deceiver, betrayer!" Over and over, she swiped at him, trying to hit him out of the air.

"My gorgeous gargantuan, I swear I've never met you before in my life!" shouted Chase.

"Byrnetha! Stop! This is one of my friends!" Try as she might, Dana's cries did nothing. Byrnetha's eyes had already changed from sparkling blue to blood red. The beast had been released.

Chase expertly weaved around one incoming hand, but was blindsided by the second. It wrapped around his whole body and squeezed.

"Bone crushing… so… cool," he wheezed.

"Please stop!" cried Dana. "Remember what you said! You can't kill a human! It will ruin your family!"

"Not a human," she growled, squeezing him tighter and tighter. "Traitor."

The world was becoming hazy. The giant hand gripping his body left no room for Chase to breathe. He couldn't go out like that. The air was his gift, his power. He couldn't lose to it.

He closed his eyes. *A strong mind breeds a strong body.* Every muscle relaxed, and the hand no longer felt very tight. He took a small breath, and with it came the sense. He could feel where the darkness was coming from. With the last bit of air in his body, he blew. A blade of wind streaked out, slashing against her neck. It wasn't aiming to kill, only to break that string around her neck. Her grip loosened ever so slightly, and Chase took a deep breath, summoning a strong gale to grab the item around her neck and send it hurtling into the distance.

The darkness was gone, but the beast was still there. Now there was no sense left. She gave a primal roar and wound up to smash Chase into the ground.

Down came her hand.

Smash.

A boulder collided with Byrnetha's face. She stumbled back and dropped Chase. Dana caught him from the air and laid him gently on the ground.

He gave her a warm smile. "Thank yeh, beautiful."

In came Byrnetha again, charging straight at the pair of them. Dana stood up and let out her own roar as Byrnetha's hand came down upon them.

At least it tried to.

Dana stood strong, holding up the woman's huge hand above her head. Byrnetha pushed and pushed, but could not win. Dana's eyes flickered from brown to red as the struggle continued.

Chase chuckled weakly. "Bloody brilliant, Dana, but I do hate to see women fighting over me." Chase took a deep, shuddering breath, and as he exhaled, a calm wind blew all around the two giants. Byrnetha was the first to relax, and then Dana. The red receded from both of their eyes as they turned to look at the chuckling Chase.

"So glad that worked."

29

Connections

Lorelei skidded through the purple field, bringing up plants and dirt as she tried to regain her footing. That gave Xin a moment to breathe. He needed that. Apparently so did she, as she stood in the waist high field just glaring at Xin, her chest heaving up and down.

"Alright Lore, it's just us. Can you please just talk to me now?"

"There's nothing to talk about," she spat.

"Come on Lore. The abused woman having a baby she doesn't want? I know what Mikhail did that day. I saw Jack. You don't have to hide from me."

"Shut up!" She charged in again, and Xin readied for impact. Punch to the gut. He blocked, but this wasn't just any punch. Cannon punch. The block didn't matter. The force of it went right through him, throwing him into the air, then into the ground.

Xin moaned and coughed, then slowly stood up, clutching his ribs. "Dammit Lore, I think you broke some ribs."

Lorelei laughed and started toward him. Before she could, a shining black gem hurtled from the sky, landing directly in between Lorelei and Xin. The darkness that had been surrounding Lorelei grew even thicker, and a dark smile came to her face. Both of them dived to grab it, but Lorelei was faster.

She placed it around her neck and was completely enveloped in the darkness. With one swift swipe of her dagger, her cast fell from her broken arm and was replaced by pure darkness. She gave the fist a couple squeezes, cocked her head mockingly and taunted Xin forward with a single blackened finger.

What the hell is this shit? Xin wondered, looking her up and down. He had seen many strange trinkets change people, animals, and things into strange shapes, but they never felt like this. This was different. He needed to get that thing off of her.

He took her taunt, charging in full force, but changed direction last second. One swipe at her torso while the open hand grabbed at the item.

Her dagger parried the sword, and her previously broken arm grabbed Xin's wrist. It was strong. His momentum was lost to him as Lorelei changed his path, his body hurdling faster than should have been humanly possible.

Once again, Xin hit the Earth, this time face-first. His mouth was filled with plants and dirt that he sputtered out as he leapt back to his feet.

She charged and punched. Xin wasn't about to be hit by one of those again. He side-stepped last minute and slammed the butt of his sword onto her nose, making her step back. She attacked again, still only punching and kicking, her sword attached to her hip.

Why not draw it? Was she trying to brag that she could beat him without a weapon? Or was there a part of her that still didn't want to actually hurt him?

No time.

Lorelei attacked over and over. There was no way he could keep holding back—he had to give it his all.

She sent a punch at his gut, and this time, he brought his sword across her arm. She wasn't expecting him to actually hit, but he did. Just a cut. She pulled her arm back and sneered. She ducked down, spinning around and taking out his feet. As he fell to the ground, her knee came up and smoked him in the chin.

The world spun, but he still caught himself, planting one hand on the ground. His foot shot toward her head. She jumped back, and he jumped up into another charge, slicing at her gut. She stepped into his attack, blocking the hilt of the sword and elbowing him in the face.

His world spun again.

Was she trying to knock him out? He couldn't let that happen. There were lives at stake.

As she was spinning away from him, he brought his sword around, slashing at her leg. Got it. She hissed in pain and limped back. She glared at him for a moment, clearly trying to rethink her strategy.

"Lore. This needs to stop," he managed to say through the panting.

"Are you admitting defeat, then?" She grinned that deadly grin. "Admitting you've been defeated by a girl?"

"Fine. You win. I don't care. It's never been about winning or losing with you. You should know that."

That wasn't what she was expecting. Her face twisted, and Xin knew her heart was at odds. Still, she shook herself out of it and scowled. "Tchah! Not good enough. This isn't over until one of us can't move anymore."

Again she attacked, though with far less fire. It was easy to dodge and strike her diaphragm to wind her.

"I don't want to hurt you, Lore."

She coughed, wheezing out the rest of her air. As she gasped in, she glared up at him, those golden eyes aflame. "Why not? You have every reason to want to hurt me! After everything I said to you, did to you, how can you just be so forgiving? I don't deserve that. I don't deserve you!"

Finally, she unsheathed her sword and swung it straight at his throat.

He didn't block.

He didn't dodge.

He didn't do anything but look her in the eye.

The sword stopped just before it bit into his flesh.

Not once did he blink as he gazed into those burning golden eyes. "I told you I wouldn't fight you back then, and I'm not going to do it now."

A scream of rage escaped her lips as she threw her sword to the ground. She hammered on his chest, and he saw the tears welling in her eyes. He didn't stop her.

"You did hurt me, Lore. You hurt me a lot. After you left, I cried for hours. I was a wreck for months—" He shook his head. "Years after that, but I kept moving on. Do you know why?"

"Because you're an idiot," she cried, her punches getting weaker and weaker.

"Because a part of me didn't believe you. A part of me hoped we would meet again someday. That my future wasn't completely torn to shreds." He softly grabbed her arms. "It tore me up some days, and I did a lot of things I'm not proud of, but I never stopped thinking about you."

She didn't fight him. She just looked up into his eyes. "It was all my fault. Everything that happened. I was too cocky. I pushed us too fast. I was too weak. You needed to rescue me, and because of that, Yuri died. It's my fault. I should have been the one that died!"

"That's not true, and Yuri would be giving you one hell of an up-cuff to hear you say it." He reached out for the item around her neck. She flinched, but let him take it.

As soon as he gripped it, the flowing darkness subsided into it, turning it into a single, solid black gem. The gem didn't matter to him at all. He tossed it to the side, staying locked in her eyes. His hand came up and pushed back her hair to see all of her wonderful face.

"I'm so sorry, Xin. I should have told you about Mikhail, but, after all our time together, I was sure I could handle him, that I could take him out of my life for good." She shook her head and placed it on his chest. "But I was just too damn weak."

He ran his fingers through her hair. "You thought you loved him once, didn't you? That's why it's such a frightening word to you—why you couldn't kill him."

Lorelei nodded and looked back up at him. "All this time, all those men. It started as a way of pissing off Mikhail, but then it became so easy to get what I wanted. I lost control. I lost… my connection," she said, recalling her conversation with Chase aboard the Oasis. "The last real connection I had was with you. But… I don't know if I'm ready for that again. I didn't want to get close to you again, but I miss that feeling so much." The tears welled in her eyes.

"You know, you really had me convinced that you didn't care about me."

"I'm sorry. I wanted to push you away to keep you safe. The truth is, I've never felt this way about anyone. It fucking terrified me five years ago, and it still does. But seeing you again, being so close to you. By the gods, all I've wanted to do was feel you again. But I don't want to hurt you. It seemed better—"

Xin's soft lips pressed up against hers, making her whole body feel alive. He pulled away, looking her once again in her eyes. "The future isn't written and the past is in the past. All I care about is right now with you."

"Are you sure about this? I don't know if I can give you the future you want. I don't know if I'll ever be able to say... It."

"It's alright. I'll wait. And even if you can't, that's alright. All I want is to be with you." He pulled her hips into him with such gentleness and care. She had almost forgotten how gentle he could be. Her heart raced and in an instant she wrapped her arms around his neck, kissing him with all that withheld passion.

She found her connection again.

"Have I mentioned I like your tattoos? 'Cause I really do."

Lorelei and Xin laid atop a well-trampled patch of crop, snuggled up beside each other, lacking all of their clothes. Lorelei ran her fingers along his body, outlining the marvelous tattoos all over his body while he stared lovingly at her.

"Me, too. That's why I got them. Met a woman that was covered in them on my travels. She said they were meant for protection and strength. Not sure if it's true or not, but I liked the look of it."

"Oh," Lorelei said teasingly. "Did you happen to see all of this woman?"

"And if I did? Would you be jealous?"

"What? The Siren, jealous of another woman?" she crowed, acting very offended as she stuck her chin in the air. "Maybe a bit." They both laughed. "But… why isn't your left arm done?"

He shrugged. "Didn't get a chance to finish it. Ah, I might get it done someday, but it takes a lot of time. That's something we don't seem to have a lot of anymore."

"Yeah…" said Lorelei, a little sadly.

Emir tried to shuffle his way through the fields to avoid their notice, but at the first rustle of the plant, Emir held perfectly still. He did not want his eyes taken for peeping.

Lorelei sat up with a sad look on her face. "Hey, Xin…"

He sat up as well, laying a hand on hers. "Yeah?"

"Thank you." There was a weak smile on her face.

Xin chuckled. "For what? Sleeping with you? I'll be honest, I've been wanting to do that for a while now…"

She laughed and gave him a light slap on the chest. "No, though I am grateful for that, too." Her eyes sparked as she looked him over. "Very grateful." Her face fell serious once again. "I meant about stopping me back there. You were right, violence wasn't the answer. I just couldn't stop myself."

"Well, that weird black stuff probably wasn't helping."

"Actually… I think it was trying to talk me down at first."

"Really?"

"Yeah, I was… I was just so focused on punishing that man. Like killing him would solve my problem with… *Him*." She shook her head. "I don't know. I guess everything just felt too familiar."

Xin wrapped her in tight, hugging her close.

She sighed. "And… you were right."

"About?"

"Jack."

"What about him?"

"Tchah." She gave him a scolding smile. "You know damn well."

"I'd like to hear it from you."

She sighed, then snuggled in tight to Xin before saying, "He's mine. He's my son." Tears welled in her eyes and she let a few spill over. "Sorry. That's the first time I've said that since he was born."

"Never apologize for that," he said, softly kissing her forehead. "But... Why did you keep him a secret?"

Lorelei sighed and looked up at the stars. "Why else? Mikhail. He can't know he has a child out here. If he knew, I'm sure there would be no keeping him in Purgatory. And I will never let him take him."

"Does Jack know?"

Lorelei shook her head as she fiddled her thumbs. "No, he doesn't. As far as he knows, he is an orphan like the other kids. It seemed safer... and... I just can't. Every time I look at him, I see Mikhail. I hate that this innocent child brings me so much hate. He didn't even do anything."

"Well," Xin began, clearly a little worried about his next question. "You obviously have no qualms against abortion, so why didn't you..."

A still silence filled the air. For a moment, her wide eyes looked up at him, but she looked away. "...I didn't want to," she said quietly.

"Why? If you knew it was Mikhail's..."

"But I didn't. Not for sure. There was a chance..." She choked, tears filling her eyes.

Xin's face fell with realization. He held her tightly. "Lorelei. I'm so sorry. I should have been there."

"It's not like I gave you a choice," she replied with a tear filled chuckle. "I thought it was fine. It felt right after realizing he wasn't yours that it was best you didn't know. But then... seeing you with him on the Oasis, and just being around you this last month. Feeling that connection. By the gods, all I could keep thinking was how much I wished you were there with me then. How much better Jack would have been with you around. Gods, I fucked up so much. Both of you deserve better than me."

"Don't do that, Lore. You did what you thought was right, and Jack... he's an amazing kid. He's definitely got your spirit. I saw that right away."

"Really?" she asked, looking up into his eyes.

"Yeah. Definitely. He's also got your ears." He caressed her ear lightly, and she smiled. "And your nose. He's even got your pinky."

Lorelei laughed. "That's a weird thing to notice."

"Yeah, I caught that one when he nearly gouged my eye out."

With another laugh, she hugged him tight. "Thank you, Xin. I… I guess I only ever saw Mikhail in him. I forgot to look past that."

"He's your boy. That's all that matters."

"Thank you," she whispered.

The ground beneath them shook. Xin and Lorelei hopped to their feet to see the mountain return itself to the Earth. They looked at each other in amazement.

"We should… probably go check that out, right?" asked Lorelei.

"Yeah, probably."

As they gathered up their clothes, Lorelei said, "Hey Xin… about what happened… for now could we just… keep it between us?"

He looked back at her, but she didn't meet his eyes. "You don't want to do this again?"

"No! No, I definitely want to do this again. It's just… I've worked kind of hard on the strong female badass persona. I don't really want to muck that up by being tied down with labels," she said nonchalantly. When she saw Xin's face drop a little, she continued, "That, and… I don't know… I guess I don't want everyone expecting something from me. Astrid will be all 'I told you so'. Gods know what Chase will say, but you know it will be perverted, definitely will be something about a threesome. I'd rather keep things the way they were for now."

"Alright," he said, though there was clearly a part of him that was disappointed. He kissed her softly on the forehead. "Come on. We really should get to that mountain."

"Yeah." She returned to gathering her clothes and getting dressed. As she pulled up her pants, she voiced a small, "ouch".

"What's wrong?" asked Xin, coming quickly over to her, pants equipped, shirt in hand.

She held out the once casted arm, and they both saw the clear swelling.

"Damn… that can't be good," sighed Lorelei.

"Guess that cast wasn't ready to come off. I'm sure Astrid can put it right. But for now…" Xin ripped his shirt in half and fashioned it into a sling, gently placing her arm inside.

Lorelei shot him a thankful smile. "It was so weird. That thing… it was like I had no pain at all."

"On that… You said the black stuff was trying to talk you down. How come it seemed to be helping you in our fight?"

Lorelei couldn't help but laugh. "I said it was trying to talk me down from killing Ricky. As soon as you stepped in, it wanted a fight. Not sure why…"

"What is with weird things wanting to kill me?"

After another laugh, something caught Lorelei's eye. She cocked her head at a peculiar item on the ground. "Hey… Xin? When did you start using three swords?"

"What? I don't. That would be stupid," he scoffed. "What would I do with the third one, put it in my mouth?"

"Well… you have three swords now," she said, pointing to Xin's two familiar swords lying beside a jet-black sword with a sapphire gem in the hilt.

Xin picked up the new sword and examined it closely. The hilt and sheath shone with a gem-like quality, and as he drew the sword, the perfect edge of the flawless blade sang in the wind. "Incredible. This is an amazing blade but… where did it come from?"

"Where is that thing that you took off of me?" Lorelei asked, and Xin smirked. "I am not talking about my clothes, ass."

Xin laughed then looked around in the dirt. "I don't know. I thought I threw it around here somewhere."

"Let me see the sword."

He went to pass it to her, but she held her hand up.

"No, no, don't pass it to me. That thing has already caused me enough problems. Just hold it so I can look at it."

Xin complied, confused.

Around the gem were carvings of an alphabet that Xin had not recognized, thinking they were just decoration. Lorelei, however, seemed to know otherwise.

"Shit…" she said, her face dropping. "I thought it could be, but… damn."

"What?" he asked, trying to decipher it himself. "What does it say?"

"I don't know, but I do know those ruins are something Ymir would always use."

"Ymir? The God Ymir?" Xin said, a little higher pitched than was usual.

"Blessed of Gaia's spirit, Ra's knowledge, and the arm of Ymir, the Godslayer was the perfect warrior," Lorelei quoted from the fairytale told to angel children. "It would seem that the Godslayer has found the arm of Ymir. Guess that explains why he wanted a fight. He was testing you."

"Don't even joke."

She tapped a finger on her cheek in mocking thought. "Well, I suppose it could be a regular old sword that showed up out of nowhere."

"Come on, we'll figure it out later," Xin sighed. He threw on his leather jacket over his bare shoulders.

Lorelei gave him an appreciative look-over. "Oh… I like that look. Let's do that more often."

Xin laughed. "Maybe. Gotta say though, it's not the most comfortable."

He attached his original two swords to his back, gripping the black sword in one hand and holding out the other to Lorelei.

Lorelei grinned, taking his hand joyfully, but as they started walking, her eyes shot to a spot in the field. She wrenched her hand away, dove into the field and came out with a cowering Emir.

"Emir?" Xin asked, more confused than anything.

She bared her teeth, getting in close to his face. "You fucking little sneaky pervert. How long have you been here?"

"I am sorry! I was just walking to the mountain to check on Dana and I heard you talking. I only saw at a glimpse you were… unclothed, and I didn't want to be punished for peeking, so I hid. Please do not take my eyes," Emir begged.

"How much did you hear?"

Emir sighed. "I… I heard everything… Including the information about your boy."

Lorelei threw him to the ground and drew her sword, a vicious rage in her eyes.

Emir scurried away, cowering from her sword. "Please! Please don't kill me! I swear I won't tell anyone. I understand the boy's father is very dangerous. I would not put a child at risk like that, I swear!"

Lorelei examined him, growled, and sheathed her sword. "I'm trusting you on this, Emir. Don't fuck it up."

Emir scrambled to his knees and bowed low. "Of course."

30

Descendants

As the three walked through the fields, it did not take them long to see the towering woman walking toward town. The trio cut them off, sprinting. They were quite surprised at her walking companions.

Dana walked beside her, rolling her eyes at a flirty Chase, who had seated himself upon the giant's shoulder. The giantess, however, did not seem to mind in the slightest.

Chase noticed his crewmates ahead of them and waved energetically. In one swift motion, he glided away and set down in front of them. "Hey! Xin, Lorelei! There you a—" Chase paused, giving Xin a once over. "Oh… heh… that's a good look for you, mate."

Xin rolled his eyes. "So I've been told. Don't get used to it."

Chase looked them both over. "Bloody hell, you two really went at it, didn't you?"

Lorelei's eyes went wide. "What? We did not… What are you talking about?"

Chase cocked his head. "I was talking about fighting." A knowing grin spread across his face as he looked between the two. "What were *you* talking about?"

"Nothing. Never mind." She snapped her head away from him to look at the giantess. "I am assuming you're the one that sent the distress bird."

"You… you found my pigeon? You came here to help us?"

"That was the plan…" Lorelei looked around, her face falling in sadness. "I'm guessing we were a little late."

Byrnetha nodded, tears streaming anew. "I am the only one left."

"I'm sorry."

"Hey, Byrn, think you could heal up these two as well?" asked Chase. "Looks like they need it more than I did."

"Of course." She bent down to her knees and held out a hand to Lorelei, who took a step back.

"Uh… him first." She motioned to Xin.

Byrnetha's face fell in sadness. "You do not trust me? Is it because I am a giant?"

"What? No. One of my best friends is a giant." Dana held her head a little higher at that comment. "I just… have general trust issues."

"Very well." She reached her hand out to Xin, but flinched away. "What is in your hand?"

"This?" Xin held up the onyx sword. "That is up for debate."

"It… it looks like my Relic."

"You mean that thing that made you mad at me for no reason?" said Chase, getting up close to it. "It wasn't a sword before, was it?" He attempted to take it from Xin, but it materialized through Chase's hand.

A chill ran through Xin's arm and he shivered. "I uh… I don't think it likes you."

"That's an understatement. It tried to make Byrn kill me."

Xin's face twisted with annoyance. "Then why the crap did you try to grab it?!"

"I was curious!"

Xin gave a grumbling sigh and shook his head.

"She also called him a traitor," Dana piped up. "Said he wasn't human."

"Yeah, that was mean," pouted Chase.

"I'm sorry." Byrnetha gazed softly at Chase. "It was what the voice was insisting."

Lorelei sighed, scratching at her head. "Well, I guess that proves it."

Xin looked at her with concern. "You think?"

"What? Proves what?" asked Chase.

"Never mind," said Lorelei, not meeting Chase's eyes.

Byrnetha gazed around, then asked, "Would you like me to take care of your broken bones now?"

"Bones?" asked Lorelei, pretty sure the only bone broken on her was her arm.

"Yes, yours and the man's two ribs. I am actually quite surprised he is standing. I imagine it is quite painful."

Xin shrugged. "I've had worse."

Lorelei slapped him on the arm. I thought you were exaggerating about the ribs! We shouldn't have..." Lorelei trailed off, looking around the group—Chase's grin growing wider. She snapped back to the smirking Xin. "Never mind! Fix him first."

Xin walked over to Byrnetha, who sat cross-legged on the ground. He removed his jacket, and her massive hand covered his whole torso as a faint glow radiating from them.

"Oh my, you have a powerful energy. Perhaps your pain tolerance is not natural. Have you been to the garden?" Byrnetha asked.

"Uh... no."

"A family blessing, perhaps?"

Xin's face went completely white.

Lorelei chuckled, and began to quote once again, "Blessed of Gaia's spirit—"

"Don't you start that again. It doesn't mean anything," snapped Xin.

Lorelei shook her head, and the rest of the group watched, confused.

"Well, whatever it is, it seems quite beneficial. You are all done," said Byrnetha.

Xin stood up, stretched and twisted with appreciation, and gave Lorelei a pat on the back. "Your turn."

Lorelei took a few steps towards her, but stopped, looking at her apprehensively.

"You can trust me," Byrnetha said with a soft, supportive smile.

"Just the arm, no snooping around my body, no feeling energies, got it?"

Byrnetha nodded. "Very well."

Lorelei stood beside her, holding out the swollen arm. The giantess' glowing hand wrapped gently around Lorelei's entire arm. Byrnetha's brow furrowed. Her breath shortened. Her eyes widened. She snapped her gaze to Lorelei in disbelief, and the ground around them shook.

"Byrn? What's going on?" Chase cried.

Byrnetha gasped and snapped her hand away, still gawking at Lorelei, who returned the look with pleading eyes.

"Byrn?" Chase prodded. "Are you alright?"

Byrnetha smiled at Lorelei and focused on Chase. "Fine. Sorry about that. I guess my body is more exhausted than I thought it was. Sometimes it's hard to control when I'm tired."

"We all need some rest," said Lorelei, already striding back toward town. "Let's get back to the village. I'm worried about Kari and Astrid out there alone."

Chase laughed, falling in step beside Lorelei. "Oh, don't worry. I took care of everyone before I left."

As the troupe returned to the village, nervous faces watched them from their windows, but no one interrupted them. They got to the docks, and Lorelei couldn't help but laugh. Five of the men from earlier were tied up tight and hanging from the flagpole. Upon seeing them, the men called for their release, but got no such thing.

Chase joined Byrnetha on her ship to make sure everything was in order, while Dana hurried off to their own ship to make up a meal for them all. As the rest of them walked up the gangplank, a distraught Kari ran over, holding out a crying toddler.

"Please take it," she said, shoving him towards Lorelei. "I don't know what to do with it anymore. He was happy playing with Chrissy for a while, but now he just won't stop."

"Why are you giving him to me?" Lorelei snapped. "Give him to the one that actually likes kids."

Kari started to pass him to Emir, but he held up his hands. "Oh no, I do not deal with children this small."

Xin laughed. "I think she meant me. Pass him over."

"Oh, okay."

Xin scooped him up without hesitation and rocked him up and down. "What's up, little man? You hungry?" He sniffed and gagged a little. "Maybe not. Let's get you cleaned up." With that, he grabbed a small pack from Kari and hurried him below deck.

Lorelei couldn't help but watch him go with doey eyes.

Kari cleared her throat.

As Lorelei snapped her eyes to her, she saw the little grin on her face. "Tchah, wipe that smile off your face. Where's the kid's parents?"

"In Astrid's room. They agreed to let Astrid look at Rebecca."

Lorelei was taken aback. "Even her husband?"

"Yep, guess he had a change of heart. They've been down there a while. I hope everything is going alright."

As if in response, Astrid and Ricky came up from below deck. Ricky saw Lorelei and flinched away from her, taking a step behind Astrid. He soon noticed Kari no longer had his son and went into momentary panic until Kari told him about 'the doo doo' incident and told him Xin would be right back.

Meanwhile, Astrid saw Lorelei, and her eyes lit up. "Oh, you're back! How are you feeling?"

"Fine."

Astrid came up close and grabbed her once broken arm. "Your arm is healed? How? It should have been another couple of weeks to fully heal."

She snapped her arm away. "Never mind about me. How's Rebecca?"

"She's fine and resting."

"That's good."

"What was going on with you? What was that black stuff?"

Lorelei sighed. "There's a lot to explain. I think we'll have to wait for everyone to be together, so I only have to do it once."

"Alright."

A soft melody floated through the air with the sound of a man's voice. Astrid and Lorelei looked over to the stairs where Xin was coming back up with the boy sucking on a bottle.

Astrid giggled. "I thought he couldn't sing."

"Huh?" said Lorelei, snapping herself away from staring. "Of course he can sing. He just doesn't like having an audience."

To prove her point, Xin snapped his gaze to all the eyes looking at him. His song ended abruptly and his face went red. "Oh... uh. Hey."

Ricky came over and took his son with care, rocking him back and forth in his arms, a smile on his face.

Lorelei sneered. "So we're just going to ignore the fact this man beat his wife?"

Astrid sighed. "I understand, Lorelei, but there's not much we can do. They both assured me it was a one-time thing. And you have to admit, circumstances were pretty extreme."

"That's no excuse."

"I know. Still, I think he is legitimately contrite. We just have to hope that they've learned enough to grow from this experience."

"Everyone deserves a second chance, right?" Lorelei said with just a hint of sarcasm.

"I still think that's true," she replied with a smile.

"And I still think you're naïve." Lorelei sighed. "But I suppose one of us should be."

The crew had helped Rebecca and her family back home. Though it was well past midnight by the time their meal was served, the crew gathered on the deck and shared an enormous meal with Byrnetha. It was both in celebration and memory for her fallen comrades, and the rightful capture of the guilty party.

Chase had sent out a pigeon earlier that day to the Gaian forces to come collect the criminals. It would be a few days before any ship could get there, so they enjoyed their night together.

As the food had disappeared, and the last tale had been told, Chase stood up and looked at Lorelei. "Alright, lass. Our bellies are full, we are all together, and there is no immediate danger. Now would you care to explain to the group what the hell happened today?"

Lorelei chugged back her drink. She leaned back in her chair, looking at the starry sky as she thought. With a sigh, she leaned in and said, "Alright. Fine. Sit back and get comfy. This is going to be a long one."

Chase did as he was told, and Lorelei stood to her feet. She held out her hand to Xin. "Relic."

"What? I thought you didn't want to touch it."

"That was before you proved you had control over it."

"I did what?"

Lorelei rolled her eyes and beckoned with her hand. "Relic."

Xin shrugged. "Alright."

He placed the sword in her hand, and she held it out for all to see. She motioned to the writings around the shimmering blue stone. "These, my friends, are the writings of Ymir."

"I did not write anything," said Emir, looking at her quizzically.

"What? No, not you. Ymir with a 'Y'. You know, the god."

"Oh… Why does it sound like it starts with an 'E' then?"

"I don't know. Because that's the way you say it."

"That is confusing."

"Let's just assume for this whole conversation, I am not talking about you."

"Very well."

"Anyway…" She shook her head in frustration and smiled. "This is important for one very big reason." She took the sword and hucked it out into the ocean.

"What the hell?" cried Xin. "What'd you do th—" His words stopped short as the sword appeared back in his hand. "Uh..."

Lorelei grinned. "The arm of Ymir has found its master."

Everyone looked around, confused.

As they all looked back to Lorelei, she smiled and continued with ecstatic energy. "Listen closely, for you are about to hear a tale reserved for the most pompous assholes in our world. The Angels.

"Long ago, the gods descended from the heavens to heal the war-torn world. They were wonderful, kind, perfect, and with them, a peace reigned like no other.

"These perfect beings were betrayed by their wayward brother—a god of trickery and mayhem. He released the treasure that had fallen along with the gods, and in so doing, caused humanity to become vicious, releasing all of the evils the gods had worked so hard to quell.

"The gods sought to punish the traitorous god, but their divine powers kept them from harming each other. For this reason, the gods worked together to create a human capable of slaying a god.

"Blessed of Gaia's spirit, Ra's mind, and Ymir's arm, the Godslayer was the perfect weapon. So perfect that the creature slew the traitorous god in a mere instant. However, after its purpose was fulfilled, the Godslayer became paranoid. He began to believe the Lost God was not slain, only escaped, and so he went on the hunt. When he could not find him, he passed the task on to his kin.

"To this day, the hunt continues. However, after so many years, the godslayers have forgotten what to look for. Now, they will take the life of any wayward Angel, so be a good girl (or boy), and stay in the fortress."

Chase, who had been watching the story with pure, child-like excitement, broke out into applause as Lorelei finished with a grand bow and sat back in her chair.

"Bloody brilliant!" Chase exclaimed. "I thought for sure I had heard every story there was. I love being surprised. I do have a question, though."

"By all means."

"Assuming the tale is true, why didn't the gods just... you know... kill the Godslayer? It seems a bit flawed to leave someone alive that can kill you."

Lorelei shrugged. "Not sure, exactly. Obviously they took away the sword of Ymir, since the giants had it, and I don't even know what the mind of Ra is supposed to be, but maybe they took that away, too. Would explain the going crazy part. But as far as I know, there is no way to take back a Blessing once it's bestowed. Maybe they just figured they weren't a threat anymore."

Chase grinned, slapping Xin on the back. "Bloody brilliant."

Xin sighed. "You... may not think so in a moment."

"What? Why?"

"Traitor, deceiver, betrayer," said Lorelei, staring Chase in the eye. "Why do you think the Relic told Byrn that?"

"Uh, 'cause I got a Blessing from the Lost God?"

Lorelei shook her head. "I have another theory. But first, how old do you think Dana is?"

"Uh..." Chase chuckled nervously. "It's not polite to guess things like that."

Dana smiled. "It's alright. I don't mind."

"Ah... haha. Well, I'd say you don't look a day over thirty-five."

Dana shook her head. "Don't be polite, Captain. I know I look at least forty."

Chase chuckled.

"And how old are you, Dana?" Lorelei asked.

"Twenty-eight."

"What?" Chase's mouth was agape. "How..."

"I told you, giants age faster than regular humans," said Lorelei. "This is because they have multiple blessings. So then, how do you have multiple blessings while looking younger than you are?"

"I... I don't know."

"Because you're not human. Not completely. You're an Angel."

Chase laughed. "Well, that's sweet of you to say, lass, but that's usually my pick-up line."

"Argh. No. I mean you're an actual Angel. Your father must have been one. And with the power you have, likely a very old one."

Chase stared at her for a moment, took out a hearing aid to ensure they were on correctly, and looked bewildered at her again. "I think I misunderstood you."

"You definitely did not, but just so we are a hundred percent clear," she said, then signed the words as well as repeated the phrase, "You are an Angel."

Chase slowly looked around the table. When he decided no one was trying to mess with him, he turned back to Lorelei, desperation in his eyes. "You're joking, you must be joking. That's not possible. Angels are perfect, aren't they? I was born defective! There's no way—"

"Actually, it proves it more than anything. All Angels are part human, but the Angels with the most divine blood end up having a high risk of birth defects. I suppose the bloodlines don't quite mesh that well. For example, Odin was born with only one eye, and Set only has partial use of his legs."

"Really? I had no idea," said Chase in wonder.

"Well, there is more than one reason the Angels tend to hide out in their fortresses."

Chase paced back and forth. "So what would that even mean? How can you be sure?"

"I suppose the only way to know for sure is to see how long you live, but that's a waiting game I'm not willing to play, especially seeing as how you already look ten years younger than you are," she said in contemplation, then shook her head. "Anyway, it means we need to make sure you can control your power, because you are going to be living far longer than any of us will. Meaning you are going to have people's lives in your hands for hundreds of years."

"Hundreds?" Chase squeaked, stopping in his tracks.

"That's right. If we assume your father is an Ancient, you may even live close to a thousand years."

"Wait, wait, what's an Ancient?" Chase asked.

"An ancient is a first generation Angel. A direct son or daughter to the primal gods. They are ones with the most numerous and powerful blessings. And the ones who have the longest lifespan. There are currently only two alive from the twelve families. Demeter Arieos of Gaia and Set Urielais of Ratum."

"So, I'm a kid of one of them?"

"No. With your unique power, and now with the reaction of Ymir's relic, I think it's pretty obvious. You're a descendant of the Lost God."

A silence filled the deck. No one knew what to say.

Chase looked at the Relic sitting in front of Xin with a sudden queasiness. "So… how did Xin prove he had control over the Relic?"

Lorelei grinned. "Because he didn't slice off your head the moment he saw you again."

Xin straightened and looked around. "What?"

"Tell me the thought didn't cross your mind when Chase tried to touch the sword."

"I…" Xin looked at Chase, then at his drink. "Maybe… for a split second."

Chase inched away from Xin.

"But I just brushed it aside. Chase is my friend. I would never hurt him."

Chase grinned.

Lorelei smiled. "Thus proving you are the master and sticking it to fate. Well done, Godslayer."

Xin furrowed his brow in thought, flipping the sword over and over again in his hand. Memories of his father swam through his mind. Did his father really know about this godslayer business? Did he really keep it from him all these years?

Chase laid a hand on Xin's shoulder. "Mate? You alright?"

He looked into Chase's worried sky-blue eyes. Xin's father always taught him that the gods didn't control his fate, but how else would his path meet up with the descendant of the god he was meant to be hunting? Maybe his father was wrong…

Or maybe his friendship with Chase really was still a way of sticking it to fate.

Xin smiled and patted Chase on the back with his free hand. "Well, I suppose if it's already attached to me, I'll keep it around." He looked at the sword. "As long as you agree we protect Chase, not hurt him."

The sword melted from his hand, climbed up his arm and onto his back. As it reformed, it sent one sword clattering to the ground, effectively taking its place.

"I guess that's a yes," said Xin.

Chase dived for the discarded sword on the ground. "Oh! Can I have this one?" Chase drew the sword and was promptly disappointed by its broken blade. "What the? Why did you have a broken sword on your back?"

Xin shrugged. "Konstantin broke it."

"But why did you still have it on?"

"Well… because I never found a good replacement. I can't just go around with one sword on my back. It wouldn't make an 'X'."

Everyone stared, waiting to see if he was joking. When he sent them all a confused look, a roar of laughter erupted.

"What? It's my thing." When the laughter didn't cease, Xin gave a grumbling sigh and downed his drink.

As the laughter faded away, Emir leaned in, waving his hand back and forth. "Alright, alright, I have one more question."

Lorelei wiped a happy tear from her eye and motioned him to continue.

"How is it you know so much about the gods and angels?"

Lorelei's smile faded away as everyone else turned their attention back to her.

"That… is a very good question," said Astrid.

Lorelei took a swig of her drink, not making any eye contact. "I like to learn things."

"That can't be it," said Chase, getting in close. "I spent half my life living with priests that served an Angel, but you know way more than any of them ever did."

Astrid pressed a finger to her cheek. "And you do seem to have a rather passionate hatred for the Angels… More than most."

Lorelei's finger tapped on the table as she glared at all of them. Finally, she sighed. "Alright, alright. But this information does not leave this circle, understood?" The crew gave an unhesitant round of agreement. Before continuing, she sent an especially dark look up to Byrnetha, who gave a nod.

"I have you and your crew to thank for my safety. Your secrets are safe with me."

Once again, a sigh escaped Lorelei's lips as she sank back in her chair. "Alright. Before I joined Konstantin's crew, I was…" Another sigh. "I was a noble."

"A noble?" squeaked Emir.

"That's right."

Astrid shook her head. "That still doesn't explain it. We've met plenty of nobility. Byrnetha's a princess of the Titans. Did you know about any of this?"

Byrnetha shot Lorelei a concerned look before shaking her head. "No."

Lorelei gave a grumbling sigh. "Ugh, why is everyone so nosy all of a sudden?"

Everyone stared expectantly.

"Fine! My… family had close ties to an Angel family. I… kind of made friends with one of the Angels and she would tell me that story. Then, one day, she died. After that, I decided I hated how things were at home, so I ran away."

Emir got up close to her, looking her straight in the eye. "But… but why would you leave a life of leisure? Of power? Of riches?"

Lorelei smiled knowingly, meeting his gaze with burning intensity. "Why would you, Prince Emir?"

Emir took a few stumbling steps back, and sights were now on him. "I—"

Astrid giggled. "Well, for love, of course. That was pretty obvious from your story."

"R-right!" he confirmed with a nod, sweat dripping down his unusually pale amber face.

Byrnetha stooped down, examining him with severe skepticism. "I believe her. She has knowledge beyond even mine, but you? I have a hard time believing you are royalty. What proof do you have? What was your family name?"

"W-well I—" Emir looked around the table. By the looks on their faces, only Astrid believed his original story. He sighed. "Alright, fine. I lied. But only about being a noble. The rest of my story is true! My princess and I fell in love. We ran off together after my brother betrayed me and were separated by the elements."

"Oh, Emir, that is so tragic!" cried Astrid.

Xin looked at her in disbelief. "Do you seriously still believe him? That story still stinks."

"It does not!" insisted Emir.

As Emir glared at Xin, Lorelei stood up with a sigh. "Well, I'm done for the night. We should all get some rest. Emir, you keep watch on those guys." Lorelei jabbed a thumb to the captured men, now tied up to the bottom of the flagpole on shore.

"What? Why me?"

"Did you fight today?"

"No."

"Did you do surgery today?"

"No…"

"Did you watch a screaming toddler today?"

Emir gave a resigned sigh. "Alright, alright, I get it. I did not do anything today. I'll keep watch." With that, he grumbled his way to the crow's nest.

Lorelei went below decks with a simple wave. Astrid, Kari, and Dana also gave their farewells and hurried off to their rooms. Chase waved them all off, and as they cleared out, sat looking into his drink. A strong hand gripped his shoulder, and he looked up at the warm face of Xin.

"Hey buddy," he said. "I know it's a lot to process. Just… keep in mind it doesn't change who you are as a person. You're still Chase."

"Yeah…" Chase shot him a warm smile. "Thanks mate."

Xin patted him on the shoulder and headed below deck as well.

As Chase stared once again into his drink, he heard a woman's voice. He turned around and saw Byrnetha giving him a concerned look.

"Sorry, gorgeous. Lost in my own world. I didn't actually hear what you said."

"Oh, I said that is a big thing to learn about yourself. Are you alright?"

Chase smiled weakly. "Aye, I think so. It's just… a lot of things are starting to make more sense now, but I just can't figure out why my ma never told me. Did she even know? I always thought she never wanted to talk about my dad because she didn't actually know who he was. You know, had an orgy or something and I was the by-product."

Byrnetha snorted out a laugh. "That's an odd thing to think about your mother."

Chase's cheeks turned red. "I… It's not like I imagined her in those instances. I dunno. Mom was pretty adamant about being open with your sexuality. I guess it didn't seem strange to me." He gave a sad sigh. "Just wish the other priests were as open as she was. Would have made things a lot easier after she died."

"I'm so sorry."

"But… Why didn't she tell me? Did she even know? She must have known something, looking back on it now. She was so worried and excited when I got my powers, but not surprised. Like she knew it would happen. So why didn't she tell me?"

"I guess you'll never really know for sure."

Chase sighed. "I guess not. Not unless I find him somehow." They exchanged warm smiles, then Chase said, "But you should really get to bed. You've had one hell of a week."

She looked over at her boat, a sad uneasiness about her. "I… suppose I should."

"I'm guessing you don't want to be alone."

She shook her head. "Not really, no."

"Well, I can stand by your door tonight, if you'd like."

Her cheeks went red. "I… suppose."

"What were you thinking?"

"That… maybe… you could stay in my room?" Before Chase had a chance to reply, she covered her face. "I'm sorry, I'm being too forward. Just ignore me."

"Too forward?" Chase summoned a wind to glide up to her shoulder. "My gorgeous woman, that is just the amount of forward that I like." He laid a kiss on her cheek and she giggled.

"Oh wait, how old are you?"

She giggled again. "Twenty-one."

He gave a sigh of relief. "Oh, good. Apparently, my radar is way off with you lovely giants. Lead the way, my lady."

31

The Escape

The ship lurched, and Lorelei sprang out of bed. That wasn't a wave. The ship groaned in protest. As Lorelei reached the deck, a familiar yet daunting sight awaited her. The ship's sails had been wrapped in rope, and Hugo's all so familiar battle ship sailed toward shore.

"Shit!" she cried, just as the rest of the crew joined her on deck. "Dammit, Emir, did you fall asleep?"

"Uhh…" Emir poked a groggy head over the crow's nest, struggling against a few ropes. "Maybe."

She did a quick head count. "Fuck. Where's Chase?"

"Not sure," said Xin. "But I have a guess." He pointed to the giant's ship, and Lorelei rolled her eyes.

"Of course. Xin, try to keep the ropes from getting too tight. From this distance, Hugo's power is limited. We need to get a move on before he gets any closer."

Xin drew both his swords, examining his new addition with some appreciation. "Alright, time to show me what you've got." He leapt in the air, slicing through a group of ropes like nothing. As he landed back down, he said, "Huh, I was expecting something fancy, what with you being an enchanted sword and all. Oh well."

As Xin continued to hack away, Lorelei barged onto the ship, then into Brynetha's bedroom, where both she and Chase were snuggled up. Upon her door being slammed open, Byrnetha screamed, and Chase leapt up and ready for battle, unabashed by his nudity.

Lorelei threw his coat at him. "Chase. Clothes. Hugo's here."

"What? How? Why?"

"Did you send that emergency pigeon yourself?"

Chase slipped on his pants. "Uh… yeah."

"That's why. The pigeon went to the nearest army ship. Apparently that was Hugo's. Probably went overtime knowing we were here. Meaning, it's time to haul ass and hopefully he'll spend enough time here to let us get away."

Chase was dressed and ready to go before she even finished her sentence, and the two raced back. Hugo's ship was almost in port, and the ropes were still reaching.

"Oh, no you don't. Not again." With an open palm, Chase chopped through the air, slicing all the ropes. They fell limp into the water.

"There's no point fighting," Hugo's voice called over the loudspeaker. "Come in quietly and I promise to take it easy on you."

"Fat chance, Hugo baby!" Lorelei called back, not actually expecting him to hear her. The sails were free, and together Xin and Lorelei kept the oncoming ropes at bay while Chase tried to send them sailing.

A giant mass of ropes blotted the sun. Xin and Lorelei readied for the overwhelming mass.

The ropes stopped.

On the docks, Byrnetha held them tight in her giant hands.

Chase ran to the edge. "Byrn, you can't!"

"Don't worry. These little guys have no authority over a princess of the titans. Leave quickly. I'll keep them busy as long as I can."

"Thank you. May the gods keep you safe, Beautiful." With a tip of his hat, the sails filled and the Water Lily was off into the vast ocean.

Hugo's voice echoed in the distance, probably demanding them to come back, but they were too far off.

That awful island vanished onto the horizon, and Lorelei let out a boisterous cheer. "Well done, Captain. I'd say that mission was a…" She gave him a knowing smile. "Rousing success."

Chase broke into a fit of laughter, clutching at his gut. "Too right."

She gave him a light punch on the arm. "So, finally got to sleep with a giant, huh? How was it?"

Chase grinned. "Great. Lots of fun…" The smile faded a little. "Different…"

"Felt a little small, did we?"

"A bit…"

Lorelei laughed. "Well, I suppose that is to be expected."

"What about you?" Chase gave her a smile. "Have you ever been with a giant?"

"Full sized? Nope. Probably never will. The half giant was intimidating enough. Kinda fun…" She shrugged before sneaking a peek at Xin and saying, "But I've had better."

Xin withheld a smirk, but Chase didn't seem to catch the glance. "You're talking about me, right?" he asked hopefully.

Lorelei chuckled. "Actually, yeah, you were better. Still though, not the best I've had."

"Well, how about you tell me about the half-giant, and your best time, and I will take notes?"

Lorelei chuckled, sighed, and shook her head. "Another time, maybe. For now, we have to make sure to get out of Hugo's range. We do not want to run into him again."

"Alright, alright, I'll get back to filling the sails." He glided off, yelling at Emir to chart their course to Olympia as the rest of the crew went about their own business.

And Lorelei had her own business to take care of.

Her eyes wandered over to her stalwart swordsman, who was leaning against the mast, trying his best not to devour Lorelei's form with his eyes, but Lorelei wanted to be devoured. She sauntered by him, locking her hungry eyes on him before heading toward the bow of the ship. Once they were out of sight from the rest of the crew, Xin slid up behind her, wrapping his arms around her waist and pulling her in close.

"So," he whispered in her ear. "Was that your way of telling me I'm the best you've had?"

"Hmm, maybe."

He ran his hand teasingly to the top of her pants, making her bite her lip anxiously.

"What do you think you're doing?" she asked softly. "Someone might see."

"They might… I suppose I should probably go somewhere else, just to be safe." Ever so slowly, he drew away. She gripped his wrist, placing his hand back where it was.

"I'm sure they'll be busy for a while," she said, urging his hand a little lower, and turning her head to kiss him.

Their interaction didn't last long, as a little red ball came bouncing past and over the side of the deck. The two didn't notice that, but they did notice Kari yell from a distance,

"I think your ball went over here, Chrissy!"

Acting purely on shock and instinct, Lorelei grabbed Xin's arm and tossed him over the edge of the boat as he uttered a single "Ak!"

Kari and Chrissy sprinted around the corner. "Hey Miss Lorelei, have you seen Chrissy's ball? I think I threw it this way."

"Nope, sorry. Haven't seen it," she replied as normally as she could muster, though her body still tingled.

"Aw man, I hope it didn't go overboard," she said, motioning to look over the edge.

"No, no, it definitely didn't. Besides, couldn't you make something to find it?" Lorelei prodded.

Kari pondered for a moment. "Maybe I could! Thanks Miss!" and ran off with Chrissy close behind. Lorelei sighed with relief and cautiously looked over the side of the boat where the annoyed face of Xin greeted her. He'd apparently found an edge to wait upon.

"Sorry," she said with a bashful chuckle. She reached her arm down to help him up, but he pulled her down instead. In one swift motion, he pinned her against the ship with one hand and threw the lost red ball back onto the deck with the other.

Satisfied that they were alone at last, Xin said with a smirk, "Now, where were we?"

A couple of days went by with no incident. They were back on course, heading straight to Olympia, but the ease would not last. Hugo's ship caught up with them. They were able to keep out of range of those annoying ropes, but they had to keep in constant motion. They would get ahead for a while, but just when they thought they were in the clear…

"Enemy ship to the aft port!" Kari bellowed from the crow's nest above as Chrissy whined circles around her. A whistling sound cut the air, followed by the splash of a cannon ball in the waters just shy of their stern.

"By the gods! Can't a guy get a moment's rest?" cried Chase, his orange hair and red bandana soaked with sweat from his constant workout. Still, he filled the sails once again with a large gust of wind.

Lorelei set down her guitar with a sigh, stretching out and heading to the cannon. "Oh man, Hugo baby, if I had known you were going to be this upset I would have… Ah, who am I kidding? I would have done the same thing." She chuckled as Xin set a ball into the cannon, giving her an eye roll with only a hint of a smile. With calm clarity, she took aim and skimmed the edge of the oncoming ship.

Another ball flew toward the deck of the Water Lily, and with a sliver of a grin, Xin drew his wondrous new relic sword and parried the thing into the ocean.

"I do not understand!" complained Emir, poring over his maps next to the wheel. "How do they keep catching up? We have wind powers."

"Well, we are in their territory," said Lorelei, taking aim once again but severely missing. "Plus, they have one of the best navigators around. Both at sea and in the bedroom."

"Is there a man you have not slept with?" Emir scolded, drawing a scowl from Lorelei.

"Excuse you. I am quite particular about who I sleep with. The Navigator thing was Hugo's idea," she said, as if that explained everything.

Chase appeared beside her with an excited grin. "Did you have a threesome? I thought you didn't do orgies."

"I draw the line at threesome," she said with a smirk, taking another shot, but once again missing.

Chase grinned. "Good to know."

"Can we please focus? We're being attacked!" snarled Xin.

Another ball flew in, but before it could hit, Chase blew it off course.

Lorelei snapped a finger at Emir. "Right, navigator, it's time to get better. Our little ship doesn't stand a chance against Hugo's."

"But how do I get away from someone who knows the currents so well? They already know the best path to our destination."

"But do they know our destination?" asked Lorelei with a knowing smirk.

"I… no. They believe we are going to Royal Derry to see the Captain's mother's grave. Wait… I have not asked. Is that where you would like to go, Captain?"

"Huh?" asked Chase, who had been redirecting a cannon ball and hadn't actually heard the question.

Emir reiterated quickly.

"Oh, nah, mate. I just used that to get us across the border. A grave is just a chunk of stone. I know ma is with me wherever I go."

"Excellent!" exclaimed Emir, a little too eagerly as he pored over his maps again. "Now, we can take this path, to make them believe we are going there, then hop to this one, hopefully throw them off the path, and then from there we can take this one to quickly get us to the city. Perfect!"

"You got this, Emir?" Lorelei asked, firing another shot.

Emir stood tall, hands on the wheel, with a prideful smile on his face. "I have got this."

He did indeed have this. The Water Lily flew through the water, its small size and favourable winds getting them quickly out of the battleship's sights.

Their path would take them longer to reach their destination, but after two days without seeing Hugo's ship, they felt they may finally be in the clear.

At this time, training had returned full tilt for Chase. Meditation in the morning, followed by strength workouts from Xin, then fighting basics in the afternoon from Lorelei.

One afternoon, the lovely Lorelei, her hair messily tied up and away from her face as it usually was on the ship, was sporting a very long shirt that went all the way to her knees. Chase wasn't sure if you'd call it a dress, but it also wasn't a man's shirt, so that was different. In fact, since they left that awful island in the Rustic Ring, Lorelei seemed to dress differently every day. Less ragged depression, more comfortable woman. He wasn't quite sure why that was, but he had his theories. Especially since a certain stoic swordsman seemed to be far more smiley than he usually was. Still, it was just a theory.

Since flirting was off the table during training, Chase needed to think of some other conversation (that didn't include her may or may not be dress) in order to take the sting away from his burning legs as he held his stances. Finally, he decided on something that had been eating away at him since the last island.

"Hey, Lorelei, I was wondering if you'd tell me more about... you know, being a noble."

"Well, that's random," said Lorelei with a cocked eye.

"First thing that came to mind through the pain," Chase chuckled weakly, his legs shaking.

"Change stance."

He complied and looked over at her, hoping she would continue.

She sighed. "What did you want to know?"

"I guess... why did you leave?"

"There were a few factors. First thing was that my father was not very fatherly. But... I guess the main reason I left was... that I met a guy. I thought all my problems would go away if I ran off with him. I guess I wasn't wrong, but it also just made new problems."

"But why didn't you go back? Or why didn't they come find you?"

"They think I'm dead. Believe me, the last thing I want is for my family to know I'm alive. As horrible as Konstantin's ship was… it was still better than home."

"I'm so sorry."

Lorelei shrugged, gazing off to the horizon. No, make that in the direction Xin was working out.

"Uh, Lorelei, are we going to switch stances?" asked Chase, his legs feeling like rubber.

"Huh? Oh, yeah. Switch to punches."

Chase complied, continuing his drills over and over. Far longer than usual. Still, Lorelei remained lost in space.

"Lorelei, how long are we doing punching?" Chase whined, but Lorelei didn't seem to notice. "Lorelei? Lorelei!"

"Huh?" she muttered, listing her gaze back to Chase. "Oh, right, uh, switch to blocks."

"Alright," he sighed.

"You know what? I think that's enough for today. I'm going to grab a snack," she said, motioning to leave.

"What? But we just started."

"Well then keep doing drills. I don't care." She strode off below deck, walking unnecessarily close to Xin on the way.

Chase stood and pouted, deciding to go work on his powers at the edge of the boat instead. He supposed it was his own fault for bringing up her past.

After what felt like forever, Chase sighed with boredom. "That snack is sure taking a while…" he muttered to himself, scoping out the deck to see if he perhaps missed her coming back out. Nope, no sign of Lorelei, or Xin for that matter. Suspicious. Although it was pretty normal for him to have a shower after his workout.

During his thought process, his stomach gave a growl. He looked around for their friendly giant, and yelled, "Hey Dana! When's supper? I'm starving."

"I'll get started on it right now, Captain," said Dana, putting down the comically small flute, then heading to the kitchen.

What to make? Dana pondered. She really loved making food for everyone, though it was quite the challenge to keep everyone happy. Astrid: no meat, Lorelei: no beans, Emir: no pork, Kari: fresh vegetables whenever possible. Everyone had their preference, but they knew being on a ship, their choices were often limited. For example, right now the only meat they had left was pork, meaning Emir would have to eat what Astrid got. She knew no one would ever be mad at her for what she had to cook, but she really did hate disappointing people. Perhaps she could ask Xin to go fishing. He seemed to enjoy that. Of course, she'd have to find him first.

Dana stepped into her kitchen, the sparkling floors glinting with sunbeams from the portholes. The silver pots and pans clanked and swayed with the rocking of the boat, and Lorelei sat alone at the dining table, seemingly quite happy.

As soon as Dana entered, Lorelei's head snapped to her in surprise, sweat upon her brow. In an overly loud voice, she said, "Dana! It's Dana. Dana is here."

Dana gave her a cockeyed look. That was an odd way to greet her. "Lorelei, you don't have to yell. I'm not Chase," she concluded with a giggle, but quickly regretted it. "Oh, that wasn't very nice. I'm sorry."

While Dana was apologizing, Lorelei seemed to be whispering something incoherently, gripping the table.

How odd, Dana thought. Still, she wasn't one to judge. "I was just about to make some lunch, but we're pretty low on supplies. Do you know where Xin is? I was hoping he could do some fishing."

"Xin?" she squeaked, once again gripping the table. "Nnnno, I haven't seen him," she said, oddly breathily.

"Are you feeling okay?" Dana asked.

"Fine! Fine, I'm fine," she said energetically, biting her lip. "Actually! You know, I think I did see Xin go below deck. You should go look for him."

"But… supper?" said Dana, looking longingly at the kitchen.

"The faster he goes fishing, the faster we get more supplies, right? Go on. Better hurry!"

Dana shrugged and did as she was told. She wasn't one to argue.

As she climbed down the stairs, she heard Lorelei cry out, "By the fucking gods!"

It didn't seem angry, but in case there was a chance, Dana hurried off. She didn't like being around Lorelei when she was angry.

Lorelei sat at the table, sweat on her brow, panting heavily.

Xin appeared from below the table and sat beside her, a satisfied grin on his face. "Phew, I thought she would never leave."

She gave him a playful punch on the arm. "I told you to stop, shithead."

"Did you?" he teased, running a hand over her thigh. "Things were pretty muffled down there. Besides, you said you needed some stress relief. I was just obeying orders."

"I'm going to get you back for that one," she growled playfully.

"Promises, promises."

Dana came back in cautiously. "Um, Lorelei, I didn't see him down th—" Her gaze landed on the smirking Xin. "Oh, here you are."

"Funny thing, Dana." Lorelei laughed awkwardly. "He came in just after you left. Anyway, I should go. Let me know when supper is ready." With the speed of someone who wanted to get out of an awkward conversation, Lorelei was gone.

"Um, is she okay?" asked Dana.

"Oh yeah, she's great. Don't you worry," Xin replied with a hidden smile.

"I was hoping you could do some fishing today, if it's not too much trouble."

"Sure thing," he replied, pulling out his toothpicks, and popping one in his mouth.

As he was about to leave, Dana asked, "Oh, I was about to make supper. Any requests?"

Xin stopped at the stairs with a smirk. "Ah, don't worry too much about me. I already ate." With that, he left the kitchen, leaving a mildly confused Dana.

On deck, Xin grabbed the fishing equipment and set up on the opposite side of the ship as Chase's antics. Hopefully, he hadn't scared away all the fish already. Chase noticed him and trotted over.

"Hey Xin! How about we do some training? Lorelei kinda bailed on me. I hope she's not mad about me asking questions."

"Ah, I'm sure she's fine. She just needs some time… alone sometimes. As for training, can't at the moment. Dana actually asked me to do something. I figure that doesn't happen often. I should probably do it."

"Aw man, well, mind if I help out?"

Xin shrugged and agreed, so Chase went and grabbed another rod. They sat in silence for quite some time, with Chase trying to strike up conversation here and there, but Xin wasn't really one for small talk. Chase sighed in boredom.

Suddenly, something caught Chase's eye sticking out of Xin's pocket. He gave it a cockeyed look, then set down his fishing rod and snatched it.

"Hey! What are you doing? Give that back!" cried Xin, completely caught off guard by the interaction. His face turned bright red as Chase unfurled the item to reveal a pair of simple women's underwear.

Chase quirked a brow. "Panties? What are you doing with panties in your pocket?"

"Would you keep your voice down?" Xin whispered. "It's not… they're not… Just give those back."

Chase looked his friend over, and a knowing smile crept onto his face. Xin reached out to snatch them back, but Chase held them out of reach, and Xin, not wanting to make a scene, just glared.

Chase grinned. "Let's see. I can see a few possibilities. First, you like to wear women's underwear."

"What? I do not!"

"Second, you hooked up with a woman back on that island and have kept these as a souvenir."

"Yes, that's it. Now give them back." Xin shoved his open hand at Chase.

Ignoring Xin's hand, Chase's grin grew wider as he examined the underwear. "Third is that you are hooking up with someone on this boat. And honestly, I can only think of one person that could be."

"You're crazy. I'm not hooking up with anyone," Xin insisted, but the bright red hue on his face told another story.

"Really? So, if a gust of wind just happens to lift up lovely Lorelei's shirt over there, she would definitely be wearing underwear?" Chase smirked, pointing out Lorelei, who was chatting with Astrid, examining her latest painting.

Xin's face turned dire. "You wouldn't."

With a grin and a flick of his hand, a huge gust of wind blew across the deck, lifting Lorelei's shirt to show her completely bare ass.

"Huh… would you look at that?"

Xin slid away from him. "Oh, you're in shit now."

Lorelei turned a deadly glare at Chase. "CHASE! DID YOU DO THAT?" she yelled, storming over to them.

"Who, me? Of course not. The wind is a mysterious mistress, you know," he said with a wave of his hand.

"Alright, you know the rules. Rule three, no peeping." She pulled out a dagger with a grin. "Consequence is loss of a body part, starting with the eyes."

Horror filled Chase's face. "No, no, no! Anything but the eyes!" he cried, running away from the knife wielding crazy person.

"You knew the rules. Time to pay up, pervert!" She jumped on him, tackling him to the ground.

As she sat with the knife poised, he guarded his face with the panties still crunched up in one hand and cried, "I was just trying to prove my theory!"

She tilted her head and lowered the dagger. "What theory?"

He grinned and unfurled the garment in his hand. "That you and Xin are sleeping together."

Lorelei's mouth dropped as she snatched the underwear from him, her ears turning red. Her gaze snapped to Chase, back to the apologetic face of Xin then glared back at Chase. "You say a word of this to anyone, I really will take your eyes."

"Alright, alright," he said, still grinning.

"And what are you smiling about?"

"You're still not wearing any underwear."

Lorelei shoved his face into the deck in annoyance. "Pervert," she growled, standing up carefully.

Chase sat up and stretched. "I just don't get it, though. Why is it such a big secret? Also, what happened to not sleeping with crewmates?"

"Number One: None of your business. Number Two…" A smile snuck onto her face as she glanced over at Xin. "Xin has always been an exception to the rules."

"Adorable," Chase laughed.

Lorelei threw the dagger between his legs. "I am not. Forget everything you just saw and heard." With that, she stormed off.

Xin watched her go with a smile. "Told you you were in shit."

Chase grinned. "Totally worth it."

32

City of Olympia

The City of Olympia. Capital of Gaia and the most densely populated island in all the nations. The focal point was the massive Mount Olympus on the Southernmost point of the island, atop of which lay the shimmering Gaian fortress with massive marble pillars, rounded, golden roofs and multiple looming statues of Gaia and her children—the heads of the four Angel families of Gaia.

The city itself was a cultural haven of the arts. The city would often put on a wide variety of shows, and people from all over would come to watch. Unlike the Rustic Ring, people of all colours and sizes roamed the streets. Many half-giants were a part of the specialized guard, making the city one of the few places Dana wouldn't stick out.

On the horizon, the crew could just see the divine wall, which looked like a foggy wall of red interrupting the once endless blue of the ocean.

Assuming their plan worked, this was as close as they would get to the wall from this side. For now, they would stop in the city to ensure their ship was properly stocked and ready for the crossover into Purgatory. None of them knew for sure what awaited them on the other side of the wall, but they were sure supplies would be quite limited.

They were now docked with some other schooners, the Gaian's flag flying from the mast. It was important that no one knew they were outlaws.

"Alright uncultured swine, tell me again the number one rule while we are in the city," Lorelei said, standing at the helm.

"Don't draw attention," they all sighed in unison.

"Right. That especially counts for you, Captain. There will especially be no bragging about finding the Holy Lands, understood?"

"Yeah, yeah," he sighed, disappointed. "Even if it is a great conversation starter."

Kari bounced in place, excitedly looking at the city. She was all cleaned up, out of her usual overalls, and wearing a pink crop top with simple shorts. "Dana! Dana, will you take us shopping? There are a bunch of parts I need for my gadgets."

"Alright, but we need to get supplies as well."

"Yes!" she cheered, and Chrissy spun in happy circles.

"I… also need to go shopping," said Emir as innocently as possible.

Kari quirked a brow. "For what?"

"Things…"

"You can come along, but Chrissy will let me know if you're stealing anything," she said, poking a finger into his chest.

Chase laid a gentle hand on her shoulder, causing her to stand stick straight, and clench her hands nervously.

"Haha, remember we are technically pirates, now," said Chase. "Don't be too upset with him for stealing. Besides, I don't think he can help it."

"I can so! I am not a klepto… something," argued Emir.

"Mhmm," said Chase skeptically. He removed his hand, (which let Kari slip away nervously), and held up a gold piece. Immediately, Emir's eyes shot to the gold, then watched it bounce between his fingers hungrily. Only when Chase hid the gold back in his pocket did Emir snap out of it.

With a shake of his head, Emir argued, "That proves nothing."

"Well, have fun, you three," Chase concluded with another laugh aimed at Emir. "I personally have other plans for this city."

As the three headed off the ship, Astrid stood at the edge of the boat, ready to go, leaning back and forth on her feet anxiously.

"Oh wow! It's huge. I've never been to the city before. It's so beautiful. I can't wait."

As she was about to follow behind Dana and the others, Lorelei stopped her.

"Whoa, whoa, whoa, where do you think you're going?" she scolded, drawing a look of confusion from Astrid.

"...Into the city?"

"Without any shoes?" Lorelei said, motioning to her bare feet.

"But... I never wear shoes."

"We're in the city now. Do you have any idea how disgusting people are in large groups? You're likely to step on some broken glass or something worse. You're a doctor, you should be avoiding things like this! That's all we need is for you to get some sort of weird infection or disease." As she went on, the disgust in her voice became more and more severe, and her skin started crawling.

"Alright," Astrid sighed. "I think I have some sandals."

"Good. Bring me back some sweets when you go," said Lorelei, finding a nice spot to sit off to the side.

"Wait, you're not coming?" asked Astrid.

"Nope. I hate the city. All those people and their germs... I'm staying right here. Someone needs to guard the ship."

Xin, who had been standing by, ever silent, piped up with, "Oh, no. No way!"

"What? Why?"

"You've been complaining all week that you wanted to get off this boat and that you needed new strings for your guitar. You're not just staying here and then complaining when we leave that you didn't do anything. The ship blends in, and there is nothing to guard on board. Dana took all the extra gold for supplies."

"But the city is gross, and there's so many people. They're going to touch me, or worse—try to talk to me!" she argued, standing back up with arms crossed.

"It won't be that bad. Come on." With that, Xin picked her up by the hips and slung her over his shoulder.

After the initial shock, she laughed, playfully punching his back. "You little ass! Put me down!"

"Just like getting into cold water, gotta dive right in," he teased, then hopped overboard with an annoyed and entertained Lorelei.

Astrid watched the two go, a sadness behind her smile.

Chase wrapped an arm around her shoulders. "It's not easy, is it? Seeing them together."

Astrid snapped her gaze up at him. "What? What are you talking about? I'm happy they're finally getting along."

"Well, yeah, obviously. Doesn't mean it doesn't make you sad." He gave her shoulder a little squeeze.

Astrid blushed and pushed him away. "What are you talking about?"

"Huh? Your crush on Lorelei, of course."

Astrid jumped in surprise. "You… I… I don't… How did you… You knew I was gay?"

"What? Of course I did! I knew you were gay since the bathhouse. Only person you checked out there was Lorelei."

"And… you don't care?"

Chase laughed. "Why would I care? You and me, we're in similar boats, you know. Well, except for the fact that I don't have a preference."

A wave of dawning washed over Astrid's face. "Oh, that makes so much sense now." She shook herself out of it. "Anyway, I knew Lorelei wasn't interested in girls. Me and her together was never going to actually happen. That never even crossed my mind."

"Yeah, yeah, alright. You know what will make you feel better?"

"Umm, no…"

"Rebound sex. I've been a rebound partner for lots of people. I've been told it works wonders."

Astrid started fiddling with her braid nervously. "Chase… you're great and all, but you're not exactly… my type."

"Huh?" His face scrunched up in confusion, then realization dawned on him. "Oh no, not with me! I know I've got the wrong equipment. I meant we find you a lass."

"Oh!" Confusion crossed her face, along with a small smile.

Chase chuckled. "Come on, gorgeous." He motioned wide to the city in front of them. "This city is huge! I bet we could find someone for you."

Her cheeks turned pink as she fidgeted with her braid. "I don't know. That's not really my thing. It seems weird sleeping with someone I just met."

"Aye, I suppose that makes sense, not that it ever bothered me." Chase sighed. "Keep in mind, we're basically on a suicide mission. May not be a lot of time to actually get to know anyone."

"I suppose… but don't you have your own plans? I don't want to get in the way."

"Oh please, I apparently have plenty of years to sleep around now." That exuberant grin slid back on his face. "I want to make sure you're happy."

Astrid giggled. "You never stop surprising me, Captain."

"Heh heh, gotta keep you on your toes. Speaking of, go get those sandals and let's find you a lass."

She gave him a sweet smile. "Alright."

Not far off from the docks lay a bustling marketplace. People of all colours and sizes roamed around, the cries of merchants calling out ecstatically to the crowd for them to see their wares. Dana, Kari, and Emir each stood at a different shop, examining the curious goods available here that were not available in Yggdria. Especially different fruits and vegetables that Kari had never seen before. As Kari examined a particular strange red fruit that the merchant had called a 'pomegranate', Chrissy went bounding off around a corner.

"Chrissy! Get back here!" Kari cried, dropping the fruit and dashing after her dog.

Three years ago, Kari had joined Lorelei on the Oasis, and only a few months after that she had found Chrissy. The Oasis had docked at an island in the

Forsaken Ring and as the adults gathered supplies and did whatever adult things they liked to do, Kari had snuck off to explore. Months on the ship had given her cabin fever, and she was not willing to wait for someone to go exploring with her.

As she walked, she heard the most horrid noise she had ever heard, surrounded by vicious, mocking laughter. Of course, her mind automatically went to cruel pirates torturing some poor woman. She knew the dangers, but her desire to be like Lorelei overcame her, racing to rescue the person.

What she found was not at all what she expected. A group of teenage boys stood round a tiny yellow puppy, tied to a fence, crying out for its little life as they beat it down. Without even thinking, Kari charged in with a mighty battle cry, expecting the few training sessions she had with Lorelei to be more than enough to take on those jerks.

It was not.

She managed to get a few hits on the boys, but ultimately only ended up cowering over the poor puppy as the boys beat her instead. Once they had their fill of chaos, they left the broken and bleeding pair to wallow in their pain, and the tiny puppy gave Kari affectionate kisses. Using the last bit of strength she had, she carried the little thing back to the safety of her home.

Today, as she ran after her furry best friend, she rounded the corner to see her and a young teenage boy together. In retrospect, the boy didn't look threatening at all, petting Chrissy happily, his shaggy, dirty blonde hair falling in front of his eyes. However, with the memories of the past still fresh in her mind, she automatically assumed the worst of the boy.

"Get away from her!" she screamed, dashing at the pair.

He yanked his hand away from the dog, holding his hands up innocently. "I-I'm sorry. She just came up to me and wanted to be pet, so I pet her. I wasn't going to hurt her."

Kari stopped in her tracks, mouth agape. This boy certainly did not look mean now that she stopped to look. His hazel eyes were soft and caring, and at the moment, full of concern.

Kari shook her head. Her wild hair—though currently tied up in pigtails—still managed to get in her eyes. "N-no, I'm sorry. I shouldn't have freaked out. It's just… Last time Chrissy was alone with teenage boys, she lost her leg."

The boy seemed a little taken aback. He glanced at Chrissy's metallic leg sadly. "Poor girl. There are some seriously bad people in this world." He stooped down to take a closer look at the leg and his lips parted into a huge smile, revealing his gapped teeth as he exclaimed, "Wow, that's a super nice leg. Where'd you find it?"

"I made it."

"Are you serious? That's really impressive. I think I'll have to get you to make me one too," he said, beaming that adorable gapped smile at Kari, making her face feel warm.

"Wh-what?"

He pulled back the sleeve on his right arm and popped off his hand and upper arm to reveal a stub. "It doesn't do much but blend in. It would be pretty cool to have something that works."

"Oh wow. What happened?"

He gave an uncaring shrug. "Accident at my parents' shop when I was young. I was playing where I shouldn't have been and got it caught in some equipment."

"Damn. How old were you?"

"Four. So honestly, I don't have a lot of memories with it," he replied, ruffling his shaggy hair with a small chuckle.

"Well, I haven't had a lot of practice with arms, mostly just legs, but I could definitely make you something. Although I'm probably not going to be here long."

"Oh, you're not from around here?"

Kari was taken aback. She looked around at all the people surrounding them, and realized, for the first time in three years, she did not stick out like a sore thumb. She liked this city.

"No, I'm not. I'm an engineer on a ship and we're just passing through."

The boy's eyes went wide, shining with excitement. "You're an engineer on a ship? At your age? Seriously?"

Kari giggled. "Yep."

"Well, I was just heading out to meet my friends. If you'd like, we could show you around the city while you're in town."

"Yes!" Her face dropped. "Oh, actually, I don't know. The people I'm with are a bit… different. I'm not sure how stoked they'd be about that."

"Well, we won't know if we don't ask, right?"

"I guess you're right. My name's Kari, by the way."

"Kari, that's a really pretty name," he said with a smile, making Kari's face feel warm again. "My name's Adrian."

Side by side, the kids made their way back to the market, where Dana was looking around anxiously for Kari.

"Dana!" Kari called with a wave.

"Kari! There you are. I was worried," she said, hurrying over and turning a surprised eye at the boy. "Who's your friend?"

"This is Adrian," Kari said, digging her toes into the dirt.

"Hello, Adrian," she said with a gentle smile.

Adrian looked up at her, slack-jawed. "Wow. Giant. Very cool."

"I was wondering if it would be alright if I went and hung out with him and his friends to see the city," Kari mumbled.

"Well, I think it's certainly a good idea to hang out with some kids your own age, but you know I'm not the one you should be asking."

"Right, we'll just go find Chase and…"

"Oh, no, no," said Dana, the smile dropping from her face. "We're going to find Lorelei."

"Bu-but Chase is the Captain! Why do we have to ask Lorelei?" Kari pleaded, knowing full well what Lorelei was going to say to the idea.

"Do you really need to ask?"

Kari crossed her arms in a pout.

Dana chuckled and ruffled her hair lightly. "Come on, I think I have an idea where she might be."

Down a different street, Lorelei and Xin strode side by side. This road was known for the arts, housing many different shops to do with art, music, dance, anything imaginable. All sorts of performers lined the street, showing off their best skills in the hopes of getting a few coins. It was an amazing sight to Lorelei, as her eyes sparkled at every turn. That is, until someone got too close to her and she turned a nasty snarl. After nearly biting the head off of some poor dancer, Xin took her hand lightly.

"Would you just relax? We have some time alone together for a while. Let's enjoy it."

Lorelei looked up at him with a small smile, snuggled in close, and continued walking down the street hand in hand until she spied a shop with a plethora of instruments on display. She dashed over to it giddily, smushing her face up against the window to peer inside. "Ooo, is that a twelve-string guitar? I've always kind of wanted one. Oh, or a lute. That's classic pirate right? Hmm… maybe not. Oh, I could get a new flute for Dana. The one she has is way too small for her."

"Have you considered getting a new guitar for yourself?" Xin asked, coming up behind her and wrapping his arms around her waist. "You've always used the same guitar."

"I… I suppose I could, but that guitar of mine… it's really important."

"Oh?" asked Xin.

"I… well, I can't be sure, but—" She sighed. "I think it might be my father's. My real father."

"You've… never really talked about your parents, other than the songs, of course. Why do you think the guitar is your father's?"

"Well, the songs my mom would always sing me—I've never heard them anywhere else, so I'm sure they were made by him for her. And the guitar… My mother had it, but she never knew how to play. She gave it to me and I figured it out, but why did she have it? I suppose it could have just been a hobby she thought she would take up but didn't, but it didn't feel like that. There also used to be a tiny carving of a rose with 'For my Wild Rose' written under it, just like my mom's favourite song. Obviously, it was a gift then, right?"

"Used to be?"

Lorelei sighed in frustration. "Mikhail. He stabbed a hole through it when he was feeling particularly jealous one day. I don't want to talk about it."

"No problem. So about the father thing, you've really thought a lot about it?"

"Yeah, well, mom never said that my father wasn't my father, but… I felt like it was implied a lot, especially by him. That, and I look nothing like the guy." Her shoulders dropped in a huge sigh. "But, since mom's gone now, it's not like I'll ever find out. Guess I'll just have to keep living in a fantasy."

Xin smiled, giving her a loving squeeze and kissing her cheek.

She turned and smiled at him. "Tchah," she scolded half-heartedly. "What if someone sees?"

"So what? I don't know anyone here, do you?"

Lorelei took a quick look around. "No, I don't." With that, she turned and gave him a passionate kiss. "Now come on, I want to go inside and look around!"

Dana and the group walked down the art street, Kari gawking and giggling at all the performers. They rounded a corner just as Xin and Lorelei were entwined in their kiss.

Dana gave a small gasp and pushed them back around the corner they came from. The three heads, (and one dog head), peeked back around the corner just as the two made their way into the shop. Dana and Kari looked at each other and laughed.

"What's so funny?" asked the confused Adrian.

Kari took a few deep breaths and wiped a tear from her eye. "Those two have been pretending for weeks to not care about each other. I mean, we all knew it was bullshit, so it's pretty funny to catch them like that."

"Oh… I think I get it," he said as he gave a forced chuckle.

"Don't worry about it," Kari smiled.

"Do… do we tell them we saw them?" asked Dana.

"What? No way. Lorelei would bite our heads off. Let's just wait here until they come out of the shop."

Dana sighed. "Alright."

After what felt like forever, the couple came out of the store, Lorelei practically glowing with excitement carrying a large bag.

"Right, time to go," said Kari, giving Dana a pathetic shove. Still, they were on the move.

Adrian fiddled with his shirt as he looked at the pair in front of them. "Oh, man. That guy is huge. Should I be worried?"

"Of Xin? Hahaha, no. It's her you have to be worried about," she said, pointing out Lorelei.

"Her? She looks pretty nice," he said, and Kari burst out laughing.

Dana tried to hold back a laugh as well. Instead she called out their names, drawing their attention over.

Lorelei bounced up, waving some papers at her. "Dana! Check it out! There's a show going on tonight. I got a few tickets. I wasn't sure who all would want to come." Her gaze snapped to the unknown boy. "Who is that?" she growled viciously, making Adrian burst into a cold sweat.

"A-Adrian is my name."

"Kari would like to ask you something," said Dana, pushing an apprehensive Kari forward.

She mumbled something incoherently under her breath, her gaze focused on the ground.

"Kari, you get nothing by mumbling," Lorelei snapped.

Kari stood up straight, arms at her side, and said clearly, "I want to go and hang out with Adrian and his friends and check out the city."

Lorelei's face darkened as she shouted, "You want to go off with a guy you just met?" A few surprised glances snapped their way from the people walking by. Lorelei didn't notice. "What do you know about him?"

"Not a lot, but Chrissy really likes him, and he's really nice, and you've taught me how to defend myself. I'm not completely helpless."

Lorelei shot a vicious glare at the boy. "Don't be fooled by how charming someone is. Sometimes it's the nicest ones that have the most evil in their hearts."

Adrian shrank a bit.

Lorelei turned back to Kari. "You of all people should know that."

"I know, I haven't forgotten," she sighed, looking back at her feet. She took a deep breath, then looked Lorelei in the eye. "But… Lorelei, it feels right."

The fire in Lorelei's eyes died down, and her shoulders softened. "Tchah, you know exactly how to play me, don't you?" She smiled weakly at the girl, who was no longer as small as she remembered.

Kari gave her a warm smile, and Lorelei sighed.

"Alright, fine. On one condition." She looked beside the group. "Emir."

"Yeah?" he responded, making everyone else jump, especially Adrian, who shrieked a little then turned and asked,

"Where did you come from?"

"Hmm? I was here the whole time," he said, and it was true.

"Emir goes with you," stated Lorelei.

"What? Why?" both Kari and Emir whined in unison.

"One, because he seems to be bored anyway, two, because he's the least likely person you could give the slip, and three, it's pretty easy to pretend he isn't there."

"Fine," pouted Kari.

"Wait, I did not agree to babysit. What is in it for me?" asked Emir.

"I don't know," sighed Lorelei. "I'll give you first dibs on shiny stuff next time we loot something."

"I am not a bird," he exclaimed, then stopped to think for a moment. "Although that could be very advantageous for me. Very well. I will babysit," he concluded, hitting a fist into his open hand.

"I am not a baby!" objected Kari, to the entertainment of Xin and Dana.

Lorelei, on the other hand, had turned her attention back to the boy and got right in his face. "Now you listen good, kid. If I hear of you or your friends hurting Kari in any way shape or form, if a single tear crosses her face, I will personally make sure you suffer every form of torture there is," she growled, sending shivers down Adrian's spine. "I mean flaying, waterboarding—mmph." Her threats were annoyingly cut short by Xin's large hand covering her mouth and pulling her back.

"What she's trying to say is have fun and be safe," said Xin with a smile.

"Thank you, thank you! Come on, Adrian!" exclaimed Kari, dragging a stunned Adrian behind her. Emir grumbled something incomprehensible and followed begrudgingly behind the pair.

Lorelei turned her glare to Xin and said, "I was not done threatening."

"You were about to make him piss himself, which would not be a great first impression. Don't worry so much, she'll be fine. I have a good feeling about him."

Lorelei sighed. "Alright, fine." She turned a smile up at Dana. "Hey Dana! Want to go to a show?"

"Huh?" Dana looked back and forth between the grinning Lorelei and the apprehensive Xin, who seemed to be giving her a pleading look. She couldn't help but smile. "Oh... no, I don't really like theatre, and the crowds that go with them. I have more shopping to do. You two have fun."

"Oh, alright," said Lorelei with some disappointment.

Dana walked off, and the couple headed for another part of town.

"You know," said Xin, "we don't have to have anyone come with us."

Lorelei lowered her gaze. "You mean go to a show... alone together... like a... date?"

"Yeah... I guess so," he replied, trying to hold back a smile while his cheeks burned red.

Lorelei thought for a moment, then shook her head. "I mean, it would be rude not to ask anyone else first, right? It's not like we get to the city like this very often. I think Astrid might want to go."

Xin sighed, his shoulders slumped. "Alright, we'll go find Astrid."

33

Adventures in Olympia

Down yet another busy street in the City of Olympia, Astrid was having the time of her life, dancing ahead of Chase, absolutely loving the crowds, the smells, the sights. She ran up to random people, introduced herself, and danced away, confusing them. Chase just watched with immense entertainment.

She paused for a moment to let Chase catch up. "The city is so wonderful! There's so many nice people! And look at all those clothes!"

"Well, I suppose if you're going to impress a girl, we should get you something that doesn't look like pajamas," suggested Chase, looking at her ever shapeless dress.

"You… you want to go clothes shopping with me?" Those big green eyes sparkled. "Lorelei never wants to go clothes shopping."

"Well, I'm not Lorelei. I'm thinking we could both use some girl time, eh? Been thinking of getting a haircut myself. What do you think?" he asked, and Astrid wrapped him in a big, excited hug.

"Let's do it!" she exclaimed, and off they went to every shop they could find.

The two tried on outfit after outfit, trying on all sorts of different looks. Chase made Astrid giggle uncontrollably at the one store that purely sold dresses as he quite admirably pulled off some very nice looks. The glares from the sales clerk said otherwise. Though, when they went to make their

319

purchases, Chase's charm did not fail to impress as he managed to get them a hardy discount.

Next on the checklist, haircuts. For the first time in a very long time, Astrid's hair came out of its braid, and the curly mess that ensued surprised everyone except Astrid. She apologized, but the man at the salon welcomed the challenge and ultimately tamed her wonderful locks, giving Astrid a wonderful curly down-doo.

Chase decided to cut his long hair right down. Something he hadn't done since he was a child. Nervous at first to reveal his hearing aids, the loving smile of Astrid gave him strength. Off came the hair and styled up neatly. Chase loved it, but his paranoia still made him return the bandana around his hearing aids.

Now dressed in shining new clothes—Chase dressed just as brightly as ever—the two walked down the street, ladened with bags full of goodies.

"That was so much fun! Thank you Chase!" chirped Astrid, once again dancing in the street.

"Anytime," he chuckled. Just then, they heard a familiar voice calling their names. They looked over to see Xin and Lorelei walking towards them.

"Here you are! I've been looking everywhere for you," said Lorelei.

"Hey Lorelei! What do you think of my new look?" Astrid asked with a spin.

"Huh?" Lorelei gave her a quick up and down. "Oh, looks good, Astrid."

Astrid stuck her lip out at the lack of energy in Lorelei's tone.

"I think she means to say you look absolutely stunning, Astrid," said Xin with a chuckle, obviously catching Astrid's annoyance.

Astrid smiled at him appreciatively.

"Tchah. That's what I said, just in my own words," she scolded and Xin rolled his eyes. "Besides, I'm more curious where Chase's hair crawled off to."

"Har har," he replied.

"Anyway, there's a show going on tonight. You guys want to come?"

"Watch people interacting? Nah, not my style. I'd rather actually go interact with people," Chase replied with a grin.

"Alright, one vote for 'rather get laid', what about you Astrid?"

Astrid looked between Lorelei and Chase for a moment. She did like the idea of seeing a show, but she was having a wonderful time with Chase. That, and she couldn't help but feel Xin's eyes asking her not to join. She smiled a cute little smile, her head cocked to the side. "No thanks. Chase and I already have plans. You two have fun."

Lorelei's mouth dropped. "Wh—really? Oh, okay."

"Come on Chase, let's go!" said Astrid, hooking on to his arm. They walked off with a wave and Lorelei watched them go a little sadly.

"Are you jealous?" Xin asked as they got out of earshot.

"What? No," she snapped, but her crossed arms and pouty lip made him think otherwise.

"Well I guess it's just us, then. Hope that's not too terrible," he said with a chuckle.

"No… of course not."

"Come on, I'm hungry. I saw a restaurant back the way we came."

"Dinner and a show?" she squeaked nervously. "What is even happening here?"

"You are so weird. Have you never been on a date before?" Xin asked.

Lorelei shook her head.

"The notorious Siren, killer and sleeper of men, nervous about a date. Well, there's a first time for everything." With that small smile, he held his hand out to her.

She took it warmly.

Xin pondered for a moment. "Did we really never go on a date before?"

"Nope. Not really. It was always the four of us if we went anywhere. I pretended to have married Yuri once, so I guess that would be the closest thing to a date I had," she chuckled, remembering the moment fondly.

"Oh, yeah. That was before we were together. I was so jealous."

"Ha, I know. It's partly why I did it," she teased, punching him on the arm.

"Seriously? Argh, why am I not surprised?" he growled, picking her up in a bear hug and swinging her around, causing her to let out an uncharacteristic giggle.

Chase and Astrid strode up to a lovely looking little bar in a quieter area of town. As they got close to the door, a loud bellow came from inside and a large man tossed a scrawny middle-aged man out the door. The small man was quite an interesting sight, dressed in ragged formal clothes with a small black kitten peeking out of his pocket hissing at the man that had tossed them out.

The scrawny man wobbled to his feet and slurred, "You don't know greatness when you see it!"

"I'll believe your greatness when you pay your tab," said the large man. "Until then, stay out."

"You know I wrote that stupid play that they're performing," said the tiny man, sweeping back his silver streaked auburn hair. "But did they give me a copper piece? No! They stole it. 'Not reputable enough,' they told me. Can you believe that?!"

"Whatever you say, buddy. Go home," said the large man, returning indoors.

"You have made a dangerous enemy, sir!" he shouted, shaking a fist at the door. "You haven't heard the last of Liam Myrdinn!" When no reply came, the man flopped to the ground with a grand sigh. A little "mew" sounded from his pocket and he gave the kitten an appreciative scratch.

Feeling the drama had passed, Chase and Astrid snuck around the strange man. Once inside, Astrid said to Chase, "Sure seems to be a lot of hype about this show. You sure we're not missing out?"

"Ah, that's not how it works. My luck makes sure that all the excitement happens around me!"

"Are you sure about that?" Astrid giggled as they found a table to sit at.

"Enough about me. Let's think about you," he said, scratching his freshly shaven, soft chin with appreciation. "Let's see, you have a crush on Lorelei, meaning we're looking for cold and uncaring."

"I do not have a crush on Lorelei," she squeaked.

"Hmm, or we should find someone the complete opposite. That might be better. Ah, but that's basically you…"

"I'm starting to have second thoughts about this…" she sighed, sinking down into her chair.

Kari and Adrian walked side by side through a residential district. Adrian had finally snapped out of the stupor Lorelei had caused and was chatting away happily with the giddy Kari.

Emir lagged behind, bored. He walked close to a woman with a large purse, but before he could reach in, the growl of the ever vigilant Chrissy made him reconsider. Along he went again in boredom.

"Your family is pretty intense," laughed Adrian.

"You don't even know the half of it," she giggled, then frowned, wringing her hands. "I am sorry about that. Lorelei really does mean well. She was just treated like crap for a lot of her life. I guess that's why she decided to help me."

"You want to talk about it?" he asked with some concern.

"No, I don't want to be a downer," she replied with a big smile. "I'd rather just have some fun."

"Well, that's good, 'cause we're here!" he said, pointing out a large run down house.

"It's uh… lovely," said Kari, suddenly a little worried about their location.

"Haha, it's not my house. It actually belongs to my friend Cai's family. Old house that they inherited and never bothered fixing up. We decided to make it our club house. You know, a place away from adults and other problems," he explained, making Kari feel a little better. As they approached the house, he opened a box that lay by the door.

Adrian chuckled at the confusion in her eyes. "You put all your worries and fears in here before you come in," he explained and Kari looked at him to see if he was messing with her. When she decided he seemed to be telling the truth, she laughed a little.

"That's kind of lame."

"Hey, don't diss it till you try it."

"Alright, I'll try," she said, looking in the box, imagining placing all her problems within it. She closed the box, actually feeling a little better. "Alright, I think I'm good."

Adrian smiled, opened the door, and motioned her inside. As Emir was about to join, Adrian stopped him. "Uh, look, at the risk of incurring that chick's wrath, we've actually all agreed that there are no adults allowed in here."

"Huh… Well, I am only twenty-one. I am barely an adult," Emir assured him.

"Sorry, still counts," said Adrian. "I mean, I guess I could talk to the others to see if it's okay, if you really want him inside, Kari."

Kari looked Emir over and turned to Adrian with a smile. "Nah, he can wait out here."

Emir scowled. "Alright, young ones, but do not think you can pull one over on me. I am a professional thief. I will have every possible escape route figured out in the blink of an eye, so do not even think about sneaking away."

"By the gods, you're all so hard-core. I promise we're not up to anything nefarious," said Adrian, as he closed the door on Emir.

Once he was sure they were out of earshot, Emir gave a great sigh. "Why did I agree to this?"

Inside the house was about what Kari expected. Broken windows, old furniture along with nests and excrement of birds long gone. Adrian led her up the stairs and stopped at a door with a sign reading 'Roxy, Dorian, Misha, Adrian, Cai and Pearce - Personal Clubhouse - Keep Out' with a bunch of random doodles clearly from different people. It ranged anywhere from rainbows and unicorns to skulls and dragons. Kari chuckled at it a little.

The door opened to reveal a group of teens all around Adrian's age. As soon as they saw him, they greeted him excitedly.

A bright blonde boy with short spiky hair was the first to notice Kari lagging behind him. "Hey, hey, who is your friend?"

"This is Kari, and this is Chrissy," he said, motioning to each one appropriately. Everyone greeted them happily, causing Kari to smile wide, and Chrissy to bark excitedly.

A girl with perfectly groomed dark brown hair and dazzling blue eyes behind black-rimmed glasses came up close to Kari. Kari was a little thrown off to see a girl so young in so much makeup.

"Wow, you're so pretty. Can I touch your hair?" she asked giddily.

"Uhh… I'd rather you didn't," said Kari, never comfortable when people would randomly come up and pat her head like she was Chrissy.

Another boy, larger than the others with a square face and brown hair, said to the girl, "Roxy, stop being weird."

She crossed her arms and pouted at him, but still sent Kari a warm smile.

"Well, Kari, this is the gang," said Adrian, then proceeded to introduce them. Roxy was the perfectly made-up hair-toucher. Misha wore no make-up and sported a loose sweater, with her hair tied up neatly and a book upon her lap. Dorian was the square faced scolder, Cai was the spiky blonde boy, and last was Pearce, a pale skinned, thin boy with unnaturally black hair.

"Hello," Kari said nervously after all the introductions.

"Kari's travelling through here on a ship," said Adrian excitedly. "I met some of her crew and they were crazy intense. It was really cool."

Kari's face was burning hot, but she managed a small laugh.

"Oh! And she is super talented. Check out Chrissy's leg! She made that," he said, pointing to the excited dog. The kids crowded around, admiring the work and giving Chrissy plenty of attention, which she absolutely loved.

"So you're pretty good with technology and stuff, then?" asked Cai.

Kari gave an enthusiastic nod. "Yep. I'm the best there is!"

"What do you know about cars? There's this old one that my dad intended to get running again, but so far it's just collecting dust."

"Sure, let me take a look."

The group led Kari to a run-down garage where an old beat up convertible car sat. The frame was still in good shape, so Kari went into the engine, fiddling around with a few things.

After a while of poking, prodding, and pulling multiple tools out of her surprisingly large pockets, she poked her once again grimy face out of the hood. "There, give that a try."

Cai, sitting in the driver's seat, turned the car over. It whined a few times, sputtered then… *BANG.* Out came plumes of black smoke.

Everyone was terrified by the loud noise, but the car continued purring away. Kari stood in the cloud of smoke, coughing and sputtering, now completely covered in grime.

"Uh… explosions are perfectly normal. And it's running now!" she said with a toothy smile.

"Alright!" cheered Cai.

"You're amazing!" said Adrian.

"Ah, it was nothing," said Kari, scratching her head. Roxy came over with a cloth to help clean Kari up.

"Awesome," said Dorian. "Can we take it for a drive?"

"Does anyone even know how to drive?" asked Misha, a little cross.

"I've driven my dad's car a few times. I can do it," said Cai.

"Sounds good to me," agreed Adrian. "And I did promise you a tour of the city. Uh, should we tell that guy that came with you?"

"Emir?" Kari thought for a moment. Eventually, a grin crossed her face as she said, "Nah. Let's go!"

Outside, a very bored Emir sat stacking a pile of rocks on his hand, trying to balance it. As the bang sounded, he jumped, dropping a few rocks on his head. He grumbled various curses under his breath and went to scope out the source of the noise.

Just as he rounded one corner, he saw the garage door opening. A car flew out.

There in the backseat was Kari, waving and yelling, "I'll be back in a little while, Emir! Don't worry!"

"Wh—A car? They had a car?" Emir wailed. "I am going to get in so much shit if Lorelei finds out." He paused in thought. "But that is only if… And Kari did say she would be back."

He sat back down, scratching his chin and pondering some more. "Ah, but what if she does not come back? Shit… I suppose I should follow them," he conceded, then sighed helplessly. "How do I catch up to a car?"

<h1 style="text-align:center">34</h1>

Hermes' Piper

The rattling old car streaked down the darkening streets of Olympia with the teens cheering with unrestrained glee. There were cars in the city, but they were not very common to find. Only the richest had them, as their fuel was very rare and expensive.

As the group drove around, enjoying the wind in their hair, Adrian, squished up beside Kari, softly wrapped an arm around her shoulder. Her face turned hot and she couldn't help but smile madly.

She was so distracted that she almost didn't see Lorelei and Xin walking down the street in front of them. At the last minute she noticed them, cried out "Shit! Turn, turn!" and grabbed at the steering wheel, quickly veering them down a side street. Cai screeched to a halt.

"Sorry guys," Kari replied abashedly at the looks snapped her way. "But if Lorelei caught me without Emir, it's game over for me."

They looked over to the crowd of people going into a giant, sparkling white building, the sound of orchestral music flowing out. Kari took a close look at the two walking together and noticed the hand holding with a giggle. She also couldn't help but notice the uncharacteristically happy smile on Lorelei's face.

"I don't think I've ever seen her smile like that before," Kari said aloud, but mostly to herself.

"Looks like they're going to the play. That's where all our parents are tonight, too," said Cai.

"They're not really my parents," Kari explained.

"Ah, blood or not, that lady was definitely acting like your mom. Or maybe more like your dad with how scary she was," laughed Adrian, and Kari joined in.

"I guess so. Come on. Let's get out of here before she spots us."

"Great, and we can go to our own show. There's a band playing on the other side of town. I've heard really great things about them," said Adrian, and the whole car cheered out in agreement.

The sky grew darker, and an ill-tempered Emir walked down the streets grumbling to himself about being the babysitter. He noticed a bunch of teens and young adults converging on one particular building, and as he approached, he heard some kind of awful, screeching, rhythmic noise. It was unlike anything he had experienced before.

"What on Geb is that gods awful sound?"

Inside the plaza, swarms of teens were jumping, dancing and having the time of their lives as the odd music blared from the stage.

"This is the greatest music I've ever heard! I love it," yelled Kari to Adrian the best she could over the noise.

"I've heard it's all the rage in Alexandria. It's so cool," he yelled back.

Song after song, Kari's new group of friends danced their hearts out. Kari couldn't help but dance closer and closer to Adrian.

As another one of the songs came to an end, the crowd cheered. The umber skinned main singer and supposed band leader, sporting curly black hair under a red hat, spoke to the crowd with electrifying energy.

"Good evening, Olympia!"

The crowd screamed back with excitement.

"Tonight, we have a very special song for you all. A song to fight against the man. To fight against oppression!" he cried out, receiving more screams of excitement, and in the background, the soft sound of a flute began to play.

"How many are sick of the rules? Don't you wish you could just say *fuck you* to everyone that has told you what to do? You know the worst of them all? Your parents. All they ever do is tell you who to be, what to do. Do they even care about you?"

The crowd roared back in seething agreement.

"Yeah!" cried Adrian. "All I am to my parents is an employee! They don't care about what I want to do!"

Kari, however, looked around nervously. That was not a sentiment she agreed with, and the music was starting to give her the creeps. "Adrian, I want to go. I don't like this," she said, pulling on his hand.

"Come on, Kari!" he cried with unexpected frustration. "Don't you hate your parents? Aren't you sick of them telling you what to do?"

"I hate my biological parents, but my real family has only ever looked out for me. Please, I don't like this, Adrian. Let's go…" The sound of the flute grew louder and louder, drowning out any other thoughts in her head. "…after this song. This is a beautiful song."

The angry jeers died away and complete silence filled the stadium. All except that beautiful flute melody.

"Come on, everyone!" shouted the singer, a knowing smile on his face. "None of your parents are home. Show them who's the boss. Go on and take all those things that they hold more precious than you. All those valuables that you aren't allowed to even breathe on. Take them and bring them here. The one who brings back the most will be granted the power of the great Angel Hermes. Now go!"

Without a word, the kids poured out of the stadium in an orderly fashion. All except Kari, who stood glued in place, her face a blank slate. Chrissy whined, running circles around her, nudging her hand, jumping up and licking her face. A look of worry crossed the dog's face as she took a large bite of Kari's leg.

"Ouch! Chrissy, what the crap?" cried Kari, rubbing her sore leg, but finally snapping out of the spell. She glanced around with mass confusion. "What's going on?"

As she looked around, she saw Adrian walking away. Pushing past the mindless teenagers, she caught up to him.

"Adrian! Snap out of it. Hey!" she cried, trying to slap him lightly, shake him. Finally she sighed and said, "Ah, dammit. I'm sorry about this," then wound up and punched him square in the face.

"Ow! What in the world? What was that for?" he cried, nursing his slightly bloody nose.

"Sorry, it was the only way to snap you out of it," she said, and Adrian clicked in with the oddity of their surroundings.

"What's going on?"

"I think everyone is in some sort of trance. It seems like pain is the only way to snap you out of it."

"Well, we can't exactly go around punching everyone. What do we do?"

"I might have a plan, but I need my gadgets. We need to get to the ship as fast as possible."

"I think the car was over this way, but I don't know how to drive," Adrian's voice was tight, "and I don't see Cai anywhere."

"How hard can it be?" said Kari, a nervous grin on her face.

Together, the two weaved through the crowd and out to the parking lot, jumped in the car, and got it running. Kari put it in gear and gave it some gas… Too much gas. She lightly ran into the side of a building.

"Oops, just gotta get the hang of it," she declared, then changed to reverse, put down the gas again and ran into a pole.

Apparently, this hit was hard enough to start the sleeping Emir up with an, "Ow, what in Duat?"

Adrian nearly jumped clear out of the car, spinning to look at the man in the back seat. "Where did you come from?"

"I was here when you got here. I figured if I camped out in your car you couldn't give me the slip again. What's going on here anyway?"

"No time. Do you know how to drive?" asked Kari.

"Me? No way. This is the closest I've ever been to a car."

"Damn. Alright, third time's the charm," she said, grinding it into gear then taking off down the road. She gave a great cry of triumph as they sped down the mostly empty streets to the docks.

Earlier that day, Xin and Lorelei walked to the grand, shining theatre where many others were lining up to enter. Lorelei came in close to Xin, glaring at all those near her.

"By the gods, there are a lot of people here," she said with a look of disgust. "I didn't think of that. Maybe we should just go back to the ship."

Xin wrapped his arm around her. "Don't worry. As soon as we sit down and the show starts, you won't even notice."

"I guess. Am I allowed to kill anyone that touches me?"

Xin let out a loud laugh. "I would advise against that."

"You're no fun," she sighed with an exaggerated pout.

As they walked by the entrance, they passed by a man in a formal black coat leaning by the door, watching the patrons enter with boredom. As Xin and Lorelei passed, his back straightened, watching Lorelei go with exhilaration. The two didn't seem to notice him amongst the crowd.

The lobby was congested with attendants pointing people to their seats. The couple made their way to theirs, and soon enough, the play was underway.

Just as Xin had predicted, as soon as the music started, Lorelei was completely enamoured with the show, getting right into it. Perhaps a little too into it, as during one of the action scenes she voiced how unrealistic they were making it.

A very fine-looking lady dressed in nothing but shades of purple turned to Lorelei, pressed a finger to her lips and shushed her with all of her purple might.

Lorelei turned a threatening grin at her. "Are you shushing me? Are you sure you want to do that? 'Cause I will show you what real violence looks like."

The purple woman gasped. "You would not. I will have the guards here in an instant."

"Keep trying me."

"Come on, Lore," said Xin, lightly grabbing her hand and sitting her back down. "If you go and make a fuss, you won't get to finish the show."

Lorelei gave a frustrated sigh. "Argh, alright." She sat down with a huff.

The woman in purple eyed her throughout the rest of the play, and when intermission came, she hurried off.

Xin watched her go. "I really hope she's not getting the guards."

Lorelei wasn't paying attention to Xin, or the vanishing purple lady. Instead, her eyes were glazed over, a smile on her face. "By the gods, that one part with the harp was really impressive." After a moment, her face fell a little.

"What's wrong?" asked Xin.

"Probably nothing. Just my overactive brain. It's just, all this music feels so familiar, like I've heard it before, but… also not? Does that make sense?"

"Hmm, maybe a bit. Some songs did sound familiar. I just assumed it was something you had sung before. You do know a lot of songs."

She thought for a moment, then shook her head and smiled. "Never mind. This was really amazing. Thanks for making me do this."

"You're welcome. Though honestly, I'm just glad for the excuse to spend the whole day alone with you."

"And the day is not even done yet," she said with a flirty grin, rubbing a hand on his leg. He smiled and went to kiss her, but was interrupted by the enthusiastic black coat man sitting beside Lorelei.

"Hello. I hope you don't mind. I switched seats with the lady here." He laughed. "She seemed very anxious to be rid of her ticket."

Lorelei looked him over. He was quite the handsome man, tan skinned, with dark chocolate brown hair neatly groomed to one side, accompanied by finely groomed facial hair, and light topaz eyes.

"What can I say? Not everyone enjoys real danger," she said with a grin, drawing a hearty laugh from the man.

"Well, that's the truth. Not to worry though, I'm no stranger to a little violence." He lounged back in his seat. "Been sailing these seas since I was a kid."

Lorelei quirked a brow. "That right?"

"Yep. My crew is docked in town for a few days on some business. Thought I'd check out the show while I was here. I've heard the score was incredible. I'm a bit of a musician myself, you see."

"Really?" she asked with a bit more enthusiasm. "What do you play?"

"Violin, and I'm a bit of a singer."

"Really? I've always kind of wanted to learn the violin, but I never had the patience. I'm a guitar girl myself." She chuckled. "And I've been known to do a little singing."

Xin laughed. "Yeah, your singing is to die for." They continued to laugh together while the man smiled at Lorelei.

"Perhaps after the show we can get together and play. I would love to hear your deadly singing."

"You may regret that," she replied with a flirty chuckle.

"I doubt it," he said with a suave grin.

Xin couldn't stop the scowl forming on his face.

The band started to play. The lights went dim, and the show began again. Xin wrapped an arm around Lorelei, who snuggled in gratefully. Xin shot the man a quick glare and received a simple cocky smile in return. He did not like this man at all.

Back in the arena filled with the henchmen of Hermes, the teenagers slowly returned with piles of gold, jewels, and anything of value, piling them in the centre of the arena.

"Aw man, these kids really were loaded. Boss is gonna love this," said the singer, sitting on the edge, revelling in their work with a grin.

The drummer, a short and scrawny man with a scarf wrapped around his forehead, was drumming nervously on his thigh. "You really think the boss will show up to give someone powers?"

"Of course not, you idiot," spat the singer. "That's just to help the enchantment work to inspire the kids. Boss never shows his face in public."

"Oh… Right."

"Any word from the new guy?" asked the singer.

"No, not a word for a while," said the guitarist, a tall man with hair down to his ass-crack. "Should we send someone to check on him?"

"Nah, all the kids are back, anyway. And if the guy deserts, the boss will take care of him."

They all turned their heads as they heard a scuffle and multiple yells. In a moment, their bass guitarist, a huge man with a bandana over his head, dragged along Kari and Adrian, who were kicking and yelling at him.

"Hey, I found these two lurking around backstage. Guess they somehow avoided the enchantment."

The singer jumped up from his seat and came up close to Kari, grabbing her by the chin and scrutinizing her. "Well, aren't you a pretty one? What's the matter? Didn't want to stick it to your parents?" he asked, and Kari growled bestially. "You know, you actually look kind of familiar."

He scratched under his hat, revealing an odd star-shaped scar on his right temple. Kari noticed it at a glance, then couldn't help but realize the others also covered their temples in some way or another.

She turned back to the leader, who was still uncomfortably close, and said, "You know you may know how to sing, but you have terrible breath."

Rather than being offended, he gave a small chuckle, then took a step back. "So what were you doing back there, sneaking around?"

"None of your business."

A hand came across her face with lip splitting force. His smile was gone as he growled, "You'll tell me or I'll kill your little buddy here."

"You harm either one of us and you'll have hell to pay," Kari yelled, straining against the brute still holding her. "Lorelei will—"

"Lorelei?" raged the guitarist. Kari swiftly realized the whole band had twisted into a rage at the sound of her name. "Lorelei the Siren? That bitch is the one—"

The band leader silenced him with a wave of his hand. He came in close again, a nasty grin on his face. "Lorelei, you say? Now I know where I recognize you from. You're that little girl the Siren abducted three years ago. Your parents have been worried sick about you, you know."

"That's not what happened! Lorelei saved me from them!" Kari cried out, tears filling her eyes from the memories of her past.

"Is that what she's told you? I've heard she has control over people's minds. Tragic that she uses it on children as well."

"Stop it!" screamed Kari, causing fireworks and explosions to appear all around. The goons went into panic mode. The huge man let go of Kari and pulled Adrian away from her.

"How is she doing that?" squealed the tiny drummer. "Does she have a blessing?"

Composing herself, she wiped the tears from her face, smiled, and said, "That's right, fools! You've angered me and now you will face the wrath of Ra!"

In response, a line of fire appeared all around the stage, lighting up the terrified faces of the band, who were now huddled together in fear. All except the leader, who looked quite pissed off at the lot of them.

"Idiots! This is obviously a trick."

The nervous drummer wasn't convinced. He looked at the girl with complete fear. "Let's kill her! That will stop it!"

"No, don't!" cried the leader, reaching out to stop him.

Too late.

He charged, pulling a dagger from underneath his shirt and aiming for Kari's throat.

Adrian was stuck. He couldn't escape the stunned brute.

Emir reached out from the shadows, almost grabbing the man's arm.

Pop.

The drummer's head exploded from the inside out, spraying out in a dazzling array of blood and brains.

Shocked and appalled, Emir slunk back into the shadows, hoping the rest had not noticed him.

Kari, receiving the brunt of the explosion, bent to her knees and puked. "What the fuck was that?" she asked once her stomach was quite empty.

"Idiot. He knew the rules. Boss is always watching," grumbled the leader. He turned to the guitarist and said, "Just use the flute. We'll brainwash her again, get rid of all her memories. Then we return her to her parents and get the reward."

"No! I'm never going back to them!" she cried, charging at the flute man. Too slow.

A haunting melody floated out from the flute, and Kari stopped dead in her tracks, her face completely blank. Even Adrian was no longer fighting the behemoth.

The leader walked up to Kari, a victorious grin on his face. "Alright kid, listen up—"

A huge explosion sounded. Everyone jumped, and the melody came to an abrupt end.

Kari snapped out of it and sounded a loud whistle.

"Woof!"

From the crowd leapt her big shaggy dog, snatching the flute from the hands of the guitarist and giving it to Kari.

"Huh, this looked really fragile," said Kari, examining the flute. "I hope I don't—"

Snap.

"Oops," she said innocently, holding the broken flute in her hand. All the kids in the stadium snapped out of the spell and started looking around, confused.

Emir passed the microphone he had swiped from the singer to Kari. Before she could talk, the singer went to grab it back, but a dagger appeared at his throat, held by a very serious Emir.

"I am on baby-sitting duty. You will not touch her again," he growled, fiercely enough to make the man stand down.

While this was happening Kari spoke to the crowd. "Evening everyone. Now let me ask you, did you enjoy being brainwashed by these jerks?"

"No!" screamed the crowd.

"Didn't think so. How about we work together and give them a lesson on how the kids around here really are?"

The crowd stormed the stage, chasing after the now fleeing members of the band.

The play reached its conclusion as the moon sat high in the night sky. Xin, Lorelei, and the stranger began their journey out of the theatre, Xin grumbling while Lorelei and the man discussed their favourite parts of the show and appreciating the spectacular musical numbers it featured.

As they were about to exit, a clamour began. Soldiers lined up to the door, shoving all the leaving patrons to the side, and separating them from the stranger. As the crowd looked to the source, they saw a refined elderly woman, her snow white hair tied up neatly with grand flowing green and white robes, and a circlet with a mixture of gold and flora around her head. Around her walked a handful of young women, also dressed in green and white, with hoods covering their heads, their gaze to the ground. One of these girls had the elderly woman's hand on her shoulder as she led her down the path. Upon closer inspection, it seemed the elderly woman was completely blind. Silence flowed through the hall, followed by whispers of the woman's name.

Lorelei, however, did not need to be told the woman's name. As soon as she laid eyes on her, she tackled Xin into a side room and peered out the door anxiously.

"Not that I'm complaining, but what was that about?" asked Xin.

Lorelei shushed him. "That's arch-angel Demeter. I can't let her see me," she whispered.

"But… she's blind."

"That doesn't stop her. Her power makes it so she can easily sense people."

Xin gave her a knowing look, unseen to her. "You think an arch-angel would remember a little noble girl from another nation?"

"I…" Lorelei glanced back to Xin, then back out the door. "…she might. That woman has the memory of an elephant."

With a suppressed sigh, he came up behind her and wrapped his hands around her waist. His face right next to her ear, he said, "Well, now that we're alone again, it doesn't seem so bad," and slid his hand into her shirt.

"Well, aren't we feeling naughty?" She gently closed the door and turned to face him.

"What do you say to getting our own room tonight, away from the boat?"

"A whole night all alone in a room with you?" She grinned. "Now you're speaking my language. But for now, we're going to have some time before that old bird disappears." Her hands slowly ran up to his chest, pushing him against the wall. As Xin moved in to kiss her, she instead went to her knees, making him forget any earlier frustrations he may have had.

Outside the theatre, Demeter and her disciples, known as priestesses of Demeter, gathered around a large, shining, gold and green carriage pulled by two stunning white horses. The priestesses helped her into the carriage and motioned to join her, but she held up a shaky, wrinkled hand.

"No, no, girls. You've done quite enough for tonight. This old lady is going to go straight to bed. Why don't you young ones go out and enjoy yourselves? You all work so hard," she said with a caring smile.

The girls objected, unwilling to leave her alone.

"Now, now, don't worry about me. Truly, I insist. Go and have fun, children." She gave a small chuckle. "That is an order."

The girls glanced amongst each other, having a hard time holding back a smile. With a curtsy, they all chimed in unison, "Yes ma'am"

35

The Priestess

"Right, I think I've got it," said Chase, leaning in close to Astrid and nudging her head over to a redhead at the bar. "What do you think?"

"I-I don't know." She snapped her gaze back into her drink, cheeks tinged pink. "I don't even know her."

"Ah, that comes later. I mean, what do you think of her physically?"

Her feet tapped the ground as she swirled her drink. "She's... pretty."

"Works for me." With that, he stood up and strode over to the woman, leaning in uncomfortably close to her. "Hello, gorgeous," he said, though far less charming and more cocky than his usual tone. "For some reason, I was feeling a little off today. But when you came along, you definitely turned me on."

The redhead looked at him with disgust. "Excuse me?"

Chase struck a pose. "Do you believe in love at first sight, or should I pass by again?"

"Look, I'm really not interested. You're not my type."

"Ah, I can be anyone's type if I try hard enough."

"Seriously, just back off."

"Alright, alright," he said, raising his hands defensively. "Maybe you're just not into guys. My friend over there isn't into guys, either. Maybe I could change both of your minds in one night?"

Utterly disgusted by the thought, the woman threw her drink in his face.

Astrid rushed over, slapping Chase on the arm and pushing him away. "Chase! What in Tartarus has gotten into you?" She turned to the woman and said, "I'm so sorry. He's not usually like this. Let me pay for your drink and I'll get him out of your hair."

Chase scoffed. "Ah, never mind. You gals are no fun. I'm going to go somewhere I'm appreciated." With a wave, he stormed off out of the bar, slamming the door along the way.

Astrid watched him go, her mind in a tizzy. As she shook herself out of it, she turned back to the redhead. "Um, well, I'll still pay for your drink."

The redhead gave a chuckle, apparently picking up on the ploy before Astrid did. "Why don't you stay for one yourself? Looks like your 'friend' is just fine on his own." She pulled the chair out beside her and gave it a gentle pat.

Astrid smiled and took her offer. "I guess he is."

From outside, Chase peeked in the window, and saw an ecstatic Astrid talking up the redhead.

He grinned, then told himself, "Job well done. Now what about you? Ah, I guess there are other bars where you didn't make an ass out of yourself. That's the beautiful thing about cities!" He looked around at the mostly empty street and shook his head. "Who are you even talking to? You're not used to being alone anymore, are you? Shite, I think we need to find you someone."

Chase strode off down the cobbled streets, continuing to ramble to himself, not paying any mind to the passed out drunk. As his ramblings faded off into the distance, another far more ominous sound pervaded the air.

Thumps, scrapes, grinding and clicking. The little kitten in the drunken Liam's pocket woke to the sound first, leaping to Liam's shoulder and hissing. Liam woke with a small groan.

"What's the matter, Ash?"

Liam listened. The sounds reached his ears, and his face went white.

"No. No, no, no, no." Liam scrambled to his feet, then fell back down.

"No. They couldn't be here. Not yet. Not now."

"Liam Myrdinn." The voice behind him was cold, metallic, monotone. He knew it too well. "By order of Lord Horus, you are under arrest."

He didn't dare look back. All Liam could do was run as fast as his legs would take him.

He didn't want to die.

Within another cozy bar in the city, Chase had found himself chatting up a few of the patrons, having a grand time drinking and telling stories. Amidst one of these stories, a group of ladies walked in, adorned in green and white robes. As they sat at a table, they lowered their hoods, looking around excitedly at their surroundings. Of course, Chase swooped right in, grabbing a chair and sliding into the table. The ladies looked at him with initial surprise, but couldn't help but giggle at him.

"Hello, ladies. What are a bunch of fine things like you doing in a place like this?" Chase asked.

"We're taking a break," one brunette announced with a smile.

"Lady Demeter has ordered it," giggled a willowy girl.

"Ooh, you're priestesses. And of Lady Demeter of all Angels. Brilliant. My mother was a priestess, you know. She was a kind, loving, gentle woman. What I wouldn't give to see her one more time." He sighed.

The girls all looked at him with compassionate eyes and a resounding, "Aww."

One particular blonde suddenly caught Chase's eye. She seemed a little less enthralled by his story, keeping to herself slightly hidden behind another girl. Chase craned his neck, trying to get a better look.

It was Astrid—he was sure of it. She had her hair up into a bun, and wore different makeup, but other than that, it was Astrid.

Chase cocked his head. "Huh? How'd you do that?"

She lifted her head a little, looking around to see if he was talking to her. When she realized he was, she asked, "What are you talking about?" Even her voice was the same.

"How'd you get into a group of priestesses? And did things not work out with that lassie? I thought you were doing well."

"I think you may be confused," she assured him, as the girls looked back and forth between them.

"Oh, come on, I was only pretending to be an arse to help you out. You're not mad, are you?"

"I have no idea what you are talking about. Please stop." She straightened herself up, holding her chin high. Actually, that was odd. Astrid almost never slouched.

"You know what? You do seem a little different," he said, getting right in her face.

"Get away from me!" she screamed, slapping him in the face. A shocked silence filled the bar.

Chase let out his pouting lip as he rubbed his sore cheek. "Oi! What in Tartarus was that for, Astrid?"

"A-Astrid? I'm not—" Her face fell, those big green eyes getting even larger. She grabbed him by the jacket and pulled him in.

"Ak!" cried Chase.

Those shimmering emerald eyes bored into his soul as she asked, "Do you know my sister?"

"Sister?"

The girl released him. "Yes. Astrid is my sister. She was… taken from me just over six years ago. I was so afraid she was dead…" Her eyes became sad, but she snapped herself out of it and smiled. "My name is Ayla."

"Ayla, huh?" Chase scratched under his red bandana, thinking hard as he leaned back in his chair. "Damn, I was sure you were Astrid. You look exactly like her."

Ayla giggled. "Yes, well, that is what happens when you are identical twins."

Chase laughed. "I can't believe she never mentioned you. I mean, I know we've only been sailing together for a little while, but it seems like having an identical twin would be an excellent conversation piece."

Ayla's hands went to her mouth as she gasped. "Is my sister in the city?"

Chase sat up and leaned in close, that large boyish grin on his face. "Bang on, gorgeous. I even know where she is at the moment."

She grabbed his hands. "You will take me to her this instant!"

"Ooh, you're a forward lass. I like that."

Ayla pulled back quickly, her face turning bright pink as the rest of the girls giggled at her.

Chase sighed and sat back again. "But in all seriousness, I don't know about taking you to her right now. I kind of just set her up with someone, and a long-lost sister might kind of put a wrench in things. It's tricky work finding the right girl for her, after all."

"Girl…" Ayla's eyes brimmed over with happy tears and a few spilled down her face. "You set her up with a girl?"

"Well, yeah. Wait, did you not know she was gay?"

Ayla wiped the tears from her face and chuckled. "Yes. Yes, I knew. Sorry. It's a long story." She sat back with a sigh and tapped her cheek in thought. Chase chuckled at the similarity, but she didn't notice. Eventually she said, "I suppose it would be rude to interrupt, but I really would like to see her again."

"Well, obviously. I was going to suggest you come back to my ship and you can see her there when she gets back."

The girls tittered, and the willowy one leaned over and whispered something in Ayla's ear. Ayla's face went pink once again, and she shot the other girl a glare. "I think I know a set up when I hear it. He obviously knows my sister, and I want to see her again."

"Set up?" Chase laughed. "Oh darlin', I would never resort to trickery to get a lady on my boat. If I were looking to get her back to my boat for my own fun, it would look something like this."

Chase rose from his chair, flicking his coat out behind him, and slowly sauntered around the table. As all eyes watched him closely, a sweet, citrusy breeze flowed through the bar. Ayla's chair was lifted and turned so lightly that she barely even knew it was happening.

He came in close. Not close enough to completely intrude on her space, but close enough to let his wonderful citrus scent fill her senses. With a suave smile and typical Chase confidence, he said, "I have sailed the oceans for years, seeing the most beautiful sights and people, but you, darling Ayla, shine far brighter than any I have ever seen."

Her eyes went wide with wonder. As he held out his hand to her, she gently took it. He pulled her to her feet and set his arm around her shoulder. "Now then, how would you like to come see the mightiest vessel in these oceans? The vessel that shall be the first in five hundred years to see—" He swept his arm wide out in front of them. "The Holy Lands."

All around the bar broke out into laughter and giggles.

Chase's face dropped, and he slapped his forehead. "Bollocks." He looked around the bar. "Do me a favour, mates, and forget I said anything about the Holy Lands. It's supposed to be a secret."

Once again, the bar broke out into laughter, but the consensus seemed to be agreement, mostly since none of them actually believed him.

Ayla looked him over, suppressing a smile, but she couldn't help but giggle. "You're very silly."

"I had someone else tell me the exact same thing." He smiled, then held his elbow out to her. "Now then, gorgeous, how would you like the soon to be world renowned Captain, Chase the Ace, to escort you back to his ship?"

She giggled and hooked her arm around his. "Lead the way, Captain."

As they headed for the door, Chase stopped suddenly, and looked at Ayla. "Wait, you didn't make a comment about my name."

"Huh? Chase the Ace? I think it's a very clever name."

Chase grinned the largest smile he had ever had. "I think I may love you."

Ayla turned bright pink and giggled uncontrollably.

As they walked along, Chase couldn't help but examine the completely different way Ayla walked from her sister. Astrid was always dancing, bouncing, twirling. Ayla walked almost rigid, taking long, straight steps. No deviations, nothing. He also couldn't help but notice the leather boots cladding her feet, that clicked on the cobblestone with each step.

By the time Chase caught Ayla up about their adventure so far, they were now walking by the docks.

"So that's what my sister has been up to. I must say I am so very glad she has found such amazing friends. It is comforting to know there are people who accept, even encourage who she is. After what our parents did..." She sighed.

"What did they do?"

"She hasn't told you? I suppose it's not something she would like to talk about," she said, wringing at her robe. "But I do feel so guilty."

"I'm sure whatever happened wasn't your fault."

Tears welled in her eyes. Her lip quivered. Finally, she took a deep breath. "When we were children, we were inseparable. We did everything together. We would cause all sorts of mischief confusing people. It was innocent fun. Eventually, of course, we started becoming interested in people. Astrid told me about a crush she had on a girl in the village. I didn't think it strange at all. Things like that weren't really discussed, and we were still fairly young. Not long after, I had let it slip around our parents. It was just meant to be harmless teasing. I had no idea what trouble it would cause. From that day on, our parents treated Astrid very differently. She was forced to do more hard labour than me. Our parents separated our rooms and made sure we were rarely alone together.

"Then we turned sixteen, and, as I'm sure you know, meant we were able to go to the Sacred Garden. However, this was a rather pricey ritual. Instead, Astrid was sold to slave traders in order to pay my way to the garden. My parents' reasoning was that if they could only afford one child, they would keep the child that would give them grandchildren. That Astrid was no use to the family."

They had finally stopped in front of The Water Lily, and Chase leaned against it, completely stunned. "I... had no idea Astrid went through something like that. I knew she was a slave, but I just thought she was kidnapped forcefully. I never imagined people would actually sell their children like that."

"It's all my fault," said Ayla, bursting into tears. "If I had just kept my mouth shut all those years ago, maybe she could have lived a normal life. Everything I have is because Astrid's life was sacrificed, all because she loved the 'wrong' people."

Chase placed his hands on her shoulders. "Hey, don't think that way. This world, it hates anything different. If it wasn't then, it would have been later. Astrid wouldn't have been able to hide herself away forever."

"I just hate our parents so much," she continued to cry. "I always did everything I could to get in trouble while Astrid was always a perfect angel—always listening and doing what she was told. Then I go and fight them at every turn and they fucking praise me? Fuck them!" she shouted to the night sky. "The moment I received my powers, I never went back to that awful place. All they got was a letter saying not to bother looking for me. I hope they're fucking happy in their hovel all alone. All they fucking deserve."

With that, she brought her gaze back down to the shocked face of Chase.

"What?" she asked.

"It's just… really weird to see those lips swearing," he said, mouth still agape.

Ayla laughed, sniffing back her tears. "I guess she's still a goody-goody then."

Chase laughed. "That's for sure. I also know she is the kindest person I've ever met. There's no way she blames you for what happened."

"Perhaps. But I won't know until I see her again. Are we almost at your boat?"

"Huh? Oh, we're here," said Chase, giving the ship a little knock.

"Oh my, she is lovely," said Ayla with a smile.

"The Water Lily," he announced with a grand flourish. "Named after my mother, Lilian Rose Burke, a priestess of Artemis."

"You were telling the truth about that?" Ayla gasped. "I thought it was just a cheesy line."

"Ha! I don't blame you."

"I've heard of Lilian," she said after a moment of thought. "She died of an incurable sickness, isn't that right?"

A sadness crossed Chase's face as he reminisced. "Yes. They had all the best healers trying to help, but no one could save her. I was eleven when she died. The saints raised me for a few years, then I went and became a cabin boy on a merchant ship. Of course, it's always been my dream to get my own crew and find the Holy Lands, but it's only now that it's looking like a real possibility."

"That's quite a dream," she said with a smile.

"Aye, I suppose it is. I'll go take a look for your sister in case she came back early." He started up the gangplank and held a hand out to her to help her up. With a small smile, she took it and joined him aboard.

After a thorough search of the ship, Chase came back to the patient Ayla sitting on the railing.

"Looks like she's not here. Sorry." He laughed. "Of course, the one time she's actually doing something for herself."

"It's alright," she replied. "I don't have to go back to Lady Demeter until the morning. If you don't mind, I would like to stay and wait for her."

"I could never say no to a beautiful lady wanting to be on my ship," he beamed, dipping into a flourishing bow.

"You are quite the charmer, aren't you?" she giggled.

"I've been known to charm a heart or two," he chuckled, sliding onto the rail next to her.

After a long night of chasing bad guys through the city, the kids had lost track of the band and decided to go home for the night. The play would have ended not long ago, and their parents would all be home soon. First stop was dropping Kari off at the docks. The car was silent along the way, everyone considering the events of the night.

Finally, Cai voiced, "That was… quite the night," and everyone in the car nodded in agreement.

Cai pulled up as close as he could to the docks, and as soon as the car stopped, Emir jumped out with joy.

"Oh, the Water Lily! How I've missed you!" he cried, speeding off to the familiar ship.

"I'll be right behind you, Emir," called Kari, slowly hopping out of the car, with a buzzing Chrissy around her.

"I do not care, little one," called Emir with a wave of dismissal. "We are in sight of the ship. You are no longer my responsibility."

With a shake of her head and a smile, Kari turned back to the car, eyes gazed to the ground. "Thank you all for spending time with me. Even if things did get a little crazy."

"You know our lives were pretty normal before you showed up," giggled Roxy, straightening her hair in a hand mirror.

"I'm sorry," Kari sighed. "I guess trouble just follows our whole crew. You're probably not going to want to hang out again."

"Are you kidding?" boomed Dorian, slapping the side of the car. "That was the most fun we've had in our entire lives!"

Almost all at once, the whole car cheered in agreement.

"I think it's unanimous," laughed Adrian, hopping out of the car as well. "You are definitely hanging out with us again." Adrian smiled warmly at Kari. "Do you mind if I walk you the rest of the way?"

The kids in the car giggled, and ooo'd at him.

He laughed, scratching his head nervously. "Aw, come on guys, it seems wrong letting her go back alone. Besides, I did promise I'd keep you safe, right?"

Kari nodded, her face once again very warm.

Adrian looked to the car. "Wait for me here, 'kay?"

"Yeah yeah, just don't take all night," replied Cai. "Our parents will be home any minute now."

Upon the ship, Chase and Ayla waited on the edge of the boat, in the unlikely chance Astrid came back early. Chase couldn't help but examine the woman a little closer. She certainly looked like Astrid in almost every conceivable way, but at the same time, they were nothing alike. Ayla sat on the rail, slouched over with an elbow on her lap and her hand in her face. Astrid never slouched. Ayla also sat almost completely still, only allowing her booted feet to sway gently back and forth with the boat. Astrid was always moving, bouncing to the unheard rhythm in her head.

Ayla glanced over to see Chase staring. "What?" she asked with a smile, straightening herself up a little.

"It's just so bizarre. You're so… still. Astrid would have bounced up and down at least five times by now and probably started dancing out of boredom."

"Oh, she still dances then? I am so glad. It always made her so happy, but I could never keep up with her."

"Ha! I don't know anyone that can." He leaned over the rail, noticing odd lights in the distance. They examined it closely, noticing a few dark figures hesitantly walking up to the boat.

"Hmm, I wonder if that's some of my crew," said Chase.

"Just Kari and Chrissy down there now, Captain," said Emir from behind them, making Chase jump and Ayla scream in surprise.

"Where in the world did you come from?" Ayla scolded.

"I just got here. Did you not see me… Oh, never mind. I think I shall invest in a bell," sighed Emir, rubbing a tired eye and yawning.

"Big night?" Chase asked.

"Babysitting is absolutely terrible. I chased a car around for half the night, then dealt with magical flutes, then Kari had me climbing up and down buildings. I am done," he said with another grand yawn.

"Uh, alright but you're telling me more about that later."

"Yes, yes, very well. Good night Captain, good night Astrid," Emir said with a yawn and a wave as he walked off.

"Oh, I'm not—"

Chase stopped her with a wave. "Ah, we'll tell them in the morning. I'm curious how many will notice."

Ayla giggled. "Oh, I haven't played that game in a very long time. How exciting."

They watched the three dark figures draw closer and eventually saw Kari and Chrissy walking along with a boy Chase didn't recognize. He cocked his head, and was about to call out to Kari to ask who she was with, but received an urgent shush from Ayla.

"No, no! You can't interrupt young love like that," she said with a warm smile, seeing the awkward smiles on the two young faces as they stopped and turned to each other.

"Huh?" Chase whispered, then laughed. "Well, I guess you do have some things in common with your sister. Just love a good romance, don't you?"

"I suppose I do. Now shush, I want to hear what they're saying!"

Down below, Adrian turned to Kari, and softly grabbed her hands with his one good hand, and looked right into her eyes. Kari returned the look, an excited smile on her face. Chrissy sat patiently beside Kari, tail softly thumping on the wooden dock.

"Well, this is me," she giggled nervously. "Thank you so much for everything tonight."

"Hey… Kari. Were you really kidnapped by that lady?" Adrian asked with concern.

Kari looked him dead in the eye, absolute seriousness on her face. "No way. Definitely not. Lorelei saved me. My parents used me for horrible things just to make money. Lorelei never forced me to do anything. It was my decision to leave, and it's my decision to stay away."

"Then you're happy, and safe?"

"Definitely," she replied with a smile. "Well, as safe as pirates on a mission to change the world can be, I suppose."

"That's good," he said, returning the soft smile. "Do you know how long you're staying? I would really like to see you again before you leave."

"I'm not sure exactly, but probably first thing in the morning," Kari said sadly.

"So soon? Damn. Well then, I'll be back tomorrow morning as soon as I can get away from my parents," he promised, squirming a little. His hand perspired as he managed to say softly, "But just in case I don't see you again, I'd really like to kiss you. Would that be okay?"

Kari's face burned brightly, her heart raced as she nodded her head. Slowly, he leaned in and gave her a soft kiss on the lips.

Up on the railing, an ecstatic Chase and Ayla watch the scene with doey eyes, a unanimous "Aww" escaping their lips as the two kissed. They lingered there for a moment, just looking into each other's eyes, then said their goodbyes. Kari walked onto the ship, eyes completely glazed over with joy, a permanent smile plastered on her face.

"Heya, Kari. Fun night?" asked Chase.

"Mhmmm," she sang.

"Who's the boy?"

"Adrian," she sighed dreamily, as she watched the blonde-haired boy walk back to the car.

"Emir mentioned something about magical flutes?"

Without looking away from the boy, Kari reached into her pocket and passed the broken flute to Chase.

"Yeah… There were some bad guys. We took care of them," she replied airily.

Chase looked over the flute, noticing a familiar symbol engraved on it. Two serpents entwined, biting each other's tail. He had encountered the symbol once before when he had met Xin. A pack of wargs had been roaming the countryside on a small island, and Xin had rescued Chase from becoming their snack. Upon killing the alpha, the pack turned into humans, and a gem with the same insignia was discovered. Xin had recognized it as the mark of Loki, a rogue angel that Xin kept finding the handiwork of. He was beginning to think it was intentional.

Chase shook his head and shoved the broken flute in his pocket. He'd have to show it to Xin tomorrow.

As the car drove off, Kari gave another dreamy sigh, and said, "I'm going to bed now. Goodnight, Chase. Goodnight, Astrid," bringing a suppressed giggle from Ayla.

Chase smiled and said, "Goodnight, kid. Sweet dreams."

"Mhmm," she sighed, then disappeared below deck. As soon as she was out of earshot, the two started to laugh.

"Oh, I am so glad I came with you. That was the most adorable thing I have seen in a long time," said Ayla.

"I think I'd have to agree. There is another couple on the ship that can be pretty adorable, but in a different way."

"You seem to have a way of attracting interesting people, don't you?"

"Well, I managed to get you here, so I must," he said with his usual grin, making Ayla giggle.

"You had mentioned earlier, about how the world doesn't accept people that are different. You tend to find people who are different too, don't you?"

Chase scratched his ear. "Yeah, growing up, I was always shunned for being different. I never want anyone to feel like that, so I guess I kind of am drawn to people that are different."

Ayla gently put her hand against his ear, making him look at her with some panic. "Was it because you are deaf that you were treated differently?"

Chase jumped back from her. "How did you…?"

"Sorry," she chuckled. "It's the blessing I received. I can tell things about the body that most wouldn't notice. It's very helpful with healing."

"You're a magic healer? C-can you…?"

"Fix your hearing? I'm afraid not," she replied sadly. "If it was caused by damage, then maybe, but you were born with it, so I'm afraid my powers won't work."

"Oh, well, it was worth a try," he sighed. "Aye, it was because I was deaf. Most of my childhood I couldn't hear at all. It wasn't until I was older that I got my hearing aids. The kids didn't know how to play with me without being able to talk, so I didn't exactly get invited to play. When I did get my hearing aids I was able to do more, but it took a long time for me to be able to talk fairly normally, so that freaked them out too.

"It wasn't until I left and started hiding the fact that I had a disability that people started treating me normally. Well, until I met Lorelei and the crew, that is. They were the first people I told about it in a very long time, and they've never treated me any differently."

Ayla looked at her swaying feet, then asked, "Lorelei, is that your girlfriend?"

Chase laughed. "No. We had a fling but we're just friends. I'm not with anyone."

"Oh, good," she said, her cheeks once again turning pink. "It is… getting rather late. Where is the rest of your crew?"

Chase tapped his cheek in thought. "Well, Dana was here when we got here. You met Emir and Kari." Chase pondered and gave a knowing chuckle. "Xin and Lorelei definitely won't be coming back here tonight. That leaves Astrid and that's our crew."

"That's all? That's much smaller than I imagined."

"Ah, we're small, but we're mighty," he beamed, flexing his arm.

Ayla chuckled. "I believe you."

"Well, I can give you my bed tonight. Being Captain and all, it's definitely the most comfortable. I think… Actually, Lorelei probably made sure she had the best bed. But then again she doesn't really sleep much…"

"Oh, no. I couldn't possibly kick you out of your bed. I can sleep on the floor."

"Ha! Yeah, right. I can see it now, 'Chase the Ace, mightiest pirate captain in the world, lets a Priestess of Demeter sleep on the floor.' Now what kind of gentleman would I be if I let you do that?"

"I suppose," Ayla chuckled.

"Oh, I guess if Astrid's not coming back tonight, you could use her—"

"Or…" Ayla slid in a bit closer to Chase, laying a soft hand on his. "We could always… share a bed. Then neither of us would be put out," she said, her big green eyes looking up at Chase.

"Oh," said Chase, completely blindsided. That was a first for him.

"Unless all that talk back at the bar was just bluster. Am I not the most beautiful thing you have encountered on your travels?" Her giggle told him she was just teasing, but that didn't matter.

He grabbed her hands and looked her dead in the eye. "I never joke about true beauty. Your absolute beauty radiates both inside and out. I just…"

Ayla sighed, pulling her hand away and looking back to her feet. "I'm sorry… It must be very strange for you. You are friends with my sister and we look so much alike…"

"Oh, no, no, it's not that. You two may look alike, but you are completely different from your sister. No, I was thrown off because I thought priestesses of Demeter were more… umm…"

Ayla grinned, looking at him through the corner of her eye. "Prudish?"

Chase shrugged. "I was gonna say proper, but that works, too."

"We like to make people think that, but come on. Demeter's family worships nature and creation. There isn't anything more natural than sex."

He brought his hand to her chin, gently turning her head toward him. "And here I thought I was going to be the one in trouble. Luring the poor defenceless priestess out to a pirate ship to take advantage of her. I'm starting to think it might be the other way around."

"Sir, I am around women all day, every fucking day. I am certainly the one taking advantage of you."

Chase swooped in, locking lips with Ayla. She pulled him in tight, gripping her fingers through his hair and knocking his bandana askew, but for once, that didn't faze him. He picked her up as she wrapped her legs around him, and without even stopping for a breath, carried her off to the Captain's quarters.

He had run as fast as he could, the threat of death sobering up the once drunken Liam. He had run, but they had found him. Of course they did. They were machines built for one purpose, after all.

Now he lay in a dark alley, the sound of the sea not far away, his precious life blood dripping from him. One pile of copper armour lay beside him. Well, it wasn't armour per se—it was more than that. He knew them as Clockwork Soldiers. They were machines with a human body, the head of a hawk, and composed of only gears and metal. Two more of the soldiers stood, still active, looking down upon him, their red lights for eyes scanning him over.

"We must bring his body back to master Horus," said the first soldier, its beak only opening slightly to let the sound out, not to form the words themselves. The second soldier did not respond, still scanning over the battered body of Liam.

"Soldier—" the talkative robot started to say, but found a sword going right through its chest from its comrade. With what little consciousness he had left, Liam looked at the soldier with confusion.

"S-s-sorry about t-t-that b-b-bucko," it attempted to say through its sparking beaked face, seemingly fighting against itself. "Try not to d-d-die, eh l-l-little Willy?"

The confusion overwhelmed Liam. He only knew one man that had called him that, and that man disappeared many years ago.

"Eddy?" he wheezed, summoning his strength to look up.

The soldier was gone.

Ash came out from the shadows, mewing and rubbing against him. Liam smiled and managed to sit himself up. He ripped apart what was left of his shirt and started hastily tying off the worst of his wounds. When that was done, he sighed and picked up Ash.

"Not today, little buddy. I won't be leaving you yet."

36

The Healers

Morning arrived, and the seabirds squawked their little hearts out as they flew above. A sunbeam caressed Chase's cheek, waking him softly. A warm smile crossed his face as he saw the glowing, sleeping face of the beautiful Ayla lying next to him. He stroked her silky smooth cheek, and silently crawled from bed, grabbing only his pants from the scattered clothes on the floor, and snuck out the door.

As the brisk morning air struck him, he took a large, satisfying breath. The wonderful smell of bacon reached his nose, signalling that Dana was already up and hard at work. Emir sat at the table, poring over maps of the area, likely finding them the best way to get to the fortress unnoticed. Kari sat in the middle of the deck, cheek in hand, half-heartedly throwing Chrissy's ball for her. Her eyes were still just as glazed as the night before, and the smile had not diminished in the slightest.

Chase saw movement at the edge of the boat. He found the familiar face of Xin climbing up the gang-plank. Well, it was mostly familiar. The satisfied look of utter happiness on his face was quite unusual for him.

Xin walked up with a quick, "Morning, Captain."

"Morning, First Mate. Did you have a good night?"

"None of your business," he replied with a grin, walking off towards the stairs.

Following shortly after was a yawning Lorelei, who leaned next to Chase, a tired smile on her face.

"Long night?"

"Like you wouldn't believe," she sighed happily.

"And you're going to tell me about it, right?"

"Hmm, maybe." She gazed dreamily at Xin, who had been interrupted by an excited Chrissy. "Have you ever gone on a date?"

Chase, taken a little aback, gave her a cockeyed look. "Hmm? Umm, yeah sure. Why?"

"I think I went on my very first date last night."

Chase smiled. "How was it?"

"It was… strange…"

"…and?"

"Wonderful," she concluded dreamily.

"Adorable," he laughed, receiving a sharp jab from Lorelei's finger.

"Tchah. I told you I am not adorable."

"Ow, alright, alright," he said, rubbing his chest.

"What about you? I know that look." She gave him a nudge. "You found someone, didn't you?"

"Haha, yes, I did. It's a bit… complicated, though."

"Ah, well I am willing to listen, but if it's going to be a long story, I need coffee first. Stay there."

Chase saluted as she walked off. "Aye, aye."

Along the still sleepy early morning streets of the city, an anxious Astrid bounced along beside the familiar redhead from the night before.

"Oh, my goodness, I can't believe how late it is already. I know Chase is going to tease the crap out of me for this. And probably Lorelei, too."

"You seem to have very strange friends."

Astrid giggled. "Yes, yes, I do. And thank you for taking me to the docks, Samina. This city is so huge. I don't think I'd ever be able to find my way around it."

"You get used to it, farm girl," Samina teased.

Astrid's giddy giggle turned to embarrassment as Samina's hand slipped into hers. She glanced around nervously, wondering if anyone would say something.

"You really are from the boonies, aren't you?" said Samina with a laugh. "It's alright, this isn't illegal or anything."

"Oh, heh, right, of course," she replied abashedly, trying her best to relax.

"I'm curious. Have you been with anyone before?"

"I'm being weird, aren't I? I did kind of have a girlfriend for a little while, but she was super clingy. And she had the most annoying laugh. And I only ever saw her on the Oasis, where I knew everyone. I guess I'm not really used to this. I had to hide it for so long."

Samina stopped, pulled Astrid in for a kiss, and said, "Well, I hope I was better than your ex-girlfriend."

"Definitely."

As she gave Samina a doey gaze, a small "mew" caught her attention. She looked down to see a tiny black kitten with a white diamond on its chest rubbing against her leg.

"Well, hello there, little cutie!" Astrid bent down to give it some pets, but it trotted from her hand and looked back at her, mewing.

"You… want me to follow you?" Astrid looked from the kitten to Samina, who shook her head, clearly apprehensive of the dark alley.

The kitten mewed again, and Astrid followed it, leaving Samina in the main street. She saw a strange metal lying on the ground and gave it a curious look-over. Not for long, as the mewing continued.

"Alright, alright, what do you want to show m—"

A hand reached out from the shadows, grabbing at her ankle. She gasped. Samina shrieked. The fighter in her told her to kick, strike and flee. The doctor in her made her pause and take a look at the terrible shape the man was in.

All caution went out the window as she dived beside the injured man. She turned to Samina and yelled, "We need to get him to a hospital, quickly."

Samina rushed to her side, but before they could do anything, the man grabbed Astrid's wrist. His beaten face looked at her with sheer panic.

"No. No hospital, no law," he wheezed.

Astrid sighed. "You're a pirate, aren't you? You're lucky I'm a doctor." She turned to Samina. "I need you to do something. Please listen closely."

Back on board the Water Lily, Lorelei had disappeared into the kitchen to make some coffee. Dana came out to let the crew know that breakfast was ready, and just as everyone moved to go down below, Ayla stepped out onto the deck, yawning and rubbing her eyes, wearing only Chase's shirt.

"Chase, I can't seem to find…" she began, but trailed off as she noticed all eyes on her. "Oh, apparently everyone is awake."

"Astrid? Why are you wearing Chase's shirt?" asked Dana.

"Oh, no, wonderfully kind healer. You didn't…" wailed Emir.

Xin scratched his head. "Damn, I know he's persuasive, but this is ridiculous."

Kari and Chrissy cocked their heads in confusion.

Chase burst out laughing. "Well, that's one way to make an entrance."

Next, Lorelei came up the stairs, nursing a cup of coffee. "Alright, Chase, I'm ready for your story…" She stopped as she noticed the ogling crew. "What's everyone staring at?"

"Astrid," said Dana.

Lorelei peeked around Dana, to see the very innocent, awkward Ayla standing on deck. A vicious scowl twisted on Lorelei's face as she handed over her coffee to Dana. Out came her silver hairpin dagger, and before anyone could say anything, she was at Ayla's throat.

"Who the fuck are you, and why do you look like my best friend?"

"I-I-I." Ayla's eyes flicked from the dagger to Lorelei's seething face. All colour drained from her already fair complexion.

"Whoa, whoa, whoa, down girl," said Chase, placing a calming hand on Lorelei's arm.

She apprehensively lowered her weapon.

"By the gods, woman. Also, I thought I was your best friend."

"Keep dreaming," Lorelei said, shooting him a smile.

"You must be Lorelei," Ayla strained, rubbing her throat. "Chase warned me, but I have to say, I'm still very surprised."

Chase laughed. "Well, that's one out of five that knew you weren't Astrid. I don't feel so bad anymore."

"Wait, that is not Astrid?" asked Emir.

Ayla curtsied with a sweet smile. "No, my name is Ayla. I am Astrid's twin sister."

Lorelei chortled, returning the dagger to its sheath. "*Twin* sister. I guess that would explain it." She gave Ayla a quick look over. "Little shit only said she had a sister, not a twin. And she gives me shit about being secretive. She is in so much trouble." She turned to Chase. "Speaking of, where is she?"

Chase shrugged with a smile. "Still out with her lady friend, I guess." Chase's gaze shifted to the docks as he noticed a figure running toward them. As she got closer, he laughed in surprise. "Well, look who paid the ferryman."

Samina sprinted up the gang-plank, panting like mad. "Help...man dying...Astrid needs your help."

Supplies were grabbed, the stretcher gathered, and the crew followed Samina back to Astrid's side.

As the rest of them loaded Liam up into the stretcher, Lorelei couldn't help but stare at the awful pile of metal on the ground. She barely even noticed her friends take off back to the ship. Her feet were frozen in place as she studied it. Her stomach did flips as she thought, *These things should not be here.*

A little "mew" sounded at her feet, snapping her out of her thoughts. She gasped and looked around quickly. Realizing she was alone, gave a tiny squeal of joy.

"Kitty! By the gods, I haven't seen a kitten in forever!" She bent down slowly, letting it come to her for some scratches. Before she could get her fill, however, it trotted off, looked back at her, and mewed again. Lorelei came closer and saw a beaten up guitar laying on the ground, strings snapped, neck cracked, and a few nasty holes in the body.

"Poor thing. Looks like you got a beating, too." She gently picked it up and examined it. "Don't worry, I think I can fix you."

"Mew!" Lorelei looked down just in time to see the kitten start to climb up her leg. She withheld a gasp of pain as it climbed its way up to her shoulder.

She laughed. "Guess you're coming along, too, huh? Fine by me."

It purred and rubbed lovingly against her cheek, making her voice an uncharacteristic giddy chuckle.

Together the two strode back to the Water Lily, not noticing the flickering red glow coming from the pile of scrap metal.

Lorelei joined up with the group on the ship, guitar in hand and kitten on shoulder. As soon as she got on board, Ayla, now dressed back in her robes, hurriedly pricked her arm with a needle, drawing some blood.

"Ow! What in Helheim?!" cried Lorelei.

"Sorry, no time," said Ayla. "He's lost a lot of blood and will need a transfusion. So far, no one has been a match." She placed the blood in a vial and swirled it around.

Lorelei's face dropped, becoming pale and sweaty. "T-transfusion?"

"Hey, Ayla, are you sure Chase's blood doesn't work?" asked Xin. "Since he's an Angel with super healing powers, I figure that would be pretty useful."

Ayla snapped her gaze to Xin, then Chase. "You're an Angel?"

"Oh… yeah, sorry." Chase chuckled and scratched his head. "I just kinda found out myself. I guess I forgot to mention."

Ayla shook herself out of the shock. "No. As much as it would be nice, the blood types were not a match."

"But… what would happen if an Angel transfused their blood with a human?" asked Xin.

Ayla furrowed her brow in thought. "Well, it would depend on how pure the Angel is, but as a general, there is a chance the receiver would gain a Blessing, likely very mild. They might not even notice." She studied her vial again and grinned. "But it would seem we don't have to worry about that. Looks like Lorelei is a perfect match!" She grabbed Lorelei's hand and dragged her below-deck.

Desperation was written across Lorelei's face as she snapped her head around, looking for any excuse for escape. She locked onto Xin's eyes, and he mouthed "it will be fine" as she was pulled away.

She took a deep breath.

Inside the sickbay, Astrid was tirelessly and carefully stitching the now unconscious man back together. Ayla grabbed a chair, put it beside the man and indicated to Lorelei to sit.

She complied, setting the guitar lightly against the wall.

The kitten, still perched on Lorelei's shoulder, watched Astrid work with great concern, spouting little chirps every time he flinched. Lorelei gave the kitten a couple comforting scratches and examined the twins hard at work.

Astrid was still stitching up all the wounds, while Ayla readied the transfusion. Lorelei had missed Astrid coming back to the ship. Did she even realize her sister was here? If she did, there was certainly no sign of it. Lorelei knew that look in Astrid's eyes. She was zoned into her work.

Ayla jabbed a needle into Lorelei's arm, then did the same to the man, effectively connecting them with a long tube. Lorelei's blood started to drain from her body, and she had to take a few deep breaths again.

It will be fine.

"There we go," said Ayla. "The transfusion has started. I'll get to work on some salve."

"Thank you, Ayla," replied Astrid, finishing up one last stitch on the man's arm. Her hands paused in shock as she suddenly looked up at Ayla's familiar face. Her eyes widened and tears started to well. "Ayla?"

Ayla smiled softly back at her. Lorelei thought for a moment that the two would put aside their work to greet each other properly, but without uttering another word, the two women set back to work.

Apparently, they had both decided the reunion could wait.

After what felt like forever, Ayla removed the needle from the tiring Lorelei.

"There, that should do it," sighed Astrid, drying her hands and looking over her patient. "Now all we can do is wait."

"Thank goodness you found him. He would have died for sure, if not," said Ayla.

Astrid turned to her sister, tears once again filling her eyes. "Ayla, I can't believe you're here." A sob escaped her lips, and she wrapped her sister in a tight embrace.

Ayla returned the teary embrace, and both of them went off, sobbing about how much they missed each other. Ayla continually apologized for what happened, and Astrid continually told her it wasn't her fault.

A soft smile crept to Lorelei's face as she watched the two. Not for long though, there was only so much crying she could handle. As carefully as she could muster, Lorelei rose to her feet, readying herself for that lack of blood dizziness. When that passed, she called the kitten—who had snuggled up with Liam—back to her shoulder with promises of treats. With a mew, it complied, motioning to climb her bare arm. She scooped it up before it got the chance.

"I'll let you guys catch up," said Lorelei. "If he wakes up let him know I've got his guitar. I have a feeling he'll be looking for it." She thought she saw at least one of them nod. So, broken guitar in hand, Lorelei left the two sisters to catch up in private.

Waiting on deck was a gathering of curious, worried eyes. She chuckled at the concerned crew and said, "He's all good. Just needs to rest now."

A relieved cheer filled the air.

Lorelei took another step, but found that dizziness overtaking her again. To her great relief, Xin was by her side catching her before she could fall.

"Thanks," she said. She wasn't sure if it was the lack of blood, but he seemed extra handsome at the moment. With a shake of her head, she pushed the thought away. As she looked around, she noticed Astrid's fling was nowhere to be seen.

"Where'd the redhead go?"

"She seemed pretty freaked out by everything," said Xin. "I'm guessing she went home."

"Poor Astrid." Lorelei sighed and shrugged. "Oh, well, I'm thinking she'll be too busy catching up with her sister to really notice."

"So, everything went alright?"

"Yeah." She looked him up and down, studying him for a moment. "Xin… do you…"

Xin bit his cheeks, trying to hold back the excitement. Was she going to do it? Was she going to tell him?

She shook her head. "Never mind. I need you to do two things for me."

Xin sighed. "Sure, what do you need?"

"First, lock up our new guest."

"Really?"

"He denied being taken to the hospital, meaning he could be trouble. I don't want to take any chances."

"Right."

"Second, take me over to Chase. I need to discuss his choice of bedmates."

They both gave a small chuckle at that. Xin helped her over to Chase, who, as usual, was entertaining himself making small whirlwinds off the side of the boat. Xin leaned her up against the rails beside Chase and hurried off to the first task.

Lorelei gave Chase a soft punch on the chest when he sent her a questioning gaze.

"Complicated, huh? That's the understatement of the year," she said.

He shot her that boyish grin.

She gave him a nudge. "Well? I'm waiting for my story, third best friend."

"What?" Chase whined. "Bollocks. Xin beats me too, huh?"

"Sorry, that's the way the cookie crumbles."

"Mew," voiced the kitten on her shoulder, now rubbing up against Chase's cheek.

Lorelei chuckled. "Oh, right, first we find a snack for the kitty, then you tell me about your hook-up."

37

The Siren's Song

Morning turned to mid-day. Astrid and Ayla still sat in the medbay, catching up on the missing six years.

A loud moan made them jump and turn to the man stirring in the bed.

"Oh, he's up already? That is some amazing medicine, Ayla," said Astrid.

Ayla giggled. "Well, I did have a wonderful teacher."

He slowly sat himself up, flinching from the pain. The familiar clinking of the chains sent the man's eyes wide. "What? What is this?" He looked desperately at his arms and weakly tugged against them. Next his gaze snapped around the room. "Where am I? Am I back in Ratum? You bastards will never take me alive!"

The girls giggled in perfect unison.

"Oh, no. You're not in Ratum," said Astrid.

"You're still very much in Gaia," concluded Ayla.

Liam looked between the two, rubbed his eyes, and looked again. In a mere whisper, he said, "Oh, dear… I must be doing worse than I thought. I seem to be seeing double."

Another harmonic giggle.

"No, you're not," said Ayla.

"We're twins," said Astrid.

He relaxed, leaning up against the wall. "Oh, thank the gods. Then what

367

are the chains for?"

Astrid wagged a teasing finger at him. "First rule of being a pirate, never trust another pirate."

"You are pirates?" Liam asked worriedly.

"Well, she is. I am actually a priestess," replied Ayla, causing the man to once again look between them with confusion.

He pressed a thoughtful finger to his cheek. "How… odd." A wide grin spread across his face. "Wonderful! I love odd."

Astrid giggled. "Well, then you'll love our crew."

"How are you feeling?" asked Ayla, coming over to examine his wounds.

"Considering I thought I was dead, pretty damn good," he said, flexing a muscle, and flinching from the pain. "Relatively, of course."

With a tilt of her head and legitimate concern in her eyes, Astrid asked, "What happened to you?"

Ayla was far less concerned, as a wicked smile crossed her face. "I bet he betrayed his crew, and they dumped him off here. Or he got caught stealing and got beaten to death as a warning."

He looked between the two again and pointed at Astrid. "I thought *she* was the pirate."

Astrid grinned. "I am!"

"Ha! Wonderful. Well, I like your imagination, girl, but I assure you my tale is far more exciting than that. I, in fact, am being hunted by Clockwork Soldiers. Mindless soldiers of Ratum with absolutely nothing better to do with their time than hunt an old man for twenty years, apparently."

"Oh, don't be silly," said Astrid. "You're not an old man, you're barely middle-aged."

At almost the same time, Ayla asked, "Ooo, what horrible thing did you do? You must have pissed off an Angel to be hunted by their soldiers. Did you steal from them?"

"Thank you, kind woman," he said to Astrid, then turned to Ayla and said, "Far better. I stole the heart of an Angel. Would you like to hear the tale?"

Both girls' eyes lit up with excitement. "Oh! Tell us! Tell us!" they insisted, getting closer and closer.

"Well, I could tell you…" He paused for a while, letting the tension in the girls' eyes grow. He grinned then exclaimed, "Or I could sing it to you!" He reached to his back, grasping at where his guitar was normally strapped, but of course, found nothing there. "My guitar! Where's my guitar?"

"Oh, my friend found it," said Astrid. "Don't worry, she's a guitar player, too. She'll treat it well. I think she was trying to fix it up for you."

"Oh." He seemed a little surprised, as well as relieved. With a shrug and a sigh, he continued. "Well, I suppose I can just tell you without the song part."

Ayla giggled. "I'm sure that would be fine."

"Well, you see, my lovely ladies, it all began twenty-eight years ago, the year 997 AG (After Gods). I was a pirate sailing as a bard on a fairly renowned ship called *The Cursed Trinity*. Obviously you've heard of it," he said, looking at the girls for confirmation.

They looked at each other, then back again. "No, sorry," they chimed in unison.

Liam's chest deflated with a depressed sigh. "Ah, well, I suppose that was a long time ago now." His disappointment didn't last long, as he raised himself tall once again to continue the tale.

"Anyway, we had landed on an island in Ratum in the Forsaken Ring. It was a haven for pirates and outlaws to gather and share stories. A wonderful island, but very dangerous if you didn't know what you were doing. One time, upon visiting that island, I found a piece of beauty amongst the thorns.

"I am telling you girls, this woman… beautiful couldn't even begin to describe her. Her smile could part the clouds, her eyes lit up the world on the darkest day. Hair was as dark as midnight, but she had a spirit that shone like the light of a thousand suns.

"That was my Anat.

"This beauty sat among the dirt and filth and was thriving. She was fairly small and frail, but she had a spirit that could subdue any man. In a place where most women dared not tread, she walked among them with no fear.

"Naturally, I was enamoured by her. I simply watched her for the first little while, but after some time, I grew enough courage to speak to her.

She was wonderfully intelligent and clever. I wrote her songs and spent hours upon hours just talking with her. Eventually, she fell in love with me as well."

He sighed, stopping to reminisce on the past, a smile of pure happiness on his face. "Those were the happiest days of my life."

Gradually, the smile faded from his face, and twisted into sadness and anger. He leaned forward, his voice low so that the girls needed to lean in as well. "Then a dark day came. Her father came and snatched her away." He snatched at the air in front of him, making the girls jump back. "He took her back to their fortress, where I was sure I would never see her again. It wasn't until then I had even realized she was an Angel."

Both girls gave a unified gasp.

His eyes became intense. "She had begged me not to follow, afraid that my life would be forfeit if I did, but I didn't care. I was in love." He remained still and silent for a moment, looking at the floorboards, leaving the girls hanging in suspense, wondering what happened next.

He gazed up with sudden intensity. "My crew had already abandoned me by this point, but I didn't care. I stormed Alexandria and demanded to see my love. Soldier after soldier, Angel after Angel I fought them off, but the force was too great, even for me. Eventually, when I could fight no more, I was sent to the dungeons. Weeks went by with no word of my fate. Finally, my love came to me, but not how I had imagined."

The steam seemed to fade out of his story, and a true sadness seemed to overtake his words. "She told me to leave Ratum and never return. That she could never be with a lowly human. I thought she must be lying, but when I looked into her eyes, it was like she didn't even recognize me. All that time together, all those memories, just faded from her once dazzling eyes."

He took a shuddering breath and gazed at the cuffs around his wrist. "I didn't know what else to do. My love had refused me, and to stay needlessly would only bring my death, so… I left."

The girls voiced a resounding sigh of sadness.

As Liam regained his composure, he looked up at them. "Eight years later,

I heard the news that she had died giving birth to a child. I was devastated. Even though I was banished from Ratum, I just had to go to the funeral—to see if it was true—to see her one last time. I was able to sneak into the funeral and see the truth with my own eyes. Anger and sadness overtook me. I spent days in the city in a daze. One night I drunkenly went to her grave, wanting to yell and scream at the gods for their injustice, but instead I found a little girl bawling uncontrollably.

"I tried to comfort her as best I could. When she finally calmed down, I discovered she was my love's daughter, and she insisted that the death wasn't natural, but that was all she would say. I am ashamed to admit I got angry with her and frightened her in my inquiry as to what happened. That's when the child's father appeared. I don't know why, but she helped me to escape. Unfortunately, since I had broken my banishment, they sent their soldiers to collect or kill me. So I stayed on the run, forever more to be hunted by the awful clockwork soldiers."

"Amazing," said Astrid and Ayla as silent tears ran down their faces.

A soft knock sounded at the door, and Dana peeked her head in.

"Sorry to interrupt, but lunch has been ready for a while. I thought I'd check to see if you two were hungry.

"Starving!" said Liam with a laugh. "Especially for food prepared by a giant. How exciting!"

Chase peeked his head in as well. "Would you look at that? He's alive. That's good news, eh lassies?"

"I am offended that you ever doubted it!" chuckled Ayla.

"Intriguing. You are quite a talented healer after all," said Emir, standing beside Liam, causing Liam to jump out of his skin then flinch in pain.

"By the gods, Emir! Don't scare the patient!" scolded Astrid.

Emir's shoulders dropped. "I did not mean to…"

"I'll go and get a plate for you," Dana said to Liam, who gave her a grateful smile.

"Wait, after lunch?" squeaked Ayla, hopping to her feet. "Oh, my goodness! Lady Demeter will be worried sick about me. I need to go!"

Astrid grabbed on to her sister's sleeve. "You can't go yet! There's still so much I want to talk about."

"Why don't you come with me?"

"What?" Astrid looked around. "But, my crewmates…"

Ayla giggled. "I don't mean come forever, silly. Just to meet Lady Demeter. I'm sure she would love you. She is a wonderfully kind woman. Not like other Angels at all."

"I… don't know. I should probably stay and make sure my patient is okay," Astrid said, tugging on one of her curls.

Liam laughed. "Don't worry about me. I feel great. I've definitely been in far worse shape in far worse places. Just give me a drink and I'll be perfect."

"Oh! No, no, no. Please don't drink any alcohol," said Astrid.

Liam gripped his heart. "No alcohol? Are you trying to kill me?"

A dark chuckle escaped Ayla's lips. "If she wanted to do that, she would have left you on the street to bleed out."

"It will slow the healing process," said Astrid. "If you want to heal quickly, you will abstain from any alcohol."

"Really? Well, that might explain a few things. Alright, then. No alcohol. You go ahead and don't worry about me," he said with a smile.

Astrid turned to her sister. "You don't think it's a bit dangerous? Her being an Angel and me being a pirate?"

"Well, maybe, but we don't have to tell her you're a pirate, now do we?" She smiled that mischievous smile that Astrid missed so much. "Besides, it's not like you're an actual criminal. There's no way you could be, goody-goody."

Astrid giggled. "Well, that's true." She stopped and tugged at her hair again. "I don't know… Maybe I should ask Lorelei."

Liam's eyes lit up with excitement. "Wait, wait, wait. Lorelei? *The* Lorelei? Lorelei the Siren?"

From the doorway, Chase laughed. "Sounds like someone else is a fan of Lorelei's work."

"Of course I am!" said Liam. "A woman who goes around killing outlaws with song? That's a woman after my own heart! I've been following her exploits for years. So then you must be the new crew I've been hearing about. This is very exciting!"

"Aw, go on, you two," said Chase to the twins. "I promise we won't leave without you."

As Astrid and Ayla ran off to meet back up with Demeter, Kari stood at the railings, gazing off into the city with a sigh.

From below her she heard, "Psst! Hey Kari!"

Excitement overflowed as she recognized that voice. She looked down to see the smiling face of Adrian looking up at her.

"Adrian!" she squealed, leaping off the boat and into a big hug. "I'm so glad you're here."

"Yeah, sorry it took so long. After that fiasco last night, my parents didn't want to let me go anywhere. But I managed to sneak away."

"Oh, yeah! I've got a surprise for you. I was working on it all morning. It's not the best, but it should be better than what you have. Come on," she said, grabbing his hand and pulling him on board.

"Onto a pirate ship?" He grinned. "Awesome."

Within the sickbay on the ship, the bored bard sighed, jangling at his chains, singing sad songs about freedom lost. He occasionally flinched from a twang of pain, but the painkillers the healers had given him were doing quite well, all things considering.

As he continued to sing his laments, a chuckle came from the doorway. He looked up to see a large muscled man holding a guitar in one hand. Not his guitar, but the style wasn't far off.

"Little dramatic, don't you think?" asked Xin.

"Well, my life has been saved, but at what cost?" Liam sighed, jangling his chains.

"Ah, you worry too much. As soon as we're sure we can trust you, we'll let you go. Besides, you shouldn't be moving around, anyway. Doctor's orders." Xin took a few steps toward him. "But Lorelei figured you'd be bored, so she said you could borrow her guitar until she gets yours fixed up."

Liam's eyes lit up with excitement, and Xin started to pass the guitar over. At the last moment, Xin snatched it back, breaking the poor man's heart.

"Oh, however it does come with a warning," said Xin. "If you put one scratch on her baby, she will find various new ways of torture to try upon you." Xin chortled at the paleness of the man's face and handed the guitar over.

Liam took it with a little less enthusiasm, gave it a quick look, and snorted. "Well, how would she be able to tell? This thing has certainly seen better days."

"It's very old and very important to her. Just be careful, alright?"

"Of course. Despite the state of my own guitar, I do actually treat my instruments with the utmost care." He accentuated his point with a vigorous strum. "You're Xin Romo, aren't you?"

Xin's eyes narrowed. "Yes."

"Now, now, no need for the famous death glare," Liam chuckled as he began to play a bouncing tune on the guitar. "You've got quite the reputation about you too, you know. Not nearly as fascinating as the Siren, but quite impressive still."

"Thanks. I guess."

"I quite enjoyed the tale of the burning nobleman," said Liam, then began to sing, "Fire ablaze in the heart of town, there came a fearsome man. Upon his hand, the nobleman he threw into the flame."

"Tch. That's not what happened."

"Is that so?" Liam leaned forward, paying full attention to Xin. "Do tell."

Xin sighed and leaned against the wall, arms crossed. "I went to collect my reward for a job I did and the 'nobleman' was just lying there, passed out drunk. When I woke him up, he freaked out and ran off. In his panic, he ran into the brazier in the town centre and since he was so soaked with alcohol, he lit up like nothing. Of course, instead of admitting their Lord was an idiot drunk, they blamed me."

A beaming grin spread across the man's face as he broke out into a jolly laugh. "Wonderful. The best lies are the ones based in truth, you know?"

"Yeah…" Xin examined the man for a moment as he continued plucking out a song. He had never met the man before, that he was sure of, but that smile seemed so familiar somehow.

"Say, how would you like to tell me a few more of your stories? I do love to hear the truth behind the fable. Perhaps I will even write another play with you as the star!" Liam gushed, suspending a beautiful chord for flair.

"Heh, like anyone would watch that."

"Ah, you let the master be the judge of that," Liam said.

With a shrug, Xin figured he would humour the injured man. Why not share a couple stories? Maybe then he could figure out why the man felt so familiar. A couple of stories turned into many, and after nearly two hours of tales, Liam sat back with a hardy laugh.

"By the gods, boy, you have been through a lot for someone so young. And so many odd tales. I wonder why this Angel Loki seems to have set his sights on you."

Xin gave a low growl. "That's what I plan to ask him if I ever find him."

Liam stopped his playing, taking a moment to work out a cramp in his hand. Through the silence, they heard a different melody being played, along with the sweet voice of Lorelei.

"Oh, my," breathed Liam. "That must be Lorelei. The rumours of her voice were not over exaggerated, it seems. How wonderful."

"Yeah," Xin said with a soft smile. "I guess she's got your guitar all fixed up."

"By the gods, I had almost forgotten this wasn't mine." Liam examined Lorelei's guitar, running his hand over the contours of its body. "It feels so… familiar. Reminds me of a guitar I had many years ago. Only thing missing is a little engraving I made." He spun the guitar around to examine the face of it a little closer. The front held many different small scratches and cuts, but, without hesitation, his finger placed itself right upon one particular repaired cut near the bottom of the guitar. "Right about here is where it would have been," he said, a small, reminiscent smile on his face. "For my wild rose."

Xin snapped his eyes wide open. "What did you say?"

Liam cocked his head. "It was something I made for my Anat when we were together. I gave the guitar to her because she wanted to learn. I wonder if she ever did…" Liam's eyes glazed over in reminiscence, which meant he missed the sheer panic in Xin's eyes.

Finally, he realized why the man's smile seemed so familiar. Xin began to pace from Liam to the door, cursing a string of swears under his breath.

"What's wrong?" asked Liam.

Without answering, Xin undid his chains, much to Liam's surprise. Liam looked at his wrists, then up to the obviously distraught man.

"Stay here. No, don't… No… shit. I don't know. Yes. Stay here. I'll be—"

Lorelei's voice drifted in once again through the open window as she sang a new song.

"We live our lives, so full of dread in this forsaken world

So long we tread amongst the dead,

Lost and all alone.

Amongst the thorny brambles, I plucked a daunting tune,

Until one day, I saw a rose, and knew just what to do."

To Xin, it was a song Lorelei had always sung, a song her mother had always sung to her as a child.

To Liam, it was something far more heart wrenching.

"How… why…" Liam shook himself out of it. "Why is she singing that song?"

Xin turned to him nervously. "It's… her song?"

"No… it's not." He dragged himself off the bed, falling to the floor.

"Argh. What are you doing? You shouldn't be out of bed," Xin scolded, picking him up off the ground. Liam grabbed his shirt and looked him straight in the eye.

"Take me to her now, or I'll drag my bleeding ass out there myself."

Xin sighed. "Alright."

The two slowly stumbled their way out of the clinic, up the stairs, and soon saw Lorelei sitting and strumming and singing with Liam's guitar. The kitten was sleeping peacefully with a full belly and an empty bowl beside it. Chase also sat nearby, watching Lorelei play with a curious interest.

"My wild rose,

protect yourself from this world

I want you close to keep you safe, even if it hurts.

My wild rose,

so full of spirit and life,

All I ask is just one chance, to stand right by your side."

Lorelei gave Xin a confused look as they came up the stairs. "What the hell, Xin? You're supposed to keep the patient in Astrid's room, not take him for a walk."

"He—"

"You. You're Lorelei?" said Liam, interrupting Xin.

Lorelei gave him an apprehensive look, then shrugged. "Yup, that's me. I got your guitar all fixed, but she still has a few little scars. But that's alright, gives it a little more character, right?" She gave a little chuckle. "I should know."

"That song you were playing. Where did you hear that?"

"My mother sang it to me when I was little…"

The man pushed away from Xin and stumbled in close to her, examining her face. "Those eyes. You must be."

"Tchah, what the hell? Personal space," she growled, placing her foot on his chest and gently pushing him back. "Don't think just because Astrid spent all morning keeping you alive that I won't stab you."

He stood a little straighter, giving an exuberant laugh. "And that spirit!"

"What the hell is wrong with you?"

With half a grin, Liam plopped down on the ground, spinning the borrowed guitar expertly around and in place. Without a moment's hesitation, those experienced fingers started playing the same tune Lorelei had been playing. She was taken aback at first, but nothing compared to when he began singing the second verse. The verse she hadn't gotten to yet.

"What brings you here, my rose, my dear, to a land of dark and fear?
You brighten my world, my life, my heart,
Like no other could.
Amongst the blood, the sweat, the tears, I plucked a merry tune
Because, this day, I saw a rose, and knew just what to do."

Eyes wide, Lorelei didn't take her eyes off the man for a second as he continued to play her song. The words were perfect… well, almost. A few words were ever so slightly different than she remembered, but hearing it now, it was exactly how her mom used to sing it to her.

Her breath became short, so Xin came in close, hoping to help calm her a little, but she wasn't paying attention to anything else at the moment as Liam continued that song.

My wild rose,
protect yourself from this world
I'll keep you close, I'll keep you safe, even if it scars.
My wild rose,
so full of spirit and life,
All I ask is just one chance to stay right by your side."

Liam strummed the final chord and looked up at Lorelei with a small smile.

She shook her head in disbelief. "How… no one should know that song. I've only ever sung it around my friends." The confusion faded, and anger twisted on her face. She jumped at him and grabbed his throat, looking him straight in the eye. "How do you know that song?"

Liam seemed unfazed by her death glare. He just smiled and said, "I should hope I know it. I wrote it."

Lorelei was shocked to her core. She let go of his throat, stumbling backwards, almost crashing into the newly repaired guitar until Xin caught hold of her.

Liam stood gingerly back to his feet, still smiling. "All this time, I thought that girl was someone else's. I never even considered she could be mine. When is your birthday?"

"A-August 5th, 999," she quavered.

"August…" He did some mental math, then started mumbling, "Just over 6 months, then. She must have known before Set came and took her away. That must have been what she wanted to talk about that night. She seemed so excited." He thought for a moment and looked up at Lorelei with an absolute glow of happiness. "I suppose she had reason to be. Look at you. You're utterly perfect, aren't you?"

"S-stop," she whispered, her hands shaking.

"You have her eyes, her ears, her fingers," he said, looking her over excitedly. "Ah, but I apologize, you seem to have gotten quite a lot from me." He laughed. "Mostly my hair. It is quite the hassle, isn't it?"

Lorelei ran a hand through her hair, then looked at his silver streaked auburn hair and nodded nervously.

Liam continued enthusiastically. "But of course it also seems you have inherited my talent, not that your mother wasn't talented, but she couldn't figure out this guitar no matter how much I showed her. Did she ever figure it out?"

Lorelei just shook her head.

"Ah, that's alright. She was good at so many other things." He sighed and ran a finger along the one scar on the guitar. "But what happened to my engraving? Anat didn't do that, did she?"

Lorelei shook her head and breathed, "It was my fault."

Xin snapped his gaze to Lorelei. *She said it was Mikhail that did it,* Xin thought. *Damn bastard, of course he'd make her think it was her fault.*

"Oh, well, that's a relief," said Liam. "The last time we spoke, it seemed she didn't know me at all. I suppose if she kept this little piece of me, and sang you all my songs, maybe she did still love me." He sighed happily.

Lorelei had no words. Xin tried to give her a supportive squeeze, but found a force trying to push him away. Lorelei's breath was quickening. Her eyes darted around, examining all of Liam. Xin tried to speak softly to her, to calm her, but she didn't seem to hear him.

Emir, failing to notice Lorelei's state of panic, appeared beside Liam and asked, "Are you saying you are related to Lorelei?"

Liam jumped out of his skin. "By the gods, man. When did you get here?"

Emir just sighed.

Liam took a deep breath, slowing his heart rate back down. "Yes, it would seem so."

"But… Lorelei said she was just a noble," said Chase, scratching his head. "Anat and Set… Those are Angels from Ratum."

"That's correct," said Liam, a proud smile on his face. "A noble, hm? That's quite a clever cover up. I suppose that explains why there are no pictures of you as well. You are just as clever as your mother. Perhaps more so. You've been avoiding your family almost as long as I have, and far more successfully. I had no idea Iabet was still alive."

"No!" An ear-piercing scream emanated from Lorelei's mouth, sending out a shockwave and shattering all the glass nearby.

Chase grabbed at his ears in pain and pulled out his hearing aids.

"Iabet is dead!" Lorelei screamed. "I am not Iabet. Never say that again!" Waves of pressure rolled off of her, and the air started to feel heavy and electrified. An overwhelming sense of dread filled everyone in sight of the phenomenon.

"I'm sorry, Lorelei. I didn't mean to," Liam cried, trying to get closer to her. "I was just so excited. I never knew I had a daughter."

Static electricity sparked off of Lorelei. "No! Get away from me! You're not real! You're just a fantasy! Leave me alone!"

"Lore! Stop!" Xin stepped in front with his hands up, hoping to calm her, but too late. A bolt of lightning shot out towards Liam, hitting Xin instead. Blood flew from Xin's hands. He snapped them back, cursing himself for that terrible block.

"Xin?" Lorelei gasped, seeing the damage she caused. Tears welled in her eyes. "Xin, I hurt you!"

Xin shook his head. "It's fine, Lore," he said, though it wasn't completely true. For now, he tried his best to ignore the shooting pain with every movement. He was sure at least one of his hands was broken and his whole body felt fried.

Her breath quickened again. She couldn't control her panic. Every part of her wanted to go to Xin, to help him, to apologize, but she was sure she would hurt him again. She grasped for her necklace and looked at it with desperation. "No… no, it's not fine. This isn't supposed to happen. I–I need to go."

"Lore! Wait!" Xin cried, but it was too late. She sprinted to the edge of the boat, threw off her shirt and shoes, and dived into the water.

"Shit!" Xin punched the rail weakly and flinched from the pain. With a sigh, he slumped down against the rail.

Chase crouched in front of him with wide, concerned eyes. His bandana hung around his neck, his hearing aids safely tucked away in his pocket.

"Xin… What happened? What was that?" Chase said as well as signed.

"Chase… I don't know sign language," Xin said.

Chase glanced at his hands, surprised. "Oh, sorry, force of habit when I can't hear. I can still read lips. Just don't talk too fast."

Xin sighed and shrugged. "She lied. She wasn't a noble. I think the loudmouth kind of explained the rest already."

"I'm sorry," said Liam softly.

Xin sighed. "I get it."

"Well, what do we do? Do we go look for her?" asked Chase.

"Probably best not to. She's an adult. She'll come back when she's ready."

Chase sat back in thought as Kari and Chrissy finally came up from below deck with Adrian excitedly sporting a brand new arm. Adrian couldn't stop thanking the grinning Kari. Her face dropped as she looked around at the damage on the ship.

"What the fuck happened here?"

38

Just a Fantasy

Far across the seas, aboard the Oasis, little Jack had a mechanical seagull—a mail gull—tight between his legs, trying to shove a massive wad of crumpled papers in its mouth, tears streaming down his face.

"Argh! Stupid bird! Go in!" He smacked it a couple of times until a firm hand grabbed his wrist. He looked up to see the stern face of James looking down at him.

"Jack, what are you doing? You're going to wreck it. Those aren't cheap, you know."

"They don' fit!" The tears and snot started to stream even greater.

James sighed and picked up the bird, pulling out wad after wad of paper, opening one to see a disturbingly cute picture. He sighed again. "Who were you trying to send these to?"

Jack sniffed back his tears. "M-miss Lowlei."

"Why?"

"To make her happy. I think she's sad."

James sat down beside Jack. "I'm sorry buddy, but even if we could fit—" he gazed around at the pile of paper on deck, "—all of this into the gull, we wouldn't know where to send it. How about we make you a big folder to keep all your drawings in, and then you can give it to her when she gets back?"

"But she's sad now."

"Maybe, but she won't always be. She has her friends with her."

A smile crept to Jack's face. "Like Mister Sin?"

"Yeah." James couldn't help but grin. "Xin's always been really good at cheering up Lorelei, so no more worrying, alright?"

Jack wiped away the snot and tears, then gave a firm nod. James chuckled and rustled his hair lovingly.

Back in Olympia, down along the shore, just out of sight of the Water Lily, Lorelei sat amongst the rocks, the waves crashing around her and misting her face. She fiddled with the silver-blue chain, scrutinizing it, contemplating why it had stopped working. That chain had always kept her powers in check.

She set the necklace down on a rock. Immediately, waves of destructive vibrations and energy flew out from her, so she snatched it back up. It was working, it just wasn't enough anymore.

Damn.

She looked out at the endless blue expanse, the place where she had always felt calm. Here, the ocean was clear, blue, perfect. Not like back home. In Ratum, especially at the fortress, the waters were dirty, filled with pollution and runoff from the Angels' countless experiments and creations. Unlike Gaia, descendants of Ra did not care about the earth, only its resources.

Still, when she was young, she would always sneak out to the shore, gazing out, dreaming of freedom.

"Iabet! Iabet, wait for me!" cried a young boy, his beige skin drenched with sweat as he ran along after a girl of a similar age. She turned to look back at the boy, her golden eyes lit up with excitement.

"Hurry up, Hibiki! I want to go to the shore again!" she cried, raising a hood

over her short auburn hair.

The boy caught up, panting and pushing his long jet black hair from his face, which revealed a small star-shaped scar on his right temple. "Are you sure, Ibby? You know we can get in trouble... Well, I can get in trouble."

"Oh, don't worry so much!" Iabet teased, rubbing the boy's head affectionately. "Life would be too boring without any risk."

As the kids jogged along the golden bricked hallways, a familiar sound reached Iabet's ears. She halted them in their tracks and listened for a moment, peeking into a room which led into a small garden with a fountain in the middle. Upon the fountain sat a woman with midnight black hair and flawless bronze skin, singing what was supposed to be a happy song. However, as was usual, tears fell down her face while she sang it.

"Uh oh, mommy is sad again," said Iabet with a sigh. She turned to Hibiki, a stern look upon her face. "Go and find a perfect flower for mommy. I'm going to go try to make her happy again."

Hibiki sighed and did as he was told without complaint. It was far less dangerous than going to the shore.

Iabet went up to her mother and slid a tiny hand into hers. Her mother looked down at her with glazed eyes and a sad smile. "Oh, hello my little girl."

"Hi, Mommy. What's wrong?"

"Hmm?" she asked with half-hearted surprise and wiped a tear from her face. "Oh... I'm not sure. I always seem to get sad when I sing some songs." She turned another half-hearted smile at Iabet. "Don't you worry about it, though, my little girl."

Suddenly, the door slammed open, and a wiry, ill-tempered man stormed in. "There you are, you fucking useless bitch," he growled, his awful dark brown eyes locked on Iabet's mother.

"Horus!" she cried weakly, retreating into herself.

He grabbed her by the arm and pulled her up. "Come on, you know what time it is."

"Horus, I don't want to. Please, you're hurting me," she cried.

He threw her to the ground. "Get up and get to the fucking bedroom, or I'm taking your fucking useless daughter instead."

Anat rose to her feet, leaving without further argument.

Iabet, however, had some argument left. She ran over and started beating on Horus' leg. "Stop it, Daddy! Mommy said she didn't want to. If you keep being mean, I'm going to tell Grandpa!"

A large hand struck her with such force that she tumbled to the ground. Horus stood over the girl, a literal fire in his eyes. The fountain beside them bubbled and boiled. Iabet just cowered.

Anat watched the scene with sad eyes, but did nothing to intervene.

"You think your grandfather gives a shit about you, you filth?" Horus shouted. "He has far more important things to worry about. He is far more cruel than I am, and your fucking mother has done nothing but piss him off. You think you're important to him? You're lucky you're even alive, let alone allowed to live here. But go ahead. Run to grandpa and see how hard he beats you and your mother because of it."

Iabet's face fell. She barely saw her grandfather, and he was a frightening man. She had no doubt Horus was telling her the truth. Her eyes slid from Horus, and settled on the cooling golden brick floor. Horus gave a small laugh and dragged Anat out of the room.

Hibiki, who had been hiding behind a bush, came out to make sure she was alright. It was his job to protect her, but there was nothing he could do about other Angels. He was just a human slave.

"Hibiki," she said weakly, tears filling her eyes. "Can we please go to the shore now?"

He nodded, helped her up and together the two went to the ocean.

Atop a cliff face, Iabet and Hibiki sat and looked out at the endless sea. Below were the crowded docks, which buzzed with human sailors and merchants. Iabet sat with her far too large, completely unmarred guitar in hand, attempting to play a tune. After many unsuccessful attempts, she cried out in anger and punched the ground repeatedly.

"Are you okay, Ibby?" Hibiki asked.

"No! I need to get this right!"

"Why?"

"It's so obvious. Horus isn't my real father. My real father made those songs for

mom. He must be the man from the songs. A sailor of the seas. So I need to learn the songs on his guitar. That way he'll hear them and take me and mom away from here." Once again, she attempted a song, receiving only terrible, clunky notes.

Day after day, year after year the little girl played and played, getting better and better. Even after the death of her mother the girl continued to play.

The man she expected never showed up, but a different man—teenager, to be exact—did show up one day, almost a year after her mother's death.

"That's a very beautiful song. You're quite talented," said the boy, surprising both children atop the cliff.

Hibiki leapt to his feet, standing between Ibby and the boy. "Stay behind me, Ibby!"

The boy laughed. "Dumb boy, what are you going to do? Cry on me? Come on. Do you even know how to throw a punch?" The boy laughed again, his dazzling violet eyes staring down Hibiki.

"I-i-it's my job to protect Ibby."

The boy just laughed as he walked up to the trembling Hibiki. Hibiki tried to throw a punch, but the boy stepped to the side, and pushed Hibiki's head the opposite direction, sending him stumbling to the ground.

Iabet watched the exchange nervously, still sitting with her too big guitar. The boy didn't bother to give Hibiki another glance as he went straight to Iabet, sitting cross-legged in front of her. He gazed right into her eyes. She felt her cheeks grow warm as she studied the handsome boy's face. The only other person she had met that was even close to her age was Hibiki.

"I've heard you a few times when we come to port. You've gotten a lot better. There's still a lot to learn, though. I don't do a lot of guitar, but I do know a few things, if you'd like me to show you," he said with a knowing smile.

Her eyes full of wonder, she nodded her head slowly.

He grinned. "Great. My name's Mikhail, by the way. What's yours?"

"I... Ibby."

Ocean spray sprinkled her face as Lorelei gazed back to the Water Lily. "This is ridiculous. That man... he can't be my father. It's a trick. Xin must have set it up after I told him."

"Right… 'cause Xin is such a prankster," spat the ever annoying vision of Mikhail, now lounging next to her, not affected at all by the ocean spray. "Besides, you never told him where the engraving was."

"That's… true," said Lorelei.

"Also, Xin didn't know you were an Angel."

"Didn't he? I had wondered a few times if you had ended up telling him."

"Please. If he knew the truth, why would he have tried to get back together with you? He would have vanished the moment he knew the truth. Your family has done the most despicable things this world has ever seen. No one will forgive you for that."

As Lorelei started to believe the words, another vision came to her other side.

"Bullshit. A child can't help who their parents are. You're still you," said the vision of Xin, sitting crossed-armed, looking out at the sea.

She looked at him and smiled. "You did know… didn't you? Mikhail must have told you… but why?"

She didn't get to ponder the point long, as the sweet sound of a violin and the deep, cool voice of a man flowed through the air. She looked around the shore, and noticed the handsome man from the theatre, no longer in formal wear, but a long leather jacket with a loosely fastened shirt underneath that revealed a large scar upon his hair-covered chest.

Lorelei listened to it for a moment, and almost instantly recognized the song as an old sea shanty about forlorn love, and the deadly sirens of the sea. Of course, it was one of Lorelei's favourites. She carefully hopped off of the rocks, singing along to the melody as she drew near.

In perfect harmony, the pair continued the song, each trying to show off their best skills, shooting knowing smirks at each other.

With a final flourish and long held note, the man lowered his bow. "I am impressed. Your voice truly is to die for."

She grinned and gave him a little nudge. "You're not too shabby yourself."

"The name's Killian, by the way," he said, holding a hand out. "Figured I should tell you before you disappeared again."

"Sorry about that. Me and Angels don't really get along, so I had to disappear quickly," she said, shaking his hand. "And you can call me Lorelei."

"Lorelei, huh? That wouldn't happen to be Lorelei the Siren, would it?"

"And if it was?"

"I'd say I was a big fan of your work. I am especially a fan of the newly instated Bard's College at the Sandalphon Academy."

"Well… I officially have no hand in that," she said with a chuckle.

"Obviously. What a scandal that would be," he said with mock formalness. As they laughed together, he couldn't help but check out her scantily clad form. "So… Going for an evening swim, are we?"

"Hmm, I suppose, though as you may be able to tell, it wasn't exactly planned," she said, giving a shiver as a chill wind blew through her.

He removed his jacket and offered it to her. "Would you like to talk about it?"

She shook her head. "No, but I think I would enjoy singing with you a little while longer if you're not busy."

With a deep bow, he said, "I would stop the world if it meant spending more time with you."

She chuckled and nudged him again. "Alright, the flattery is lovely, but let's play some music."

Killian complied with a smile.

39

One with the Earth

Earlier that day, just after lunchtime, Astrid and Ayla raced together down the streets, hurrying to meet up with Arch-Angel Demeter. They winded through crowds, up and down massive hills and finally ended up at a grand wooden gate, weaved with gold. On the other side laid a gathering of buildings, all made to look exactly the same. Behind those laid an oddly thin and tall mountain, which shot up all the way into the clouds.

Astrid looked up in awe, but her body was shaking. "We're… meeting her at the fortress?"

"Where else would we find the Arch-angel, silly?" Ayla chuckled and went to speak with the guard.

Astrid stood back and gawked. This was the place her crew was planning to break into, and Astrid was just casually strolling in. Her heart was racing. What if they found out she was a pirate? What would they do with her? She supposed this could actually be an excellent thing. She could scope it out, maybe figure out the best way to get to the portals. Maybe Lorelei's plan would work out.

Ayla passed her sister a rope with a small green gem wrapped around it, quickly explaining that it was a tracker for her to wear inside the fortress. Without it, she would be kicked out or imprisoned. This, of course, did not help Astrid's nerves.

Ayla noticed the panic in her sister's eyes and took her hand softly. "Don't worry so much."

The gates creaked and groaned as they opened just far enough to let the sisters through. They walked up the extravagant walkway lined with perfectly sculpted bushes and trees. The interior was layered with shimmering marble floors and walls. Immaculate and detailed sculptures of who Astrid assumed were all the Angels lined the halls. At least the ones of importance.

As they weaved and wound, Ayla smiled and waved at many of the others dressed similarly to her. Many of them stopped and gave the two of them a second confused glance over, but Ayla wasn't stopping to chat. There were others she seemed to pay no mind to who were dressed far more simply, usually doing menial tasks, with odd star shaped scars on their temples. Astrid had never seen that before.

Finally, they stepped into a room, and Astrid's jaw dropped at the marvel before her.

She stood in a colossal, radiant garden with massive trees and plants of every shape and size. There were lemon trees, orange trees, apple trees, and those were just the ones she recognized. There were some trees she had only seen in books, like the palm trees. There were bushes, shrubs, vines, and herbs. Every single type of plant Astrid knew was here.

Yet, somehow it felt odd.

Everything felt so structured. Each plant had its perfect place. There was nothing wild about this garden, and it felt so strange to Astrid.

Clover covered every inch of the ground, with only a simple stepping stone path to lead the way toward the centre where an ancient, massive tree stood proud. Its trunk was as wide as she was tall and it stretched all the way up to the ceiling, its branches canvassing the entire garden.

Beside the tree, sitting in an intricately carved, wooden bench, was an old woman, dressed in thick, flowing white and green robes. Around her were a handful of young women listening intently to her words. Apparently they were in the middle of a lesson.

The lesson paused as the sisters neared. A withered smile spread across the old woman's face. Not needing to look over to them, she said, "Ayla, my dear girl, when I told you to have fun last night, I did expect you back in the morning, not late afternoon."

Astrid's eyes grew wide. How did she know Ayla was here?

Apparently, Ayla didn't find it odd at all. She just curtsied and said, "Deepest apologies, my Lady. I ended up having a very eventful morning and lost track of time."

"Ah, would it have anything to do with your sister you have with you?" she asked, a knowing tone in her voice.

Even Ayla was a bit taken aback by Lady Demeter's perceptiveness. "I… yes. This is my twin sister, Astrid."

"Twin? Ah, no wonder your auras are so similar. I do sense, however, that you have not received a blessing like your sister. Why would that be?"

"Because our parents are evil, selfish assholes," grumbled Ayla, making Astrid turn to her with concern.

"Oh, dear," sighed Demeter, "Ayla my dear, what have I told you about holding on to grievances so strongly?"

"That it will rot my mind from the inside out," Ayla recited.

"That's correct. You must forgive, else your mind will never be at peace. It seems your sister understood this," said Demeter, and all eyes turned to Astrid.

"I… Well, I'm not happy with them, but I do understand… I suppose. In a way, it was for the best. I found a new family that loves and accepts me," she concluded with a smile, then gasped a little. "Oh! But Ayla was always very loving and accepting."

The priestesses tittered.

Demeter smiled. "Come, have a seat, girls. I was just finishing up a lesson."

They both curtsied and took a seat in the clover. Astrid ran her hands through it, revelling in every little detail. It was so lush and full. Astrid just wanted to roll around in it.

She pushed the thought out of her mind as Demeter resumed the lesson.

"Now then, where were we?" Demeter scrunched her wrinkled face up in thought. "Ah, yes."

In between the group of girls, a small tree with deep green leaves sprang up. The girls got in close and examined it, but Astrid didn't bother.

"Now then, who can tell me which plant this is?"

Astrid shot her hand up in the air, and the girls tittered. She was confused a little until she looked over to the smiling Demeter and her milky eyes. She had forgotten she was blind.

"I assume, by the sounds of it, that our new arrival would like to answer. In the future, my dear, you may simply say, 'I do.'"

Astrid looked at the ground, her face burning hot. "Yes, ma'am."

"Now then, you have an answer?"

"Yes, it is ginkgo." Astrid sat a little taller, feeling her confidence return. "Used in medicines to help the mind. Especially those with dementia."

"Very good. You didn't even have to examine it. I am impressed."

Astrid gave a small laugh. "It's an easy one. One of the first plants I learned about."

"Ah, so you'd like a challenge?" Another smile crossed Demeter's face, but this one seemed a little more playful. The gingko tree retreated back into the Earth, and in its place rose a shrubbery. One with large berries with red and green skin.

One of the priestesses giggled. "They look like mini apples!" Some of the others laughed and agreed, but Astrid shook her head.

"No, it's a camu camu plant. These berries aren't used very often and can only be found in the Ratum Jungles. They are used as an anti-inflammatory and can be used to treat viral infections, certain eye conditions and hardened arteries. However, it hasn't been fully tested."

"My, my, my." Demeter seemed quite impressed. "You certainly are knowledgeable. You must have had a brilliant teacher."

Astrid tugged at her curls. "Well, yes, but a lot of these things I learned on my own. Plants have always fascinated me. Even more so when I decided to become a doctor."

"Fascinating." Demeter seemed to consider Astrid for a while. At least, that's what it felt like. Eventually, Demeter asked, "Tell me, my child, does anything here call to you?"

Astrid cocked her head, looked around a little, then replied, "Umm... I'm not sure... Why?"

"Well, it does seem a shame to let one with such a strong aura continue to go on without a blessing. Especially someone that seems to know more than my own students."

Astrid gasped. "Wait. This is the garden? The Sacred Garden? *The* Sacred Garden?" Astrid squealed. She looked about with vibrating excitement.

"It is, indeed. So again I ask you, does anything here call to you?"

Astrid's face grew dire. "But... I don't have any money..."

Another knowing smile. "And I never asked for it."

Astrid nodded nervously, rose from the ground, and took a slow look around the room. She went up to each tree, each shrub, each sprout and ran a cautious finger along them. She felt that they were different, powerful—felt the usual connections she did with plants, but nothing special to her.

Something did feel special.

That massive tree. It felt like it was calling her. She shook her head. That couldn't be right. That was the only plant in here she didn't recognize. Clearly, it was something far more special than her. Perhaps something was calling her from the other side.

She bounced around to the back of the tree, but still found the same feelings from the other plants. Again, the tree felt like it was calling to her. Like it was singing. Astrid shook her head again. There was no fruit on that tree, anyway. It wasn't like she was going to eat its bark.

Finally, she came back around to the patient woman and bowed her head. "I'm sorry, my Lady. I can't seem to find anything that calls to me."

"Hmm..." Demeter scratched her withered cheek in thought. "Well, it is not unheard of, but it does seem a bit odd for someone with an aura like yours to not feel a connection with the Earth."

Astrid cocked her head. "But I do have a connection with the Earth. I feel its every breath in my step. It talks to me and I talk to it." Astrid removed her sandals, letting her bare feet slip into the luscious green clover all around.

Instantly, she found her connection and started swaying rhythmically. Her eyes gently closed, and she took a deep breath, letting the wondrous smells of the garden fill her every pore. "It has a rhythm. It always changes, depending on its mood, but I can always feel it. It's wonderful. It completes me."

Astrid slowly opened her eyes again, only to be greeted by many confused stares. All except Demeter, who had a regal smile upon her face.

"Oh… oh I'm sorry," said Astrid abashedly, reaching for her sandals. "That probably sounded really odd. I—"

"Would you dance for me?" Demeter asked.

Astrid stopped mid-motion, turned to check if Demeter was being serious, then straightened back up, leaving her sandals on the ground. "Umm… but there's no music."

"You just said the Earth makes your music. I would like to… 'see' it," she said, giving a soft chuckle.

The faces around her stared intently. Some were confused, some were anxious, some were excited. Astrid looked at her sister, and saw the worry and confusion in her eyes. She smiled at her. It had been a long time since she danced for her sister. With another deep, fulfilling breath, Astrid closed her eyes and listened for that rhythm again.

A smile spread across her lips as she found it. She was in a good mood today. Very upbeat.

It started with a sway, then her hands felt the flow, rising up and over, then out wide. Her feet sprang to action, first skimming through the soft clover—leaping, jumping, and spinning flawlessly around the immaculate garden. Under the branches, over the shrubs. The flow of this garden was absolutely perfect. How did she not see it before?

Without fully realizing it, the flow had taken her back to the giant tree. Her eyes were barely open. They didn't need to be. She knew the Earth wouldn't lead her astray.

Unseen to Astrid, beneath her feet, the clover began to glow. It followed her dance, reacting to her movements, seemingly dancing with her. As she ran her hand along the tree, the glowing spread out from her fingertips and followed her motions once again. It branched away from her, weaving in and out through the bark and all the way up into the canvasing branches.

The music reached its crescendo. Astrid spun and leapt, feeling the beat in her core. Then it began to fade, to calm, and finally, to end. Astrid took her final step, resting down to her knees in a flourish, her dress fanning out all around her, and the glow rescinded to a single point upon a branch above Astrid's head.

Sweat upon her brow, her chest heaving up and down, Astrid looked up to the group with a smile. "Wow, that felt amazing!"

Her smile faded as she saw the gawking looks from the women before her.

"What?" she asked with a cock of her head.

There were no words. A few eyes looked to the point above her head, so Astrid did the same. Slowly, she stood back to her feet and plucked the fruit from its perch.

"What kind of fruit is this?" asked Astrid, examining the odd thing that seemed like a cross between an apple, a plum and perhaps a raspberry. It was nothing she had seen before.

"I don't know," said Demeter. "This tree was the very first thing my mother planted when she came from the heavens. It has never borne fruit until now."

"Do I... eat it?" asked Astrid, very airily, like she was in an almost dream state.

"I believe that is what my mother has intended, yes."

Astrid brought the fruit up to her lips. All eyes watched with burning curiosity. Ayla took a step toward her sister, terrified by the strange events happening, but Demeter laid a comforting hand on her arm. Ayla bit her lip and just watched.

Astrid took a bite, the juice squirting and running down her chin. Everyone stood in an intense silence, expecting something miraculous to happen. Astrid chewed carefully, swallowed, and smiled.

"Neat!" she chirped. A resounding wave of relieved sighs escaped the priestesses. That was, until Astrid's eyes rolled back into her skull and she slumped to the ground. The girls shrieked in surprise, barely noticing the strange fruit roll from Astrid's limp hand and absorbed back into the earth.

"Astrid!" Ayla screamed, diving to her fallen sister. She cradled her and closely examined her smiling, unconscious face. Ayla turned a pleading look up at Demeter. "Lady Demeter, please help her!"

"Oh, my dear girl, there is nothing I can do for her. Her future is in her own hands now."

The Water Lily swayed gently back and forth, now repaired from her little assault from Lorelei. Xin and Chase sat on opposite ends of the ship, scanning the horizon for Lorelei's return.

Liam sat against the cabin wall, bottle of booze in hand. At the moment, he didn't care how fast he healed. It had been a hell of a day. Kari sat on deck, busily trying to repair Chase's hearing aids, while Adrian opened and closed his new arm in awe.

"You are so incredible," Adrian breathed.

Kari looked up from her work, a cheesy smile on her face. "Heh heh, thanks, but it's really nothing special. I could get it to do more if I had more time."

"No, this is amazing. Way more than I've ever had. Thank you so much. I should pay you for it."

Kari shook her head. "It's fine. I made it out of stuff I already had, so it didn't really cost me anything, and I like the challenge."

"That won't do." He grinned nervously and scratched that mop of hair. "How about I take you out for supper tonight?"

An unexpected giggle escaped Kari's lips. "Alright, we could do that."

"Great!" He hopped to his feet. "I should get back so my parents don't completely freak out. I'll come and pick you up later, alright?"

Kari nodded, a goofy smile still on her face. Adrian gave her a quick kiss on the cheek and left with a wave.

He ran down the gangplank, over the creaking docks and onto the solid cobblestone roads. As he did, he heard a strange scraping sound. He looked curiously over to what seemed like a metal torso pulling itself toward the docks. The curiosity in him sent him wandering over, until, from its head, sprung a bright blue light. It shifted and formed into a huge, swirling blue circle. As soon as it settled, an army of mechanical men flowed from it, seemingly appearing from nowhere.

Their target: The Water Lily.

Adrian's heart raced. He wanted to run back and warn them, but there was no way he'd make it there before them. All he could do was hide and watch.

"My Lady, it's been over an hour. Are you sure she's alright?" Ayla asked, nursing her still unconscious sister.

"Oh, don't worry, my dear. My mother was a very talkative woman, and I imagine she has a lot to tell your sister," chuckled Demeter.

"Wha–"

Ayla stopped as Demeter's face shifted. Her wrinkled brow furrowed, and those milky eyes shone with rage. "What in the hell are those abominations doing in my lands?"

The girls looked around, confused, seeing nothing in the room.

Demeter rose to her feet with power and grace, and pulled a small mechanical dove from her pocket. With a turn of its tail feathers, it opened its mouth.

"Connect me to Horus this instant," she demanded to the bird, and its eyes flashed different colours, eventually ending on flickering red. As the bird's eyes turned solid, the grating voice of Horus came from its mouth.

"Demeter. To what do I owe the pleasure?" he said, with a hint of venom in his voice.

"Don't you give me that. You know very well why I am calling. What are your clockwork abominations doing in my land?"

"I assure you, I have no idea what you're talking about. I've been too busy organizing this year's hunt to be worried about the day to day. Don't tell me you've forgotten about the hunt?" This time, his words were laced with condescension.

"Insult me again, and you will find your bed filled with poison ivy," she snarled. Everyone knew Demeter's memory was perfect.

"Of course. Now, as for the soldiers, they have likely tracked down a dangerous criminal and are working on apprehending them. As soon as they fulfill their task, they will return home."

"One or two I can handle, but you have sent a whole army. I could consider this an act of war."

"War? Oh, no, no, they are programmed to stay well under the allotted soldiers' cross-borders agreement. Your mighty army would have no issues dispensing them," he assured her with seething sweetness.

"If those abominations are not gone within two hours, I will make sure they are dispensed of."

"Very well. They should only need a few minutes, anyway. Good day, Demeter."

Demeter turned the tail feather back without bothering with a farewell, and the bird's eyes ceased their glow.

Without turning her head, she said, "Hugo Markham, just in time."

The girls looked to the door, where a gruff, grumpy man in Gaian uniform and a rope wrapped around his arm stood. Behind him, a skinnier, rigid man stood at attention, sweat upon his brow. They both bowed deeply upon being spoken to.

"I assume you are here for the pirate girl," she said, making Ayla snap a betrayed look at the woman.

"Yes M'lady," he replied. "Though it seems things have gotten far more complicated. Would you like my men to take care of Ratum's soldiers?"

"Luckily for you, the two issues coincide. I assume you have found the

Siren's vessel?"

"Yes ma'am. It would seem Miss Galenson needs to take more care of the company she keeps," he said with a grin, and Ayla was sure he was talking about that red-head Astrid had spent the night with. If she ever saw her again…

"Take young Astrid back to her ship and keep an eye on the abominations. I will give Horus his two hours. After that, you have permission to destroy them," said Demeter.

"My crew may not be enough," said the General.

"No, which is why you will be commanding my son's soldiers while he is away."

The General's eyes lit with excitement, then a hint of worry. "Forgive my questioning of your orders, Ma'am, but are you sure you want a mere border guard commanding your elite soldiers?"

She gave a regal laugh. "Mere border guard? My dear Hugo, I placed you at the border because you are one of the most competent and trustworthy humans we have."

Hugo seemed to grow a foot taller from the pride welling in his chest.

She sighed. "And I am afraid Ares is the only one of my children with a head for combat. No one else would have a care for this situation."

His chest deflated a little, but he still took the compliment where it was due. With a deep bow, he said, "Thank you, Ma'am. I will not disappoint you." With that, he waved his man over to collect Astrid.

Ayla laid her body over her sister, screaming "No!" and gripping her tight.

"I believe what young Ayla is trying to say is that she would like to go with her sister. She is quite distraught and confused, I do not believe she means to go against the Arch-Angel's wishes," said Demeter, sweetly, but with an obvious air of annoyance and threat about her.

Ayla sat up cautiously, tears coming to her eyes at her complete powerlessness. As the men gently lifted Astrid away from her, Ayla followed close behind.

"Oh, one more thing," said Demeter as Ayla walked past her. "I would like you to give Iabet a message for me."

On the Water Lily, Chase witnessed the circle of blue energy swirl to life. The thing was almost as large as the ship, and unlike anything he had ever seen before.

"Uhh… Xin?" He jumped as Xin appeared beside him. He almost forgot his hearing aids were MIA. The two continued to watch the portal as a stream of metal men with glowing red eyes poured through the portal.

"What in Helheim are those?" asked Xin, the worry and confusion clear in his eyes.

Without having to look, Liam's face turned to panic as he heard the all-so-familiar mechanical noises. "Clockwork Soldiers. Automatons devoid of human emotion." His face fell into his hands, despair washing over him. "I didn't think they would track me down so soon. I'm so sorry. I should just turn myself in. I've had a good run."

Xin smirked, drawing both swords with his bandaged hands. "Ha, nice try. You're not getting out of talking to Lorelei that easily."

"No! You can't fight them," Liam cried. "They've taken out entire crews just to get at me. By the gods, I've doomed us all."

"Wrong," Xin grinned, slicing off the head of the first soldier to come aboard with ease. "They've doomed themselves."

40

Clockwork Soldiers

A jaunty violin melody with the harmonic voices of Lorelei and Killian filled the air. They had gone over every piece they both knew, and were starting on introducing new songs to each other. A blue light caught the corner of Lorelei's eye. She snapped her gaze down the shore, and her gut twisted. She knew exactly what that was. Without a word, she tossed Killian his jacket and ran off.

"Wait!" he cried out, but she was already long gone. A scowl twisted on his face and his right eye twitched. He rose to his feet, slung his jacket over his shoulder—after giving it a prolonged sniff—then followed in her footprints.

Clicking and grinding, clanking and clashing. The sounds of battle filled the usually populated docks. But every soul had fled. All but the crew of the Water Lily.

Soldier after soldier stomped aboard their ship, those beaked faces and lifeless red eyes scanning over each of them droning their warnings over and over, not actually giving anyone the chance to do anything but fight, as swords and spears came flying at every vulnerable part of their body.

"YOU HAVE BEEN CHARGED WITH AIDING AND ABETTING A CRIMINAL. SURRENDER NOW—"

Shing.

Off went its head. Sparks and oil flew from its severed head as its body writhed, then fell.

Xin stood above it with a smirk. "Nah."

More clanking and whirling sounded behind him, and he swung around just in time to block an oncoming sword and slice at the automaton's chest.

Clank.

Xin's sword vibrated from the connection of the solid plate armour adorning the creature. Pain shot through Xin's injured hand, forcing him to drop his sword. One hand out wide and one hand unarmed, the machine took another swipe at Xin.

A massive gust picked the machine up and sent it hurtling overboard.

Xin looked over at Chase with a smile. "Well done, Captain," he said, then picked up his fallen sword.

"What's wrong?" Chase asked. "You never drop your swords."

"Nothing," Xin insisted, picking up his sword with a withheld flinch.

"Shite, it's your hands isn't it?"

Another machine came in, droning about surrender, and Xin stabbed it right between the plates, severing its core. "I'm fine. Focus."

As Xin glanced over at the concerned, hearing-aidless Chase, he saw a clockwork soldier behind Chase, mid-swing. No time to help. His sword was still embedded in his last victim. Before he could shout out his warning, Chase deftly swung around with a wind-filled back-fist and sent the attacking soldier's head flying off the ship.

"Yes!" Chase jumped in the air, absolutely ecstatic. "Did ya see that Xin? I'm getting just as badass as you!"

Xin's mouth dropped. "How… Never mind." No time for conversation as more bird-men swarmed the deck. After decapitating a few more, Xin looked over to the swirling blue portal, only to see more of them marching out. "Argh! This is never ending!"

"I'm sorry!" Liam cried from the shelter of the upper deck. "This has never happened before."

"It's part of their programming," said Kari, sending a few gadgets to explore the scene. "They can only have so many Ratum soldiers on Gaian soil, so each time one is disconnected, another comes out of the portal."

Xin's sword started to slice through another neck, but once again, the shooting pain in Xin's hand made his grip falter. With a growl, he came in and swiftly sliced through the other way with the far cleaner slicing relic sword. As he snatched up his discarded sword, he asked, "And how do we stop that?"

"I need you to disable one so it can't attack me, but leave it running. I might be able to tap into the circuit and close the portal."

Xin smirked. "Oh, is that all?" Starting to favour his new relic sword, Xin sliced off an oncoming soldier's limbs with surprising ease. He motioned Chase to send it to Kari, and with a wave of his arms, the struggling machine rolled to Kari's feet. Without delay, she set to work on checking out its grinding insides.

Along the cobbled streets of Gaia, Ayla held her unconscious sister close to her as they bounced along in the back of a reinforced, Gaian sanctioned vehicle. The wind whipped about in the topless car, making Astrid's free curls fly about. Ayla made sure to keep them out of her eyes. Every so often, Ayla couldn't help bringing her focus from her sister, and shooting daggers at the General sitting in the front passenger seat.

Markham glanced at her in the mirror during one of those glares. "Do you really need to continue looking at me like that?" he asked. "I assure you, I have no intention of harming your sister."

Ayla scowled. "But you want to send her to Purgatory."

"I don't *want* to do anything like that, but Lorelei forced my hand with her ridiculous tricks!" he bellowed, rage in his eyes. Ayla shrunk back, and the man took a deep breath. He lit a cigar. "I am sure I will be able to get a lesser sentence for Astrid. She isn't even officially a criminal yet. I should be able to find her some cozy slave work in the city."

His words seemed honest enough, and Ayla relaxed a little. She didn't like the idea of Astrid being a slave, but it was far better than Purgatory. Ayla sat back, brushing Astrid's hair from her eyes once again, and thought about the events of the day. Especially the last words that Demeter had said to her. She glanced back up at the grouchy man. "Sir? Do you know who Iabet is?"

"Iabet?" He looked at her in the mirror again, his eyebrow cocked, taking a thoughtful drag of his cigar. "I haven't heard that name in a long time. Horus' daughter, I believe. Died almost twenty years ago now. Why?"

"Lady Demeter… figures she's a part of Chase's crew."

"What?" He began coughing, whether from a gasp or a laugh, she wasn't sure. After regaining himself, he continued, "That's ridiculous. There's only a few of them on that ship and none of them could possibly be her. Astrid and Kari are far too young and Lorelei…" He paused, the gears seemingly grinding in his mind. Sweat formed on his brow as his face dropped. "No… no, she can't be…"

Ayla wanted to pry further, but also felt she may have said too much, already. There was so much she didn't understand about the situation.

As they got closer to the docks, Ayla saw the solid line of soldiers, blocking access in and out of the docks. Many curious citizens had crowded around, hoping to see what the fuss was about. As the car came to a stop, Markham stood up in his seat, examining the scene below. She was sure she saw a hint of concern in his eyes.

"How are they holding out?" he asked one of the soldiers on scene.

"Well enough, it seems. There's been no sign of Lorelei, though."

"Keep the girls in the car safe. We hold out here until time runs out. Hopefully, they last that long." The concern faded from his eyes, and a smirk appeared. "Doesn't look great for the reputation if they're already dead when I take them in."

Ayla was about to snap. How dare he be so casual about people's lives. Someone else beat her to it.

"Tut, tut. And here I thought you were actually worried about me," said a familiar, melodic voice from behind the group. All heads spun around, and there sat Lorelei on the trunk of the car, barefoot and shirtless, a cocky grin on her face.

"Lorelei," Hugo growled.

"Now, now, Hugo baby, no need to bare your teeth," sang Lorelei. "I just want to get to my crew, and your men seem to be in the way. You also seem to have my best friend unconscious in your car. So really, I should be the one upset." In an instant, a shimmering silver dagger appeared in Lorelei's hands, pointed at Ayla's throat.

"I would like to take myself and Astrid to our ship. Make one wrong move, and the lovely priestess will become collateral damage," she purred with pure venom on her lips.

Hugo scoffed. "You're bluffing. You wouldn't kill Astrid's sister."

Lorelei twitched with annoyance. "Wouldn't I? I've had quite the shit day, and she works for the Angels. Honestly, I have no problem with the idea at the moment. And I could just blame you for doing it. Astrid would believe me."

Tears of fear filled Ayla's eyes.

Hugo growled, and the ropes started to inch around on his arm, like a snake waking from its slumber.

She gave him a knowing grin. "You could try and tie me up, Hugo baby, but would it be fast enough? Imagine the headlines. 'General Markham, responsible for the death of a priestess of Demeter'. Wonder how far they would demote you for that? Really just seems easier to let me through and take my chances with the Clockwork bitches."

Hugo let out a frustrated roar and ordered the men to clear the way. She motioned Ayla to get out of the car and swung Astrid onto her shoulder. Together, the three moved through the soldiers, the silver dagger never leaving Ayla's throat.

As they moved past the soldiers and into the empty docks, Lorelei spoke softly to her. "Little further and then you can head back," she said, the friendly tone returned to her voice.

Was that really all a charade? Ayla wondered. She was quite impressed. "No, I'm coming with you," she said, the confidence returning to her.

"Are you fucking stupid? You see what's on that ship, right?"

"I know, but I can't leave Astrid right now. Her vitals are weak, she needs someone to watch over her. I don't know what Gaia did to her, but it's really taking a toll on her body."

"Gaia?" Lorelei groaned. "For f— I let her go off on her own for one day and she manages to get knocked unconscious by a dead woman. Typical."

Ayla couldn't help but snort a laugh.

A small smile slid to Lorelei's face. "Alright, do you think you can manage to carry Astrid for a bit? It's a bit easier kicking metal cans with all your limbs available."

"I can… try," said Ayla hesitantly.

"Let me assist you," said Emir, appearing beside Ayla, causing her to screech in surprise.

Lorelei smiled again. "Wonderful timing Emir. Alright. Stay close." She slid Astrid off her shoulder and the two took an arm each.

On deck, Kari, still busily trying to figure out the soldier's insides, nearly got smacked on the head by an incoming sword attack. Xin managed to send its head flying, but once again dropped his sword.

"Argh!" he cried, snatching it back up. "Anytime now, Kari!"

"It's not like I'm trained in Ratum soldier technology! I fix boats! You'll be lucky if I can do this at all!" she bellowed, not taking her eyes off the work at hand. "And it's a little hard to concentrate with swords swinging at my head, you know!"

"Doing my best here, kid," said Xin, weakly blocking another attack.

Chase, oblivious to any conversation, kept knocking away soldiers, occasionally greeting a fist or the edge of a sword to a non-vital area. He was getting better at fighting, but he was still just a novice. As if to prove the point, a swarm of three machines charged past him. He was able to knock back one, but two more got through and aimed at Kari, who shrieked and covered her face in defense.

Chrissy was about to jump at one, but found herself grabbed by a giant hand. Kari looked up to see Dana's weak, smiling face as she sat down in front of Kari, the soldiers crashing uselessly on her back.

"Dana! What are you doing here?" Kari asked.

"Just—" Dana flinched slightly as another soldier hacked at her back. "Just thought I'd see what you're up to, Kari."

"But… they're hurting you!"

"Ah, I've got thick skin. They're just like little bugs. Like little mosquitoes," Dana chuckled, then flinched a little greater from a sword being jabbed in her side. Her eyes flashed red for a moment, and Kari hovered her hand over her pocket.

Dana took a deep breath and closed her eyes. "One cup sugar, two cups of flour…" she mumbled under her breath.

Kari sighed with relief and continued on with her work. Now with Dana protecting her, Kari would be able to properly focus.

Kari was safe, but Liam was still exposed, and the focus of the soldier horde. One particular abomination made its way past the defence, though losing an arm along the way. It grabbed at Liam with its one good arm, and started to drag him away.

Liam twisted and turned, punching its solid hand uselessly. "No! You bastard! I've got too much to live for now!"

The machine stopped in its tracks, and for a fleeting minute, Liam thought his words got through to it. That was until it fell to a heap on the ground. Standing over its body was a pissed off Lorelei, holding the core of the machine—a glowing blue cylinder—in her hand, a swath of soldiers behind her.

"You came back!" he cried, his heart leaping to his throat with excitement. Those wonderful golden eyes glared at him.

"Don't get too excited. I'm here for my crew," she said, pushing past him.

Emir and Ayla laid Astrid down beside Kari, under the partial cover of the still mumbling Dana.

"Did no one think to give the pirate a sword?" Lorelei yelled out.

"Didn't really have time to think about it," replied Xin.

Lorelei sighed and pushed one of the walls of the cabin. It slid in and rotated to reveal an arsenal. Liam's eyes sparkled.

"I'm assuming you're a sword guy," said Lorelei.

"Uh, yes. Shortsword. Rapier, if you have."

"Ha! What kind of pirate ship would we be without a rapier?" she exclaimed, tossing one at him. He caught it and gave it a few practice swings.

Lorelei studied her weapons for a bit, trying to decide the best tool to dispatch this crowd. She decided on two different weapons. The first, a rope with a small metal dart on the end, she took and wrapped around her waist. The second, a large spear-like weapon, with a large sword blade and a speared tip at the opposite end. It was known as a guando, or horsecutter's sword. Seemed appropriate for the current situation.

Lorelei walked back up to Liam. "You know how to fight?"

Liam held his head high. "Of course I know how to fight!"

"Good. You're the last line of defence. Keep them safe. I'm counting on you."

Liam's eyes lit up, and he stood a little taller as the pain from his wounds seemed to disappear.

"Emir," said Lorelei, tossing the glowing blue cylinder at him. "Make yourself useful, and steal some hearts, alright?"

"Do you have to say it like that?" Emir grumbled, but received no response.

In the flash of an eye, Lorelei charged out into the crowd, twirling the guando over her head and slicing three machines in half. She stabbed the weapon into the chest of another, swept up her discarded shirt off of the deck, and aired it out.

"Pretty rude, tromping on a ladies shirt," she said as the soldiers intruded on her position. She ducked down, allowing a couple of the attackers to hit each other, and sent a spinning hook kick at the last one standing (while also putting on her shirt), sending its head flying into the ocean.

Liam watched with mouth agape. He had heard the Siren was a legendary fighter, but it was incredible to see her in action. The fact that she happened to be his daughter made it even more exciting. He couldn't help himself from cheering out, "That's my girl!"

Lorelei took a few steps back, standing in the gap between Xin and Chase, both looking quite relieved to see her.

"Have a good swim?" quipped Xin, slicing the head off a soldier.

"Pretty good. Looks like Hugo's caught up with us, though," said Lorelei, impaling two machines, and losing grip of her weapon. She pulled off the rope around her waist, twirled it, and sent it flying with perfect accuracy at the vital areas of the machines.

"Damn, so even if we get rid of these, we still have them to worry about?"

"Yep, but on the bright side, they're keeping civilians away." She tapped Chase. "Tornado, portal," she signed to him.

"But what if I lose control?" he asked, ducking beneath a swipe coming in from his rear.

"Keep it small and keep your head in the game," she said, and partially signed. She knew enough to get by, but she wasn't perfect at sign language.

"Right. Try to keep them off of me."

Xin and Lorelei flanked Chase as he took a deep, calming breath.

Sure enough, after a few moments, a small funnel cloud appeared, and a tornado touched down just outside the portal, causing the unloading soldiers to fly in every direction.

Onlookers watched and gasped, and Lorelei gave Chase a cheer, which he didn't actually hear.

The two held off the flow on the ship until one soldier took a swing down at Xin. He blocked it, but lost his grip. The blade cut deep into his collarbone.

"Fuck," he choked, kicking the soldier away and pulling the blade from his bone.

"Xin!" Lorelei cried out. "Why… Shit, your hands. I'm so sorry."

"Don't worry about it. This would be too easy without a handicap," he smirked, quickly trying to tie up the wound before the next attack.

"No, if I hadn't freaked out… If I didn't lose control, you'd be having no problem. I told you that you're better off without me."

Xin grit his teeth, not from the pain, but from the comment. Anger filled his eyes, and the relic sword that was on the ground became engulfed in darkness. A darkness that could only be compared to the utter abyss of the deep, dark ocean. It floated upward, standing ready beside Xin, though he did not hold it.

"Don't say that," Xin growled, apparently not noticing the sword as he blocked another soldier with his still armed... arm. The relic, still not being held, severed the core of the attacking soldier. "I never have been and I never will be better off without you."

"Xin? Are you... mad at me?" she asked, a little shocked about the sword, but honestly more shocked about the anger.

"Of course I'm mad. Why don't you understand that we are better together? Look at all we've done in just these last few months," he said, and the sword continued working as if Xin were still holding it, though his left arm lay useless at his side.

The relic, it's reacting to his anger, Lorelei thought. *Is that good? It seems to be right now, anyway. Shit... he's not going to like this.*

"Please, what we've done is just a fluke," she yelled. "Hell, it's probably all thanks to Chase. Just think, if you two didn't find me you'd probably already be at the legendary treasure. I'll just bring you down."

Xin scoffed. "Be at the treasure? We'd still be floating around the outer ring figuring out which end was up. It's because of you we've gotten as far as we have." He crossed down with his right arm, the relic sword crossing down as well. The darkness around it sliced out and continued on its path, severing multiple assailants.

"No, I can't be around anyone. I'm too dangerous. I should just leave!" She realized her mistake in an instant.

The anger faded from Xin's eyes. "You can't. No, you can't. We can figure out your powers together. Please don't leave." The darkness in the sword faltered and clattered to the ground.

She turned to look at him directly. "I'm sorry, Xin, I didn't mean it. I won't leave again, I promise." As they looked at each other and smiled, a soldier came up from behind, about to strike. "Xin, look out!"

Xin spun on his heel, ready to defend. There was no need. Vines and flowers sprouted from its every cog, completely immobilizing it. He looked around and found all the soldiers having the same issues. Chase's tornado faded away as he too, observed the scene.

The three fighters looked at each other with utter confusion.

"What the fuck?"

41

Mother Gaia

All around them, clockwork soldiers were being bent and torn apart by what could only be explained as Nature. From behind everyone, a familiar giggle sounded.

"You two. When are you going to figure out that you're meant to be together?" said Astrid, stepping past the crew in cover and walking toward the fighters. As she walked, flora grew at her feet and spread outward, eventually covering the whole deck in clover and flowers.

Lorelei looked her friend up and down, a look of dread in her eyes. "Astrid… What have you done?"

"I just had a very pleasant conversation with Gaia. Sorry it took so long," she giggled. "She is quite talkative. She said she'd like to help us on our journey."

Lorelei stepped toward her. "Astrid, this isn't safe. Humans can't have powers like this."

Astrid giggled again and booped Lorelei on the nose. "Oh, don't be such a worrywart. This is special. I know what I'm doing."

On the dock, the portal fizzled closed.

"Uh… I figured it out…" said Kari. She grumbled, "Not that my thing's very impressive anymore."

"If it makes you feel any better, I collected these for you," said Emir, appearing behind Kari and placing a pile of clockwork cores at her feet.

She squealed excitedly and hugged him.

Upon the closure of the gate, Astrid, with a sweep of her hand, completely engulfed the soldiers with vines, and blew a kiss. The vines turned into flower petals which floated off in the wind, leaving no trace of enemies behind.

Next, Astrid bounced up to Xin, running a hand over his collarbone, instantly mending the gash. She removed the bandages on his raw, broken hands and held them softly in her glowing hands. The bones snapped painlessly back into place. Every wound healed. Not even a scar remained.

"Better?" she asked sweetly.

"Much," he replied, looking at his hands in amazement.

"Right," said Lorelei, trying to shake herself back and make a plan. "Ratum soldiers are taken care of, now we have to worry about… Hugo…" she trailed off as she saw an armada of ships enclose their location. "Alright, no time to sit and think. Time for action," she said, pointing and signing at Chase.

He nodded, set out orders to the crew to unfurl the sails and prepare to launch. He sent a gust of wind to pick up Ayla and bring her beside him.

She looked at him wide-eyed, her cheeks turning pink. "Chase? What are you do—"

He interrupted with a passionate kiss. As he pulled away, he looked deep in her eyes and said, "You need to go."

Snapping from her surprise, she shook her head violently. "No! I want to stay here with you and my sister!"

He sighed, running his thumb over her cheek. "While I would love that, the kidnapping of a priestess of Demeter is going to send a lot of trouble our way."

Tears came to Ayla's eyes. "B-but…"

He took off his bandana and wrapped it gently around Ayla's neck. "You hold on to that, alright? I'll come and get it after we find the legendary treasure."

"You'd better," she said with a teary chuckle. She wrapped her arms around his neck and kissed him.

As the two untangled from each other, they found a rather cross and pouty looking Astrid glaring at them. "Really? You hooked up with my captain? You failed to mention that."

"I'll tell you about it when you get back, alright?" Ayla giggled. "And you can tell me about all your adventures, and this crazy new power."

Astrid smiled and nodded. She wrapped her sister in a big hug as tears streamed down her face. "I love you, Ayla."

"I love you, too, Astrid. Come back safe, alright?"

"Of course," replied Astrid, wiping away the tears.

Ayla gasped. "Oh! I almost forgot. Demeter wanted me to give a message to someone named Iabet."

Chase's face dropped nervously, glancing over to Lorelei, who seemed to have had a similar reaction.

Astrid just looked confused. "Iabet? There's no one here by that name."

"That's what I thought," sighed Ayla.

"How about you just tell me the message?" suggested Chase.

"Well, she wanted Iabet to know that she was sorry she missed her at the theatre, and that while it's not the path she expected, nor would have suggested, she is glad that Iabet found her own path in life. Though she still believes she missed out on a golden opportunity."

"Ha! Old bat wishes." Lorelei's face fell as all eyes turned to her. "Ahem... we don't have time for this. Just... tell Demeter..." She thought for a moment, then sighed. "Tell her thanks."

"Oh, um, alright," said Ayla.

Astrid turned her confused expression at Lorelei.

"Alright, time to go," said Chase, cracking his knuckles. "This is going to look a lot worse than it will feel, so go with it, alright?"

Ayla nodded, and with a sweep of his hand he sent Ayla flying to the docks, causing a huge, explosive gust, crashing into the soldiers and onlookers.

Ayla lay on the docks in mock unconsciousness.

"Be gone, useless mortal," boomed the voice of Chase all through the docks. "The gods have deemed you unworthy to assist the chosen on their journey. Only I, Chase the Ace, Angel of Gales, know the wishes of the gods."

The crowd murmured and whispered in excitement. Whispers of, "How is he making his voice so loud?" "That poor girl," "Did he say Chaz? Or maybe it was Kayne?" flowed through the crowd. Another burst of wind pushed people back, knocking some on their asses.

"Listen well, mortals! My crew, the crew of the Angel of Gales, will be the ones to find the Holy Lands and claim the legendary treasure as our own. The world is about to change."

Then, with perfect timing, the sails unfurled and an unnatural wind blew, sending the ship sailing off.

"That was lovely, Captain, but do we have an actual plan?" yelled Lorelei.

"Make a break for the fortress," he yelled back with a huge grin as he took the wheel.

"That's great, but what about the—" As she was about to finish her thought, multiple shots sounded off all around them, and the sky filled with cannon fire. "—ships..."

The crew looked on hopelessly. There was nothing they could do.

"Got it!" said Kari, pulling a button from one of her many pockets and pushing it. A wall of electricity surrounded the boat, deflecting all the cannonballs. The field fizzled out and died after a few moments.

"Shit... that didn't last as long as I hoped," said Kari with a sigh. "Oh well, at least it didn't—" Of course, from the core of her contraption a huge explosion sounded, sending pieces of wood and metal flying into the ocean and into some surrounding ships. "—explode..."

"Good enough!" laughed Chase, sending another huge gust of wind to send them flying at full speed towards the fortress. Closer and closer, the sea gate to the fortress came, and the crew became ecstatic.

Too early for celebration.

The sea rumbled. From the abyss shot a huge cliff face.

"Shit! Titans? No time to turn!" cried Lorelei.

"Don't worry," said Astrid, bouncing up to the bow of the ship, standing at the very edge. She reached out her hand, and the crew readied themselves for impact against the rock-face. As soon as her finger touched the rock, it turned into sand, and the crew blasted through without a scratch.

Everyone let out a huge cheer in relief, and Astrid pumped her fist in the air.

"Yes! Bring it, Titans! I can do this all… day…" she trailed off, her eyes growing heavy. She fainted away, her body falling from the bow of the ship.

"Astrid!" Lorelei sprang to action, racing to the edge of the ship, and caught her friend by the foot. Astrid hung unconscious from the bow, Lorelei was at the end of her reach, grasping as hard as she could. Xin ran to the edge, prompting her to swing her his way. With a grunt and some maneuvering, she was able to do it, and Xin grabbed hold of Astrid's arm and hauled her up.

"What happened? Is she dead?" cried Kari, running up to check on them.

Xin set her lightly down on the deck and checked her breathing. "She's alive."

They all breathed easier.

"Of course she's alive," said Lorelei. "She just pushed herself too far. Humans are not meant for this kind of power. What was she thinking?"

More rock walls formed around them, slowing and then stopping the ship. They were trapped, and the only person able to free them was unconscious.

The crew looked around, unable to solve their problem.

Lorelei fell to the ground in a huff, burying her head in her hands, muffling a frustrated scream. She snapped her frustration at Chase. "Argh! Why did you tell them our plan? Now they'll have all the fortresses under lock and key."

"I'm sorry! But I figured it was easier than having them potentially torture Ayla for that information."

She groaned. "Gods dammit. I hate when you make sense."

"Not that it matters anyway," said Xin, pulling out a toothpick and throwing it in his mouth. "Doesn't seem like we'll be making it to any fortress."

"But… isn't this good?" Chase asked eagerly. "We want to go to Purgatory. They'll just send us there, right?"

"Wrong," snapped Lorelei, "They might send Emir and Xin there, but that's about it. Kari is too young—she'll probably be made a slave. Dana is a traitor, and a giant, so she'll likely be executed. As for you, Chase, probably execution as well, assuming they aren't curious about your lineage. In which case, pray they don't send you to Ratum. I have no idea what they'll do with Astrid. We'll just hope Demeter keeps her and my awful cousins don't get a hold of her."

"What about you?" asked Xin.

"Well, being that Demeter apparently knows I'm alive, I'm guessing I'll be sent back home. From there, probably torture and imprisonment within the fortress walls for the rest of my life. Basically, what they did with my mother." She groaned. "Or she'll try to marry me off to Ares again. I guess that would be better than going back to Horus."

"Well, well, we can't have that happen, now can we?" chimed a mostly unfamiliar voice, accompanied by an energetic violin riff. All eyes turned to the handsome dark-haired man, leaning against the rail, violin poised upon his bristled chin as the man continued to play a lamenting tune.

"Killian?" asked Lorelei, in a confused tone that said, *What the hell are you doing here?*

"Killian?" asked Xin disgustedly, looking at Lorelei in a tone that said *How do you know his name?*

"Killian?" asked the rest of the confused crew, in a tone that said, *Who the hell is Killian?*

"Killian," he stated with a smile and a bow. "Killian Rees, fabulous musician, and apparently your saviour."

"Saviour?" they all echoed, some with eagerness, others with skepticism, some with just pure confusion.

He pulled out an odd-looking trinket from his pocket and tossed it to Lorelei. It looked like a large pendant with a shimmering amber gem. Beneath it lay the symbol of two serpents intertwined, biting each other's tail.

"What is this?" asked Lorelei.

"You smash it against the vessel you would like to teleport, and it takes everything and everyone aboard it near the castle of my boss," Killian explained, once again playing on his violin. "Call it… an emergency exit, if you will."

"Near?"

"It's not a perfect tool. It usually takes you about a day or two from the castle. It's a bit tricky pinpointing a moving castle, after all."

"What's the catch?"

"No catch. Well, unless you count having to meet my boss as a catch. I figured you'd want to, though, being that he has some portals you can use," stated Killian, bowing along with a suspenseful tune.

"Are you serious?"

Xin had had enough. "Let me see that." Xin snatched the trinket from Lorelei, and with a glance said, "Oh, fuck no. This is the mark of Loki!"

"Loki, Hermes, Seth, he's known by a lot of names," said Killian, still playing away, unfazed by the multitude of stares his way. "But, the way I see it, you don't have much of an option. You take a chance with my boss, or you take the fate you already know will happen if you stay here."

Lorelei looked at Xin with concern.

Xin furrowed his brow. "You can't seriously be considering this. There's no way we can trust this guy."

"What other choice do we have?" she asked.

They both looked at Chase, who was trying his very best to keep up with what was being said without his hearing aids. Lorelei gave him the abridged version with her limited sign language.

"What do you think, Captain?" she finally asked as she wrapped up the summary.

"Certain death or unknown adventure? I think you already know my vote," he said with a weak smile.

As if in response, the cliffs around them began shifting, meaning the armada was in position and about to take them out. There was no time left. Lorelei looked pleadingly at Xin, who cried out in frustration and smashed the gem against the ship.

In an instant, and with far less show than anyone had expected, the ship was gone.

Back on the docks, a nervous, shaggy, blonde-haired Adrian watched the action out at sea. As the cliffs disappeared, he breathed a sigh of relief at seeing no ship within it.

Down on the docks, he saw the man who he figured was in charge, talking into something in his hand. He was far enough away that details were not clear at all, but he could practically see the steam escape from the man's ears and heard him roar very clearly, "How the fuck did they escape?"

With a chuckle, Adrian said, "Well, there go my supper plans." Leaving for home, a buzzing little machine flew into the back of his head.

"Ow!" he cried out, rubbing the bump on his head. He turned to look at the odd object, which seemed to be carrying a piece of paper with his name written on it. "This must be from Kari," he said with some excitement, snatching the paper and opening it.

Sorry about supper.
When I come back with a better version of your arm, you can take me out for two suppers.
~Kari

With a big, goofy grin, Adrian said "Definitely," under his breath and walked home, reading the tiny note over again and again. He almost didn't notice walking by Cai until he heard his name being called. He looked up and saw his buddy waving him over to a bush. When he joined, Cai pointed to a group of soldiers and healers gathered around at the theatre.

"What's going on?" Adrian asked in a whisper.

"I guess they just found this lady's body earlier today hidden in the bushes. Seems like it was one of the people at the play."

"Was it a mugging?" Adrian asked.

"Doesn't seem to be. Sounds like the only thing taken was their ticket," said Cai.

"Who would kill someone over a ticket? The show wasn't even full."

"Who knows? Probably some kind of psycho."

Both boys ducked down quickly as the body of a woman was loaded into a body bag, her head placed in separately. They couldn't help but notice she was wearing far too much purple.

Epilogue

"I'm sorry, Boss. We failed. Please. Please give us another chance."

The band leader's forehead was pressed against the cold stone floors of the throne room. They had just returned from Olympia, and his face was filled with cuts and bruises from those little brats they escaped. His little red hat lay beside him as that star-shaped scar lay bare.

Before him sat an enormous stone throne, woven with engravings of snakes, and littered with yellow gems. A tall, thin man sat upon this throne, looking down upon his minions, his cloud-grey eyes glazed over with boredom.

"Bested by a child. Why am I not surprised?" He sighed and stretched, his arms reaching higher than they should have been able. As he sat tall, he nearly reached the top of the throne. "Now then, I don't think I'll kill you, but someone needs to be punished." His voice was lower now, and far darker.

The men trembled in fear.

"The new guy," said the guitarist, not daring to raise his head. "The new guy went completely inactive right in the middle of the job. He should be punished. He can't be trusted. Why isn't he back yet?"

The man furrowed his brow in thought and shrunk back to human size. "Hmm…" He flipped up a worn leather bracer upon his wrist, and a soft, green glow radiated off of it. "He's not far off. I suppose the trinket may have missed the mark a little." As he tapped and swiped, his face twisted into a grin. "Punish him?" He let out a ringing laugh. "My dear boy, I'll be giving him a medal when he returns."

The men slowly raised their heads, looking up and around with confusion. "Why?"

"Because he is bringing home something far better than gold."

The men waited in eager suspense.

The boss's eyes grew dark as a wicked grin twisted on his face. "A Godslayer."

Grins spread across all the men's faces as they looked around with eager glee.

The boss clapped his hands. "Time to redecorate. We want to make a good first impression now, don't we?"

His throne warped and shifted. The room followed suit. The men gripped the floor, trying not to become queasy. When the warping stopped, the throne room had shifted into a cozy office with armchairs and carpet. The boss's throne was now a huge armchair sitting behind a long desk. He spun around in it a couple times and, upon the last rotation, had changed his face into that of a balding man with a moustache.

"What do you think?" he asked cheerfully. He leaned in with a serious scowl and a different voice. "I'm going to make him an offer he can't refuse."

The men looked at each other in confusion.

"Get it? Godslayer, Godfather?"

The men shrugged.

Their boss sighed. "I suppose that is a little too obvious, isn't it? How about this?"

The room shifted again. This time the floor and walls turned shiny and metallic, and his armchair shifted from short and brownish red to tall and black. The desk disappeared, and a huge pool filled with sharks appeared. The boss shifted his face once again to that of a bald man with a scar.

He placed his hand on his chin, and in yet another voice, said, "No, Mr. Romo, I expect you to die."

He broke out into another grin, hoping for some praise, but all the men could conjure was a weak thumbs-up.

The boss gave a defeated sigh. "You're right, you're right. This is all too pre-Calamity. No one gets this stuff anymore. Christ, I miss television so much." He slumped with despair and thought for a moment. His eyes lit up. "Ah, I know!"

For the last time, the room shifted—this time a little closer to what it had originally been. Now, however, the floors were checkered marble, with a long, blood-red carpet reaching from the door to the throne. The throne grew tall and thin, once again made of stone, but covered in a red velvet cushion.

A pair of black stone wings grew out either side of the throne, and red drapes lined the walls. The boss's body shifted once again—transforming into a tall, slender man with pasty white skin and long black hair.

He grinned and stood up to examine his work. He clapped his hands together. "'We learn from failure, not from success!' Too true, too true. This is perfect."

The boss looked at his wrist again, and the smile faded away. "Oh… It appears another special guest is coming along as well. This might make things difficult…"

"Who is it, Boss?" asked the band leader.

He looked up, a mixture of happiness, sadness, and confusion on his face. "My son."

Like it, Love it, Hate it

Hey! You did it! You read all of Heart of Gaia. I hope you had as much fun reading it as I did writing it. I am so happy you chose my book out of everything out there.

You know what would be extra, super awesome? If you shared this book with everyone you know! Facebook, Instagram, Twitter, you name it! Every share helps me to release my next book in the series, so get sharing.

Also, don't forget about a review. Reviews are a major help to us independent authors. Even if it's not a glowing review, I want to hear it! Learning helps me become a better writer for all you lovely readers. Let me know what you think of the story, the characters, anything! (Well, maybe keep it book related. We can discuss other things later.)

Here's a link to Heart of Gaia. https://a.co/d/gaRf2oT

About the Author

Misty R Phillips is a woman of action. She tackles each day—head on—with a blanket and a cup of coffee. Armed with her wit, far too many cats, and a curious faced dog, she battles the wonders of family life. She takes all of her flaws, insecurities, and failings, wraps them in little bits of paper, gives them personality and names, and shoves them into her books. She may be graphic, vulgar and a wee bit asinine on paper, but all of her friends and family know her to be sweet, kind and loyal.

You can connect with me on:
- http://www.mistyrphillips.ca
- https://twitter.com/MistyRPhillips
- https://www.facebook.com/MistyPAuthor